Also by Michael Burn

The Labyrinth of Europe

Mr Lyward's Answer

The Debatable Land

The Age of Slate

Mary and Richard

Fiction

Yes, Farewell

The Midnight Diary

The Trouble with Jake

Poetry

Poems to Mary

The Flying Castle

Out On a Limb

Open Day and Night

Play

The Modern Everyman

Autobiography

Turned Towards the Sun

Childhood at Oriol

Michael Burn

Childhood at Oriol

Turtle Point Press

New York 2005

Copyright © 2005 by Turtle Point Press

LCCN 2004108025 ISBN 1-885586-32-9

Frontispiece courtesy of the author

Design and composition by Jeff Clark
at Wilsted & Taylor Publishing Services

Printed in Canada

to Mary

All those great words . . . trust, marriage, wife, husband, children, lover, friend . . . they are attacked and return secure, are smeared and return untouched, are made mercenary and return pure as when they first were minted . . . organization has its fling at them, but they return . . . and in their first meaning.

Part

One

1

In the summer of 1920 an elderly man called Arthur Friedmann came to Oriol, on the north coast of France, to attend the consecration of the British cemetery, in which his only son was buried. The service over, he went for a walk alone in the deserted pine-forest.

He came upon a wide clearing, covered with Army huts no longer occupied, the gunnery camp where his son had been trained. His son had loved Oriol; "after the war," he had once written, "we must turn it into something." In many letters he had described its quiet and lonely enchantment; and now the father began to understand what he had meant. Between the forest and the Channel straggled a soft wilderness of dunes, thick with clumps of esparto grass and sprawling shrubs, out of which the sand emerged in smooth curves, like flesh from rags, white and silken to the touch. When there were storms the sea could be heard in the forest, above the creaking trees; now only a light breeze blew off it, lifting into the air the sticky scent of the pines. The dark trees spread for many kilometres; the branches grew at the tops, leaving bare the tall trunks, which the sun turned gold and copper and bronze. So many winter winds had swept them that not one tree seemed to grow upright; they were like copper ladders left resting against the sky.

Arthur Friedmann lit a cigar and went further. The forest floor of pine-needles, speckled with sunlight, looked like innumerable sleeping lizards. The sand slipped into his pointed shoes, under the spats, and the pine-scent mingled with the aroma of his cigar, the first ever to be smoked there. He was unused to walking; he liked, and owned, a large car, and now and then took a constitutional on foot along a boulevard or a promenade, or in a garden. He was an entrepreneur and a speculator, who envisaged all that he saw as something more or something different. He was ready to leave people, but not things or places, as he found them, and in changing the things he changed the people, not always for the better. The impulse was not avarice, though he had made several fortunes, but a restless creativeness which had no other outlet.

Between two dunes, about a mile away, glittered a strip of sea, and invisible beyond was England, fenced in with a rim of hotels and boarding-houses nearly all hideous to him; even after forty years of living there the absence of desire in England either to woo or be wooed still amazed him. He took from his wallet a letter of his son's, dated June 1917, written perhaps near this very point, and full of projects for building and development. The boy had had ideas; perhaps, he thought, I will carry them out myself. He climbed a sandhill, and looked across a dark swath of tree-tops at the blue slope of the Channel.

There was a cabin on the hill-top with a corrugated-iron roof and a chimney from which smoke was rising. It had a garden with roses and marigolds and hollyhocks, all very unexpected. He did not want to interrupt his mood, half reverie, half prospectus, and was about to move on, when a woman dressed in black came out, followed by a girl of about nineteen, also in black. He remembered having seen them at the cemetery the same morning. The coincidence was too striking; several of his greatest successes had sprung from the recognition of coincidence. He took off his grey Homburg hat and said "Good day."

The older woman replied; her voice, her looks, the kind of garden, suggested that she was English. He went on: "Did I not see you this morning?"

"I remember seeing you."

"I came to visit my son's grave. He was killed at the Marne."

"My husband was wounded there. My husband is also buried in the cemetery."

She opened a small white gate leading from the loose sand into the garden and said: "Won't you come in? My daughter and I live here. Perhaps you would like some tea?"

The cabin was simply and pleasantly furnished, with a wood fire burning; a number of pictures hung from the walls and others were stacked against them, and an empty easel stood in one corner. While the daughter made tea Mrs. Weatherby introduced herself and explained that her husband had been a painter, had come to Oriol several years before the war, and built the cabin himself.

"He showed excellent judgment," said Arthur Friedmann. "It is the first time I have been here, but my boy often spoke of Oriol. It has great charm."

"Anne and I are very happy here. We could not live anywhere else, even now."

With reticence and sympathy he asked a question or two about her husband, to which she replied calmly, interweaving similar questions about his son. She and Anne had worked in the hospital during the war, and she had been nursing her husband when he died. Apologetically she confessed that she had not known his son; the two of them sat for a time without speaking, while the girl brought in cups and plates and looked with curiosity at the dapper stranger. She was pretty and fair; he liked her quietness and her friendly smile.

They spoke of the morning's ceremony and agreed that beautiful ground had been chosen for the soldiers' graves, over-looking the estuary of the river Oriol.

"But it is dead," he added. "There should be some living memorial."

"I would like that, and my husband would have liked that. A garden, or a park . . ."

"Or a whole area."

She did not understand him, and the thought was still only germinating. He stubbed out his cigar and drank some tea.

"And you'll be staying on here, Mrs. Weatherby?" He had an old-fashioned almost pedantic politeness; his voice, though low, was rather hoarse, as if he had asthma, and still a little guttural.

"Oh, yes. We have many friends here, and very few in England."

"Aren't you a long way from anywhere?"

"Not as far as it seems. The road is only five minutes away, and a bus

5

goes into Oriol. We have neighbours within easy walking distance; they have been very good to us. My husband was so fond of France."

She paused, and then asked the question which everyone sooner or later asked: "Are you English?"

"I am a British citizen. I was born in Czechoslovakia, and my name is German. I was in business in the City of London when the war broke out, but being of German origin, I was asked to leave it."

"But with your son . . . ?"

"My son served in the British Army. He was a major when he was wounded, though he was only twenty-two. That was not taken into account then."

"How shameful."

He had become quite a connoisseur in the accents of commiseration; hers sounded sincere. He liked the whole household; the husband a painter, the level-headed calm woman, the pretty girl, the air of dignity. The project in his head grew; he skirmished cautiously to discover more facts. Nearly all the land, she told him, belonged to the Baron de Moutiers, who spent most of his time in Paris; his château, the Château d'Oriol, was falling to pieces. Oriol was little more than a fishing village. There was a wonderful beach, two miles long. The pine-woods were deserted except for her cabin, a villa or two on the outskirts, "and of course the nightingales."

"Nightingales? Here?"

"Certainly. Not in the pines, but in the thickets. Our house is called Les Rossignols."

Nightingales? They would be an asset. And a beach two miles long, and a decaying château, and an owner who took no interest in but might be glad to take some out. . . .

"We had a studio first at Etaples," she went on. "My husband loved to paint the fishing-fleet. Would you care to see some of his work?"

Friedmann admired the canvases with divided attention, wanting to know more about the land. They went outside.

"The nightingales are there," she said, indicating a lighter green among the pines. Far off the dunes dipped into V's and U's that revealed the Channel.

6

"What was your husband's name?" he asked suddenly.

"James," she answered, surprised.

It was strange; that had been his son's name.

The light was beginning to die along the dunes, the leaning pine-trunks turned red, and the tops of the trees grew darker.

"He always used to say that this would make a wonderful holiday resort," said Mrs. Weatherby.

"It will," he answered.

~

Anne had come out of the house at this moment, and it was thus that she always remembered him. There and then he unfolded for them his picture of what Oriol would be, improvised, rough, corrected in motion, but in all the main lines the place that a few years later it became. The village of Oriol was to be a fashionable *plage* with a sea-front, swimming-pools, and a Casino, the decaying château of the decaying Baron a hotel, and the pine-forests the setting for a golf-course. Napoleon-like he pointed this way and that, making a gesture as if throwing down a carpet, and finally turning to their own home and remarking with unforgettable grandeur: "And here there must be a view. You"—to her mother, the morning's ceremony forgotten—"you have been the discoverer of this place. I shall build you a village. This will be the centre of the golf-course, and the players shall have their view of the sea from here."

And a view it became. As there was light when God said so, so there were greens, fairways, a club, hotels, and finally a Casino, when Arthur Friedmann said so. Lorries came and went all day, month after month, year after year. The landscape was invaded, yet never spoiled. Dunes were levelled and shaped, but the wilderness along the coast stayed wild. Many of the pines were felled, but the forest stayed forest and the nightingales still sang, but to an audience. Beyond the swimming-pool and fashionable beach the golden miles stretched untouched. He built the Pine Hotel on the forest edge, and beside it the cottage for Mrs. Weatherby and Anne; and one day workmen arrived upon their little hill, took the cabin to pieces like a packing-case, carted it away, and built the bits into something else; and the two of them moved into their new home. In the wings and on the

7

stage of this vast scene-shifting wandered Arthur Friedmann, known to everyone as the *patron*, a rose in his button-hole summer and winter, always in spats, always in the grey Homburg hat that really had come from Homburg, bringing the faubourgs into the forest, an elegant restless Jew with slightly weary eyes, and to Anne Weatherby romantic. He would arrive in his long open Rolls-Royce at the limit of the half-made road, walk to some high point and give directions. He understood the atmosphere of places, of people, of works of art, and was sensitive to moods and possibilities which most men miss. He had what in women is called instinct, in matters of taste a flair; in business he had the Midas touch.

He wrote to friends of his dead son's and told them that if they ever wished to return to Oriol they were to come to start with as his guests; they came, and returned later as his clients. Johnny MacManus arrived among the first. He was a very young cavalry N.C.O., robust and good-looking, the son of a riding-master. Soon he set up a stable there, grooming the horses and giving lessons himself, and began to do good business. Anne rode with him. Beach, sea, forest, all were theirs. Memories of the war, like dark curtains looped back into the roof of their lives, faded and began to be forgotten. She fell in love, he was attracted by the idea of marriage, and married they were, in Paris, in 1921. Arthur Friedmann bought them a suite at the Crillon Hotel and paid for all the champagne. Looking earnestly at her as they went away, he warned her, "Be careful of him, my dear"; and she laughed and replied that she would be able to manage him. Three years later she was to wish she had asked Friedmann to explain himself.

In 1924 the Pine Hotel was opened with a splendid banquet, attended by a French Cabinet Minister, the Prefect of the Department, all the local Mayors, and a number of well-connected Englishmen, as well as Mrs. Weatherby and Anne and the "old inhabitants," invited as Arthur Friedmann's guests. The project turned to gold. Streams of louis began to slither across the green tables at the Casino. The Prince of Wales came for a week-end and the place was made. About this time Mrs. Weatherby died, and Anne and Johnny moved into the cottage; he enlarged his business and kept two hirelings specially for the Pine Hotel guests. During the season he gave lessons all day long, and now the money came in regularly. A son,

8

Merrick, was born, and it seemed to Anne that they had all they could want. The cottage was big enough for them; together they pushed back the dunes and made a garden, hung chintz curtains in the windows and her father's painting on the walls; and she saw no reason not to be happy for the rest of her life.

The change in Johnny came rapidly. As Oriol flourished he deteriorated, becoming the victim of a vanity and a wilfulness she had hardly been aware of before. People began to frequent Oriol who flattered, with more subtlety than Anne had ever shown, his ease, his vigour, and his good looks. His riding-lessons became popular with women, often many years older than himself, who did not care about fresh air or horses and perhaps assumed that a riding-master—elsewhere it might be a ski-ing instructor or a skating teacher—was thrown in with the hotel bills. They wore smart jodhpurs and tweed jackets cut by Paris shops, and Johnny took them for long rides along the beach and in the forest. At first Anne thought nothing of it; she laughed with him at the stories he told about some of them. Besides, he charged fifty francs an hour, a good sum then.

He came home later. He had drinks with his clients in the decorative little bars with window-boxes and striped awnings that enterprising *restaurateurs* were building in the village of Oriol, now a town; the Normandy, the Perroquet, the Matelot d'Or. He began to relish high-sounding names and titles. He talked aloofly of meeting the Comtesse d'Harcourt, who entered horses for the big races at Auteuil and Longchamps and might appoint him to her racing-stable; and of somebody else with a palace in Italy, and an apartment in Paris, and a villa now building at Oriol, and of this and that important or wealthy personage, all in a tone as if it were something out of Anne's ken. He became a snob; she had deceived herself into thinking he would be content so long as he had the open-air life and could be more or less his own master. She grew jealous. Some of the women he took riding were attractive; and they courted the side of him to which it was neither her wish nor in her capacity to appeal.

This continued for a while, with awkward excuses on his side, awkward remonstrances on hers, and long silences. In the end it had not been even a beauty who took him away from her. There appeared one fine day, in one of the fashionable magazines that had started to advertise the new resort, a photograph of a Mrs. Irene Hooper "with the popular riding-master Johnny MacManus." A feeling of anger and shame, unknown to her before, rose up in Anne when she saw it. Mrs. Hooper was a rich woman, divorced, who drove fast cars, raced slim yachts, and liked powerful young men. She had a reputation for drinking too much. She wore trousers, at that time still thought rather shocking, and not at all becoming to her large thighs. Her face, once said to have been handsome, was now heavily made-up and running to fat, and when she had been at the bottle almost lurid. Anne thought her blowsy and vulgar; and she had not the humorous good nature which often goes with floridity. And there in the photograph stood Johnny at her side, his arm in hers, looking very tall and lean, wearing a smile which readers of the magazine doubtless found engaging, but which gave Anne the impression of a smirk. Any initiated person would at once have taken it for granted that Johnny was Mrs. Hooper's lover.

Anne showed him the magazine. In a few months her second child would be born. It was an insult, she said, to allow such a photograph to be taken, let alone published. He lost his temper and let fly a whirl of counter-accusations about his "rights" and his "independence," mixed up with excuses about business and the importance of "getting on with people." This revelation of petulance, arrogance, and lack of straightforwardness filled her with a disgust for him which alarmed her. She tried her utmost in the ensuing days to get rid of it, but he gave her no help. Oriol had bewitched him.

She thought of going to Arthur Friedmann. Business on his side, domestic life on hers, had kept them apart; and suddenly, when she most needed his counsel, he left Oriol for good. Stimulated only by the conception and the making, bored with the success, he went off to Canada, there, it was said, to "open up" the Arctic territories, and "turn them into something." He sold most of his interest in Oriol for about ten times the amount he had put into it, and left behind him the Villa des Roses, with his daughter Judith inside it; a signed portrait of himself, button-hole, grey hat, spats, stock, and diamond pin, in the Casino and the club-house lounge; and always, for Anne, a faint smell of cigar, a faint blue thread of

10

cigar-smoke coiling among the pine-trees. There was no one now to whom she could turn.

In the cottage, row followed row. What happened frequently in the modish world surrounding her happened in her home too, and she had not the same nonchalance about it nor the experience to meet it. Johnny ended by not coming home some nights at all. She found in their room a gold cigarette-case with a diamond monogram, which he could not have afforded to buy himself. Gossip was wafted back to her, murmuring and poisoning, as if determined that there should be pleasure, gaiety, elegance, at Oriol, but never a home. She felt ashamed of him and even of herself, unable to face his obvious lies and later his callous admissions. The situation bewildered her, and she brooded over it too intricately and too long. He provided the solution himself; three months after the photograph had been published he disappeared.

She divorced him, and heard afterwards that he had married Mrs. Hooper and, not long after, that he had left her; and others later. He became a playboy ready to be kept by anyone who would pay for him, exploiting his charm, entirely flexible to his own convenience. He acquired horses, and she saw photographs of him at race-meetings. Once or twice he wrote to her about the children and sent Merrick presents on his birthday; but when the daughter, Sarah, was born, he never came to see her, and soon the presents to Merrick ceased. Anne answered the letters through lawyers, and learned that he had gone to live in America; when the children were old enough, this was what she told them. Arthur Friedmann, in Toronto, heard what had happened and sent her a cheque for five hundred pounds, merely remarking that she was well rid of Johnny; after a while she was sure of it herself. When Merrick was six and Sarah five, Arthur Friedmann died in New York, confirming the cottage in his will as a gift to her; and on the day the news of his death came, she sent Merrick and Sarah to the beach with friends, shut herself in her bedroom and cried.

She had the cottage, and fifty pounds a year from her mother's estate; Johnny sent her next to nothing. Judith Friedmann, out of affection for her father's memory, recommended Anne as secretary to the secretary of the golf-club, and she was given the job. She learned to do shorthand and to type, and saved money like a peasant. She became "the admirable Mrs. MacManus" or "the indispensable Anne." The club members saw the small and still-pretty face through the windows of the secretary's office, the hands busy at the typewriter, the head turned with a welcoming expression when they opened the glass door, and they felt that everything was informal and well looked after. She was neither superior nor obsequious. To Hillier the caddie-master, to the old greenkeepers, to Guillaume the concierge at the Pine Hotel, to all who had been at Oriol from its birth, the place could not go on without her.

Each morning she walked across the main road in front of the cottage to the gold-club, each evening she walked back; when it rained she took her bicycle. The town of Oriol was a mile away along the road, which in the other direction curved on through the forest, and across the estuary, and so joined the arterial road to Paris. The sea-front, the swimming-pool, the promenade, the bathing-huts, all that part of the beach where the crowds went, were now known as Oriol-plage. The part she loved most—the forest, the golf-course threaded through but not destroying it, the dunes, the solitary reaches of the beach where now and then the riders and the sand-yachts, the women fishing for shrimps and those who knew went—was called Jacques-plage; Arthur Friedmann had named it after his son. Oriol was for the shops and the people, Jacques-plage still wild. Everywhere were memories. As she came along the pergola walk from the road to the club-house, the old white horse that lived in the adjoining field thumped along beside her; she remembered the white mare, his mother. She remembered Fifi the goat, whose daughter Frou-frou was still trying to eat the cabbages in her back garden. She remembered the Italian workmen who had come to build the Pine Hotel, living in huts among the trees and singing round their braziers; Emilio, who could imitate the nightingales, was still a waiter at the hotel. And opposite the pergola walk was the pillar-box by which she had first met Johnny.

She was thirty-five now, and for her Johnny was dead. The unavoidable memories no longer gave her any pang on his account; they merely recorded that he had existed. Her life was with the two children. She knew that they discussed him sometimes in secret and invented tales about him.

12

They were growing up now, Merrick fifteen, Sarah a year younger, becoming accessible to other influences. She dreaded that Johnny's worst traits might creep out in them and the conflict of her early married life be resumed in the next generation; but so far there was little sign. He was like a room into which no one went or had cause to go, a sudden shadow, not a regular or haunting presence; a sound heard faintly far off in another valley. Yet now and then the sound could be heard, the shadow would fall, the room was there; in her life as she now lived it, little else disturbed her.

2

Both children were bilingual. Sarah went to classes organized by the resident British colony in Oriol, Merrick to a small school in the south of England. He spent his holidays at Oriol, and three times a year Anne and Sarah met him at Boulogne harbour. He had crossed the Channel so often now that most of the crews on the passenger steamers and all the French porters knew him. His friend the purser, Mr. Harris, would allow him off by the luggage gangway, while the smart crowd of week-end visitors had to push and shove behind. This experience of travel won him prestige at school, and he made the most of it. It gave him the reputation of a globe-trotter; yet each time he saw the French coast approaching, each time he heard the women crying their baskets of fruit in a different language, and among the local guides, the interpreters, and the porters in their blue blouses, picked out Sarah and Anne waiting for him, each time he felt a fresh excitement.

All three could have found their way home blindfold. Sometimes they took the Paris train and scrambled off during the two-minute stop at Etaples, but more often M. Philippe drove them in his taxi. It was only fifteen miles: cobbled streets out of Boulogne; villages where they knew every level crossing, every turning, every advertisement for Cinzano and Byrrh; the ten red-brick houses opposite the cement works half-way; the military cemetery along the estuary, with pine-clad Oriol on the far side; the fishing-boats moored by the quay at Etaples, the white bridge; then the forest, studded with gay villas called by ridiculous fantastic names, like Harlequin, Zizi, Polichinelle; and at last the cottage. This journey, with England only two hours away, could never be monotonous. Merrick was not of a melancholy or even emotional nature; but when the day came to drive in the reverse direction, and all that had been on the left was on the right, he always felt sorry to leave.

The children paid little attention to the fashionable world which surrounded them. They lived their own life, familiar with the caddies as with the golfers, with the attendants almost more than with the court, with their mother more than with anyone. On summer evenings, when she had finished at the office, they often bicycled a few kilometres into France— Oriol was Oriol, and France something beyond—and sat outside a village café gossiping with the peasants; or on Sundays they took a picnic to the beach or the forest of St. Mathieu, where within Anne's memory the Baron de Moutiers had hunted the boar. In the midst and at the edges of Oriol and Jacques-plage Merrick and Sarah created their "castles," places known only to them and a few elect, whom they called the "citizens"; here they could watch and plan their conspiracies without being overlooked.

It was the summer holidays of 1937.

"To-day is the golf competition," said Merrick. "We must go and look at it."

They were in their "sea-castle," a ruined hut half-swamped in sand where the dunes ran down to the deserted beach between Oriol and Berck-sur-Mer. They had tried in vain for months to reclaim it from the sand and make it habitable. The tide was out, exposing the pools that made bathing so dangerous to those who did not know the coast; high-water mark was a thin reef of seaweed, twigs, and shells, and the hard sand beyond brown and ribbed. A quarter of a mile away the flat sea made lazy snaps at the shore, and one or two fishing-boats were out. This part of the coast was a kind of bluff, and the children had been told that if they set sail due west they would not strike land till they reached America; they liked to believe this, but doubted it, for England appeared to be straight in front and further up the coast could be seen on a clear day.

Sarah was reading *Jane Eyre*.

"What's the time?" she said.

"About half-past eleven," said Merrick.

"How can you tell?" She knew he had no watch.

"From the sun."

"How?"

"You get used to it."

To avoid awkward questions he banged busily at a plank and put some nails in his mouth. After a while Sarah said again:

"Yes, but how do you tell?" No reply. "I don't believe you can tell at all. You're just guessing."

He took out the nails one by one and hammered them in. Then he said:

"If you don't believe me, go back home and see. We ought to go anyhow, if we want to watch the competition."

"Let me finish my chapter."

She was usually finishing a chapter. She finished it, started the next, promised herself she would not go on with it, went on with it, and finished that too. She lay back in the sand arm-chair she had made for herself, gazing at the little white waves and wriggling her bare feet in the sand. She was in love with Mr. Rochester, as she had been with the hero of most novels she happened to be reading. Once it had been Heathcliff; last winter, whenever a storm got up, she had gone out into it, transforming the dunes and forest into a moor and calling out "Heathcliff!" against the thunder. When Anne began to read them *Pride and Prejudice*, Heathcliff was supplanted by Mr. Darcy, so accomplished, so disdainful, and so rich. Sarah had never ceased to love Rupert of Hentzau, and at the height of this infatuation had waited outside the Casino to see a foreign nobleman she expected to look like him; but he had turned out to be a small fat fellow who had to be helped into his car.

Now she loved Mr. Rochester, so dark, so lonely, and so tragic. She imagined him riding towards her along the sands at that moment, full of sombre thoughts. He would pass her with scarcely a glance, but further along he would rein his horse and look back; and later, in the woods, they would meet by accident and recognize one another. All her lovers came to her on horseback: Heathcliff on a wild moorland pony, Mr. Darcy driving a carriage, Rupert of Hentzau on a prancing Arab. She had never seen a prancing Arab, but knew what she meant by it. If only she could ride better herself! Merrick had a good seat and had won a prize at the local gymkhana. The two of them rode when the season had either ended or not yet begun and the horses were not in demand; they hired them cheap from

16

the stables that had once been their father's. Sarah still had to have an escort, and was usually fobbed off with the sleepy old chestnut Percy, who had shamed her under Merrick's very eyes by walking straight to the edge of the sea and rolling.

"Come on, then," she said, closing *Jane Eyre*.

Merrick did not answer. He was playing a game with himself which he had played since he was a small boy. He was lugging inshore a heavy sheet of scrap from the old wreck that lay bare at low tide. If I reach high-water mark without a rest, he was saying to himself, I shall become the most famous man in the world. Whenever he undertook any special exertion he played this game, and now it had become quite a serious test with him; if he failed, he felt humiliated and wondered if he had some fatal weakness which would always prevent him from making the final effort. Sarah had once played it with him, but had now forgotten it, and he told nobody that he kept it up. His arms and finger-tips ached, the iron plate cut the skin; his grasp weakened and slipped, but he dragged it on, vainly trying to think of something else. He got a fresh grip. "I will hold you, I will hold you," he muttered. He just reached the line of seaweed and dropped the sheet.

"Whatever's the matter, Merrick?"

"It's heavy."

"What's it for?"

"To keep the sand back." He stretched his arms and rubbed his hands ostentatiously. "Come on, let's go," he said, as if he had been waiting for her.

"Where shall we watch from?"

"The Camel's Back, of course. We'll be there just as they're coming over."

She put on her shoes and followed him inland by their "private" path. The rioting yellow gorse and low prickly shrubs caught at them, and now and then they started a rabbit. Sarah stopped to pick the flowers, like white buttercups with green veins, that smelt stronger than honey and flowered in the sand all summer.

"Come on, Sarah," said Merrick.

Pushing back the branches, they passed the fringe of low pines, the frontier between the golf-course and their wilderness, and, emerging from it, stood just above the cottage and the low elongated pavilion of the Pine Hotel. Players and caddies speckled the links, the sun flashed on the shafts of lifted clubs, and the sound of the struck ball came to them an instant after they had seen it hit. People crouched on the greens, putting for all they were worth, while the caddies held the red-and-white flag above the hole. More people, in gay clothes, were lounging outside the clubhouse, watching departures from the first tee and arrivals on the last green; and smart women sat at round-topped tables, admiring and being admired. Top-knots of smoke drifted beyond from villas half-hidden in the forest, and on the inland horizon the road cut through the pines led into France. They skirted the club-house and reached their hide-out in the woods.

Above the fifteenth hole, on the sandhill known as the Camel's Back, this was their "forest castle," their viewpoint over the inhabited world. They could see the tee on one side of the sandhill, the green on the other. A good player was expected to reach the green in one, but to drive into the sand was to be lost; Sarah had never done the hole in fewer than ten and had once taken twenty-seven. The sun burned through the bright-green pine-quills and warmed the children's backs. They lay on their stomachs, sucking heart-shaped lollipops bought from Madame Menard's stall opposite the Casino; Merrick was fiddling with his new camera, and Sarah began to read again.

Players arrived upon the tee and sent their caddies up the sandhill in advance. Invisible, the children watched them. They knew nearly everyone. Their ideas of what all these people did when not on holiday were extravagant and luridly coloured by liking or dislike. Sarah almost believed that swarthy Mr. Mazarian, whose wife had died very suddenly, and who had married again soon after, was a murderer. Even Merrick, much more matter-of-fact, had assured the waiters at the Pine Hotel that Sir John Gregson's wife, who happened to be Russian, was a ballerina and often danced on tables. They picked up gossip and embroidered it with their own fantasies. Nobody was colourless to them. They had a character for everyone, vivid and partisan.

"Someone new with Major Bryant," said Merrick.

A broad-shouldered man with a lean merry face was walking up the duckboards, a pretty girl on his arm; he was looking down at her and laughing.

"French this time," said Merrick.

"How can you tell from here?"

"It's obvious."

Major Bryant bent and kissed the girl behind the ear.

"He's very familiar," said Sarah. "He does it in front of everyone."

"Hello," said Major Bryant, hearing a low whistle from the branches. "So you two are there." He was a "citizen," one of the few permitted to detect them. "What are you up to?"

"Watching the competition," said Merrick. "Are you going to win?"

"I'm not playing in it."

"Why not?"

"I'm not serious enough. What about you? You're better than some of them."

"I'm not allowed to. I'm too young."

The French girl smiled, amused at the two faces peering through the branches, and Merrick thought it necessary to assert himself.

"I've got a handicap," he said. "Twenty-three."

"It's too much. Bring it down to eighteen and we'll get you in."

"All right. I will, too."

Major Bryant laughed and walked on. Merrick saw him laugh again as he talked to the girl, and wondered what was being said about him; he took it for granted that something was being said.

"I got a photograph of him," he said. "It's the fourth. And a different girl each time."

"Don Juan," said Sarah.

Merrick said nothing. He had not read Byron; Sarah knew it and had hoped to be asked what she meant.

They watched the pair descend to the green, Merrick with curiosity and Sarah with suspicion. Major Bryant chose a club for the girl, and, standing behind her, folded his hands over hers while she addressed it.

19

"She's not much good at *golf*," said Sarah.

"They aren't any of them any good at golf. They're awfully pretty though. He's very popular with women," Merrick said knowingly. "Look ... the Rat and the Mouse."

They peered out at the tee again, like Indians at a covered wagon; Miss Marples and Miss Wells had arrived.

These were two more of the "old inhabitants." Miss Marples, the Mouse, stooped, being very tall, and had a gentle, vague, peaked face. Miss Wells, the Rat, was squat and walked as if in seven-league boots. They went through their familiar routine. Miss Wells had a whole quiverful of clubs and took time to choose the right one; Miss Marples had only two, both of them irons, one flat, the other scooped. They stayed at the Pine Hotel, and though well off always carried their own clubs; they had played a round a morning every summer since before the children remembered, and had been at Arthur Friedmann's opening dinner. On Sundays Miss Marples went to morning service in the English Church and Miss Wells played alone; she was a scientist and a free-thinker, and had once gained a brief hold over the children by showing them how to dissect a frog.

At last Miss Wells chose her club.

"Lift it, lift it higher," muttered Merrick, and then, as the ball scudded into a bunker, "They're hopeless. She will stand too far in front of it. They never get any better." His forehead was puckered at her stupidity.

Miss Marples built her steeple of sand, balanced the ball upon it, chose her scooped club, and drove straight through the steeple, sending the ball high but not far.

Merrick shook his head, impatient with both of them. "They'll never learn, never. Why don't they let Jerry teach them?"

"Why don't *you* teach them?" said Sarah.

"I will one day. Look at them. . . ."

The two ladies stalked over the top, their voices intermingling in calm, never-ending chimes; they were talking about the political situation. Their faces were leathery, but kind, and they thought of golf as a brisk walk interrupted by blows.

Now came the serious competitors. Here was the Australian General

Grandison, loud-voiced and burly, to whom dozens of cups had fallen in all corners of the world. He had given up the Army long ago for financial buccaneering, and his partner was André Lemaitre, a French banker and a director of the club, to whom he was talking about an audacious project in Africa, which Lemaitre was to support. Next came a succession of young men in shirt-sleeves, with knotted silk scarves, who flew over from the City for the week-end and returned on the Sunday night boat. They were cheerful, dashing, a little wild, and now and then made love to one another's wives. After them came the young de Moutiers, son of the old Baron to whom Oriol had belonged. Golf and baccarat had rescued the family from ruin; and from the proceeds of their tumbledown château, now the Grand Hotel d'Oriol, he had built the modern Villa Panache. He too was a director of the golf-club and the Casino. There were one or two lesser theatrical and film stars, and one or two Americans; all sent their caddies ahead to the summit of the Camel's Back, and sat down in the little hut by the tee for a drink, until the pair in front had left the green. And all of them were welcomed by Mr. Glanville Wake, the secretary of the golf-club and the children's pet aversion, who had arrived to watch the game. He wore, as ever, a canary-coloured waistcoat and plus-fours, which the children said had been dug out of one of the greens.

"Here's Jerry," said Merrick.

Sarah wriggled forward on the pine-needles; secretly she worshipped Jerry. His father, who had been professional to the club since its beginning, had lately died, and Jerry had taken over from him; he was a lanky fellow of nineteen, and one day would be a champion. Her heart beating faster, she watched his easy light swing. The ball soared directly above the red guide-post, dropped sheer on to the green, and stopped dead.

"Cut," said Merrick. "That's the way to do it."

"Oh, I do hope he wins, Merrick. He's much better than all of them. And General Grandison's so certain always. I do hope Jerry wins."

"He can't, stupid."

"Why can't he? Of course he can."

"He's a pro. The cup's only for members. A pro can't win the cup."

She stared at him indignantly. "Whatever's the difference?"

"A pro's paid. Didn't you know that?"

"Well, I think it's just unfair. And he's much the best. Look, it's almost in the hole again."

She lay in the sand, brooding silently over this new injustice. Everywhere, without looking for them, she found things that were unfair.

Jerry kept an eye out for them in the bushes as he came loping past, expecting to find them there. His freckled face took badly to the sun, and his forehead was peeling. He carried his own clubs.

"Hello," he said. "Coming bathing afterwards?"

"Can you come?" Merrick asked.

"His Nibs," Jerry jerked a thumb back towards the green-and-yellow secretary, "is very busy. Oh, very busy today."

Sarah brought herself to speak. "It was a wonderful shot, Jerry."

"Sure you didn't move it on?"

"Quite sure," said Merrick.

"You two'd do anything."

One day Jerry had played a similar stopping shot, right up against the flag-post, and when he reached the green had found it in the hole. The children confessed later that they had put it there.

"Mr. Wake's a pig!" Sarah exclaimed suddenly.

"Of course he is. We all know that."

"He's a pig, a green pig." She began to write it, but the white sand was too loose and the letters fell in. So she lay on her back and repeated vehemently to the sky, "Mr. Wake is a green pig."

He was down there on the tee, being amiable to everyone. There was nothing pig-like about his appearance; he had a waxed moustache and an upright figure, maintained by rowing exercises.

"Parrot. Old parrot," said Sarah. "Mangy old yellow-and-green parrot."

"He's coming over," said Merrick. "Better get back."

They pulled their palisade of branches closer, as Mr. Wake stalked past, swinging his shooting-stick, his eyeglass on its black cord stuck into the breast pocket of his yellow waistcoat. He was talking about the opera at the Casino Theatre to the Baroness de Leverson, who had driven her ball into the trees; while her caddie looked for it, she took off her dark

22

glasses and made up her face. She was playing with Sir Maurice Wilden-stein.

"An excellent performance," Mr. Wake was saying—"quite excellent. It is really quite a good little theatre." He called out to the caddie, who grimaced and shrugged her shoulders. "This rough is getting too thick," he said. "Several of the membahs have mentioned it."

Merrick nudged Sarah and winked. "The membahs," he whispered.

The Baroness soon gave up the ball and walked delicately off down the duckboards, followed by Sir Maurice and Mr. Glanville Wake, bending and clicking his teeth at the loose rungs, with Josette, the caddie, behind; that evening Josette would return and find the ball, even if she had to search for hours, and sell it at Jerry's store.

"The membahs, the membahs," Merrick sang.

"Oh, do him, Merrick. Do do him."

"He's the pelican now," said Merrick. "Look at the way he screws his head. His shirt-collar's always too tight. You be someone smart, and I'll do him being polite to you."

She cajoled her awkward limbs into the melodic contour of the mannequins, as she had seen them in the fashionable papers and sitting in real life outside the big hotels. She rested one wrist on her waist, extending the other arm with the fingers parted for an imaginary cigarette-holder, and smiled alluringly, her eyebrows slightly raised. Merrick clenched one eye as if he wore a monocle, assumed a false smile, and advanced upon her with his head on one side like a magpie's.

"Good morning, Baroness. And how is the game today?"

"Oh, so-so. So-so."

"The weathah is being very kind to us. Very kind indeed."

"I hope it stays like this for the Horse Show."

"Which Horse Show?" Merrick asked, becoming himself.

"Oh, don't be so lit'ral, Merrick. I'm only inventing. They're always having Horse Shows."

"Don't stand right out there. He can see us."

"S'pose he does?"

"He'll blame it on Mother." The boy cleared his throat portentously.

"Er ... Mrs. ah MacManus ... those ... hum ... those children of yours...."

"Go on, Merrick, go on. It's just like him."

"I think it would be ... hum ... advisable if they were to keep off the fairways. The membahs ... the ... ah ... the membahs ..."

Her face became radiant at this word. "Oh, do go on, Merrick. That's just it."

"The membahs," he continued gravely. "The membahs have ... ah ... been complaining ..."

"Do 'and what is more ...'"

"Not now."

"Oh do," she prompted him. "And what is more, it has come to my ears ... go on."

"Later. I've got to be inspired. Look, Sarah ..." he pointed back to the tee. "It's the Maharajah. And Cacouette's caddying for him. Come on, get into the hide again. I've got to photograph the Maharajah."

They lay down side by side. Merrick wore grey flannels and a white shirt, and Sarah had on a print dress rapidly becoming too small. Both were fair; Merrick's hair was close and neatly cut, the nape of his neck free. Sarah's was uncombed, tangled, and falling over her forehead. Physically she was to him like a loose-leaf folder to a compact book, and still growing. Already she was as tall as he was; Merrick's body waited for itself and had method in its growth, but Sarah seemed to develop only upwards, and this physical lankiness had contributed to make her shy. She could not be direct with strangers; yet if something went to her heart, she would look up and a warm affection overspread her whole face, more captivating because less expected than Merrick's regular look of candour.

The Maharajah advanced, attended by his equerry, Mr. Achmed. Over billows of fat the Maharajah wore a blue silk shirt, patched with sweat, and blue trousers; he resembled a bulging stormcloud swathed in blue and crowned with a small green turban. He was fat on a grand scale and had stepped complete from Sarah's illustrated copy of the *Arabian Nights*; she saw him on a voluptuous divan with the Princess Scheherazade and a hookah.

24

"Poor man," she said, "having to carry all that about."

"It's his fault," said Merrick. "He doesn't have to be like that."

The Maharajah could only swing his club in a cautious semicircle no higher than his waist; when he drove, it was surprising that his ball even topped the hill. It rolled into an armpit of sand near the children. Cacouette, laden with a huge bag of clubs, came after it.

"Hello, Cacouette," said Merrick. "How goes it?"

"No *bon*," said Cacouette, wrinkling his monkey face and sniffing. "No drink. And I'm hot."

A fisherman's son, like most of the caddies, he walked three miles to Etaples and back each day, and though the same age as Merrick, was much smaller and looked ten years older; his face had the pinched, wrinkled look of dwarfs and monkeys. He stood by the ball, awaiting the Maharajah's groaning progress up the duckboards.

"Take a photo of Cacouette," said Sarah.

"Why should I?"

"I'd like one."

"Later."

"Oh, don't be so putting off."

"You take it, then."

"You know I don't know how to."

"I'll show you. Come on, stupid; it's easy."

He pulled the camera open, supposing that she wanted to be shown. She tried to follow his explanation, since she had asked; but what she really enjoyed was to have him take this trouble over her, to be teased, and finally, with his laughing incredulous look, to be given up.

The Maharajah appeared, puffing. Merrick lay straight behind the camera, like a machine-gunner. Sarah's nose began to itch. She contorted and compressed her nostrils, buried her face in her elbow and heard a grunt, then silence, then a bellows heaving, and at last the crack of the hit ball and a violent expulsion of breath. The sneeze died a painful death, and she saw the Maharajah, dewy with sweat, rolling down to the green. The leather cylinder-full of clubs followed, looking as if it was walking on Cacouette's patched boots and trousers. Merrick did a war dance round her.

25

"I got him," he cried. "Right in the very act. Absolutely right at the moment. We'll blackmail him, Sarah. He'll have to give us hundreds of francs."

"What happened?"

"You don't mean to say you didn't see?"

"I began to sneeze."

"Oh, you are *hopeless*. He cheated, Sarah, right under my nose. He lifted the ball and teed it up."

Envious and chagrined, her pale long face scarlet, she sat on the pine-needles with her legs tucked under her, looking up at him; grains of sand tattooed her cheeks and stuck to her eyebrows and eyelashes.

"Cacouette winked at me. I got him just as he was doing it, teeing it up. It's evidence, Sarah."

"What shall we do?"

"Get it developed, of course! Oh, Sarah, fancy sneezing just at that very moment."

"I didn't sneeze," she said indignantly. "I stopped myself sneezing. I nearly choked."

"I told you how to stop sneezing. Just hold the bridge of your nose."

"I did."

"That's what stopped it, then. Lucky I told you."

He managed to turn every event so that he scored off her, and her own struggles to assert herself collapsed.

"Come on," he said. "There's going to be a shower."

The sun ducked into a black cloud and the pine-woods seemed to hold their breath. The first raindrops fell with a thud like apples, making dark-brown pock-marks in the white sand. Along the fairways the brilliant turf went sombre and players ran for trees. And everywhere, in the open and under trees, came out the brightly coloured mushrooms of golf umbrellas, red, blue, black, and orange, twirling like roulette wheels. Under one of them, close together, stood Major Bryant and his French girl; bright rain-drops fell in tassels round them. Soon only Miss Marples and Miss Wells were left on the course, ploughing on, playing their low raking shots through the rain.

26

"You'll get soaked, Merrick," Sarah said, peering at him under her matted hair. "You ought to have brought a coat."

"Nothing's better than this beastly shirt. It just sticks to me."

"Merrick!"

He had taken it off and stuffed it into his trouser pocket, and stood there under the thin trees, naked to the waist.

"You're just showing off, Merrick. It's to invite pneumonia."

But she knew that none of the catastrophes due to incaution ever came to him. He had bathed immediately after a big meal, although everybody had heard about the waiter at the Beach Hotel who did this last year and exploded in the sea; and he had not exploded. He had fallen through a frozen dune-pool last winter and not so much as caught a cold. He had put his foot through the glass roof of the Pine Hotel lounge and never even got a cut. He was always lucky. The rain slithered coolly over his shoulder-blades and down his chest, while she felt clammy drops between her skin and her dress. If only she were a boy!

"Rain's just like anything else," he said carelessly and strolled out of the trees. A thick gust drove him back grinning and dripping.

"There, Merrick. You're just pretending you like it. It's all going down your trousers."

"It'll soon stop. Look at *you*. Dying duck in a thunderstorm. Lucky this has got a case," he said, patting the camera. "I bet that old black cheat has taken cover."

"He's used to monsoons," said Sarah. She had been reading *The Ascent of Everest*.

"Monsoons are different."

After the shower the turf was emerald, the scent of the pines pungent and fresh. Sitting at her typewriter Anne saw them returning along the last fairway. Merrick had put on his shirt, but not tucked it in, and it was open in front. Sarah came a few steps behind, furtive as she approached people. "Don't slouch," Anne said out loud. She pointed towards the cottage and rubbed her back with an imaginary towel. Merrick waved cheerfully back.

"They'll be hit, of course," Anne said to herself. "Then I shall be blamed."

27

Fortunately Major Bryant and the French girl were the only couple near; and they were walking in, arm-in-arm.

"Are you in charge here?" said an irritated voice behind her. An elegant woman had entered the office; she had a hard face, of the kind that is called handsome, but rather a long nose. "I'm Anita Ferguson of the *Spyglass*," she said, as if this was an event.

"Oh, yes. Can I help you?"

"I want to see the secretary."

"I'm afraid he's out on the course."

"Please tell him I'm here. I flew over this morning."

Anne disliked gossip-writers; since the days of Johnny and Mrs. Hooper she had had a prejudice against them, which acquaintance had not softened.

"I want to know who's here this week-end," declared Miss Ferguson. "This Maharajah, for instance. The paper wants a photograph of him."

"He's particularly asked that he should not be photographed," said Anne.

"We'll see about that. Who the devil's that?"

An unusually tall woman with an ungainly crow-like walk was crossing the course. She wore a large felt hat, and her hands were dug into the pockets of a grey cloak; golfers called out to warn her, but she paid no attention.

"That's Judith Friedmann," said Anne, watching her curiously. "She owns the golf-club, and most of Oriol."

"She hardly dresses the part. What is she, a recluse?"

"I scarcely know her. She's very unlike her father."

The children had stopped to stare at Judith, who did not look at them; Merrick nudged Sarah and laughed. When Judith had passed, he held up the barbed wire so that Sarah could get into the field with the white horse. Sarah's hair became caught, and he disentangled it. A few feet away a large notice in French and English said: Please do not cross this field.

"Not my idea of Oriol at all," said Miss Ferguson, still gazing after Judith.

"You don't really know what Oriol is like," Anne replied thoughtfully.

"What do you mean by that?"

28

"Oh, there is another Oriol, but there's no one important to photograph there."

"And do people like that scarecrow inhabit it?" asked Miss Ferguson. "Come on, let's see your list." Anne handed over the visitors' book, but she did not look at it. "Isn't that Baroness de Leverson?" she said, peering out of the window. "Yes, it is. And old Sir Maurice Wildenstein with her. They were together at Deauville. Are they going to get engaged?"

"I don't know."

"You don't know?" Miss Ferguson made it clear that in her opinion Anne ought to know. She snatched up her camera and hurried off to greet the Baroness.

Anne looked at the clock; it was nearly time to lock up. Judith was striding towards the Villa des Roses. The children were getting through another forbidden fence and Sarah's hair was again entangled. Anne sighed happily; she would soon be home.

3

Wh   hen Anne reached the cottage gate, a face was peering
       through the sitting-room window; the front door opened and
       Sarah ran out to meet her.

"Hello, darling," Anne said, kissing her.

"Hello. What happened today?"

"Nothing much. Miss Ferguson has come."

"The awful one?"

"Yes, the awful one."

Arm-in-arm they walked indoors; and at once everything was warm, intimate, accustomed. The season had only just started, the nights were still
cold; an open fire was burning, and Merrick and Sarah's wet clothes hung
steaming over a tall fender as old as Anne. Blanche was humming opera
in the kitchen; a smell of onion-and-marrow soup made their mouths
water.

"Where's Merrick?" said Anne.

"Upstairs, I think."

"What's he doing?"

"I don't know." She was hiding something, not giving him away. He
came in that moment, and not down the stairs; he had been rigging up a
dummy in Blanche's room to frighten her when she went to bed.

"Where were you?" Anne asked.

"Me? In the bathroom." He said it quite naturally; he lied much better
and more often than Sarah. "How was old Wake?" he asked.

"Much the same."

"*We* saw him."

"And I saw *you*. Getting under the wire. What do you think notices are put there for? You'll get me into trouble."

"No, we won't, Mother. Everyone thinks you're wonderful."

He gave her a hug; she had meant to be severe with him, but felt herself yielding and him aware of it.

"Go on," she said. "You're all cupboard love. And you're up to something, I know." A quick glance betrayed the two of them. "There. You can't hide it. All right, I don't want to know."

She went into the kitchen.

"She always knows," said Sarah.

"You always go red, that's why. You're scarlet now. Anyone could tell if *you* did a murder!"

He sat at the upright piano, strumming out the notes Blanche had been singing.

"Come on," he called out. "Sing some more."

She came to the doorway in her greasy apron, as big as overalls. "*C'est de la musique, ça*," she said knowingly, nodding her head.

"Well, sing it, then."

"Go on, Blanche," said Sarah.

"I've got your suppers to get. No time for singing."

They heard her praising his playing to Anne; he played by ear, usually with the loud pedal, and had a tuneful voice.

Sarah sat in the bow-window, devouring the next chapter of *Jane Eyre*. The sun had set, the last golfers were coming in. Streaks of dying light turned the window-panes amber. The fairways grew dark as the heather in the rough, and heavy shadows smothered the greens, till the course began to look weird and the trees were a black barrier. Two hundred yards along, lights were going on in the Pine Hotel and chandeliers glittering behind plate-glass windows, where Pierre, in a white coat, mixed drinks and the golfers lingered before changing for dinner; in summer nobody thought of dining before nine at the earliest. A taxi brought someone back from the afternoon session at the Casino; at night it was not fashionable for the women to arrive before eleven, and the men in the hotels and villas liked to sit over their cigars and brandy, discussing sport, people, business, politics, the danger of war. The cottage squatted like a tiny dinghy

34

alongside an illuminated liner; in the hotel rows of lights with everybody round them mellow, on holiday, in a good temper, and then one little light for Anne, Blanche, and the children. Opposite were the lonely dunes, and the nocturnal melancholy of the sea beyond.

The children laid the table. Blanche entered, beaming, and sweating from the vapours of a huge soup-tureen. Anne ladled it out, the children's eyes following her movements like a dog's; they had never been taught, as were some English children at the hotel, not to stare at the food. On wet Sundays they often ate their midday meal at a small hotel in the town, among the French bourgeois who made it a ritual. They took food as pleasure and had no sense of impropriety about it.

"*Bon appétit*," said Blanche, like a benediction.

She was a fat red girl from Boulogne, with innumerable distant relations who died so frequently that (although she scarcely knew them) she nearly always was in black. Every other afternoon-off she laid flowers on the family grave. She loved Monsieur Philippe, who drove the Pine Hotel taxis, and Merrick teased her relentlessly about it, pretending she was off to an assignation when he knew quite well she was going to the cemetery. She was his butt. He would jump out on her from behind doors, creep round the house at night and tap like a spook or a burglar at her window, and tickle her to distraction in the passage.

"Oh, Monsieur Merrick, Monsieur Merrick," she would cry, writhing and weeping and slapping his hands. "Stop, stop! You'll be the death of me."

But he guessed that she enjoyed it. Sometimes Sarah was scandalized, yet could not help laughing; and Blanche was so good-natured. She loved children and longed for several of her own. Anne was her one real friend.

"Are you going to read, Mother?" asked Sarah after supper.

"If you like."

"One game of Initials first," said Merrick.

"You only play because you know you always win," said Sarah.

"You could win if you concentrated enough. You've got much more imagination than I have."

"It isn't imagination. It's facts."

It was no good protesting. Already he had got out the pencils and paper and given them each a sheet; obediently they wrote the letters of the alphabet down the middle.

"Now, what's the letter to be?" he said. "You choose it, Sarah."

"No, you."

"Go on. Do something yourself."

She closed her eyes and stuck her pencil into a newspaper.

"It's S."

He began to write at once, and had a dozen words down before either of them had written one. Three heads crouched over the table; looking up, they caught each other's eyes, stared abstractedly, and suddenly scribbled a word.

"I can't think of anything," said Sarah.

"Go on, Sarah. There's hundreds."

Anne was thinking about tomorrow's meals, and that she would have to go into Oriol, and that Merrick needed a pair of shoes.

"You're not concentrating, Mother."

"Yes, I am."

"You've hardly written anything down."

"We're not all as clever as you."

"It isn't cleverness," he expostulated. He really wanted them to do well. "It's just concentration."

She bent her mind to the game and opposite the letter A wrote South America. The warm room, Blanche's humming, the fire, the children's seriousness, gave her a deep sense of peace. She too became serious, pressing the pencil against her lips. The children could not forgive condescension; if she had not seemed to throw herself heart and soul into the game, had she given an impression merely of humouring them, they would have been disappointed in her.

"Time's up," said Merrick. "You read out first, mother."

"South America."

"Got it."

"So have I," said Sarah. "And South Africa."

"Well, then, Saint Antony."

33

"Got it, Sarah?"

"No."

"One for Saint Antony, Mother."

At the end she had a total of twelve.

"Now you, Sarah."

"Sister Anne."

"Who's she when she's at home?"

"Merrick! In the story of Bluebeard. . . ."

"Never heard of her. *Never* heard of her."

"Sister Anne is perfectly all right," said Anne, always pleased when Sarah got the better of him. "I used to read you the story of Bluebeard when you were little. That shows what a memory you've got."

" 'Sister Anne, sister Anne, do you see anybody coming?' " Sarah quoted. "I thought everybody knew that."

"Well, I suppose it will do. But why not Sister Alice or Sister Agnes, or . . . ?"

"I've got Sister Agnes too," said Sarah.

"And who might she be?"

"She was a famous nurse in the war, wasn't she, Mother?"

"She was indeed. That's another mark for Sarah."

Merrick sat back, putting on an outraged look. "It's got to be famous names or expressions in common use," he said. "I don't call Sister Agnes either."

"I do," said Anne. "Count it, darling."

"Well . . ." He yielded, but pretended to look injured, and anyhow they all knew that he was sure to have most. "And what else, pray?"

Sarah went through her list, mostly quotations and names from fiction and history . . . Silas Marner, Sir Galahad, Samson and Delilah, still waters, sirens' song, Solly Joel, soft answer, Scarlet Pimpernel of course . . . a total of twenty-five.

"Nothing from V to Z?" asked Merrick.

"Nothing."

Obviously he had something. He read his list. They pretended not to be impressed with it, but his enjoyment spread to them. . . . Sally in our Alley, splice the mainbrace, stove pipe, stop press, ship ahoy, stark terror (not granted), Solomon Grundy, shock troops, Swiss roll, Santa Claus....

"It's K," said Sarah. "Santa Klaus with a K. It's German."

"I've got it with K too."

He flowed on, swamping them . . . saddle of mutton, safe as houses, sailing-boat, steeple-jack, certain winner (not granted), sea legs, single rein, sliding seat . . . and at the end, triumphantly, sal volatile, Suitable Woman (not granted), Saint X....

"Who's Saint X?"

"The unknown saint. If there's an unknown warrior, why not an unknown saint?"

They laughed, and Anne saw Sarah admiring him from the coverts of her hair.

"South Zanzibar," he finished.

"No."

"Why ever not? There's Zanzibar, isn't there? Isn't there, Mother?" he asked, posing as simple.

"Yes, darling, there's Zanzibar."

"Then there must be north and south."

His total came to forty-eight. "And I do have some more, if you want to hear them," he said casually.

"Oh, I know what it is," said Sarah. "It's the kings and queens again. You know none of them count." All the same, she was longing to hear them.

"I won't read them if you think it's waste of time."

"Go on," said Anne. "Don't be a hypocrite. Read them."

"Well, for A, there was a very famous king called Simon the Awe-Inspiring, with his queen called Salome the Angular, from the shape of her hips."

Sarah looked shocked.

"What do you know about hips?" said Anne.

"This queen's hips were like the edge of a table. Just like Miss Ferguson's hips."

"Miss Ferguson's figure is much admired," said Anne.

"Not by me."

Anne wondered how long he had been noticing such things.

"Simon the Bow-legged, Saul the Cautious, Solomon the Morbid, Sarah the Well-meaning . . ."

The kings and queens were his personal joke; whenever they played Initials, they had to end it like this.

They went into the garden afterwards to say good-night to Frou-frou. She lay on the straw in her shed, her red eyes burning. The moon was full, a little blue, ringed with a rust-coloured halo. From far off came the constant lowing of the sea, and behind the glittering hotel millions of frogs croaked.

Anne felt Merrick's fingers touching her ear.

"You've got a grey hair, Mother."

"I've got several. I'm getting old."

"I like grey hair, and I don't think you look at all old. Nor does Major Bryant. I heard him say so."

His arm rested on her shoulder now, sending its warmth through her; his face was level with hers, frank and affectionate, and for an instant he might have been her lover. She thought about that moment in bed, touched by his gallantry and treasuring it. One day a girl would feel that stir; once she had felt it from his father. How quickly the years had passed; and she, though watching Merrick from her inner self in all his gestures, words, and acts, and reading between the lines of his letters from school, had no inkling how he would turn out when boyhood passed. She could not imagine the children except amidst beach, dunes, and forest, or here at home, teasing Blanche and playing Initials. Gradually he would move away into the built-up areas of manhood, where the world would have its giant ambush waiting for him. Was she doing all she could to prepare him? Would he be armed? Would he be, as his father had been, too well armed?

Bands played in the town of Oriol-plage, the moth-life roused there, roulette wheels were turning, and on the front the hurdy-gurdies of a midnight fair; but the cottage soon lay still. Fat Blanche looked sadly through her open window at the moon. She was unhappy because she had no dowry and the complexion of a beetroot, and Monsieur Philippe did not love her. She had found Merrick's dummy in her room, a draped swaying figure with a football for a face, and though she was pleased that people thought about her, she felt sad that it was only to make jokes. Ah, if only the children could understand! One day they would know what it was to love, and then they would remember her.

She said her prayers. She was very devout, and went to Mass three times a week and twice on Sundays. Every night she prayed for a quarter of an hour, kneeling by her bed, her large feet in blue felt bedroom slippers, her large red hands sprouting from a white nightgown tied with elastic at the wrists. She prayed for the peace of the world, because she had a brother in the army; and for Anne and the children; and for Monsieur Philippe, asking forgiveness in the same breath for having imagined herself married and in bed with him. A crucifix and a coloured picture of the Virgin hung above her pillow, and a postcard on the chest of drawers showed a beautiful young man, with pink cheeks and almost purple hair, breathing down the neck of a girl with pearly teeth and a permanent wave. It was entitled *Tendresse*. Monsieur Philippe had given it to her, out of the blue, on her name day; but that was six months ago, and he had not followed it up. She would wait for him for ever, but feared that he deceived her; indeed, at that moment he was with Baroness de Leverson's maid, driving to a night out at the Café Excelsior.

The children slept upstairs on the other side of the staircase. For some years they had had separate rooms. When Anne was reading them *The Count of Monte Cristo* they used to pretend that they were prisoners in a fortress, in adjoining cells, and communicated by signals on the wall. This they had outgrown, but Sarah was still scared of the dark. She looked under the bed; nobody there. She said to the cupboards in a loud clear voice, "Come out. I know you're there." Nobody came; so she locked them. She leaned out of the window; no one lurking in the currant-bushes. There was a rustle in the goat-shed, and Frou-frou stared up at her with glassy red eyes.

"All right," she said. "It's only me."

The eyes closed again. Merrick came in to say good-night. He was in his brown jaeger dressing-gown and bedroom slippers, and moved so quietly that she jumped.

"You are horrible, Merrick. You did it on purpose."

"I didn't. It's you that's nervous. You're worse than Blanche."

"I think it's unfair to go on frightening her. She'll have a fit one day. Then you'll be sorry."

"I like that. And it was you painted the face on the football." He leant out of the window at her side, sniffing the air. "It's getting milder, Sarah. We'll be able to bathe at night soon." He made a noise like a cat, bringing out Frou-frou's red eyes again. "Miss Friedmann's a funny old stick," he said. "I think it's time we investigated the Villa des Roses."

"We can't while she's there."

"She's going to Paris tomorrow. The postman told me. I had a look, and it's quite easy to get on to the roof, and somebody always leaves a skylight open."

"What did you do with the photograph of the Maharajah?" Sarah asked.

"I gave it to Jerry to develop. He's going to sell it to Miss Ferguson. If she buys it, we might do a lot of photographs for her."

"Then we could save up to buy Cacouette a bicycle," said Sarah. Ever since she had discovered that the caddies had to walk three miles to and from home each day, this had been one of her ambitions. Merrick said nothing; he had a carpentry shed in the garden, and if he made any money he was going to spend it on tools.

After he had gone to bed Sarah watched cars swinging on to the road from the Pine Hotel gates, carrying the gamblers to the Casino; women sat in the back, glowing in furs and jewels. She got into bed and tried to do a sketch of Jerry. Round her walls were pictures of people she was in love with or wanted to be like; prints of her novel-heroes, a portrait from a life of Byron, photographs of mannequins and society beauties. She had sketched a good likeness of Merrick, but Jerry's would not come. She opened her diary and tried to go on with a story which began "Once there was a sailor who had a goat called Frou-frou, of which he was inordinately fond . . ." Inordinately was a new word to be proud of, but the story had stuck there. "His wife was very jealous of Frou-frou," she added, "and re-solved to do away with her." And what then? She had no idea, except that the sailor was Jerry and she the goat, and they would run away together; the middle was the difficult part and seemed unnecessary, once she had a beginning and an end. She put it away, slept, and dreamed of gypsies, while headlamps swung their beams along the walls, as if searching for her, until, returning from the opposite side of the house, they woke up Blanche. Merrick read a chapter of a sailing book, wondered how they would get inside the Villa des Roses, and went to sleep; he did not dream at all.

4

The postman had misinformed Merrick. Judith Friedmann did not leave for Paris the following morning. She had been reading all night, and only when the sun came round to her bedroom window had she gone off into a restless doze, closing the shutters; at noon she was lying on the bed, awake, haggard, and still dressed as on the evening before. Emily, her ancient maid, was out shopping at Oriol-plage; nearly seventy, terrified of burglars, she had locked the doors and closed the windows, and being also terrified of fire she had raked out the ashes in the kitchen grate. No smoke was coming from the chimneys; the Villa des Roses appeared abandoned.

A letter from Sir Maurice Wildenstein lay on Judith's bed-table; as she reached out for it the light slanting between the shutters made stripes across her hands. She sat up, arranged a pillow at her back, and began to read for the third time. The blow came in the first sentence: "Dearest Judith, I am writing to tell you that I am going to marry Helen Leverson." The rest was apology, explanations, references to his past friendship with Judith, and hopes that it would continue; he was a scholarly man, and had put it neatly. Angrily she crumpled the letter. For many years she had taken it for granted that one day, when it suited them both, she would marry Sir Maurice Wildenstein; a convenient alliance between two civilized people of similar tastes, who had known each other all their lives. Both were at root strangers to the country of their adoption, she to France, he to England, and looked upon the world with the cosmopolitan range of a central European Jew. They were fastidious and had read widely in several languages. They loved Mozart and were hypercritical of Wagner. Judith was nearly fifty, Sir Maurice ten years older; he had been something of a gallant, but it had been almost understood between them that when his philanderings ended he would come to harbour pleasantly with her.

Judith had few acquaintances in the Baroness de Leverson's world. She knew her slightly as one of the most superficial among the fashionable set who visited Oriol during the season; elegant, at first glance attractive, a woman of skin-deep culture, in her opinion entirely unsuited to Sir Maurice Wildenstein, and about half his age. She imagined him married to this new wife, with a home and many friends, giving parties, seated at opposite ends of the dinner-table, arranging their passage through middle age into age with the height of comfort. She would never visit them, never. She would live on now in this barracks of a villa, turning into a hermit, but she would never invite them. An almost invisible hand, which time and again had diverted from her the stream of life, appeared now to have dammed it irrevocably. There had been, years ago, an old woman, an aunt of her father's, whom she had often been dragged to visit in her childhood. This old woman, never married, had lived alone with a housekeeper in a large apartment, and seemed to spend her whole time stitching tapestries; to call on her had been a burden. Judith now saw herself preparing for this role. Gradually her activities would dwindle; ten, fifteen years, and she and her great-aunt would be the same.

Legendary figures had come to Judith Friedmann's christening. You shall have riches, one had promised her. You shall have brains, another had said; you shall have the sense of beauty, you shall have the power to love and to enjoy, another and another. And at the end the witch at the back had stepped forward and cried, "You shall be ugly." All these promises had been fulfilled, but the curse had been the strongest. The obsession of her ugliness had become a fountain of gloom, bursting out when something quite different had made her wretched, and dominating the wound which had released it. She was gaunt, with flat feet and too large a nose. She was six foot, and her body resembled a plank. Her eyes were the colour of garnets and she had fine honey-coloured hair; kind friends praised these features in a manner she resented, since it emphasized their silence about the rest of her. She alarmed ordinary men, because she was so tall and so clever. A few admired her brain and enjoyed her talk, but at the frontier of her looks they halted.

She pushed the counterpane aside, lifted herself wearily, and without troubling to put on her shoes walked over to the window and peered between the slits. She recalled some play—O'Neill's *Mourning Becomes Electra*—in which a disappointed woman walls herself up in a deserted mansion. At no time had she been in love with Sir Maurice; it was precisely because the prospect of life with him represented the paring-down and final economy of her hopes, that their frustration weighed so harshly on her. A sunbeam had come in through the shutters, and the motes of dust whirled in it like snowflakes in a child's glass toy. She held her hand there; it was well-shaped, with fine long fingers, the fingers of a harpist, which the sunlight made almost transparent. But when she turned back to the room, she caught sight of herself in a mirror, the room's shadows deepening the shadows of her heavy features, marking the downward lines. Her hair hung in untidy streaks. She went nearer and stared at the reflection, as if at a mortal enemy, her lower lip moving in little thrusts. Suddenly she seized a candlestick off a table beneath the mirror, and began to smash the glass. "Hideous, hideous!" she shouted. "Yes, I am hideous." She smashed at it, until the entire reflection had gone and only a few jagged teeth clung to the gilded frame. But immediately the fit had passed she felt ashamed. She tore up the letter, threw the pieces into the waste-paper basket, and lay down again on her bed. A new mood came over her, equally sombre, but rising from another distress.

For the last few years Judith had been receiving accounts concerning the persecution of Jews in Germany. She had sent money to societies organized for their relief. Her own kindred had long ago moved westwards and were prosperously established, the second or third generation, in France, England, and America, so that she had no personal connexions with these sufferings except through a young friend, a violinist called Hans Mayer. She had not seen him for five years; it had been summer then, he had played in her Paris apartment, and people had stood under the window to listen to him.

Judith had had many protégés and been in love with several of them. None had been in love with her; but with one or two she had made an arrangement, paying for them to publish their poems, or show their paintings, or give a concert, and they in return had lived with her. Hans almost alone had asked, expected, and been asked for nothing, and given her affection; he was twenty-five years younger, and in his company she was merry and forgot her complications. He had come as a boy to Paris, and she, before 1933, had gone to Germany, and together they had walked among the trees at Fontaintebleu, or by the banks of the green Ysar, talking about music, having supper together, and made complementary to one another, she by her understanding criticisms of his work, he by his light-heartedness. There was a photograph of him in her room; he had a white face with a thin arched nose, and his fuzzy hair made him look like a gollywog. She had called him that; and to him she had been "the giantess."

This friendship had illumined her life. She had treasured it secretly, allowing none even of her most intimate circle in Paris to get hold of it, not out of jealousy, but for fear that they would at once assume she either was or wished to be his mistress and pin the living sympathy between them into a tabulated category of either sex or sentiment. When he played in her apartment, she merely let it be known that she "had a gifted young violinist coming in," and let them, if they felt like it, pay their court to him; he was not good-looking, and so many people had "gifted young" somebodies coming in constantly, that no more had been thought of it. He had always refused to take a penny from her; he would make his own way, he said. When Hitler seized power, he was not yet well known, and by 1935 life had become difficult for him. She had implored him to leave, but he had preferred to remain until he could get his mother out of the country with him. A month ago all had seemed ready, and Judith had rooms in Paris waiting for them. A note had arrived lately from his mother informing Judith that he had been taken to prison, accused of "decadence"; nobody knew what had become of him since.

Thus the world's tragedy, of which she had known well enough at a distance, had come close to her own door, intensifying, not obliterating, her personal disappointment. She had never been a profoundly happy woman.

43

Her heart, denied requital, had withdrawn to a small corner in a well-ordered mansion of intellect; but the chance of a companionable marriage and the hope of getting Hans out of Germany had seemed to leave two avenues open for its exercise. Now across each an iron gate had closed. In the past she had escaped from her frustrations into some "movement" or artistic project, shaking off an emotional with a mental fever. Her world had been a group of intelligent dilettanti, to whom for a time an idea could be almost as exciting as emotions, indeed was a kind of emotion, purer, finer, as exacting, and less liable to betray. Many people give themselves to ideas in flight from some personal distress, and a number of the best and the worst crusades in history have gathered their supporters thus. Judith had surrendered to half a dozen of them, political, aesthetic, and religious. But never before had she felt, as now, that a darkness and a deadness had settled upon the world outside her as well as upon herself. Her last letters to Hans had been almost frenzied in their urgency, but she had never really visualized him caught. The conception of what it meant, in physical detail, enlarged itself now, until it seemed to speak for the entire universe; and the desire to persecute, of which she had been made aware by birth but never, because of her wealth, been a victim, appeared as part of an all-pervading cruelty, a "law of nature." It seemed to her that she herself could achieve nothing of value, that she was not wanted, and that savage forces over which she had no influence were in control.

Last night the nightingales had been singing near by, and Keats's line had come to her:

Now more than ever seems it rich to die.

These few words and the song of the wordless sirens outside had sunk into her heart deeper than the book of her favourite Proust, which she was trying to read. She had put it down, and the mood had nearly mastered her then; it returned now, tranquil and caressing as the sunbeam between the shutters. Through the open door into the bathroom she saw bottles on a shelf above the basin, her sleeping draughts among them. She began to think of her friends, of the societies and the charities, and the struggling groups of rebel artists that had always attracted her, to whom even a small share of her fortune would be a blessing. Perhaps they would have better use for it; rational arguments flocked to the side of her despair, and no firmly held principle opposed them. Her head ached and she was shivering; death presented itself as a haven of peace. She even took off her rings and placed them on the bed-table, as if bequeathing them. At this moment a slight noise startled her, coming apparently from the roof. She lay still, listening, and heard it again, this time louder and above the bathroom. She raised herself a little, and through the open door saw the skylight in the bathroom roof cautiously lifted. A piece of dislodged tile fell and broke to pieces in the bath. Whispering could be heard; there were people on the roof. After a minute the skylight was lifted clear and a pair of legs, in grey flannel trousers, lowered themselves and began to grope like antennae for the cupboard. Amazement scattered everything else in her head; she could think nothing except "burglars."

Her mood, despite its blackness, had seemed to have a kind of clarity and even nobility. Angered at the distraction, she went to the door. The dangling feet found the top of the cupboard and painstakingly established themselves. The rest of Merrick followed. He sat down, and Sarah, peering through the hole in the roof, was the first to meet Judith's eyes.

"Oh!" Sarah gasped.

Merrick looked down abruptly, and the cupboard rocked.

"I'm frightfully sorry," he said, crouching like a monkey against the wall. "We thought it was empty. We were exploring."

"How dare you?" she exclaimed. She recognized the MacManus children. A stream of words poured from her. Her over-wrought nerves gave way and she scarcely knew what she was saying. Two pairs of eyes gaped at her, widening in amazement; her appearance alarmed them more than the shock of being discovered. She grew conscious of herself, and became calmer. "Go away," she almost shouted. "Get out of this house."

"I'm afraid I shall have to come down," said Merrick.

"Get out the way you came in."

"I can't," he said. "I can't get the leverage." He made an effort and nearly dragged the cupboard over. He looked at her helplessly. "I can only come downwards."

"And scratch your feet all over the furniture. How dare you come in like this!"

"We weren't going to steal anything," Sarah protested from the roof. She was evidently lying precariously on the tiles; her hair hung through the skylight like a silken rope.

"I don't care what you were going to do. You've no right to be here, you know quite well. Go away, or I'll send for the police."

"My shoes are quite clean," said Merrick. "I could drop from here."

"Well then, drop."

He began to lower himself, facing towards the cupboard.

"Stop!" she called out. "You'll pull the whole thing over." She held it while he dropped.

Scarlet in the face, he began to dust himself. "We're frightfully sorry," he repeated.

"I should think so. I know who you are. What will your mother say about this?"

"Oh, please don't tell her," exclaimed Sarah pathetically. "We only did it for fun. It's the first time we've been here."

"Where else have you been?"

"Nowhere else," said Merrick untruthfully.

"I don't believe you. Just look at yourself. Are you proud of behaving like a hooligan?"

Suddenly Judith felt nonplussed, as if she had arrived in a country not a word of whose language she knew. They were watching her, and she began to be ashamed of her outburst. Merrick had a grey smudge on his nose and a wisp of cobweb hanging from his hair. Sarah's hand slipped, and a second piece of tile fell into the bath.

"I'm frightfully sorry," said Sarah, nearly falling through in pursuit of it.

Merrick picked up the pieces. "Shall I put them in the waste-paper basket?" he asked virtuously. He looked into her bedroom, and a slight change in his expression showed that he had seen the disorder there. "Hello, the mirror's broken," he said. "I'll pick up the bits for you." He went past her and knelt on the carpet, saving time until he had a plan. On no account must this get back to their mother; it would mean an end to all

46

their explorations. He had never seen a woman in such a rage, not even Sarah last year when she threw the egg-cup at him. He noticed the candlestick, lying under the little table where Judith had dropped it. What did it mean? Had there been a fight? The detective always near the surface pressed eagerly forward.

"That's enough," said Judith impatiently. "Now you can go."

"Are you sure there's nothing else I can do?"

Visions of chivalrous rescue presented themselves.

"Yes, quite sure. What about your sister?"

"Oh, she can get down all right," he replied carelessly. "We really are awfully sorry. I do hope you won't tell my mother."

He looked at her with a worried solemn air, and went to the door with such an atmosphere of debonair contrition about him that she could not let him leave; nor, now, did she want to be alone with herself again.

"Have you had tea?" she asked.

"No, we haven't."

"Well, you'd better have it here. Tell your sister to come round to the front door."

"Oh, thanks very much, Miss Friedmann. It's awfully good of you."

"So you know who I am?"

"Oh, yes. Shall I tell her now?"

"Yes."

"Go round to the front door, Sarah," he called up from the bathroom, and whispered, too low for Judith to hear, "It's all right, I think." Instructions followed how to get down.

Judith heard the skylight closed and scrambling noises above the ceiling.

"Will she be all right?" she asked anxiously.

"Oh yes. She'll go the way we came. Shall I open the front door?" he asked obligingly.

"No, it's locked. Stay down there, and I'll get the key."

"If you don't mind my saying so," he remarked gravely, "I should be careful where you walk. There may be some splinters lying about still."

When he had gone out, she at once put on her shoes, feeling like a rebuked child herself. His good manners and grown-up, almost old-fashioned solicitude touched her and seemed to break a little string in her heart. He was someone from a world she had long since lost. She began to weep, rocking her head in her hands, and it was some minutes before she could collect herself. Her hysterical onslaught upon him had disgraced her. Children were impressionable. They would repeat what they had seen with embroideries of their own, and in a few days the story would be all over Oriol, making her ridiculous. People would say that she, who prided herself so on her reason, was going mad.

At the front door Merrick and Sarah were talking through the letter-box.

"Will she tell Mother?" Sarah asked.

"Not now. She wouldn't have asked us to tea."

"Wasn't she furious, Merrick! You were awfully calm."

"I think there's something going on," he replied.

"What?"

"I don't know. Something. She must be rolling in money," he said. "You could get the whole cottage into here."

He looked round the hall, which was almost as large as the golf-club lounge. The furniture, most of it under dust-sheets, was heavy and Victorian; it looked like a dump-heap of torsos waiting for disposal. A carpeted staircase with a heavily carved oak banister led up to the upper rooms, and the vast dark pictures in gilt frames, the indistinguishable tapestries, and the pewter chandelier, gave him the impression of a family tomb. He had read about careers which had begun with some weird accident, and though far less romantic than Sarah, was always prepared for some uncanny stroke of luck. Perhaps Miss Friedmann would adopt him.

"Does she live here all alone, Merrick?"

"I don't know. It's rather spooky."

They squatted on either side of the door, their noses almost touching through the slit.

"I'm sure there's something fishy," he repeated. "There was a mirror smashed, a valuable one too, and a candlestick lying on the floor, and the bed all anyhow. I shouldn't be surprised if she's a bit off her head. Ssssh . . . she's coming."

The slit flapped back as Judith appeared at the top of the staircase. She had washed her face, combed her hair, and made herself up; she still looked haggard, but no longer frightening. She descended the stairs with exaggerated composure, like an ancient butler, unlocked the door, and let Sarah in.

"Well, you're a nice couple," she said, almost jovially, trying to let them see they were forgiven.

"We didn't mean to burgle you, really," said Sarah.

"Do you spend a lot of time on other people's roofs?"

"Well, we do rather," Merirck answered candidly. "We like roofs."

"And attics," added Sarah.

"They're the most interesting part of a house," said Merrick.

"Well, you'd better come up and tell me all about them."

The stair-carpet was like moss, and their feet made no sound on it. She led them into her sitting-room, sat them down in deep chairs, and went to fetch tea. She knew that children liked rich cakes and quantities of jam, but she could not find them. She had seldom been inside the kitchen and had no idea where anything was kept.

"Is this all hers?" asked Sarah.

"Of course it is. She owns the golf-course." Merrick, having got into the house first, had assumed a proprietary interest in it. "There was a picture of her father in the hall," he said.

"How do you know?"

"It's the same as the man in the golf-club. He started it all."

"Look at that picture, Merrick!"

"She *must* be a bit cracked," he decided.

It was a small Picasso.

"I rather like it," said Sarah.

"You would."

The room had been entirely rebuilt to suit Judith, and was now at violent odds with the rest of the house. The walls were whitewashed, a few cactuses stood in pots in the window, and the furniture and upholstery had been made when the fashion was tubular and angular. Judith had grown impatient with it, and the chairs in which the children sat were evidence of a cosier mood. Merrick did not care for the room, and found it disappointing after the lush nineteenth-century vegetation downstairs. He would have been amazed and indignant to know that the pictures were worth several thousand pounds. There was one photograph, showing a thickly moustachioed man with a high white collar, posed sedately in profile against a high-backed chair. Not liking to get up, Sarah leaned forward to read the signature sprawled across it: "*à mon amie Judith, Marcel . . .*" she could not make out the surname. It was Proust, but would have meant nothing to her.

Judith returned with tea. "I'm afraid I haven't been able to find much," she said apologetically.

"Oh, that's all right," said Merrick, but she could tell they were both surprised, in that large house, that she had only managed to provide a half-eaten sponge-cake and not even thought of making toast. The girl's eyes roved about the room, always returning to the cake, and now and then she furtively grabbed a piece. The boy ate steadily and solemnly, and gulped down cup after cup of tea. He was much the surer of himself, and Judith felt more drawn to the shy and awkward girl, who asked questions from behind her hair about the pictures and other objects in the room, and when they were answered fell into long reflective silences. But she enjoyed the boy's studied exercise of good manners and his air, as he lit a match for her, of a practised cavalier. He was telling her about carpentry.

"Yes," he said. "Once you've got the design, it's really quite simple. People think it's much more complicated than it is."

"Yes, I suppose so."

"But that's not hard."

"I could never learn it."

"Oh, I expect you could," he said with cheerful politeness.

"I can't do it," said Sarah.

"What do you do?" Judith asked.

"Oh, I draw sometimes. I don't know what I do."

"She forgets what she's doing," said Merrick sympathetically, "but she's very good at drawing. You should see some of her things. And she reads a lot too. She's read much more than I have."

He was obviously used to acting as her interpreter; something assertive in his voice made him sound like a champion.

"You must come back and look at my books," Judith said.

It was an invitation for the future, yet half an hour ago she had almost wished to annihilate the future. Merrick went on talking about carpentry, but she did not listen, thinking of the long journey of life that reached between them and her, and amazed that she could ever have started from the same point. In her exaggerated disgust for the airless warren that her own thoughts had become, she imagined the children to be more open than in fact they were, especially Merrick. Enviously, and disliking herself, she pictured them as untouched. When they said good-bye, she sent her regards to their mother and promised to come and visit them, helped by an eager invitation from Merrick; and when they had gone, she realized that she had meant it. She walked for a little round the sunny garden; and there, outside the shuttered house, ordinary events were continuing as they had all day. Jacqueline, the gardener's wife, was hanging up the washing. Cars rustled towards the golf-club, and now and then a fiacre passed clippity-clop. The sun thrust long swords through the dark arras of the pines, and birds, alighting on swaying branches, sang aimlessy. She remembered Hans Mayer and, though grief mounted her heart again, she no longer experienced the ghastly illumination in which the whole universe had seemed to be a torture-chamber. She knew people who would have told her that the children's arrival had been the hand of God, and though of course it had only been an accident, she could not help reflecting upon it as something very strange and unlikely to be forgotten. Her intellect began to savour it. One day, perhaps, she would tell one of her writer friends, and he would make a story of it. When she came back to her room, and saw in the shuttered light the cracked mirror, the tumbled bed, and next door the empty cups and plates, she thought, "A tea-party in the grave." She put on her rings again, saying to herself, "Poor Marie-Louise" (the cousin to whom they were to have been left), "she will have to wait"; and she smiled. She threw back the shutters and stood for a long time in the sun.

Merrick and Sarah walked back past the golf-club, talking excitedly about their adventure.

"She won't tell anyone," said Sarah finally.

"Oh no, not now."

"She's awfully nice," said Sarah. "Wasn't she furious, though, to start with!"

"It wasn't much of a tea," said Merrick. "It's much better at home." His forehead was puckered, the detective still at work. "I wonder what she'd been up to, Sarah."

"Up to?"

"There was something fishy. The mirror smashed, and the mess . . . you didn't see all that. If you ask me, she'd been drinking. A lot of people do."

5

Extract from "What the World is Doing" (Miss Ferguson's gossip column in the *Spyglass*), over the signature of Anita (Miss Ferguson):

Well, dear readers, how I wish you were all here. Oriol has never looked so lovely. The season is in full swing now, the villas are all open, and there is a big dinner-party every night. Really, it is quite a problem to know which to choose. On Monday it was the Duchess of Mendoza, on Tuesday Sir Maurice Wildenstein, who (as I announced last week) is going to marry the Baroness de Leverson ... what a party that was! Sir Maurice has taken the Villa Harlequin for the season, and we dined on the terrace with a band playing somewhere not too near. I don't like a band that interrupts conversation, do you? The sweet was a chocolate ice made in the shape of the Oriol lighthouse, with a real revolving lamp inside, and the wines were everything you would expect from a connoisseur of Sir Maurice's discrimination. They tell me they are off to Ceylon and the East Indies for the honeymoon ... the East seems to be becoming quite fashionable. Mary Stiles tells me she is thinking of a trip to Bali. And talking of the East, the Maharajah of Rawalpur had a very popular win in the bogey competition at the golf-club. He is spending the summer here, and has taken a whole floor of the Grand Hotel d'Oriol ...

On another page she published the children's photograph of the Maharajah at the fifteenth hole. The *Spyglass* came out in London on Friday, serving as a sedative during the week-end to the international news.

Every Monday it was on Mr. Wake's breakfast table with the other pictorial magazines, and in order to make a thorough study of them he did not go across to the office until eleven. His monocle screwed in, he read Miss Ferguson's column with intense satisfaction, devouring the great names, and at first did not see the photograph.

Mr. Wake and his sister Charlotte lived in a good-sized bungalow on the edge of the links. It had been built as an army hut and still had a corrugated-iron roof. Charlotte had given it a hedge, some rose-beds, and a lawn; but every winter the sand swept across it from the dunes, defeating her and reclaiming it. On fine mornings during summer Mr. Wake rose early, in order to have time for the two-mile drive to the beach and a short swim. He did his exercises on the sands, wearing flannel trousers and a singlet. His job called for a good deal of attention to his personal appearance, and at the height of the season he seldom gave it less than three-quarters of an hour, not including massage. Hillier, the caddie-master, who had once been a prize-fighter, massaged him twice a month, and on these mornings Mr. Wake rose an hour earlier.

Charlotte cared for his suits, shirts, and socks with the demureness and dedication of a nun. She was a kind if rather mournful woman, reconciled to spinsterhood, but still with a submerged craving for activity, which the brilliant world of Oriol failed to satisfy. Its extravagance shocked her; secretly she was not sorry when the season came to an end. She preferred the company of Mr. Ridgway, the vicar, of Miss Sadler, an ex-governess who now kept a *pension* in the town, and of the unassuming British colony who lived at Oriol the whole year round (not because it was fashionable, but because the rate of exchange made it cheap), like a dusty clump of evergreens in the middle of an orchid house. She was a little strange and, though her brother had not noticed it, becoming stranger. She had got into the habit of talking to herself, but still knew when she was doing it, and stopped if anyone came into the room. She had no social ambitions, read quantities of improving novels, and played the harmonium in the English Church.

The best room in the bungalow was Mr. Wake's bedroom. A long window ran across one wall, so that he could lie in bed and survey his domain, the golf-course, as a squire his farms or an admiral ashore his port. The other wall had been scooped into a deep cupboard, where his suits, cleaned and pressed, hung like a file of flattened Grenadiers. He had a number of pomades, and took great pains with his moustache, which was ginger, pruned like an Elizabethan box-hedge, and twirled slightly at the ends. In his office, perhaps out of deference to it—he did not himself play golf—he invariably wore his canary-yellow waistcoat and one of the three suits of green plus-fours; but at home, relaxing, was usually to be found in flannels and a well-made sporting jacket, with padded elbows, though he did not himself shoot. His monocle, whether lodged in his eye or suspended, like some distinguished order, on a black silk ribbon, pointed a general impression of firmness and authority which caused people to take him for a soldier. Though he had not himself actually engaged in warfare, he did have a little the air of a nineteenth-century general who in late life might take to stays.

Mr. Wake thought his job complex and important; inside this inflated envelope of responsibility his personality rattled like a small dry pea. He plumed himself on his discretion. There came to Oriol so many people well known in so many different ways that, in order to suit them all, he must know how to play on several instruments of compliment, and at crowded week-ends, such as Easter and Whitsuntide, conduct a symphony. He tried himself to offend none; but now and then, through lack of time, he could not help being a little rough with less important people, and the priorities for his courtesy did coincide in general with the order of the peerage, which he studied for its elevating influence as well as business. Some of the members had intricate private lives. He kept himself well posted of their latest turn, so that he should not be caught inquiring after the health of husbands and wives who were no longer together; and for this intelligence he drew on the gossip columns and on talks with the gossips themselves. He could honestly flatter himself that so far he had never dropped a brick. His tenure had gone smoothly. Membership of the club had slowly increased, but remained select. Two royal personages had presented cups, one for the men's, the other for the ladies' competition; and this year the Maharajah might stump up for the mixed foursomes.

It was a warm morning. After breakfast, a Panama hat shading his eyes, he sat out of doors in a deck-chair examining the photographs and mentally noting what yachts had set out on cruises, and might be expected in Etaples harbour; which members of which royal families might be heading in his direction; who the year's beauties were; what engagements, marriages, and divorces there had been or were to be, and who was being seen where and with whom. He noted with dismay that the Portuguese Count and Countess Carvallo, over whom he had taken such trouble last season, had gone to the south of France; what could have diverted them? Against their defection he could set the arrival of Mary Stiles, the world's wealthiest heiress, whom Miss Ferguson had photographed on the first tee with a dispossessed archduke. On the whole he thought he had scored. The Carvallos brought no one but themselves and a few servants, but a long retinue of admirers pursued Miss Stiles; and it was conceivable that, if she married the Archduke, she might invite Mr. Wake to the wedding.

"A good photograph of the Baroness de Leverson," he said, passing the magazine to Charlotte.

"She is with Sir Maurice," his sister replied in flat tones.

"It will be a good match."

"I always thought he should have married Judith Friedmann."

"Oh, out of the question, my dear. She has no elegance. A man of his kind, a man of the *monde*, needs someone with elegance, and poor Judith really has no idea of that." He called her by her first name at home, as he did a number of people whom in their company he knew only by their surnames. "She is a very intelligent woman, without a doubt, and cultured, but without elegance."

"I think we should ask her to dinner one night," said Charlotte.

"When the season is over, perhaps. There are so few with whom she would mix."

"All the same," Charlotte began. . . . She was about to say that Judith was her brother's employer, but stopped because he did not like to think of himself as employed.

"We might ask the Baroness and Sir Maurice," he ruminated. "It would be rather a special little party."

Charlotte sighed. She knew these special little parties, which took her several days to prepare and made her brother infectiously agitated. There was cutlery, linen, and glass to be borrowed, and flowers to be bought, and precedence to be thought of. Even when all had been done, and the guests arrived, she usually became too nervous to enjoy either them or what they said, and had to rely on her brother afterwards to tell her, which he was very glad to do. She admired his success and thought him one of the most distinguished men in the club, but did not enjoy herself. She knew she was a poor hostess; her mind wandered, she could not keep up with his flow of talk, and felt his eye upon her, signalling. But since he liked to play the host and it was valuable to him in his job, she thought it would be selfish to hinder him, and in the season went through it for him once a week.

"Dear, oh dear," said Mr. Wake, clicking his tongue behind his teeth.

"What is it, Glanville?"

"Dear, oh dear. But this is very tiresome. . . ."

She waited patiently to be told. After a minute or two he pushed one of the illustrated papers across to her and indicated the photograph of the Maharajah.

"He particularly asked that he should not be photographed," he said irritably. "I gave most explicit instructions. Miss Ferguson knew perfectly well." He began to make himself indignant. "You can never trust a journalist; they stick at nothing. They recognize no such thing as a private life. She has completely abused my confidence. I am in two minds whether I should not forbid her the club."

"Isn't it unwise, Glanville? She will only write something unpleasant about you."

"I have to protect the membahs. If the membahs come to hear of this, they will certainly expect me to take some action. I wonder if the Maharajah is still here."

"I saw his car yesterday in the town."

"Oh, dear. Perhaps it would be advisable to make a call upon him."

The idea appealed to Mr. Wake, and might lead to something; he was on the look-out for a winter job.

"There is a nice photograph of you, Glanville."

"Is there?"

Sometimes the camera caricatured him, and he looked anxiously. He was pleased. Although the photograph had only caught a little of his profile and his back, being really intended as one of the Duchess of Mendoza, to whom he happened to be talking, his air of being at his ease was unmistakable, even from behind; and had it not been written underneath "Mr. Glanville Wake, the popular and immaculate secretary," he might easily have been taken for an ambassador. Charlotte cut the photograph out; she kept all references to her brother and the club in an album.

"I foresee a troubled morning," he sighed.

At eleven o'clock, carrying the newspapers, he walked across the links to the club-house. Warranted pride stirred within him for the cropped turf and the well-raked bunkers. The emerald grass stretched as smooth as green baize in a butler's pantry. On the seventeenth he noticed three or four leatherjackets, head down in the spotless grass; putting on a glove he carried for such purposes, he stopped and plucked them out.

As he walked he glanced at the *Continental Daily Mail*. In the evening he would receive *The Times*. He would go through the dinner-parties and Court Circular thoroughly, and glance at the political news; he thought it decorous not to show too pronounced a political opinion, unless someone of position expressed it first, and never to be drawn into an argument. The rising membership, the large group waiting round the first tee, the smart women sitting under big orange umbrellas in the sun, the knowledge that all the main hotels were nearly full, told him that things were getting better; not yet as good as 1929, but better than 1931. The early thirties had been very depressing to him. People had not been able to afford the week-end trip across the Channel so often and had taken their holidays in England. Several Americans who had rented large villas in the boom had been ruined in the crash; poor Ogden Manvers, for whom Mr. Wake had given one of his little parties, had even committed suicide. M. Pinceot, a French business man who had built the Sunset Hotel, was now in prison for fraud. He would soon be out, however, and things in general were obviously improving. There was still a war in Spain, but only a civil war. A mob had sacked a palace belonging to the Duke of Mendoza, and the Duchess herself had told Mr. Wake that several priceless tapestries had been destroyed; this story he had re-told in an outraged tone at several dinner-parties, but he did not really expect the crowd at his own gates, or anywhere near them. Thank Heavens, no Germans came to Oriol. He had nothing against Germans himself, and preferred them in some respects to the French; but one or two members, and a number of visitors, were Jews, and Judith became agitated on this subject.

The lawn round the club-house was gay with marigolds and nasturtiums; the small posts and rope between them were painted white. He watched players driving off the first tee, congratulating or commiserating on their shots. A caddie, evidently new, stood directly behind Sir Peter Lawson, who fluffed his drive; Mr. Wake severely reprimanded the boy. He talked for a while to the groups sunning themselves outside the club-house. He knew that they felt flattered by his personal attention, just as—though he did not himself make this comparison—they enjoyed a special bow and distinguished word from M. Nicolini, the head waiter at the Pine Hotel; it was a certificate of importance, and set everyone else wondering who they were. But when he saw Miss Ferguson approaching along the pergola walk, he went hastily into his office.

"There's a message from the Sunset," said Anne. "The Maharajah of Rawalpur's equerry is coming to see you."

"Has he seen the photograph?"

"What photograph?"

She could not bring herself to call him Sir; since she was popular with the members and indispensable to him, he had not insisted on it.

"This."

"He didn't mention it. He just said he was coming. I suppose it is about that."

"If Miss Ferguson tries to see me, you must tell her I'm busy."

"She's out there now."

"I know. I can't see her. She has betrayed my confidence."

He went into his office.

Usually his little worries entertained Anne; she would have relished this one, had the children not been involved. She saw it all. Of course, they had been selling photographs; well, it was an advance, morally and commercially, from an earlier day when she had caught them outside the Casino, trying to sell gladioli stolen from the hotel garden. They had certainly caught the Maharajah in a most clumsy attitude. She looked at it again, then more closely. The caption announced that he was teeing-up, but the photograph did not show him on a tee. She recognized an umbrella-shaped clump of pines in the background. He must have been in the big bunker on the fifteenth hole, and there he was, placing his ball on a neat little pile of sand; it looked very much as if he had been caught cheating.

Others had noticed the same. In came Sam Bryant.

"Well, Anne"—he was her friend as well as the children's and had known her husband. "What do you think of this photograph?"

"What about it?"

"The man's teeing up in the middle of a bunker."

"It does look like it."

"And he won the competition. We must have an inquiry, Maharajah or no Maharajah," he said gaily.

"I'll tell Mr. Wake."

"Impossible!" said Mr. Wake. "Out of the question."

"Major Bryant wants to see you about it."

"Really! I should not have expected it of him."

It was not in taste to accuse a Maharajah of cheating; it was like accusing a royal personage of adultery. She did not hear the interview; but she saw the two heads bowed low over the photograph, and Mr. Wake examining it with his monocle and even getting out a magnifying glass. He came into her little room with Sam, trying to pacify him.

"I shall insist on an inquiry," Sam was saying, enjoying himself. "And I am not the only one who has noticed it," he added ominously, and went out looking very severe, but with a wink to Anne.

At midday the Maharajah's equerry, a slender Oriental in European clothes, drove up, and was met by Mr. Wake at the end of the pergola walk. His manner was aloof and cold when he went into the office, and aloof and cold when he came out; he had come for a written apology.

"I shall get to the bottom of it," Mr. Wake was saying, with the gravity of a musical-comedy police chief. "Please assure his Highness that we deeply regret the mistake, and that all the necessary instructions were given in accordance with his wishes. I shall not rest until I find out how this happened." After Mr. Achmed had gone, "This is most regrettable," he said. He had not yet dared to tell Mr. Achmed that his master was under suspicion. It was a dilemma, it called for diplomacy, *savoir-faire*, for all his gifts, if he was not either to offend Sam Bryant and his wide circle of friends, regular week-end visitors, some of them even on the Committee, or permanently estrange the Maharajah. The prospects of a princely goblet for the mixed foursomes grew faint and sad. Whatever happened, he would have to speak to Miss Ferguson; and she was a sharp-tongued woman, not of good birth, who could do him a great deal of harm.

Miss Ferguson's manner broke Mr. Wake's affectation of patrician calm. She had her money to earn, and if her newspaper wanted a photograph, nothing this side of the grave would hinder her. She had pulled her way ruthlessly up the rungs of her profession, determined to force a passage into "society" somehow, and if it would not accept her as an equal, at least to make it tremble at her approach. Ever since her early days, when she had stood at the porches of London churches taking the names at fashionable weddings, she had resented being merely one of the Press. She could look better and could talk a great deal better than most of those whose monotonous comings and goings and philanderings she had to record. She despised them, yet wished to be one of them; she saw straight through Mr. Wake, and made no pretence of veneration. The two voices were raised so loud that Anne could hear what they said.

"I can discredit this place," she threatened. "I can discredit it entirely. I have only to write a paragraph or two, and people will soon begin to go elsewhere."

"You seem to forget," said Mr. Wake, "that you are not the only writer. . . ."

"I am the only one anybody reads."

"Nonsense." Then, as if he had gone too far, "Now come, Miss Ferguson, we are all very glad to see you here. Your photographs are quite the best, and you give your readers an admirable picture of what the world is doing. I should very much like a copy of the photograph you took of me with the Duchess of Mendoza. I only ask . . ."

"I must have complete freedom to photograph whom I like when I like."

"But this was a special request. The Maharajah is a little touchy who he is seen with."

"Why?" asked Miss Ferguson, hoping for some scandal.

"He has millions of subjects in Asia, who are very particular. His position is very much that of a king," said Mr. Wake grandly.

"I've photographed dozens of kings, on and off their thrones. They love it."

"But this is different. He is an Oriental."

"So is the Aga Khan. He's never objected."

"Miss Ferguson . . ."

But all he could get out of her was a further clue. After she had remade her face and gone to the bar, he emerged and said angrily, "Tell Weston to come here."

Jerry was giving a golf lesson to the Baroness de Leverson, who took it mainly for her figure. Sir Maurice was watching, and Cacouette stood a hundred yards away to pick up the balls, few of which reached him. As Anne arrived, the Baroness missed the ball entirely.

"I shall never learn," she said blithely. She was as slim as Mr. Achmed and like him wore a white suit; on her small dark head was a red beret, with a diamond brooch.

"I'm sick of it," she said in French, slipping her arm into Sir Maurice's. "Go on, you have the lesson."

"Me? Never."

"You're lazy."

"I'm no longer young enough, and not yet old enough for golf."

"You never take any exercise." She turned to Jerry. "You show him," she said, smiling.

Irritated by both of them, Jerry took a club. Cacouette scampered off another hundred yards. Jerry played.

"Ah, what ease!" cried the Baroness.

"You'll be able to do something like that if you practise," said Jerry.

"Will you excuse me if I speak to the professional a moment?" Anne asked.

"Of course, of course. I'll take you for a little walk, Maurice, and afterwards perhaps I shall do something brilliant."

They sauntered off, all time, all money, in their hands, joking about the muscles necessary to become a lady golf champion. Cacouette sat on a bunker and lit a cigarette stub. By a personal favour of the club barman he was permitted to forage the ashtrays every evening; and since many of the women threw away their cigarettes half-smoked, he would often be seen puffing at a fag-end red with expensive lipstick.

Jerry laughed when Anne told him about Mr. Wake's visitors.

"I thought somebody would notice something," he said. "Very smart of Major Bryant."

"You're to be the scapegoat, Jerry."

"Am I?" He tried to look serious.

"You gave Miss Ferguson the photograph?"

"Oh yes."

"But you didn't take it . . . did you?" He looked at her doubtfully. "Merrick and Sarah took it. Didn't they?"

He grinned. "Well, yes."

"Did you pay them for it?"

"Yes. Miss Ferguson gave me a hundred francs. Merrick and Sarah shared it. I'd better tell Mr. Wake."

"Oh, no, you won't. We'll go in and see him together."

"Is he very angry?"

"He's worried about the membahs." She gave her voice the slightest satirical note, to show that she was on his side.

"Oh, the membahs."

They both laughed. It pleased him to be treated so naturally, without condescension, by a woman old enough to be his mother. When the golf lesson was over, he came into her office. He had put on a coat and tie and run a comb through his close tight hair.

"Now for the high jump."

They went in together. Mr. Wake looked up and frowned ponderously, as if they had surprised him.

"Ah, yes, Weston. Mrs. MacManus, please say I am not to be disturbed."

"I should like to stay. You see, it's really my fault. . . ."

"Yours . . . ?"

"Yes."

She smiled, vainly attempting to make the whole fuss absurd. They should all three of them be laughing about it. Yet there was Mr. Wake, screwing in his monocle, tapping with a pencil on the desk, looking from one to the other as if they had been caught misappropriating the club's funds. Her opinion of him passed from ridicule to contempt. Her lips tightened, her expression became hostile. She saw the shrivelled tributary of his existence, dependent upon the trickles which reached it from the glittering lakes of rank and wealth that had seduced her husband. In this mood, had Jerry or the children been charged even with some serious offence, she would have defended them stubbornly and passionately against such an accuser.

"My children took the photograph," she said calmly. "They sold it for a hundred francs to Miss Ferguson. Jerry has nothing to do with it, except that he took it to her."

"Your children, Mrs. MacManus?"

"Yes, Merrick and Sarah. Merrick has just got a camera."

Mr. Wake looked nonplussed.

"How did they get such a photograph?"

"I've no idea. I expect they hid in the bushes." She picked the magazine off his desk. "Yes, it's the fifteenth hole. There are some bushes just beside the bunker; they often go there."

"They have no business, interfering with the players."

"They do not interfere," she said, although she knew they did, moving on the balls of people they liked and occasionally treading in those of their enemies. "I have never had any complaint about them. Have you?"

"I cannot permit this," said Mr. Wake. "I really cannot permit it. I shall have to ask you to keep them off the course."

"They are life members," she replied. "Mr. Friedmann made them both life members when they were born."

"I am the secretary, and I have a responsibility to see that people are not troubled. This . . . this prank is going to cause a great deal of unpleasantness for me."

"It *was* rather an unlucky moment to catch the Maharajah," said Jerry cheerfully and with intent to sympathize.

"I did not ask for your comments, Weston." He rounded on Jerry. "So you gave the photograph to Miss Ferguson?"

64

"Yes, sir."

"And took money for it?"

Anne interrupted. "The children took the money."

"Weston procured it." He turned back to him. "Have you had other dealings with Miss Ferguson?"

"I've never spoken to her before, sir."

"You had no business to do this. I take an extremely serious view of your action. An extremely serious view," he repeated. "That will be enough for the moment; but I assure you the matter will not rest here."

Jerry turned abruptly on his heel and walked out, and Anne feared that he would slam the door. He did not, but seeing Mr. Wake vindictive against him, she decided on conciliation.

"Jerry has nothing to do with it," she said. "I'm sure he never heard that the Maharajah didn't want to be photographed. And of course Merrick and Sarah ought not to have taken any money. I'll get it back from them."

"That will hardly provide us with a solution. Your children are privileged, Mrs. MacManus, very privileged indeed."

"If you don't want them to take photographs on the course, then I'll tell them. But really it has nothing to do with Jerry."

"That will be for me to decide. For the moment let us say no more about it; it is a most distasteful affair. I can recall nothing in my experience like it."

She went out, thinking of Mr. Wake's experience. Before he came to Oriol, he and Charlotte had kept a boarding-house at Eastbourne. Charlotte had done most of the work herself and supported the two of them. Mr. Wake had taken money as a professional bridge partner at the big hotels, and in crowded months had earned enough to pay the laundry bills. That was his experience.

Jerry had disappeared. She did not want him to get into trouble. His father had been one of the "old inhabitants," and she had a soft spot for everyone who had been at Oriol since the beginning. She wanted to find him, but several people came into the office, and she had no opportunity. Judith was among them. Anne saw her stalking along the pergola walk, her large flat feet spread out, her cloak pulled awkwardly round her tall figure, giving no heed to the elegant women who stared at her and whispered to one another as she passed. She opened the glass door into the office and said good morning.

"Good morning, Miss Friedmann. We don't often see you here. Mr. Wake is in his office."

Mr. Wake, always much less busy than he pretended to be, had already seen her.

"Good morning, good morning," he said, bustling out. "Well, this is a pleasant surprise. Are you going to take up golf again, Miss Friedmann? You used to be a good player, I recall."

This was not true, and he knew it; but she was the chief shareholder, and he had to be polite to her. He felt ill at ease, conscious that his conversational tactics made no impact on her, and fearing that she was hostile to him. He took it amiss that she played no part in the life of the club and last summer had not even turned up to present the Arthur Friedmann cup for the men's foursomes. She was a crank with cranky ideas. There had been that undesirable young Spaniard whom she had commissioned to paint the bar; and at one time she had tried to refuse Germans entry into the club, although she had a German name herself.

"I came to see Mrs. MacManus," said Judith curtly.

"Ah." He gave Anne an unctuous smile. "Everyone comes to see her. Is there anything I can do?"

"Nothing, thank you."

He retreated into his room, offended and suspicious, and watched them through the glass.

Judith sat down, tugging the pockets of her coat shapelessly together, and Anne swivelled in the office chair to face her. The children had told her about the tea-party, without saying how they had come to be invited, and she was afraid that Judith too had arrived to complain about them; perhaps they had broken a window, or been stealing flowers again.

"Well, and how are you enjoying the job?" Judith asked, as if Anne had been there only fifteen days, instead of twelve years.

"Oh, I enjoy it," said Anne. "I've seen a lot of changes here."

"Yes, there've been a lot of changes."

66

They were silent. Judith had a specific question to ask, but wanted to bring it in casually.

"How are your children?"

"They're very well. It was kind of you to ask them to tea. They told me all about it."

"Next time I must be better prepared for them. They've grown a lot. I scarcely recognized them. Sarah will be beautiful, I think."

"Beautiful?" Anne repeated doubtfully.

"Not in a classical way, of course. Anyhow, I find that kind of beauty rather monotonous, and often there's nothing behind it. She will be a painter's type."

"Her grandfather was a painter."

"Ah yes. You and I are like aborigines here," said Judith. "I hardly recognize any of the visitors now."

They talked a little about the past. They scarcely knew each other. In the old days Judith had spent most of her time in Paris or abroad, and Anne had a suspicion that she and Arthur Friedmann had not been on good terms. Had he lived, a man like Mr. Wake would never have been made secretary. She too regretted, even resented, that Judith took so little interest in Oriol. Few people were lucky enough to get an inheritance like that, and those that did should accept responsibility. She had a lot of letters to type, and Judith's reminiscences made her impatient.

"I should like you to bring your children to see me one day," said Judith suddenly. Her awkwardness caused her to talk in rather a royal manner.

"I'm sure they'd like to go very much."

"Have they ever been to the opera?"

"Why, no. They're a little young still."

"I was taken to *Bohême* when I was fourteen. I see they're giving it at the Casino theatre next week. Would you all come?"

"We should love it," Anne replied, smiling, though practical questions about the children's clothes at once confused her. "They'll be terribly excited. Merrick is quite musical."

"Merrick is musical? I should have expected it more of Sarah."

"Sarah is really the artistic one. She takes after my father. But Merrick has a very good ear."

She wondered what could be the real cause of this visit; and Judith was wondering if Anne could be as straightforward as she seemed. The more she thought about the children's descent upon her villa, the more extraordinary it became. She did not believe that people or events were "sent," yet had that moment not come, she did not know what she would have done; she might no longer be alive. And the same evening a letter had arrived from Hans Mayer's mother, telling her that if enough money were offered it might be possible to bribe their passage to freedom; she had written to political acquaintances in Paris and found that this was so. She alone could arrange this, and again there had appeared to be some value in her life. She had become inquisitive to see the children again. They might be company. If Anne's welcoming smile and clear blue eyes bespoke her character, she might be refreshing company after the intricate psychologies to which Judith was accustomed. They might all be extremely dull, and so she had asked them to the opera to find out. It was agreed that they should go next Wednesday, after a high tea at the Villa des Roses; and Judith left, thinking that Anne was pleasant enough, but wondering if after all she wanted them.

6

On the evening of the opera the children and Anne arrived punctually in Monsieur Philippe's taxi at the Villa des Roses. Emily, grumbling as usual, had put on a starched cap and apron and went upstairs in front of them like a befrilled snail. Anne wore an evening dress several years old with a small cameo brooch Arthur Friedmann had given her, Merrick a dark blue suit. Sarah had on her pale blue velvet party frock, which she had always hated, and hated more now she was growing out of it. "I can't wear it, I can't," she had cried when trying it on the night before, hot angry tears oozing down her cheeks. All day she had refused to come, and it was Merrick who persuaded her by telling her that Judith would be offended if she did not, and that anyhow, in the darkness of the theatre, nobody would notice her. Round her neck was a thin coral necklace. She refused to wear a slide, but had permitted Anne to comb her hair, and for the time being it was off her face.

Judith would have preferred to eat in the sitting-room on the top floor, but Emily, in spite of the service lift, had declined to bring food for four people so far; and so they sat in state round the mahogany dining-table, under a pewter chandelier, with the rest of the chairs, still in dust-sheets, lining the walls like ghosts. Merrick took it that ease and gallantry were the special duty of the only man, and had anyhow a natural desire for them all to be at their best. He managed the *finesses* of behaviour with little apparent effort, choosing the right knife and fork without being caught looking, diverting Judith's attention when Sarah dropped a potato on the floor, and praising the food, this time with sincerity, for Judith had made certain there was enough. He even mollified Emily by helping to clear away. Without conceit he relished the awareness that it was he who kept the conversation running, even though he forgot each sentence after he had said it. He just talked. His assurance was self-generating. He ardently wanted Anne and Sarah to shine, and tried to bring in subjects they enjoyed. Sarah most of the time was speechless. Judith ate voraciously and shared a bottle of white wine with Anne. Now and then she rose and called down a tube that looked like a hose-pipe to the kitchen. She spoke French, and, as Emily was deaf, sounded as if she was shouting and in a bad temper; Merrick could hardly keep himself from laughing, and Sarah, infected, bent her head and went scarlet in the neck.

Judith complained about the absurd size of the house and the clumsiness of the furniture, and again Anne had the impression that she had not got on well with her father. She seemed to be nervous, but now and then a flash of humour gave a hint of something generous and enjoying. Anne did not notice then, or later, what she wore, apart from a string of large amber beads stretching almost to her waist, and a number of rings. Towards the end of the meal she said:

"I thought we would arrive before the performance begins and go behind the stage."

Sarah looked up eagerly.

"Listen to that," said Anne.

"Is anyone allowed to?" asked Sarah.

"Well, not anyone; but I telephoned, and they're expecting us."

Even Merrick was silent, impressed by this immense privilege. He was secretly disappointed that Monsieur Philippe drove them to the Casino in the taxi and not a chauffeur in a private car, and the plot of the opera, which Judith tried to explain to them on the way, sounded perfectly ludicrous. But it was very special indeed to be driven up to a side door, and be met by an expectant porter in the green-and-gold Casino livery, and have people turning to look at them and bowing respectfully to Judith, and to find themselves among stacks of scenery, and switches, and pulleys, and an air of bustle and suddenly to be upon the stage. It was rather dirty, he thought. It had been set with a table and a stove and a few rickety old chairs, and looked like a lumber-room; even the backcloth, which de-

70

picted a large window opening on to a labyrinth of roofs, was shabby and old. The canvas was patched, and several of the roofs had holes in them. Violins and trumpets tuned up somewhere out of sight. The children peered through a spy-hole in the curtain and saw people in evening dress taking their seats; the auditorium resembled the inside of a vast cake.

The narrow corridors between the dressing-rooms were thronged with extremely sunburned people in fancy dress, the ladies in bonnets and crinolines, the gentlemen in tight trousers buckled under their shoes, velvet coats, black silk neck-ties as broad as ravens, and mossy grey top hats. These were the members of the chorus, and it shocked both the children that nearly all looked middle-aged and some positively old; but it delighted them to recognize a number of friends. They saw Emilio, the waiter. They knew him chiefly as a hurried swerving tadpole, balancing trays above the heads of customers at the Pine Hotel; but here he was, in a blue frock-coat, a top hat, and sporting an elegant walking-stick with a silver knob. And there was Madame Menard, who in other life sold the lollipops, rustling and resplendent in a violet silk crinoline, with black gloves stretching beyond her elbows, a jewelled necklace, jewelled earrings, and in her hair a bunch of artificial cherries. Jacquot was there too, the old commissionaire who kept the huts on the beach, Madame Jeanne, who sold tickets at the Cinéma Metropole and always got the money mixed up in her knitting, and two or three other Italian waiters from the Pine Hotel, all glowing and sun-burned and chattering together in fancy dress, as if they had never worn anything else. They stopped talking when they saw Judith and whispered to one another *"la patronne."* They bowed and smiled respectfully to her and surrounded the children.

"So you've come to see us?"

"Wait till the second act. Then you'll hear some singing."

"Is this your favourite opera?"

When they heard that it was the children's first opera, they all became excited, trying to explain the plot, the moment to wait for. Judith, surprised at the children's friends, and Anne, who never had been, found themselves in the middle of a discussion with a waiter about Puccini.

"I prefer *La Tosca,*" he said, and sang a few bars, placing his hand on his heart and then throwing it out in an expressive arabesque.

71

"What are you doing here?" Merrick asked Emilio. "Don't you have to be at the hotel?"

"Ah, it's my night off. I come here every night off. They have no voices here. They sing like this," he added, turning away so that the French could not see him, and pinching his nose. "Only we Italians can sing these operas. Where are you sitting?"

"I don't know. We've come with Miss Friedmann."

"Ah, you'll be in the centre box. I shall sing for you and your sister tonight."

"We'll look out for you, Emilio."

"You'll hear me," he said proudly.

Madame Menard was explaining to Sarah that it would have been better to come next week, when they would hear a star from Paris. This one— she shrugged her square shoulders and the others shook their heads and pursed their lips so emphatically that Sarah felt quite despondent. "But the tenor," went on Madame Menard, "he has something." She filled out her bosom and gave it a slap. Her gold teeth flashed. Suddenly she drew Sarah aside. "You know Miss Friedmann well?" she asked.

"She's—well, she's a friend."

"I want to present my daughter," Madame Menard whispered, and swinging round so abruptly that the artificial cherries in her hair struck her cheek, she laid her hand on the wrist of a young girl and drew her into the circle. "Introduce us," she hissed.

Sarah had never before introduced anyone; but Judith happened to be near, smiling and trying to listen to everyone, and she managed to get out, "This is Madame Menard. . . ."

"And this is my daughter Julienne," said Madame Menard at once, pulling the girl forward. "She will have a voice, ah, one day she will have a voice. She is learning now, Mademoiselle, but in two, perhaps three years. . . ." And up went her eyebrows.

The rest of the chorus looked at Madame Menard resentfully and one or two of them whispered behind their hands. Julienne stood with downcast eyes, pulling at her crinoline and blushing.

"Where is she studying?" asked Judith.

"I teach her, naturally. Don't I, Julienne, my dear?" said the proud

72

mother, and then, with pointed disapproval, "It's too expensive to have a teacher, and in the week one has to work. But she will have a voice. It will be recognized, M'amselle."

"We shall hear it tonight."

"Ah, tonight! Tonight she is with *us* again!" and she swept the others with a contemptuous eye. "If the manager knew anything about music, M'amselle, she would have sung Musetta. She has studied the part, haven't you, my darling?" Again without waiting for an answer, she went on indignantly, while the chorus frowned and whispered, "But the management would not have it. They say she has not enough temperament. My daughter, not enough temperament!"

The cherries shook excitedly. The heat of championing her daughter made it necessary for Madame Menard to open her fan, which she proceeded to employ fiercely and quite naturally, as if she were never without it. What a pity, thought Sarah, that she looked so elderly; even under her thick sun-burn the lines were visible, and the blonde curls round her ears were false.

A bell rang, a man in ordinary clothes appeared and called out something in a peremptory voice, and after farewells, pressing of hands, and exhortations to watch out for them in the second act, the chorus bustled off, crinolines rustling sideways along the passage. From behind one of the closed dressing-room doors a voice could be heard spouting practice bars. Anne and the children were escorted to their seats in the theatre, which was now beginning to fill.

The auditorium was marble and gold and red plush. Miss Friedmann, as daughter of the man who had built it, had the best box in the centre of the first balcony. Two giant figures, tapering beneath the navel into slender columns, and representing mermen, towered above them, and more mermen completed the semicircle to right and left. All round, below the rim of the boxes, gilded brackets held lights shaped like candles and protected with red silk scallop-shells. Sarah could see little of the balcony above except a brass rail, across which the townsfolk of Oriol were leaning in their day-clothes, staring at the people in the stalls and boxes. A festoon of small chandeliers hung beneath the roof like a diamond watch-chain.

The children sat in front, with Anne between and a little behind them. Judith had chosen to sit at the back; Sir Maurice would probably be there, in a neighbouring box, and she did not wish to see or be seen by him. Although the opera was billed to start at eight, and the hour well past, people were still arriving at leisure in the stalls, and the boxes were half-empty. Merrick craned over, pointing out acquaintances to his mother and asking the names of people of distinguished appearance he did not know. He felt embarrassed by his blue suit and straight tie; he wished he were older and could have a dinner-jacket. Mr. Wake arrived, starched and monocled. The nonchalance with which the beautifully dressed women entered, looked about them, and allowed themselves to be admired, and the attentiveness of the men as they drew back the women's furs and cloaks, filled Sarah with envy and despair. She could never be like that; how could they not feel nervous with everyone staring at them? Even crouched beside the marble merman, she felt exposed, and ducked her head whenever anyone's eye fell on her. She glanced sidelong at Merrick, but he did not seem to mind sitting there in front; he was enjoying it.

Just before the lights went down, a stout woman of middle age came into the stalls by herself and, having found her seat, remained standing for at least a minute, turning this way and that, smiling gracefully at friends, and waving a small plump hand towards the boxes. Having let her wrap fall, she stood another minute, apparently to have her shoulders admired. She wore a light pink dress glittering with sequins and much too young for her; even Sarah, who found it hard to believe anything unkind, could see that her golden-yellow hair was dyed.

"She looks like a pink pig," said Merrick.

They noticed her again between the acts; again she managed her entry just before the lights went down, again she stood smiling and waving. They were to notice her on many evenings in the future, always arriving alone in a dress that was too tight and too sprightly for her; and they discovered that although she invariably gave the same little flutter of her hand to the boxes, no one in the boxes ever waved back. The name they gave her that first night stuck. She remained the Pink Pig. They never knew her real name and never saw her in the daytime; some years passed before Sarah understood her profession.

The chandeliers in the roof, the ruby-shaded lights smouldering along the gold-and-white balcony, grew dim, till nothing could be discerned along the semicircle of boxes but white braceleted arms resting on a red plush ledge, and the white shirt-fronts of the men. A marionette bobbed up among the orchestra, bowed jerkily to a ripple of applause, tapped with a wand, and held it poised like an admonitory finger over the heads of the musicians. They struck up, and Sarah's heart beat faster. The music throbbed with romance and tragedy. Protected by darkness, she leaned forward, gazing eagerly at the heavy folds of the curtain, which soon swept upwards in two majestic curves, disclosing what she had been told would be an attic, and in it two stoutish gentlemen, busily singing at one another in their shirt-sleeves. From that moment till the act ended, everything off the stage was out of mind.

Judith watched the children. Anne sat between them, her hands folded over her programme, calm and happy, like a child at a treat herself. After a few minutes first Merrick, then Sarah, moved their chairs forward and rested their elbows on the ledge, their chins in their cupped hands. Judith saw Anne look from one to the other of them and smile. All three were rapt, the children in the opera, Anne in the children's rapture, so deep that Judith felt sad and isolated, deprived of the power to forget herself. A tedious whisper within insisted on telling her that it was Puccini and not "good," her friends in Paris would have been amazed to see her there; yet she would have exchanged her whole critical machinery for the children's absorbed delight.

Mimi appeared, played by an ancient prima donna called Waluska, who shirked the higher ranges and would have been wiser to have stayed at home with André Lemaitre, Judith's co-director, who had married her. But Sarah never noticed the chasms in Waluska's voice. She loved it all. She loved the attic; one day she too would live in an attic and look out over the roofs of Paris. She loved the artists the opera was about. They were all poor; she too would be poor. They were painters, musicians, unacknowledged and dedicated to a hopeless search; she would be the same. To and fro the violins swayed, a forest of parallel undulations, the voices soared and sank in melodies which Judith's prompting whisper told her were hackneyed and repetitive; but the two heads in front of her never moved, the two faces gazed steadily at the stage lovers now locked, as far as their bulk permitted them, in each other's arms, and when the act ended Merrick said, "Wonderful," and Sarah was too enthralled to speak.

"They're loving it," said Anne, as she walked with Judith in the foyer. "It's a wonderful treat for them. There'll be no sleep tonight."

"It's not at all well sung, I'm afraid. They say that Maria Waluska pays now to be allowed to sing."

"The orchestra are drowning her. Still, the children don't notice it. Merrick may, but Sarah is in the seventh heaven."

"Are you fond of music?"

"Yes, very, though I don't know much about it. I get too little time to come during the season, and there's the difficulty of getting home. I don't know how many years it is since I was last here. I was just thinking when we came into the box. I believe it was with your father."

"He was very fond of you. He used to say you were the original member of Oriol."

"I've never forgotten him. It all seemed to be more fun in those days, before it became so fashionable. I must be getting old."

Mr. Wake approached. She noticed his surprise at seeing her with Judith. Instinctively both women turned away and walked out into the hall under the glass dome. Footmen with white cotton stockings and gloves, in green-and-yellow liveries, flanked the gilded doors that led into the gaming-rooms. It was still too early for the big gamblers, who probably had not yet even started dinner. They played only baccarat, and would not be arriving until the opera had nearly finished. The boule-room and the big dance-hall were crowded, mostly with townspeople, who gambled with rigid concentration, following systems which either lost or won them a few hundred francs a month. The original portrait of Arthur Friedmann hung between two palm-trees, looking down at them with amused weary eyes and the shadow of a smile lurking beneath the thick moustache.

"It doesn't do him justice," said Anne. "He had more character, and he was so kind."

"Yes, I have none of his gaiety," replied Judith, though Anne had not mentioned gaiety, and turned away.

The second act, on the boulevards, began. The children were so excited picking out their friends that they forgot about the plot. The stage was crowded with ladies in crinolines and gentlemen in top hats, all in a state of merriment it was impossible to think feigned. Madame Menard, her daughter, Emilio, and the rest, soon detected and pointed out with nudges and whispers, were laughing, singing, and flirting so enthusiastically that this was obviously the life where in spirit they belonged. It was meant to be evening. On either side of the stage were two cafés, festooned with Chinese lanterns, and tables at which ladies coquetted with their escorts. Emilio had his top hat on sideways, and a girl sat on his knee; he held her with one arm and waved a glass in the other hand, a thing he could never do at the Pine Hotel. The rest of the company strolled to and fro in front of the footlights, arm-in-arm, throwing their best looks towards the audience as they passed the middle of the stage. The older ones looked twenty years younger than they had in the wings, and their sunburn glowed. Madame Menard was superb. As she passed the centre she came right down to the footlights, lowered her parasol, and still hanging on her escort's arm, but leaning well away from him, gave the audience the full benefit of her gold teeth above her fan. This was her only prominent appearance, and she had clearly rehearsed it so thoroughly that if that instant did not bring all Montmartre to life it should not be her fault. Her daughter followed, imitating her, but without the same abandon, and for some time Sarah's eyes kept wandering off the chief singers in search of Madame Menard. They always found her, even when she could scarcely be seen, acting for all she was worth. When surprise was called for, Madame Menard looked astounded; when indignation, she tossed her head like a stallion; when pity, she mopped her eyes.

The plot detached itself. Musetta emerged, all ringlets and caprice. Merrick pushed his elbows forward and stared at her; perhaps, Anne thought, this will be his type, but hoped not. A slight noise to her left made Sarah look away from the stage. Sir Maurice and Baroness de Leverson were arriving in their box; she thought it outrageous that they should dare to turn up so late and make so little effort to do it quietly. She accepted without hesitation the amazing plunges on the stage from ecstasy to disaster; but Merrick, who was enjoying the music as much as she was and could even hum Musetta's waltz during the second interval, thought the

77

plot unlikely and wanted to have several things explained. The English translation of the programme synopsis took too much for granted and was even misprinted and wrongly spelt. "Musetta, a waywood beauty," it read, "recaptures the heart of her old flame, Marcel, by singing the famous waltz-melody. . . . But in the next act we find them mad with jealousy, while Mimi, congealed behind a tree, learns that Rudolf wishes to dessert her. . . ." Why? Mimi's "congealment" had anyhow been unconvincing; the tree had been no wider than she was, she had made no attempt to hide behind it, and had been singing within a few feet of Rudolf at the top of her voice. Why, too, in her low state of health, did she walk about in the snow in such thin clothes! Her shoes, he had noticed, were unsuitable for a winter's morning, and he could see no reason for the Bohemians to be so careless about their meals. At the beginning of the last act he was indignant to discover that Mimi, whom they had last seen penniless and in the final stages of consumption, was now driving about in a carriage "just like a duchess," but still without medical attention.

Sarah by that time had become both Mimi and Rudolf. She identified herself completely. She was the wasted figure lying on the couch under the attic window, through which appeared the lights of Paris, held behind the holes in the backcloth by the chorus now no longer wanted on the stage. She felt the anguish of knowing what was going to happen, and could have rushed on to the stage and herself implored the thoughtless Bohemians to fetch a doctor. She heard the coughs. She saw the white arm fall by the side of the shabby couch, and knew what it meant; she too would die like this, or almost die, and so bring Rudolf to repentance and everlasting devotion. Finally she became the wretched lover himself as he saw the white faces of his friends, darted an agonized look to the couch, and ran stumbling across the stage, pressing the lifeless hand to his lips, touching the cheeks and heart, sobbing and calling out—too late. The music swelled, and the curtain fell across an ultimate wave of triumphant grief.

Sarah buried her face, shielding it with her hair so that her own tears might not be observed. Merrick was applauding furiously.

"Clap, Sarah!" he cried. "Go on, clap!"

"I can't," she murmured.

The people in the next box made a few rather disdainful comments; she

78

could have killed them. Sir Maurice and Baroness de Leverson had already gone, but her heart went out to someone in the balcony above who was frenziedly shouting "Bravo." The curtain rose, fell, and rose again. Mimi, restored to life, received a bouquet which she herself had paid for, and detached a rose for Rudolf, now quite normal again, and delighted because anyone could see he was the one getting the applause. The friends, standing at a discreet distance behind the two principals, bowed and smiled. The chorus, hustling and jostling, with Madame Menard well to the fore, her teeth glittering, grouped themselves wherever they could find room. The Pink Pig made her exit from the stalls with the same stateliness as she had made her entrance. Anne and Judith hovered in the back of the box, smiling as the children applauded in competition with the young students in the gallery. The curtain fell for the last time, the programme-sellers bustled along the rows of stalls with dust-sheets, and it was over.

"Wasn't it wonderful?" sighed Sarah.

"Pretty good," said Merrick.

Outside the big domed hall they joined the throng of men in evening dress and women in long dresses, furs, and gleaming jewels, who were going into the gaming-rooms. Mr. Wake was busy bowing. A river of cars poured slowly past the porch, now brilliantly lit, and dazzling people stepped out and crossed the hall. One or two of them stopped to speak to Judith, and Sarah again became aware of her hateful dress, Merrick of his blue suit. The liveried footmen ran to the doors and swung them open on to the porch for Judith and her party to go out. The night outside, the lights, the cars, all seemed magical and buoyant, and Sarah almost expected the opera to be continuing there.

On the way back, in the darkness of the taxi, Merrick voiced some of his practical objections to the plot. Sarah was indignant, but had not the words to convince him.

"Don't you see, Merrick? It couldn't help being like that."

"Well, I know there wouldn't have been any opera otherwise. But I don't see why . . ." He wanted reasons, and they argued.

Judith kept silent, her sympathies with the girl; certainly Merrick was right, and the plot, like the plot of most operas, was absurd, but it was important all the same to keep a respect for tragedy. When they had no more to say, and Merrick was leaning out of the window and could not hear, she leaned forward and whispered to Sarah: "You're quite right, my dear. It couldn't help being like that."

She said good-night at the gate of her villa. It had been an evening of pure enjoyment for them; and for her too, for whom such a sensation was rare. The same rapture with which the children had watched the opera had gradually enveloped her as she watched them, as though a warm clear light had been shed round her, dispelling the nagging shadow that for ever observed her while she herself observed; and she slept better that night than she had for a long while.

M. Philippe took the children back to the cottage. On the way Sarah remembered something that had puzzled her.

"Why were they all so sunburned, Mother?"

"Sunburned, darling?"

"Yes, when we went to see them behind the stage." Merrick began to laugh.

"It's their make-up, Sarah. They have to have it because of the lights."

"Wasn't it real, then?"

"Of course not. If they didn't have it, they'd all look green."

He went straight to the piano and strummed out Musetta's waltz, and for an instant Sarah saw the whole scene revive. She envied him desperately; she could not sing a note in tune herself, and yet she was sure that she had enjoyed the evening far the most. Before she went to sleep that night, she had added Judith's name to her list of "citizens"; and after a moment of hesitation Madame Menard's too, as a tribute to her enthusiasm in the crowd.

7

After the evening at the opera Judith began to visit the cottage; not often, perhaps once a week, hesitating to presume upon the entrance she had made into their self-contained household. She would have liked to get round their turnstiles of politeness; the fetching of chairs, clearing of the table, and making of tea whenever she arrived suggested to her that she had interrupted them. She had an exaggerated fear of being unwanted, and self-consciousness made her go about this new friendship like a conspirator.

She need not have troubled herself. She was welcome there, as was almost anyone except Mr. Wake. In happy homes friends are always welcome; it is only where the family is at odds that they need to give warning. If the children had not liked her, she would soon have known about it by unmistakable signs; she did not guess that she had an air of strangeness for them. She imagined that Anne might not want them to see too much of her, although Anne accepted it with pleasure and quite without surprise. The children were almost an institution. At one time Miss Marples and Miss Wells had taken them up. Charlotte Wake had been sentimental about them. Sam Bryant had taught Merrick golf, and sometimes took them swimming. They always went about together, which was attractive. They were indedependent and had a deceptive guilelessness; it was not odd for a childless woman living alone in a big villa to be drawn to them. Anne merely added Judith to the list; if there were intervals between the visits, she took it that Judith had gone to Paris, or had someone staying with her at the Villa des Roses.

So Judith's behaviour was that of an army planning to enter by stealth a city whose gates are wide open. She would mention to Anne that she would be passing their way and "might look in." She would "happen to meet" the children on the golf-course and, if shopping in Oriol-plage, would go down to the beach, hoping to "come across them by accident." It never occurred to them that these were ruses. They had once or twice taken pity on other children who seemed to lack friends, but Judith was quite different. She owned most of Jacques-plage and a good part of Oriol; it was impossible that she could be lonely.

Sometimes she took them out to tea in Oriol. They had plenty to do in the summer afternoons, invitations to tea belonged to their more formal past, and at first they did not like the idea. She did not know she had made a mistake, and luckily she made it interesting. They liked a ride in a taxi or a fiacre, and as Monsieur Philippe was usually busy and they wanted to do Paul, the old cabman, a good turn, they hired him for the afternoon. They sat in the back with the hood down, with Paul on the box, his ragged whip decorated with a yellow pom-pom, and made a stately procession, clip-clop, clippity-clop, through the forest from the Pine Hotel to Oriol. Often Merrick took the reins. The horse was a dilapidated grey, flea-bitten and fly-blown, called Jamais because Paul said he would never part with him or, according to the children, because he never got anywhere. He wore blinkers, looked half-starved, and would scarcely even jog; when a car swished past him, he gave a sudden start, like an old man dreaming in front of the fire, and Paul would turn round indignantly and talk about the days when everyone rode in cabs.

The season was at its height, and they had plenty to stare at. Sleek cars nosed round the great hotels, where some of the richest people in the world sat drinking coffee and liqueurs under striped awnings. The children got out and walked, leaving Paul and Jamais to their reveries. At the smart end of Oriol, where town and forest met, the perfumers, dressmakers, jewellers, and antique dealers of Paris had laid their traps; diminutive Trianons, in whose windows kings' ransoms glittered behind delicate iron grills and women like birds of paradise were waited upon by other women like butterflies and moths. Some were a little paunchy, and, despite all the efforts of the beauty parlours, sagged at the waist and under the eyes; but there was nothing tawdry about their plumes. And some took the children's breath away. Merrick could stand in front of these windows for many minutes, watching as a ring was lifted off a black-satin cushion and slipped over a red-manicured nail, or the soft wave of a fur laid over a pair of shoulders that turned and were reflected in half a dozen mirrors, or a minute hat, priced at more than Cacouette earned in a whole season, perched upon some lovely head. The attendant spirits recognized Judith, and emerged from their pavilions to wish her good-day, hoping to lure her in; but she only went into the antique shop, and then seldom bought anything. Merrick thought that with all her money, and owning a villa the size of the Villa des Roses, she might have managed something better than her string of amber beads, but he did not say so. He was struck by the insignificance, in contrast with the women, of their escorts. Up at the golf-course and on the beach they were like Sam Bryant, robust, cheerful, handsome; but down here they all looked worn out and were either very fat or very thin, with sallow faces. They carried thick bunches of notes in their breast pockets, which they peeled off like banana skins.

He never forgot one afternoon, when Sarah and he were with Judith, gazing into the window of a famous jeweller. An ancient squire appeared, almost dragged along by two flashily dressed women. One of them indicated a diamond bracelet and said:

"That's nice."

The other pointed to a diamond watch, and said:

"So's that."

They went inside, there was a great deal of smiling and bowing, and a hand lifted the diamond bracelet and the diamond watch off their cushions. When the two women came out, each had one of them on her wrist, and the old gentleman was putting back his wallet.

"Who are they?" Merrick asked Judith.

"I think they're in a cabaret."

"And what about him?"

"He's Mr. Ingram, who owns the multiple stores."

"I wish I owned some multiple stores," said Merrick. "There seem to be a lot of them," he added, as the hand behind the window reached forward and put out another diamond bracelet and another diamond watch.

The ordinary shops, which merely sold commodities, were in the side-streets at the end near the beach. The citizens of Oriol owned most of them, and they were open all the year. They had no window-boxes or floodlit show-cases, but even they made the dullest purchase an occasion; to buy merely a cabbage or a pound of carrots seemed not a necessity, but a temptation. As for the main street, the rue St. Jean, it was a gauntlet of temptation. There were little tables on the pavement, and gardens with pots of geraniums in iron brackets, and at the Matelot d'Or a band in white suits played softly; you could sit there for hours and order nothing but a grenadine. Stout ladies in tight silk dresses presided behind polished counters, working immense coffee-machines and handing out rainbow-coloured liquids in carefully measured glasses. And the sweet-shops! Mountains of pralinés, pyramids of nougat de Montélimar, marrons glacés in white ruffs, chocolates shaped like bottles with liqueurs inside, chocolate buttons in glass bowls, and in the windows of the Confiserie des Fleurs a sailing-ship with masts of barley-sugar, an iced flag and a chocolate hull, and a map of France in coloured marzipan.

The children introduced Judith to their friends. Madame Menard was the most impressive, and since the opera they held her in awe. She sat outside the Casino under a vast umbrella, selling sweets and newspapers, looking much poorer than she was. She recognized Judith, and at once began to scheme how she could turn the acquaintance to good account. She had two ambitions; to buy the Confiserie des Fleurs and to make a prima donna out of Julienne.

"And did M'amselle enjoy the opera?" she asked, after she had sold her three times as much barley-sugar as the children ever bought when alone.

"Parts of it," said Judith.

"Ah, that Waluska is no good. What money will do!" She sighed spectacularly and wagged her head. "If my Julienne had money, M'amselle, what a singer she would be!"

Judith was not to be drawn; ever since she could remember, people had been after her for her money. Madame Menard respected her caution, but did not abandon the pursuit. When the children came alone, she interrogated them.

"Mademoiselle Friedmann is a very nice woman," she would say.

"Yes, isn't she?" said Merrick.

"And you have known her long?"

"Oh, only a few months."

"*Tiens!* Only a few months? And you go to the Villa des Roses? They say it has twenty bedrooms."

"Fourteen."

"And she lives there all alone. With a piano, doubtless?"

"Yes, there is a piano."

"What sort?"

"I don't know."

"A good one, I am certain. And my poor Julienne has only an upright. I will bring her one day to sing to Mademoiselle Friedmann, yes?" she hinted, flashing her teeth and gripping Sarah by the wrist. She played chiefly upon Sarah, guessing her to be the more susceptible, and suspecting that Merrick knew what she was after. Had she but asked him direct, he would certainly have made a plan to introduce Julienne into the Villa des Roses; Sarah did not grasp her meaning, and would have been too shy. They realized that Judith was rich, but drew no mercenary conclusions from it. It was her characteristic, just as Mr. Wake was pompous, Sam Bryant merry, and Blanche always either in mourning or in love. Merrick still thought, and once said to Sarah, "Perhaps she'll adopt us"; but it was only dramatic supposition.

And Judith, in their company, began to believe that she was undergoing a cure. Her illness had been introspection. It is easy to advise people suffering from it to turn themselves inside out and gaze a little on the exterior world; she had been so advised by her doctor in Paris, to whom she paid a large sum for so simple a remedy. Unluckily the exterior world meant to Judith not the seasons, but politics, not the forest and the beach, but Germany, the fate of Hans, and the follies and cruelties of mankind, for which her doctor in Paris had no remedy. No more had Merrick and Sarah; yet with them she managed to stabilize herself.

They gave her a fresh interest; fresh in itself, and fresh to her. She became deeply fond of them, although she tried, as with others older than them in the past, to hide the growing strength of her affection. They had prejudices against people, not against ideas, which had not yet come within their scope; but she could tell, from the silence which followed and

the questions asked after she had said something contrary to these prejudices, that they were vulnerable and still only weakly held. This she
found as delightful as rare, but she took care not to say too much, not wishing to dominate them or, as her father might have called it, to "make something of them." It was they, she preferred to think, who had the influence
upon her.

In their company it dawned on her that Oriol was a beautiful place. She
walked among the pine-needle-strewn slopes of the forest and watched
the sun set along the dunes. How much of all this had escaped her! If pre-
viously she had gone for walks, it had been with unseeing eyes, her hands
dug into the pockets of her cloak, her head heavy with the world's misery
and her own. But now that her nets were let down into a wider circumam-
bience of life, she thought less, and judged scarcely at all; and every cast
made, every length of rope paid out, was a coil loosened, a knot in herself
untied. The children became her relaxation. Her mind, her energy, she
gave entirely to the rescue of Hans and his mother. Through a friend, a
kindly busybody called Gérard, she was in indirect touch with a man in
the German Embassy in Paris believed to stand well with some of the
leaders in Berlin. She had no such connexions herself; her name alone,
and her politics, would have made even the attempt impossible. He had
reported hopefully to her; but a little more money might be needed, and
then a little more, and then a little more. She was shrewd, and refused to
sign any cheques until she saw some results. In early autumn Frau Mayer
wrote that a mysterious stranger had brought her a letter from Hans and
made inquiries about his politics; since he had cared for nothing in the
world but music, Judith was optimistic.

Judith Friedmann to Elizabeth Mayer, August 1937.
Thank God at least that you have heard news of him, and I believe it
will soon be more than news, not just persuading myself or trying to persuade you, but from all that I have heard. Everything, everything that
can be done is being done. Oh, Elizabeth, think of the day when the two
of you step down on to French soil, when we meet and embrace one another, and know it is true. Only keep up your heart, say nothing, speak
to no one, because there is jealousy and hatred everywhere, and if someone in another group hears of what is being done they might stop it just

86

for the pleasure of stopping it. Every day and night I dream of your arrival, and here you will find so many friends. I shall not speak of this until it has happened, but I shall never rest; it is something better than I have ever tried to do before. . . .

This was from her heart. She could not save the world; she might save Hans. For years she had not believed in God, but distress had forced something into existence to which she prayed; afterwards, as if to help this something carry out the good intentions she attributed to it, she would promise a little more money to Gérard. She paid visits to Paris to meet him, but the atmosphere threw her back towards despair. Once she had enjoyed the parties, and had made political epigrams. She had held a miniature salon herself, and a number of politicians were her close friends. She had financed a magazine at some loss, for original young writers, and had helped to launch a "revolutionary" theatre, where the stage, instead of facing the audience, was set in the middle like a boxing-ring; and this had done surprisingly well. There were always plenty of messages for her, but now she replied only to those that had to do with Hans. When one evening she did go out, and was caught up in the current of her customary life, the conversation irritated her. It was as witty and as well informed as ever, but went too fast for her, and she could no longer give it her full attention. Hans's face appeared to her; the room with its smart folk and civilized talk seemed to break into pieces, as if an immense weight had crashed upon a glass palace. She did not mention his name, and those few friends who knew what had happened were too busy discussing the next Cabinet or the last play to remember him. Though all were shocked, of course, about what was happening in Germany, their horror sounded banal and perfunctory, and when the hostess presented a new guest, or a footman offered a cocktail, they forgot what they had been saying and ran smoothly off on to another subject. Her unaccustomed silence was noticed, and put down to some private gloom. Someone guessed that it was due to Sir Maurice's marriage, and soon this interpretation was "all over Paris"; she was ready to leave it at that, and glad when she could get back to the Villa des Roses.

Paris and her friends seemed stale. In company with the children at

Oriol so much was new. Madame Menard was new. So was Cacouette, to whom she was presented on the road to Etaples. One afternoon they gave Emilio a lift home in the fiacre. The children prompted him with stories he had told them when alone, trying to get him to repeat them to Judith. He was reserved with her; she said with a smile that he need not be afraid.

"Go on," said Merrick. "We're all friends."

So Emilio told them all about life in the kitchens of the Pine Hotel. It could be a good job, he said, but depended on the head- waiters and the people to whose tables he was allotted. Some were *"très gentleman,"* that was to say, human, and Major Bryant always gave him a good tip; but others did nothing but complain. It was not his fault, or not always, if the plates happened to be cold, or the meat incorrectly cooked, or the wine not at the right temperature. The fault might be the chef's, yet when things went wrong everyone had a habit of sniping at him. One day the chef wanted the customers to choose *escalope de veau*, because they had too much and wanted perhaps to keep the beef to sell or to eat themselves; but the customers might not want *escalope de veau*, and then he would be sworn at for not persuading them. It was good to be a wine-waiter; you wore a medal made like a bunch of grapes in your buttonhole and were someone apart, looked up to even by the customers. The wine-waiter knew which customers understood wine and which merely pretended to understand; the former treated him as an equal, the latter he could hoodwink, and so he made money out of both. But to be a *maître d'hôtel*—that was the real thing, that was Napoleonic. He had been studying the part for over twelve years. All the *maîtres d'hôtel* at the Pine Hotel had moved on later to bigger jobs in the south of France, except one who had been caught stealing and gone to prison. He had studied them all and recorded their technique in a note-book.

"How do you mean?" Judith asked.

"Well, you see, M'amselle, different customers have different fads. Some like to be flattered. Now . . . well, I shall mention no names, you understand . . . such and such a lady has on a new hat. . . . Monsieur Nicolini will compliment her on it, and that may mean another hundred francs on the tip. To some this will be disrespectful. One must know. Not everybody can be put at the tables by the window—the best tables, you will understand. Some customers like to talk to the waiter. Perhaps they are bored with one another, so they like to talk to the waiter, they like to hear his jokes. About politics, it may be. They like perhaps to say to their friends, the waiter told me this or told me that, and they think it is the voice of the common people. One must know what it is they like to hear, or if they do not want to hear anything, but only to eat."

"And what are your politics?" Judith asked.

"Ah, M'amselle, the waiters cannot tell the clients their politics. They can only tell the clients what the clients wish to hear."

"But supposing the clients' politics are the same as the waiters'?"

"M'amselle," he answered politely, "if you will pardon me, is that possible?"

"Of course," said Judith, thinking of herself.

Emilio knew she had an eccentric reputation; but he could not imagine that anyone with a lot of money would want to have it taken away, and that was the essence of his politics.

"It may be so with very exceptional people," he said, inclining in her direction, and changed the subject.

What the waiters most disliked, he told them, was the English gentleman's habit of sitting late after dinner over cigars and brandy, when the waiters wanted to go to bed. "I must be up at six o'clock," he exclaimed, "and if I am waiting till midnight to clear away. . . ." He expostulated with his hands. When they were still, he held them together, the fingers inward and pressed together against the top button of his coat. From this position he improvised a succession of roulades, scrolls, and baroque inscriptions upon the air, now with the whole arm extended, now with only the wrist or forearm bent, occasionally pointing a single finger, or bringing back the whole hand with a sweep, as if playing the harp or drawing a line across his body, returning them always to the position of rest on his breastbone. Every movement had so precise and lyric a continuity, that his gestures seemed to be a poetic expression rather than the mere accompaniment of words.

"What a rhythm in his hands!" Judith said, after they had left him at the hotel.

Sarah, who had often noticed them before, was pleased; it pointed to an inner bond between Judith and her, unshared by Merrick, who noticed nothing except that "Emilio waves his arms about a lot. Most foreigners do."

"I don't expect you've ever seen an Indian dancer," said Judith. "They can express an entire story without uttering a word. Everything is in the hands. The more sophisticated we become, the less we use our hands, and yet the hands are lyrical. We have an inhibition against them. It is considered bad form. You shouldn't talk about foreigners in that way, Merrick. After all, I'm a foreigner myself. Emilio is an Italian and does it quite naturally. I thought it a joy to watch." She spoke sharply, and Sarah gave a side-look at Merrick, who had gone red; he did not like to be pulled up. His tone of voice had provoked Judith, and she was not sorry to have offended him. Uncertain of herself though she was, she would be prepared to offend him more if she could freeze the buddings of intolerance.

He respected her. Had the brilliance of Oriol been his background, rather than the freedom of Jacques-plage, or had he met her at a later age, having acquired settled views and become uneasy in face of the eccentric, he would have sheered away and probably laughed at her. But at that time he was accessible to anything, including the unconventional. He respected her experience, her stories of foreign countries, the glimpses she gave unwittingly of a wider world. She had sailed no seas in open boats, but her mind had travelled and she had seen things. He respected her intelligence. She had a flair for Initials, inventing combinations which defeated even him, and never playing down to them. She taught them several new games of her own, among them one called Analogies. They had to think of a person well known to all of them and, without giving away the name, suggest the kind of flower he or she resembled, or kind of animal, or book, or piece of furniture. They were playing it one evening at the cottage, and Sarah had thought of someone.

"What kind of an animal?" Merrick asked.

"Slug," said Sarah.

"I know. . . ."

"You're not to say, Merrick."

"All right. What kind of country?"

"Somewhere nobody wants to go."

"What an awful person," said Judith. "He or she?"

"He."

"What kind of a joke is he like?"

"A very good question," said Merrick appraisingly. As usual, he had taken over the game himself. "Very original."

"What sort of a joke?" Sarah repeated. "Oh, I know. The kind of joke that isn't really funny, but the one who's telling it laughs at it himself."

"What sort of a game?" asked Anne.

"Doesn't play games. Only looks at them."

"You *must* know, Mother."

"You say, then," said Anne.

"Mr. Wake, of course. Isn't it, Sarah?"

"Yes."

"That's very rude of you," said Anne, thinking she should have stopped them in front of Judith. "You oughtn't to say such things behind people's backs."

"Mother . . . that from you!" said Merrick, drawing down his eyebrows and smiling slily.

Anne felt herself blushing, but Judith laughed and thought it was not an unfair picture of the secretary.

"Why don't they like him?" she asked Anne.

"Oh, you know how children get these aversions. I'm used to him, and after all he does his job well. He's rather a little tyrant sometimes, and Sarah can't bear people to be unfairly treated," said Anne. "She's been like that ever since she was little. I took her to Oriol market once, and she howled the place down because there was a piglet tied up in a sack. Merrick is different. He explains things away better. I expect he'll be more successful than Sarah." Anne said this in a cheerful way that surprised Judith. Judith had imagined that she alone, by an exceptional perceptive flash, had recognized the difference in temperament between Merrick and Sarah; she realized that Anne had probably been aware of it since their birth.

"It might be a dangerous trait," she said.

"Yes, it might."

"What does one do about things like that?"

"I don't know. I don't think there's anything one can do, even with children. They just grow up in their own fashion. I try to keep them out of harm's way—lasting harm, I mean—and I try not to say 'don't' too often. The only thing I hope is that when they do get into serious trouble I shall be able to talk to them as a friend. I should hate to be out of their confidence. That would mean failure."

"Perhaps they won't get into serious trouble."

"Oh, that *would* be dull," Anne laughed. "I *should* think there was something wrong with them then."

Judith described Anne and the children to Hans's mother in long letters sent through a friend in the diplomatic service. Across a thousand miles she tried to keep her spirits up and provide her with a companion, and at the same time these letters were an outlet for herself.

> The rooms in Paris are still waiting for you (she wrote), but it is here, at Oriol, that I most long to see you both, and it is here you will both get well. I never realized till now how beautiful it is, and how restful. I had always thought that Father spoilt it by ever touching it—and yet there is a whole expanse as free and wild as if there had never been a hotel within hundreds of miles, and there Hans will forget everything and be his gay self again, and play better than he has ever played. I know it will be so. And I have two new friends here whom you are to meet—not painters, or poets, or musicians for once, and certainly not politicians. No ... one is just fifteen, and the other fourteen. ...

One night that summer these two friends made her a "citizen" of Jacques-plage. She had already been enrolled in Sarah's book, and now came the ceremony. A large sealed envelope arrived at the Villa des Roses, looking like the envelope which Alice, in the Tenniel drawing, hands to the Frog Footman, with an elaborately decorated invitation inside.

Oyez! Oyez! Oyez!

To Judith Friedmann, spinster, of this parish. You are hereby requested and required (this was copied from their passports) to present yourself outside the main gates of the Pine Hotel at nine p.m. next Tuesday, there to be conducted, weather permitting, to another place, where the freedom of Jacques-plage will be conferred on you. Please come in your oldest clothes and sand-shoes. R.S.V.P.

She replied.

Judith Friedmann, spinster, of this parish, is deeply honoured by the invitation and will present herself at the time and place appointed, in her oldest clothes and sand-shoes.

She bought the largest envelope she could find, sealed it with a seal of Bohemian workmanship that had belonged to her grandfather, and sent it round to the cottage in a fiacre.

"She's answered," cried Sarah, running in with it.

"She's taken a lot of trouble," said Merrick, admiring the seal and the tall Gothic handwriting.

They were both relieved. They had invented the ceremony several years before, and were not sure whether they had grown out of it. Now that Judith had taken it seriously, they had to do the same.

At nine o'clock she arrived at the gates of the Pine Hotel, just as the sun was sinking, and was met by Sarah and Jerry, who carried bathing-trunks. Wolf the Alsatian was with him.

"Merrick's waiting for us there," said Sarah.

"Where are we going?"

"Only to the beach. It won't take more than twenty minutes."

They walked off along the main road to Oriol. The lighthouse had begun to revolve, scything the dunes with intermittent beams; six seconds between two flashes, then eleven, then six again. After a few hundred yards they turned off the road into the trackless dunes. Night, like a mass movement, merged the separate identity of the pine-trees into black smudges, stars were coming out, and millions of frogs croaked in the marshy hollows. Sarah went ahead, finding their private path.

"I feel as if I were going into an ambush," said Judith.

"It's quite a ritual," said Jerry, laughing. "They did it to me last year. We ought to consider ourselves flattered."

"Have you known them long?"

"As long as I can remember. They've always been a rum couple. Careful of these shrubs. They'll tear your stockings."

They went through the belt of pines, and now the frog-chorus was all round them in the dark, like the ticking of a gigantic watch. Wolf dashed off, scenting rabbits. The air seemed to open as they advanced, and the dullest sense must have known that the sea was near. The spiky shrubs fell back; a last ridge of dunes arose, free of vegetation except for clumps of the sharp esparto grass. Not a breath of wind stirred; the tide was only a whisper, but the freedom felt immense. Suddenly Merrick sprang up, naked except for his bathing-trunks, and brandishing a long stick like an assegai.

"Who goes there?"

"Friend," Sarah replied.

"Who comes with you, friend?"

"Judith Friedmann, spinster, as per invitation."

"Pass."

"You have to run the last bit," said Sarah to Judith, and raced ahead up the dune.

"You'll have to," said Jerry, giving her a hand.

She scrambled up, laughing, sliding in the loose white sand, sinking in almost to the knees, and suddenly the four of them stood silhouetted on top of the last dune. The tide was right in at their feet; a wide moonlit water lay beyond, not like the sea, not at all like the Channel, but like some sacred African lake. The tiny waves burst softly, with a rustling inrush afterwards, throwing out a fringe of white foam-flecks for miles along the coast.

"*Thalassa, thalassa!*" cried Merrick, shaking his assegai.

"Do you know what that means?" whispered Sarah.

"It's a Greek word for the sea, isn't it?" said Judith.

"Yes, Merrick learnt it at school. It's what Xenophon's men cried when they finished their march. We always say it when we come here."

"Light the fire," Merrick ordered Jerry. He leapt straddling down the dune, waving his assegai and uttering wild whoops. Sarah threw off her clothes and followed in her bathing-dress, which she had on underneath.

94

They dashed into the water, splashing and striking it with arms and legs until flying fish of phosphorus danced all over them. A red flame leapt up between the dunes, where Jerry had lit the fire, and Judith imagined she was about to be roasted.

The children dried themselves in front of the fire, their teeth chattering, and dressed without paying any attention to Judith. The night was warm; she watched them in the shadows of the fire, the small waves bursting at their feet, and tried to recall another quotation.... What was it? "The longed-for splash of waves ..."? It had occurred to her the moment she saw the sea, but she could remember no more.

"Umslopagaas!" called Merrick, in a commanding tone.

"Here, master," Jerry replied gravely.

"Is all prepared?"

"It is, master."

"Then let the honoured one be presented."

"You stand up now," said Sarah. She stood at Judith's side, already above her shoulder. Merrick handed Judith a pine-branch. He rested it on his outstretched arms and held it out to Judith.

"Take it," whispered Sarah.

She took it.

"I give you the pine-branch," said Merrick, "in token of the freedom of the forest."

"Hold it in your right hand," whispered Sarah.

Merrick scooped up a handful of sand and held it out. "I give you the sand, in token of the freedom of the beach."

"Hold it in your left hand," whispered Sarah.

Jerry gave Merrick a long necklace of shells.

"Advance." Merrick slipped it over Judith's bent head. "I give you the necklace of shells," he said, "in token of the freedom of the sea."

"Now you must give him something," whispered Sarah.

"I don't know if I've got anything."

"Your own necklace will do," said Merrick. "You can have it back afterwards."

She took off the amber beads and hung them round his neck.

"Now stand still," whispered Sarah.

9 5

"Welcome," cried Merrick. "Freewoman of the forests, the beaches, and the seas."

"Welcome," the others repeated after him.

"That's all," said Merrick, giving her back the beads.

"Well, I really do feel initiated. What an impressive ceremony! Did you think of it yourselves?"

"Most of it. Bits of it are out of books."

They lit the rusty lantern in their hut and cooked some sausages over the fire. While they waited Jerry undressed and plunged out to sea, swimming with long powerful strokes that lifted his body. They watched the black dot of his head, bobbing among the white feathers of moonlight, two hundred, three hundred yards out, while Wolf barked at him from the beach.

"He's a wonderful swimmer," sighed Sarah enviously. "I expect one day he'll swim the Channel."

The Villa des Roses seemed unusually lonely when Judith got home that night. She sat down and wrote a long letter to Frau Mayer describing the ceremony, and among her poetry books she found the quotation:

> till at last
> The long'd-for dash of waves is heard, and wide
> His luminous home of waters opens, bright
> And tranquil, from whose floor the new-bath'd stars
> Emerge, and shine upon the Aral Sea.

Those were the words she had been looking for; that too was the emotion.

8

Judith did not forget what Emilio had told her. She was a chief shareholder in the Pine Hotel; to test his complaint she asked Anne to dinner there.

"We ought to have an escort," she said. "You invite someone."

Anne suggested Sam Bryant; she knew that he would get on with anyone, though she did not put it to Judith that way.

"All right," said Judith. "I hardly know him, but he's got a good face."

They had a pleasant evening. Many strong men might have been intimidated at the prospect of three hours with Judith, but nearly all women interested Sam, and Judith was a type out of his ken. He had a reputation for charm, of which she knew; she doubted whether it would succeed with her, and expected an agreeable bachelor with conventional views and the usual aversion of an Englishman for art. Such at least had been her experience of most of them. She found him a man of unexpectedly liberal and diverse views. At present he was attached to a firm with big trading interests in Africa; he spoke several dialects and, to her surprise, took the side of the natives in several issues against the Government. She mentioned an exhibition of African art and its influence upon painters of her acquaintance; about them he knew nothing, but about it he could tell her a good deal, speaking with the deference of amateur to expert. Schools and trends meant little to him, but he had travelled, kept his eyes open, and interpreted what he had seen with understanding; she felt ashamed of the slightly patronizing opinion she had formed of him in advance. He in turn liked her. He had met far too many people in his life to be embarrassed by such company. He noted her fine hands and eyes and her appalling clothes. She was a genuinely attentive listener; and he found something challenging and evocative about a woman who obviously passed over his looks and manner and sized him up solely on his intelligence.

When they had finished dinner Judith said to Sam: "Now I want to ask you something." She nodded towards the far corner, where André Lemaitre and his wife the prima donna were giving a party to General Grandison. She looked at her watch. "It is now nine-thirty," she said. "When do you suppose that party will be over?"

Emilio was just bringing the meat. The wine-waiter had bent to hear M. Lemaitre's instructions, and M. Nicolini, the *maître d'hôtel*, hovered in the neighbourhood.

"I should say by ten o'clock," Sam replied, puzzled.

"The eating may be finished by ten o'clock; but that does not mean the dinner is over. Can the table be cleared?"

"Of course not," said Anne, taking Judith's side without knowing her motive. "The men'll be sitting there and puffing away and gossiping for hours."

"Are you jealous?" Sam asked.

"We have our own conversation," said Judith, "but that isn't the point. Now look over there. You see that waiter? In an hour and a half I bet you he will still be here. Why? Because M. Lemaitre and his friends can't be bothered to move. They must have their cigars and brandy in here, even if the waiters want to go to sleep."

"It does seem rather unnecessary," said Sam.

"It has only just occurred to you. Well, it had not occurred to me a week ago, and I own most of this hotel. If it hadn't been for your children," she turned to Anne, "it would probably never have occurred to me. That little waiter is a friend of theirs."

"Ah," Sam smiled at Anne. "Merrick and Sarah again."

"And quite right too. Your children have a natural sense of fitness, which experience has not yet corrupted," said Judith, rising. "It is not fitting that Emilio, who incidentally has a much better voice than Madame Lemaitre, alias Waluska, should be kept up half the night listening to her husband's contemptible opinions about the crisis. And I shall see that it is stopped."

They continued their own conversation outside. After an hour and a half Judith brought them back and showed them M. Lemaitre and his friends still gossiping, huge brandy glasses cupped in their hands and several liqueur bottles on the table. Emilio leant against the wall, staring at them as pointedly as he dared and yawning.

"Give me a pencil," she said.

She scribbled a note and handed it to the night porter for M. Lemaitre. M. Lemaitre read it, puffed out his lips angrily, and glanced towards the door. Judith went out, and as she did so switched off the lights.

"Serve them right," she said. "I wish I'd thought of it before."

The next morning she gave instructions that no one was to be served with drinks in the dining-hall after ten-thirty; the hotel manager demurred, but was told that he must either agree, find another job, or engage a night staff, and the note, retrieved by Emilio from underneath the table, found its way back to Sarah, who stuck it triumphantly in her album. She was by now devoted to Judith, and spent more and more time with her.

Summer passed with fêtes, tournaments, and gala nights. A world-famous diver gave an exhibition in the floodlit swimming-pool. The fortunate carried away thousands from the Casino, the unfortunate saw thousands more vanish for ever behind the croupiers' long rakes. Senorita d'Alvarez won the tennis tournament, but those who had seen Suzanne Lenglen play her last match there maintained that no one would ever be the same. The ladies from the cabaret dragged Mr. Ingram up and down, up and down the rue St. Jean, till their wrists and forearms were almost invisible for diamonds, and the jewellers rubbed their hands and forgot about the crisis. Mr. Wake gave several little parties, to one of which the Duchess of Mendoza came; and Charlotte read more tracts, played more hymns at the almost deserted English Church, and grew quietly stranger. Sam Bryant won the men's twosomes and presented Cacouette with a tip of five hundred francs, and Miss Marples and Miss Wells plodded painstakingly round the sunlit links. The fashionable beach was crowded, and everybody sunburned. The long miles beyond kept their virgin beauty; Jerry and the children went there to bathe in the moonlight, splashing the phosphorus with their arms and feet. Now and then Judith saw Sir Maurice and his new wife; at the Battle of Flowers they appeared

99

together in a fiacre entirely brocaded with roses. She took the children to the opera again. This time it was *Carmen*, and there was Madame Menard in the chorus, more Spanish than the Spanish, swinging down to the footlights to give the audience a flash of her eyes and teeth, and singing for all she was worth in a mantilla, with a rose above her ear. Autumn came; photographed in all its glamour by Miss Ferguson, the social season drew towards its close. At the beginning of September Emily brought Judith a telegram:

HANS RELEASED PASSPORTS GRANTED DEEPEST GRATITUDE WILL INFORM DEPARTURE PROBABLY EARLY OCTOBER FOND LOVE ELIZABETH MAYER.

Tears welled behind her eyes.

"Is it bad news, M'amselle?"

"No, Emily, it is wonderful news."

"They are coming?"

"Yes, they are coming."

Judith thought back through her life, and could remember nothing that had brought her comparable happiness. At this moment he must be free. Soon would come their last night in Germany, soon they would be in the train to France. Her heart flooded with gratitude to someone, to something, almost to anything; to Gérard, to God, to Gérard's friends, to her bank balance. She wanted to tell everyone, but a last-minute dread that there might be some trick, or some mistake, or that the order might yet be revoked, made her keep it to herself. She left for Paris to make the arrangements for their welcome, warning Emily that she would probably be bringing them back to Oriol.

One evening just after her departure Jerry came to the cottage and asked to speak to Anne alone. He seemed angry. The children, highly inquisitive, went reluctantly into the kitchen.

"What is it, Jerry?" she asked.

"I was wondering if you could speak to someone on my behalf."

"What about?"

"About getting another job. I thought, if there was some golf-course in England, perhaps someone you know would give me a recommendation."

"But surely you're not leaving us?"

"I don't want to." He looked at his shoes. "I don't want to, but I've got to. I'm sacked," he said, looking up at her. "Mr. Wake told me today. I'm to go at the end of the month."

"It's not true."

"Hadn't you heard anything about it?"

"Nothing. It's a great shock to me."

He seemed relieved. "Yes," he went on. "He came into the shop this afternoon and told me a new fellow would be coming."

"It's disgraceful. Why, everyone says what a good teacher you are."

"Oh, I'm too young," he said caustically. "That's not the real reason, all the same. He's always wanted to get rid of me."

He sat moodily with his head down, hands clasped between parted knees, talking into the ground.

"Did he give any other reason?" Anne asked.

"Oh, no. He's going to be kind enough to let me have a reference, but he can keep that." He paused. "I've lived here all my life, like you. Long before he ever came here."

She rested her hand on his.

"We can't let you go, Jerry. I'll speak to Miss Friedmann. I'm sure she doesn't know anything about it. Major Bryant too—he'd be on your side."

"It's very kind of you, but I couldn't stay now. But if I could find a decent place in England . . . the trouble is they'll put Wolf in quarantine. Will it be easy to get a job in England, Mrs. MacManus?"

"But do you want to go?"

He was silent a moment. "I must," he said. "Still . . . if it wasn't for him . . ."

"The children will never allow it."

"Oh . . ." he grinned. "Yes, they'll have to keep their eyes skinned now. No more climbing over fences and hiding in bunkers!" He brightened up a little. "Perhaps it will be the best thing for me. I suppose this isn't much of a career, and I might go on year after year never learning anything new, never seeing the world. I fell into this job. I enjoy it all right, but I didn't choose it for myself. Now I shall have to make a bit of an effort."

He was in two minds; he would have been ready to go off that afternoon, but he would not accept dismissal. Anne was with him in this; even if he went, the manner of his going must be of his own choosing and in his own time. She was incensed with Mr. Wake, and he went away encouraged. The children were enraged. Anne told them that Jerry would be properly championed, and they allowed themselves to be persuaded upstairs, far from satisfied.

"We must do something," said Sarah desperately, sitting on the edge of Merrick's bed.

"We could write Wake an anonymous letter."

"He'd think it was Jerry."

"But he might get rattled. We'd go on and on at him."

"He won't pay any attention unless we do something. What could we do?"

"Set fire to his bungalow."

"Oh, Merrick, do be serious."

"Well, it wouldn't be difficult." He began to turn the pages of his sailing-book, and she saw that he wanted to read; the failure of her fellow humans to come up to her own level of indignation constantly upset her. Seeing this, he said, to placate her, "Mother's going to do something."

"But it'll be too late."

It was not the practical urgency that worried her; it was the moral duty of everyone to vindicate Jerry immediately. He had long been one of her heroes, and now she wreathed him with the crown of martyrdom. She lay on her bed dressed that night, thinking about the detestable secretary; if she had had a statuette of him, she would have stuck pins into it.

"Beast, beast, beast!" she hissed into the dark.

She wanted him to be pilloried. Everyone must be shown what a wicked man he was; in the small hours, when the cars were beginning to return from the Casino, and below in the cabbage-patch she heard Frou-frou tugging at the chain, she was still conspiring how to humiliate him, expose him, and make him apologize; and when she slept, it was the sleep of an exhausted crusader.

Next day Merrick went early to the beach. It was fine and the tide would be low enough for him to walk out to the wreck. The seashore was at its best in the early morning, shimmering and empty, the small waves sliding idly in as if for him alone, the pools still, the arms of the sea gently but rapidly withdrawing from them, and far out over the deep blue and at either extremity of the long sands a haze over three horizons. By eleven o'clock children and nurses would have come, and by midday the fashion parade; the beach at Oriol would be thronged, and even the sea wear a prepared look.

Sarah stayed behind to help Blanche with the house. Her sense of injury as strong as ever, she told Blanche the story.

"*Tiens!*" said Blanche, busily scrubbing.

"And there's absolutely no reason. He's just been told he's got to go."

"*Tiens! tiens!*"

"We're going to do something, though."

"Don't you get into trouble, dear."

"I don't mind, nor does Merrick. Nobody can do anything to *us*."

New plans had come to her: placards proclaiming Mr. Wake a villain, caricatures which she would draw herself and leave lying all over the course, threatening telephone messages. . . .

Blanche listened to her with the proper degree of amazement and sympathy, now and then exclaiming "*Tiens!*" and "*Alors!*" She was on Jerry's side, but he was not the first person to have been turned out of a job. Sarah's impulsiveness touched her; and immediately, love being uppermost in her own mind, she pictured it bursting out one day in the pursuit of love, and foresaw a tragic future for it. Men will cause Sarah suffering, she thought, and sighed heavily, thinking of her own. But she was not going to be involved in any emotional plan, unless Anne took charge of it; she continued stolidly with her pots and pans.

A whistle sounded from the dunes outside the back door. It was Cacouette and three other caddies. Sarah ran out.

"*Bonjour*, Mademoiselle."

"*Bonjour*, Cacouette. Have you heard?"

"About Jerry?"

They all nodded, taking their lead from him. They were a delegation; at last she had supporters. They would not come in, they were not supposed to be there, and would be wanted any moment for the morning round; so she sat down with them in a hollow of the dune and went over the whole story. They listened intently. There were two other boys, whose names she did not know, and Marie, a strapping girl in shawl and sand-shoes. Cacouette wore his cracked boots and a jacket Major Bryant had given him, and sniffed frequently.

"Is it true?" he asked.

"Yes, Cacouette. It's absolutely disgusting."

An argument began. The caddies talked slang so fast that she understood little; but clearly they were angry, and against Mr. Wake, and keen to do something about it. Their voices rose, Marie and Cacouette gesticulated at one another, they lapsed into moments of silent and hopeless gloom, they forgot about Sarah; she understood that it was a conspiracy and longed to join it, but could not make out what was going on except, from the words "*les autres*" repeated several times, that they were not sure about the rest of the caddies.

One of the boys jerked his head towards her and said, "What does *she* think?"

They all looked at her, their eyes travelling over her craftily, as if she were something at a cattle show.

"Do you think we can do it, M'amselle?" asked Cacouette.

She said that she did not know exactly what "it" was. They looked at one another.

"Say nothing," muttered Marie, "we shall see."

With her shawl pulled across her heavy bosom, her stalwart build, ill-kept hair, and patched dress, she looked like one of the more respectable women in pictures of the French Revolution.

Cacouette did not agree. The *argot* began again, the raised voices, the gesticulations, the hopeless silences, and Sarah was again forgotten. The caddies got up from the sand, and looked anxiously towards the club-house.

"Well, thank you, M'amselle," said Cacouette, wiped his hands on his trousers, and shook her hand.

They trooped off, still arguing, and leaving her with no idea what she had done to be thanked, except to tell them what they already appeared to know; but something was in the wind, and she the only one to have been told of it. When Merrick came back, she kept it to herself. The caddies did not call on her again; however, she noticed groups plotting, in the forest, among the dunes, and in the caddie-house.

Cacouette was the only one who wanted vengeance on Mr. Wake purely out of friendship for Jerry. Like the other caddies, he loathed Mr. Wake, whom they knew from what he said to them as a bully and from what he said to others as a toady. But this would not have been enough to mobilize them, had not their pockets been concerned. It was not just a cause, it was an interest; for Jerry bought the lost golf-balls which they found, and resold them to the members. This was a valuable source of income, for some the only undeclared source, since their parents knew what a caddie earned as fee and tip for a day's round, and often took both off them when they got home. Anything extra to be squeezed out of the golf-club was welcome; and here was Jerry, the middleman and an honest one, about to be turned away. How could they be sure of his successor? Cacouette could convince and provoke them along these lines; but what were they to do?

Jerry began to pack. He did not use his coming departure as an excuse to be rude to Mr. Wake, but the contempt he had always felt, and hidden under a mask of polite correctitude, burned icily through. There is something condemning about sincere contempt in a young face; the depth of insult felt, and the control needed to prevent an outburst, give it a compressed force that makes even a fairly insensitive object of it uneasy. A man as vain of his personal appearance as Mr. Wake could not be entirely insensitive. Years of obsequiousness, accepted for none but his own small purposes and without the least saving sense of absurdity, had dispossessed him of principles; but he liked to please everyone, even (when he was not too busy) his subordinates. He felt uncomfortable with an enemy, and this malaise often produced in him the same effects as a guilty conscience. He longed to be quit of Jerry; but having once dismissed him, and done with the awkward interview, he could now afford to be affable and hoped to "part as friends." He wrote him out a handsome reference and undertook to use his influence with the membahs to find him a new post.

He was even generous enough, after noticing him one day giving Cacouette a lesson, to say nothing about it; though his generosity was mixed with the dread of a public scene. Jerry saw all this, and saw through it.

He continued to give his regular lessons, telling none of the members that he would be leaving. Every morning at midday he solemnly took the Baroness de Leverson (now Lady Wildenstein) out on to the ladies' course, solemnly repeated the same instructions, and watched her gaily failing to obey them. He realized at last that her ambitions did not lie on a golf-course, but enjoyed her company in a detached way, and liked listening to the adroit flattery Sir Maurice practised on her and the conversations they had about last night's gambling, about the opera, the people they had met at the races, the dresses, the witty scandal. They talked very openly, as if he were only there as a machine, and he learned a great deal which he had missed when taking her seriously as a pupil. He wrote letters to an uncle in Kent, who would board him for the first few weeks, and made inquiries about boarding Wolf. When he had no lessons to give, he went off on his own, swam and sunbathed. He spent most evenings with Anne, Merrick, and Sarah at the cottage. Having scarcely known his mother, and remembering no home except lodgings, he lived their home life, learning their games and their enthusiasms; and while his experience in his job helped him to grow up, so on these evenings he belatedly enjoyed a kind of childhood and adolescence he had missed. After the children had gone to bed, he would stay for a while talking to Anne, and then bicycle home between the moonlit dunes, happy, and looking forward to the future all the more because he now had something to leave behind him with regret.

When he had only a month to go, something began to happen that kept him unexpectedly busy at the golf-club. The caddies, who had usually brought in a dozen or so golf-balls for sale each day, suddenly started to bring in two dozen. The numbers grew; three dozen, four dozen. The players were much the same, he knew of no large arrival of beginners who might account for the losses. The wind had not become violent, the fairways had not shrunk; and yet every evening, when Mr. Wake had gone home and the last couples were strolling in, a queue of caddies appeared outside the shop. Jerry was within his rights to run this market; it had been his father's perquisite, passed on to him. He bought; and each morning the queue of players coming in to buy from him increased similarly. He sold. He became observant, marked some of the balls, and noticed that several which he had sold in the morning came back in the evening for him to buy again. He asked Cacouette what it was all about, but Cacouette merely shrugged his shoulders.

Members began to complain. M. Mazarian had lost three balls in one round, General Grandison four, Monsieur Lemaitre six in one day. The smooth movement of the players round the links was being slowed down by groups of men, women, and caddies, wandering about in the pines and dunes. Couples accumulated on the tees, impatient to drive off. Tempers rose. Some players lost so many balls that they were unable to finish the round, and arrived back furious at the club, threatening to withdraw their subscriptions. The caddies received smaller tips, or no tips at all; but in the gloaming, when their employers were in the hotel bars or dressing for dinner, they would furtively disperse about the course, find the balls, and make good their reduction on tips at Jerry's shop. Obviously there was a conspiracy; but it was difficult to prove.

Mr. Wake became rattled. The mixed foursomes, one of the club's most popular fixtures, was approaching, and he had received a particularly large entry. The Maharajah had not come near the club since the unfortunate affair of the photograph, and was reported to be interested in a rival course recently opened along the coast. Mr. Wake had prevailed on Mary Stiles to present a cup for the competition; she had no title, but several people who had were to take part in it, and her name was worth a great deal more than her weight in gold. The foursomes would coincide with a race-meeting, a polo match, a gala dinner at the Casino restaurant, and a charity performance at the opera, for which some famous members of a Paris company had consented to sing. The gossip-writers would converge on Oriol. There would be dresses and jewels to describe, and splendid parties to scheme their way into. A large public, composed of those who had gone this season to other resorts or never had the money to go to any, but liked to read about them, would be waiting to hear whether Miss Stiles wore her dresses on or off the shoulder, whether the ex-king of Ruritania was still with Madame Constantinescu and if not why not, what the flowers had cost at Madame Agyropoulos's dinner-table, and all the other tantalizing paraphernalia of the great world. Miss Ferguson, who had gone off to Deauville in a pique, would have to pocket her pride and come back. And here was chaos.

Mr. Wake suspected sabotage, but did not like to accuse anyone of it. He sent for Hillier, the caddie-master.

"Do you think Weston is behind this?" he asked darkly.

"Weston, sir?"

"I have reason to think that Weston harbours a grudge against me. He must be doing extremely well out of all these sales."

"The club must be doing pretty well too, sir. Twenty-five per cent comes to us."

"Yes, yes. But Weston gets the rest. It was a foolish arrangement made by my predecessor with his father. There is nothing on paper about it, and when Weston has gone I propose to bring it to an end."

"Some of the players prefer to buy second-hand balls, sir. New ones are expensive."

"I did not say we shall cease to sell second-hand balls. In future all must be bought and sold direct, through the club." He spoke of the club as if it were some mystical entity incorporate in himself. "I shall discontinue this percentage to the professional."

"The new man won't like that, sir. It's usual at every club I ever heard of."

"That is no reason to continue it here. We do not follow the fashion here; we set it."

Hillier said nothing. Talk of this kind seemed to him high-falutin nonsense; he could imagine no professional who would not expect to increase his salary, by any and every means, from his shop. He disliked Mr. Wake, and considered that he had shirked the war; and from a number of ex-officers who frequently visited him for a talk about old times, he well knew what the members thought of him. Hillier was one of those ex-regulars who had fallen in love in and with the country where he had campaigned; he lived contentedly with his French wife and his bilingual children in the town, never intending to return to England. He had transferred the strong sense of tradition and discipline without which he could not exist from his regiment to the club. Jerry's dismissal had angered him; it was an insult to an old comrade. But he said nothing about it, banged his punch-ball about more vehemently, and went on with his work.

"I shall address the caddies," said Mr. Wake.

"Yes, sir."

"We have the tournament this week-end. Today is Monday. I shall address them tomorrow, in the evening. Please see that they remain."

"Very good, sir."

The caddies were duly assembled. It was a fine evening, and Hillier marshalled them in the "yard," a patch of sand where the boy-caddies gambled, fought, and flirted through a wire fence with the girls. They were mostly poor, and some of them ragged. They wore patched blue overalls and torn coats mixed up with expensive jackets and sweaters, worn threadbare and cast off by the members. Here and there one of them had been given a quite new pair of shoes or a pair of obviously English grey flannels. The boys wore berets, the girls gaily-coloured scarves. Some of the girls were heavily and smudgily made up, although Hillier had forbidden it, and affected rakish little caps, imitating Lady Wildenstein. Even the youngest smoked, keeping their fag-ends in tin boxes and puffing them right down to the finger. Two of the girls were going to have babies; opportunities occurred and were taken in the woods on the walk home. When the baby was about to be born, they would go away, but probably return afterwards if they could not get work on the farms. They were like a collection of cheerful young vagabonds; they gambled in the sand with worn and dirty cards, giggled, and pushed one another about, until Hillier, whom they respected a little and were afraid of even more, shouted at them to keep quiet. He saw Mr. Wake, at a distance a military figure, approaching from his bungalow, and thought haughtily of the parades he had once called to attention, the commanding officers he had saluted; what a difference now!

Mr. Wake had decided upon the appeal to honour; it was no good threatening to sack them all, since there were not enough boys and girls anywhere near to take their place. He had seldom spoken to a caddy before, except to give a reprimand, and never to them all together. He had never spoken to any large group, but felt more than enough confidence in his own authority and appearance not to feel nervous. He entered the concrete caddie-house, and was at once struck by the sweaty smell of too many people in too small a space. His handkerchief was permanently scented—Charlotte saw to that—and he touched his nose with it.

"We must have this place disinfected," he said to Hillier. "There may be disease."

Perhaps there was disease; certainly there was in the homes to which some of the caddies returned. But since no infection had spread to the members, and there had been no epidemic, and the sea air was healthy, he had not heard about it. He returned his handkerchief to his breast-pocket and went into the crowded yard.

Complete silence, never before known there except at night, greeted his arrival, his address, and his departure. Many of them scarcely understood him; he spoke excellent French, but it was not theirs. Their eyes, like midges, wandered all over him, over his monocle, his green plus-fours, his canary waistcoat, his brogues; but they listened carefully to what he had to say. Some of the girls thought him handsome; an English milord, perhaps.

"As you all know," he began, "we are going to have a busy time this coming week-end. It is the week-end of the competition, and I need not tell you—why, some of you have been here longer than I have—that we all do our best here to give our visitors a pleasant impression of Oriol and France. I think we have succeeded, as the large crowds of well-known people who come here testify; your co-operation, and Hillier's ..." the eyes all switched to Hillier, muttering inwardly, "and the whole staff's, have made this possible, and the committee are grateful to you."

There was more of this, and then something about their mutual interest. He had rehearsed the address to Charlotte earlier, and asked for her comments on it, but not waited for the answer. He cleared his throat, and went blandly on: "As you all know, a great number of balls have been lost lately, and I must tell you"—what they already knew—"that some of the members have been complaining. Well, we have our good players and our bad players, and it is not our fault if some of them go off into the woods more often than others." This phrase, as he translated it, was misunderstood and taken to have something to do with sex. "I am blaming none of you, I make no accusations; let that be clear. But I do ask you, in view of what has been happening lately, to make a special effort this week-end. Shall we try to have a record low number of balls lost?" He concluded: "I am sure you will all support me in this for the sake of the club and for our own sakes. Good-night."

He was gone, followed by Hillier.

"I hope this will have gone home to them," he said.

"I hope so, sir," said Hillier without expression.

"We shall see tomorrow."

"Yes, sir."

The caddies watched him out of the compound, then collected round Cacouette, jabbering, swearing, scoffing, doing imitations of Mr. Wake's all-too-perfect French. They remained some time before starting off home. Next day the results were worse than they had ever been. Not a single player reached the eighteenth green without having lost at least one ball. Lady Wildenstein lost three in the pine-trees at the turn. General Grandison lost two in the first half-hour, stormed into the club-house, and resigned his membership.

9

Anne and Jerry guessed what was happening, but kept well in the background. Jerry was anxious not to compromise Anne, and Anne did not know for certain if Jerry was an active member of the plot, or merely its passive cause. Consequently their conversation became a kind of vocal wink.

"Things were no better today," Anne would remark innocently. "Several people have gone to play along the coast."

"So I hear," Jerry would reply. "I had over fifty lost balls in last night."

"Really? It's extraordinary. I've never known anything like it."

"Nor have I."

"I think it's because of you, Jerry. They're angry because you've been sacked."

"Do you think so?"

"I'm sure of it."

"Well, there's nothing I can do about it."

Mr. Wake's discomfiture pleased Anne; she hoped it would do him good. She sympathized with the members and used all her tact and pleasantness of manner to calm them down. Dutifully she passed on them and their complaints, but did no more for him. She was prepared to type his letters, arrange his appointments, and deliver his instructions to Hillier and the green-keepers, but she would not raise a finger to help him out of the mess. He was entirely in the wrong; and for once the children were not involved.

The children kept themselves well posted. Merrick had record of the mounting toll of lost golf-balls. They knew about General Grandison's resignation. They knew what Mr. Wake had said to the caddies, and Merrick had developed an exaggerated version of it, monocle, throat-clearing, and all, beginning "*Mes enfants*" and ending "*vive la France.*" They told everyone. They told Emilio, more than ever their friend after Judith's intervention at the hotel, and amazed to find even authority on the side against itself. They told Madame Menard. She sat under the umbrella outside the Casino, surrounded by sticks of barley-sugar, and listened to their excited narrative.

"*Non? C'est pas vrai? Mon Dieu, quelle affaire!*"

Her gold teeth glinted as she laughed. She would nod her head vigorously, as if giving her closest attention, and then pick up a newspaper to see if she had won the lottery. She liked the children and thought them comic, and did not forget that they were friendly with *la patronne*. They continued to hope that she would give them barley-sugar free, but her affection never went so far as that. She did not quite believe the stories they told her, nor did she take their enthusiasms seriously; and she considered the caddies to be disreputable.

Two evenings before the competition Jerry was at the cottage. The cards had been brought out to play whist, but no one had dealt them; Merrick had not even suggested they should play Initials. Sunset lingered along the dunes, and the curtains were not yet drawn. On the wall the colours in their grandfather's paintings glowed in the evening light, as if illumined from behind the canvas. Now and then a barefooted fisherwoman padded past along the main road, her basket, laden with shrimps, high upon her back. Wolf lay under the table, his eyes closed; when anyone spoke to him, he opened them lazily and his tail thumped upon the floor.

"I just think there won't be any competition," said Merrick. "There'll be such a mess-up nobody will be able to finish."

"Of course there'll be a competition, darling," said Anne. "Nobody's scratched."

"General Grandison has."

"Well, nobody else."

"They'll never get round the course if someone loses a ball at every hole," he said cheerfully. He was in shirt-sleeves, his sun-burned forearms resting on the table. "How can they, unless they go on playing all night?" He looked at the others triumphantly; Anne felt antagonistic to him in this mood. "They can't, can they, Jerry?"

"Oh, I expect they'll manage. It'll be rather a muddle, though."

"It'll be a muddle all right. Sarah and I are going to watch."

"Now, don't you two start getting in the way," said Anne. "Mr. Wake's suspicious enough as it is. I'm sure he thinks you've got something to do with it."

"I'm sure he does, too," said Jerry.

"Why ever us?"

"You're always up to something."

"Us!" Merrick looked them virtuously in the eyes. "It's Cacouette who's done all this, I'm sure."

"Cacouette's never told me anything about it," said Jerry. "I've asked him two or three times."

"Of course he's not going to tell *you*. You're just the one who mustn't know, that's obvious. If *we* were doing it, we wouldn't tell *you*. When we made you do the hole in one, we didn't tell you till years afterwards, did we?"

"Cacouette *is* doing all this," said Sarah suddenly.

"Of course he is," said Merrick. "He's always the chief one."

"You're just saying that. I *know* he is."

"How do you know?"

"Because he told me." They all looked at her. "Well, more or less told me. Days ago. It was a secret, really. You were on the beach." This was her moment. She leaned forward, smoothing her hair back from her forehead, and with glances of superior knowledge at Merrick told them of Cacouette's visit and the meeting in the dunes.

"Well, you're a dark one," said Jerry.

"I promised I wouldn't tell anyone. You mustn't either."

"You might have told me," said Merrick. "I wouldn't have said anything."

"I couldn't, Merrick."

Anne felt a flood of love for Sarah and her secret loyalties. She had nothing of Johnny, except the long eyes and occasionally, when she had made up her mind, a surprisingly obstinate look.

"So they *are* doing it for me," said Jerry. "Well, I'll be blowed. I'd better clear out right away."

"Oh, Jerry! You can't do that." Sarah was horrified; Cacouette's plot was a mission.

"Well, I dunno. . . ."

"You stay where you are, Jerry," said Anne. "Don't you dream of going."

It was a pity that Judith had gone to Paris, but Sam would be back for the competition. She intended to see him, and had no doubt that Jerry would remain.

"No, you can't go now, Jerry," said Merrick. "That'd just mean that old Wake had won. We've got to show him that he can't turn you out."

Jerry was confused; gratified and flattered to be the pivot of such a conflict, but embarrassed by the members' annoyance, the club's bad name, and the money he was making out of the lost balls. When they were brought in as usual next evening, they seemed to burn in his hands, and when he sold them to the members the franc-notes began to look like a robbery. He decided that he would accept for himself only an average of his takings before the trouble began, and put anything in excess in a separate drawer, but a new instruction from Mr. Wake destroyed his scruples; the secretary, seeing the fiasco of his appeal to honour, declared open war, and forbade the caddies to sell balls at all.

"Now we shall see," he said to Charlotte the morning before the competition. "When they discover they can't sell, they'll soon start finding them again."

"They'll sell them in the town, Glanville, or hang about the back-doors of the hotels."

"I have provided for that. I have asked the membahs to buy from Hillier in the future. I am laying in large supplies of new and second-hand balls, and we shall sell them direct through the club. Neither Weston nor the caddies will have anything to do with it. You may be quite sure they'll stop their little game when they see there's no money in it. The nearest course they could sell at is twenty miles away."

Jerry took this instruction as a direct slight upon his honesty, closed his shop, and refused to give up the key. Mr. Wake ordered Hillier to break the lock; Hillier refused. Anne typed a letter, which was pasted on the club notice-board; it announced with regret that for the next few days no lessons could be given "pending the arrival of a new professional." Excited meetings were held in the sand-patches at the back of the caddie-house, where Cacouette tried to persuade the boys, Marie the girls, to remain at home during the critical week-end as a protest. They were unresponsive. Smaller tips already, and now no balls to sell; and if they stayed away the loss of their fees for two rounds a day. Besides, many of them enjoyed caddying, had their pet employers, and laid wagers on the competition. They thought of their parents, and felt scared. It had been a good joke; they had even done quite well out of it, but now it had gone too far. There were some fights, and Cacouette got a black eye.

"They'll have to give in in the end," said Merrick as he and Sarah walked across the links.

"Oh, they can't, Merrick. We can't let Jerry go."

"I never said Jerry would have to go. But there's nothing more the caddies can do."

"Why not?"

Painstakingly he explained the economics.

"Couldn't we pay them, Merrick, to make up for it? I've got two hundred francs at home."

"That wouldn't go far."

"Perhaps somebody would lend us something. Or I could sell my coral necklace. It's worth quite a lot."

"It'll be all right, Sarah. Come and look harmless. There's old Wake on the prowl." There was a splash of canary among the pines, and the sun caught a sparkle from the dangling monocle; Mr. Wake was doing a reconnaissance. He withdrew into the trees, but they knew he was watching them and sat demurely on a bench beside the twelfth tee.

"It's a pity, all the same," said Merrick. "I'd like to have scored off him."

Disconsolately he kicked the little white disc, with an arrow painted on it, which indicated the direction of the green. In the distance Miss Marples and Miss Wells plodded their eternal round. The whole disturbance had passed them by; they seldom hit a ball far, and never crooked, and therefore could not lose one. Suddenly Sarah, who had been staring vaguely at Merrick's foot, had a feeling in her head as if two little wheels had interlocked.

"Merrick!" she gasped.

"What?"

"I've got an idea. Look what you're doing. . . ."

His foot had gradually kicked the disc out of place, so that the arrow now pointed to the seventh instead of the twelfth green. She began to talk rapidly and eagerly, and a slow smile spread across his face; soon it was he who was doing the talking, taking over the idea from her. He brought out a pencil and paper, and they moved off to the rise above the fifteenth hole, where Arthur Friedmann had first met their mother and their grandmother, and from here surveyed the whole course. They came back late to supper; after Anne was asleep, and the moon up, they slipped out of the cottage, and it was well past midnight when they returned.

They were about unusually early in the morning, and from the whisperings upstairs, the suppressed laughter in the bathroom, the speed with which they finished breakfast, and the familiar look of transparent innocence, Anne at once became suspicious.

"What are you two up to?"

"Up to?" asked Merrick. Sarah did not dare look her in the face; she left all the acting to Merrick.

"You're plotting something. I can tell."

"What should we be plotting, Mother?"

"You are, all the same. What are you going to do today?"

"Oh, we'll probably watch the competition a bit. Who do you think will win, Mother? Now that General Grandison has scratched, it might be anyone." Successfully he changed the subject.

After she had gone to the club, they raced through the washing-up with Blanche and then, Merrick with his camera slung from one shoulder, hurried off to the shrubs above the fifteenth tee, taking a path through the woods in order not to be seen.

At ten o'clock the competitors began to drive off the first tee, and a large group collected at the club-house, waiting for Hillier to call out their names. Mr. Wake bustled about, wishing everyone luck, praising the fine weather as if he had organized it himself, and being affable to the gossip-writers. Miss Ferguson had arrived, and was telling everyone about Deauville; she always had one eye over the shoulder of the person to whom she was talking, so that she should not miss somebody else. Sam Bryant was there, partnered by his brunette. The gay young men were there; the sun shone on brightly coloured pullovers, and club-shafts glinted as they made practice swings. Lady Wildenstein was not playing in the competition, but wore a new suit specially designed *"pour le golf"* by her Paris dressmaker; Miss Ferguson photographed her and wrote underneath that she was a "keen sportswoman." Sir Maurice had been at the Casino late, and would not be up until midday. Mary Stiles arrived, and was at once surrounded and admired. Her beautiful still face had a slight expression of melancholy which put men on their mettle, especially the least well off, and caused the far-off public, who only saw her photograph, to tell one another that riches did not always mean happiness. A number of people had come for the week-end who had never played at Oriol before; their entries had been made by friends, and Anne was kept busy in the office taking their fees and registering them on her lists. The younger Baron de Moutiers was there from the Villa Panache, more English than the English, in a coat of the loudest check with two slits at the back, as he had seen it in an advertisement. Anne remembered him years ago as a boy of natural chivalry and polish, his bow as he kissed a woman's hand a movement from a distant century, his sentences rounded and epigrammatic, his gesticulations restrained. But since he had decided to become anglicized he had ceased to finish his sentences at all, slurred his words, and shook hands abruptly. The barman went along the terrace, putting up the orange umbrellas, and Hillier, in a white coat, called out the names of the competitors.

Some twenty couples had played off when a caddie came running across the links. He hovered behind Mr. Wake, trying to get a word in; then hurried into Anne's office.

"Please, madame," he said breathlessly. "Could you tell the secretary to come . . ."

"Come where?"

"There, over there," he panted. "At the eighth hole. People don't know where to go."

"Don't know where to go? What are you talking about?"

"Yes, madame. The holes have been changed. *Mon Dieu!* . . ." He threw up a hand in despair.

"I don't understand. Nobody has changed the holes."

"But yes . . . yes. . . ."

Other emissaries were on the tee by now, and a crowd had gathered, looking accusingly at Mr. Wake, who had gone very red in the face. Anne joined them; only Miss Ferguson, Lady Wildenstein, and their coterie remained aloof on the terrace, discussing a *fête-champêtre* and the jewels worn last night at the Casino by Madame Agyropoulos.

Several returned players began to talk at once; the secretary turned from one to another, trying to make some sense out of it. He saw Anne and scowled at her.

"What's the meaning of this?" he almost shouted.

"I don't know, Mr. Wake."

"Someone's been up to some tricks," said Hillier. His eyes met Anne's, flashing the same thought.

"It's not Mrs. MacManus's fault," said Sam Bryant calmly. "You're the secretary."

"I assure you I know nothing about it. It's some damned piece of tomfoolery." He glared at Anne again, this time with a threat; the thought had reached him too. "I shouldn't wonder . . ." he began, but stopped.

"Nor should I," said Sam Bryant softly at her elbow. "Little devils."

"They can't have . . ."

"Can't they? You know best."

He grinned, but her heart sank; now there would be trouble.

About a mile away, among the dunes, the children lay convulsed. They had done their work well. Any changes on the first seven holes would have been reported to the club-house too soon to have any effect, and so they had left them as they were. The eighth was the furthest off, and here they had begun. It had not taken long; all they had to do was move the arrows.

From their hiding-place they watched the foursomes approach. It was their luck, and Mr. Wake's misfortune, that the first two were made up of strangers who had never seen the course before. When they reached the eighth hole, the caddies pointed to the arrows, looking bewildered, and all of them consulted the score-card. The children had expected this, and had arranged their plan so that the holes to which the arrows now pointed were as far away as the correct ones had been; and no one could deduce, from the length shown on the card, that there had been some mistake. So the caddies were overruled, and the first four drove off cheerfully from the eighth tee to the eleventh green; from the ninth tee, which was near by, they drove back, in obedience to another altered arrow, to the eighth green. The second four followed. Lemaitre and de Moutiers, who came in the third four, paid no attention to the arrows, drove in the direction they were used to, and met the first four returning along the eighth fairway. It was a long stretch, and some minutes passed before the two groups realized that they were playing into each other and in some danger. They advanced on one another like opposing armies. "Fore!" cried the strangers, and "Fore!" cried Lemaitre and de Moutiers. "Fore!" cried everyone, but no one would give way. They met and argued. Couples began to collect in the fairway, some playing the way they had always played, others the way the arrows pointed, and the turf was spotted with disputing figures. A crowd accumulated on the eighth tee, a decision was come to, and the game resumed; but nobody put the arrow back. Soon another foursome arrived who did not know the course, and again they found themselves threatening and being threatened by a foursome behind who did. Again there were shouts, balls whirring past ears, disputes, hold-ups, and a ripple of congestion spreading backwards.

Tears ran down Merrick's cheeks. He had a stitch from laughing and had to roll about in the sand, clasping his stomach. One side of his face had gone red, the other white; this usually happened when he had a laughing fit.

"Oh, Sarah, it's worked . . . it's worked! Look at them all. . . ."

She peered over the dune and ducked down again, helpless.

"M. Lemaitre . . . waving his arms . . . look . . . dozens of them . . . all together. . . ."

"What will old Wake do? Look, Sarah, look . . . they're coming to the thirteenth."

The children had turned the arrow of the thirteenth tee to face the fifteenth green; the fairways were close together, and the conjunction not surprising. The leading couples arrived, and again the caddies looked bewildered, again there was a discussion, the card was looked at; again the first two fours drove in the direction of the arrow. They proceeded to the fifteenth tee, where the children had turned the arrow back to the thirteenth green, now being approached by Lemaitre and de Moutiers, playing as they were accustomed to play. The green lay on a plateau, and the children in the dunes above. The strangers advanced, unaware of the Frenchmen approaching from the opposite side. Plop, plop, plop, plop . . . four balls landed on the green from one side; then plop, plop, plop, plop . . . four more from the other. Caddies and spectators included, nearly twenty people followed them, and the green began to look like a bazaar. They pointed, argued, apologized, could not make out who owned which ball, while behind them other foursomes steadily converged. De Moutiers practised what he thought was English sang-froid, but was really a French shrug of the shoulders; Lemaitre began to lose his temper. The children laughed so much they could scarcely follow what was going on, and Merrick felt really sick. People were again playing into each other on the eighth. Confused groups shouted "Fore!" from greens without tees, tees without greens, and fairways without either, and one green, the eleventh, from which all the arrows had been diverted, became entirely deserted. The competition was like a game of snakes and ladders; the players went forward, and rushed back, and shot on again, at the bidding of an unseen whim, and most of them took it good-humouredly. After all, no one was in a hurry to get anywhere. Had General Grandison been on the course he might have had apoplexy; it was left to Lemaitre to throw down his club, take up a dramatic stance athwart a fairway, and refuse to move until the secretary had come out to explain himself. Hotfoot the delegation arrived; Mr. Wake, Hillier, and two green-keepers. Jerry, now badly needed, had been looked for, but could not be found. Forewarned by the children not to be seen that day, he had provided himself with his usual alibi on the beach. The delegation went round the tees, and in half an hour all was well.

But that was the end of Jerry's dismissal, for Anne told the whole story to Sam Bryant, and Mr. Wake, sensing a contrary opinion in influential places, became alarmed. It was decided that Jerry should remain, and as this coincided with his twentieth birthday, there was jubilation at the cottage. The children admitted their guilt to Anne, Sam Bryant, and Jerry, who had all guessed it. They wanted to tell Hillier, but Anne knew what he thought about breaches of discipline, and told them not to; so he was left merely to assume, and assume he did, and kept an eye on them from that day. Anne found it hard to play the stern parent; their exultation was infectious. Cacouette winked at them whenever he saw them, and tried to get a confession out of them. The next time they had a meal at the Pine Hotel, Emilio nudged Merrick and whispered as he handed the vegetables:

"*C'est brave, donc, ce que vous avez fait au Golf Club.*"

Madame Menard took a stately interest and asked them what they had been up to. To all these hints they replied with a look of amused but innocent amazement; and when Marcel the *coiffeur* said that he heard there had been a lot of fun on the links, Merrick remarked that he thought it had been scandalous.

Many moons waned before Mr. Wake forgot or forgave. He had been baulked of vengeance upon everyone, side-tracked, and humiliated; the directors had even suggested that he was to blame. An edge was put on his exasperation by his sister's exhortations to accept all his trials in a Christian spirit. However, he was photographed at the prize-giving by the side of Mary Stiles; this, and a luncheon-party at which he sat within five of the ex-King of Ruritania, did something to console him.

Part

Two

10

It was not till the season was over and Merrick back at school that Judith returned and heard the story of the competition; during these weeks the arrival of the Mayers and Hans's condition put Oriol and the children out of her mind.

Radiant with excitement, she met them at the station in Paris. Elizabeth Mayer was a stalwart German, square in body and face. Hans was pale and thin, but he had always been pale, and Judith had not expected him to look robust. It was his manner that shocked her. He recognized her, but no more than recognized; there was not a trace of eagerness or pleasure in his welcome. Their luggage consisted of two valises and a violin-case; he made no effort to look after it, but stared blankly at the platform without appearing to understand where he was or what he had come for, leaving his mother to take charge of everything. She drew Judith aside. "He is ill in his mind," she said. "I do not trouble about his bodily health, but for the time being he has lost his spirit."

His initiative had gone. The organism from which decision and action originate had been enfeebled, and no circumstance, however new or strange, stirred spark or echo in him. He showed no interest in the streets and squares of Paris, and did not observe the flowers with which Judith had crowded her apartment in their honour. Most of the actions he did attempt he left unfinished, picking at food and vaguely turning the pages of books and magazines. The windows of Judith's living-room looked on to a small quiet square; it was autumn, the falling leaves were withered gold, and here he took to standing for long periods, his ankles crossed, his head sunk, staring out like someone who had sent part of himself on a journey and could do nothing till it returned.

"He has been like this ever since he came home," his mother told Judith. "A complete stranger brought him home. He had been found wandering in the streets, and when he saw me he behaved exactly as he did with you at the station. I was alarmed at first that he had lost his memory."

"Did they maltreat him?"

"No more than by taking away his liberty. The doctor was sure of that; there were no signs. But he has seen things, and for someone of his nature that has been enough."

"And his playing?"

"He hasn't touched the violin since he returned."

Judith shook her head wretchedly. "What you must have been through, Elizabeth."

"That is all over and done with," replied Frau Mayer firmly. "Now we must get him well again, so that he can get back into practice; after that we can begin to think of arranging concerts. He had improved immensely in the last three years. His playing had become clearer and more precise; and I am sure that one day this recent experience will emerge in it and give it greater depth."

Frau Mayer's definiteness was a relief. She neither fussed nor despaired; she took her disorientated son aboard and set her own compass the more firmly. She had arrived with a plan and she meant to carry it out.

"First of all," she said to Judith, "there must be an arrangement about money."

"This apartment is yours as long as you need it," Judith said.

"You have saved our lives, and you are very kind," Frau Mayer answered without emotion. "We are already immensely in your debt, and when Hans begins to give concerts we shall pay you back."

"On no account . . ."

"We shall pay you back," Frau Mayer interrupted with a slight but emphatic lift of her head. "But at the present moment we have nothing. The immediate necessity is that he be put into the hands of a doctor."

"Now that I see what he is like," said Judith, "I know the man to undertake his cure. He is a friend of mine, a musician himself, and Hans can be perfectly at his ease with him."

"And when can we see him? He is in Paris?"

"He is in Paris, and we can see him at once."

"At first only you and I."

"I agree."

"*Gut*," said Frau Mayer in a satisfied tone.

"And for yourself, Elizabeth? You have no clothes, no income. And your books . . ."

"My books I hid. If we ever go back, I shall know where to find them. Once Hans has been put into good hands, I shall try to find work here. I can teach, or do secretarial work, or if there is need of someone with organizing ability—we shall see. Meanwhile I shall have to ask you for an allowance, Judith. I suggest . . ." she mentioned an extremely small sum, and refused to consider more. "If you wish to give me more," she said, "then you must give me some work. For the moment I shall be busy enough with Hans."

"But Elizabeth, there must be something you need. . . ."

Frau Mayer looked at Judith, pursing her lips. There was a slight twinkle in her eyes. "There is something," she said gruffly. "I had to leave my cats behind."

"Your cats?"

"My white cats. Do you dislike cats?"

"Not particularly. How many did you have?"

"Three. Sanka, Sarita, and Groll."

"I shall buy you three," said Judith.

"Thank you." Frau Mayer inclined her head. "I shall keep them in my room."

Her lack of sham scruples and false politeness made her an easy companion; she stated her intentions bluntly, and spent the rest of her time visibly adapting them to the possibilities. Her chief obstacle was her son. She and Judith called on the doctor, who came to the apartment incognito, studied Hans, and announced that he must at once enter his clinic. A few days later Hans went docilely and unsuspecting as far as the door; but the

127

moment he had got inside, his dulled senses awakened, he knew what was happening, and refused to stay. He stood mulishly on the pavement, shaking his lowered head and repeating softly in German "No, I won't go in" until they took him home, where he began to detect behind every suggestion a ruse to lure him back to the clinic; in other respects he stayed listless and lifeless as before. The doctor paid another visit, asked Hans to play, played the piano himself to show that he was a kindred spirit, and displayed understanding in various ways, but it was no good. Hans slouched by the window with his ankles crossed. "Why don't they leave me alone?" Judith heard him say.

"He will come to me in the end," the doctor declared confidently. "He must go away from Paris and have complete rest. Don't try to make him play. Find somewhere quiet in the country and keep him there till he's better."

"I have the house at Oriol," said Judith, "but it'll soon be winter. He would be better in the south."

"On the contrary. There will be no one at Oriol at this time of the year. He can do what he likes there, and nobody will be there to stare at him. Besides, he will be at your own house. Take him to Oriol."

They went: Judith, Elizabeth Mayer with three white cats, and Hans with an unopened violin-case. M. Philippe met them at Etaples station, and the story soon came back to the cottage, of an extraordinary young man with fuzzy black hair and a dead white face, who had been seen wandering among the pines like a deranged ghost. According to Blanche, he was a half-starved gypsy, whom kind-hearted Miss Friedmann had discovered by the roadside and adopted. When Sarah heard this, her eyes sparkled and her heart gave a bound, for had not Heathcliff been a gypsy and come to Wuthering Heights as an adopted child? She hovered on the road outside the Villa des Roses, hungry for a glimpse of him.

Emily, stirred to grudging pity, had prepared for him the room that had once been Arthur Friedmann's; the dust-sheets had been taken off the grand piano in the gloomy hall downstairs, and the violin-case placed upon it; and while outside the sea-winds groaned among the pines and Elizabeth Mayer sat upstairs telling Judith of the bitter years that had

128

passed, Hans was left to do as he pleased. Colour came into his cheeks, and they believed that he went for walks without telling them.

"He is getting better," said Frau Mayer. "He does not want to admit it, but I notice a change in him."

She seemed to Judith to be singularly phlegmatic about him. Her own experience had been so harrowing that she wanted to put it behind her as soon as possible, and her practical mind, leaping ahead to the moment when the Western capitals would acclaim him, was irritated at the slowness of his recovery. She had become impatient of pity, even for Hans and herself; the tone in which she told Judith of the persecutions had been almost that of a chairman reading an annual report. "And what about these children of whom you wrote to me?" she asked.

"They are two English children. Their mother is a secretary at the golf-club."

"Is there golf in this weather?"

"No, but they live here all the year round. The boy is at school in England. The girl is the more interesting, and later I shall tell you a plan I have for her. It concerns you."

"Ah? And what does the mother do in the winter? It must be very dull."

"I really don't know what she does. She always seems cheerful."

"What are her politics?"

Judith laughed. "You're talking like a central European, Elizabeth. Like me. I don't think she has any politics."

"I suppose that is permitted to the English," said Frau Mayer. "And when am I to meet these fortunate people?"

"I'll invite them. It'll be good for Hans to meet somebody calm."

"Am I not calm?"

"You appear astonishingly calm, but your background is stormy and it will be in your blood for at least three generations."

Sarah did not take to Frau Mayer at first, and Anne had the impression, at their first meeting, that she was being put through an interrogation by a hostile examiner. Frau Mayer had a bludgeoning inquisitiveness about everyone and everything; and though she shared the traditional German admiration of Byron and Shakespeare, and the German envy of British imperial achievement, she also had something of the Nazis' delusion that all contemporary British were degenerate. She felt a great deal of rancour against British foreign policy, blaming it for the evils that had befallen Germany and attributing to it an indirect responsibility for the Nazi movement. Like Judith, she held strong views on social problems, and looked down on those who thought about them less intensely; like Judith too, but more deeply, she resented the comparative security of England and the haphazard optimism of the British, and frequently she repeated Anne's answers to her questions with a caustic and censorious undertone. She sat squarely in her chair, facing Anne; she had almost no neck, and reminded Anne of a bullock.

"Your son is at school in England?" she inquired. "A public school?"

"A small grammar school."

"What is the difference?"

"I don't know that there is much difference, except in the fees."

"Except in the fees. H'm. And your daughter?"

"We have a small school here for the British residents. Mr. Ridgway, the parson, is in charge of it."

"The parson? So. She learns history, of course?"

"Oh, yes. History, mathematics, and the usual things."

"Science?"

"I don't think Sarah would take to science."

"I am sure that every child should be taught the rudiments of science," declared Frau Mayer. "An exclusively classical education leads to false romanticism."

Anne resented the word false in connexion with her children. She never thought it worth the energy to take offence at an objectionable detail, and had a habit, which had worked excellently on Mr. Wake, of treating people who mildly provoked her as an entertainment. Frau Mayer interested her. It was a long time since she had met a German, and she had heard her story from Judith; she admired her forceful downrightness, wondering that anyone who had been subjected to such experiences should have surmounted them so well. Frau Mayer began to expound her theories of education, obviously challenging Anne to contradict them, and Anne gave her answers from her own practical handling of Merrick and Sarah. Judith

130

saw that they were at cross-purposes, and set herself to interpret one to the other; understanding, from her own background, Frau Mayer's preoccupation with systems and general principles, and having seen enough of the English to understand Anne's empirical approach, she was a natural intermediary. Hans stood at the window; and Sarah, thinking she was unobserved, began furtively to sketch him.

Suddenly he said: "May I look at your drawing?"

She started and went red. "Oh, it's nothing, really," she answered, and tried to hide it.

"Please let me see." He came and looked over her shoulder. "But it's good," he told her.

Frau Mayer paused in full spate, watching Hans. This was almost his first moment of animation. In order not to check it, she resumed her dogmatic flow, but Anne could see that she was watching him all the time. It pleased her that Sarah should have prompted this little stir in him, and obscurely she felt it to be a vindication of her upbringing. Frau Mayer was surely not the best companion for a rest cure, even though she was Hans's mother; she was too assertive, and they had too many memories in common. At the moment Sarah, with her reticent but profound sympathy, might do a great deal more for him.

In the following days this happened. Sarah did not realize what had unbalanced him, nor did Anne attempt in detail to explain, but she could see that he was in mental anguish, and her heart went out to him. Like Judith and like Jerry, he began to come round to the cottage. He did not come in or ring the bell; but they would see him standing awkwardly at the gate, expecting them to fetch him. Sarah would run out to him. He raised his eyes with a faint flicker of pleasure, they began to talk, and gradually they walked away, disappearing towards the forest or the dunes. There was a resemblance between them: Sarah shy and confused of speech by nature, Hans made confused by circumstance. He became the first person who stimulated a feeling of compassion in her over a long period; it had stirred many times, but had lasted only the duration of an impulse. Of prisons, of the world, she knew nothing; she merely longed to say or do something that would help him. His lost attitudes and mumbling voice were a misery to her. Timidity led her to the course which the other women knew from reason and instinct to be the wisest; she made no effort to force him into life, waiting until it roused of its own accord in himself. He would fall in with any suggestion, and seemed to be waiting for suggestions to be made. They walked together through the forest and along the sea-coast. A small object such as a fir-cone or a sea-shell would attract him and he would draw some generalization from it; at the end of these walks his pockets would be full of them. He stood among the dunes gazing at the plunging white sea, solitary and regardless of the cold; once he told her that it was like Beethoven. He could not continue a conversation, but uttered joint-less remarks which he did not develop; they sprang from troubled origins she did not understand. Sometimes he lifted a curtain-corner of his ear-lier life and for a few minutes confided in her. Once, as they passed the tennis-courts, he said that he used to play tennis well; and though a high wind was blowing and he wore his walking-shoes, he would willingly have played then and there.

"I used to drink a lot," he told her. "One night I had to be carried home." He laughed, as if carrying on a conversation with some person locked in-side himself, and said no more about it. Another time Sarah was at the Villa des Roses, Judith and Elizabeth Mayer were having a political dis-cussion, and Hans stood at a window in his accustomed manner, his an-kles crossed, his hand to his cheek, as if trying to remember something. Suddenly he interrupted them. "Do you remember that inn by the river where the men used to play chess?"

Judith and Elizabeth stopped talking, and glanced significantly at one another.

"Of course," said Judith. "We always used to go there on our walks. It was called The Owl."

"Was it?"

"Why don't you have a game of chess with Judith?" his mother pro-posed.

"If you like," he answered in his dead voice. When the board was fetched, he turned the pieces upside down and looked them over, but made no move to put them in their correct places; he paid no attention to the game, which soon ended.

Occasionally his mother, on the pretext of taking him for a walk, would coax him into the hall downstairs, sit at the piano, and begin to play an accompaniment.

"Come on, Hans, come and play," she would say in German, as if to a child. "This is one of your favourite pieces." He would stand by the door, unable either to go out or to take up the violin, while she played the whole accompaniment as if for her own pleasure; but it had no effect, and the violin-case remained on the piano.

"Still, he is getting better," she declared. "This sentimental friendship is waking him up."

"The touch of innocence?" said Judith.

"Possibly. The girl is certainly a very sweet child. Are you sure she has no foreign blood?"

"I don't think so."

"I am sure there is something," Frau Mayer proclaimed. "A touch of Slav, perhaps. She is too warm-hearted to be English."

Frau Mayer also went for walks. She nearly walked Judith off her feet, wishing to be shown the whole estate of Oriol, and whenever Sarah and Hans saw the two women, one sturdy and compact, the other tall and lumbering, Hans made Sarah hide. He poked sly fun at his mother behind her back, calling her "the steam-engine" and making Sarah do drawings of her. Flashes of impishness came out in him, and at times he was indeed like a child.

Frau Mayer asked Judith questions. "Here you have all this beautiful property," she remarked on one of their walks, "and it seems to me that you know very little about it. Now, if it were mine I should administer it. Don't tell me you have no head for business, because you know that isn't true. Besides, women have a better head for business than men."

"I spend most of my time in Paris," said Judith.

"Ah, yes. Your artists. Your other Hanses. You are a great benefactress, Judith."

Although Frau Mayer meant this sincerely, her interrogations made Judith uneasy. Most people might have thought it enough to have spent a large sum in getting the two out of Germany and starting them up in France; Frau Mayer asked nothing for herself, but her demands upon Judith's conscience appeared to be insatiable. With an off-hand air, but as carefully as a note-taking sociologist, she slowly laid the economics of Oriol bare. She collected data on wages, rents, and the price of land. She proclaimed the caddie-house insanitary. She inquired about the villa- and hotel-owners and the sources of their wealth, until beneath this eagle all-relating eye Oriol no longer seemed a secluded island of delight, but a minor view of history. She filled in the limbs and veins that connected it with society (not Miss Ferguson's "Society"), and delineated the true occupations of those who came thither to relax from them and enjoy their fruits. The stage swung round, thrusting the bright spectacle out of sight and revealing some of the activities from which the money came to have devised it all and keep it going; not all were discreditable, yet this probing and stripping operation, which reveals a worm in the building even of the Pyramids, the Parthenon, or the Sistine Chapel, deprived Oriol a little of its glamour. Judith, one of its owners, was embarrassed. She had a reputation as a woman of advanced ideas, but the more questions her insistent companion asked, the more she wondered if she had any claim to it. Although Frau Mayer made no direct attack, she found that she was defending herself; she was even driven to bring the service she had done the Pine Hotel waiters as witness to her enlightenment. As a further gesture, she decided to give a Christmas party and invite all her employees, with their children, who remained during the winter months.

Merrick's holidays began a few days before. He had a rough crossing, and the road from Boulogne was slithery with ice. He began as usual by telling Anne and Sarah all his own news, but when Oriol came in sight it occurred to him that something might perhaps have happened to them.

"Well, what's been going on here?" he asked.

"Nothing much," said Anne. "It's been very cold. We're all invited to the Villa des Roses on Christmas Eve."

"Judith's asked everyone," said Sarah.

"Oh, so you call her Judith now."

"She asked us to. She's been awfully friendly, Merrick."

Anne knew that Sarah was bursting to talk about Hans. "Sarah's got a new friend," she said.

"Oh? Don't tell me you've given up Jerry. Are you in love again, Sarah?"

"Why do you always have to think I'm in love? It's so silly."

"There's nothing wrong with it. Who is it this time?"

"He's a German violinist," Sarah replied grandly and refused to say more. Merrick's bantering tone annoyed her. She had given Hans an enthusiastic account of Merrick, whose sympathies she was longing to enlist; but she wished Merrick to understand that Hans had to be taken seriously, and it was not until the evening that she thought he was in a suitable mood. Incoherently she tried to explain Hans. There was so much to explain. "He's a German," she said, "but he doesn't live in Germany now. He can't. He's been turned out."

The children's low opinion of Germany was an after-effect of the first war; Germans were the enemy, who had invaded France, tried to conquer England, and killed Anne's father. It was a great disadvantage, Hans coming from Germany; but he had redeemed it in her eyes, and she hoped in Merrick's, by being turned out, and Merrick would soon see that he was not at all "like a German."

"Why has he been turned out?" Merrick asked.

"He's been persecuted. He's awfully ill, Merrick ..." she tried to give an idea of his illness, but floundered deeper and deeper and felt that she was making him ridiculous. "You'll think him peculiar and funny," she ended hopelessly, "but he can't help it, and you mustn't show that you notice anything."

When Merrick met Hans next morning, he decided at once that he was a problem and that the only solution was to treat him as a normal human being and get him to do things. Anne and Blanche watched the three of them disappear along the Oriol road. It was a frosty blue morning. They all had red noses and wore scarves, and Sarah evidently could not make up her mind whether to slouch behind with Hans or stride ahead with Merrick. He and Sarah carried skates; they were going out to the frozen pools between the dunes.

"Can you skate?" Merrick asked, turning back to Hans.

"Oh, I used to," he answered dully. "We had an Ice Palace. A lot of people used to go there."

But when they got to the pool he meandered off and stared at the sea from a high dune.

135

"Just leave him," said Sarah. "He'll be all right."

Merrick gave her a lesson. His compactness and sense of balance made him seem better than he really was; he could move fast and smoothly along the straight and round mild curves, bending from side to side with hands clasped behind his neck, but when he attempted figure-skating he fell over. Sarah fell over frequently, whatever she attempted; her lankiness was against her, and she forgot his instructions in her longing to succeed. They saw Hans watching them with a furtive smile.

"Why don't you have a try?" Merrick suggested.

"Oh, I've forgotten it all."

"Well, have a try, anyhow."

Hans sat passively in the sand while Merrick strapped on the skates, but the moment he was on the ice the necessity of doing something galvanized him. Reflexes came to life, and he sailed along to the manner born.

"Good heavens!" said Merrick. "He's an expert. He damn nearly did a figure of eight. Why didn't you tell us you could do that?"

"Oh . . ." Hans mumbled.

"Go on, do some more."

"No."

He took off the skates.

"I don't see that there's much wrong with him," Merrick said, after they had left him at the Villa des Roses. "A fellow can't be desperately ill if he can shove on a pair of skates and move like that. He'd probably be just the same with his violin."

"He *is* ill, all the same," Sarah insisted. "You can tell from the way he walks and stands about."

It pleased her that Merrick had taken to him; but she treated Hans's troubles as her own property and wanted Merrick to see them at their worst before they were cured.

"He walks rather like you," said Merrick, "and nobody says you're ill. We'll go skating again after Christmas, and I bet you he'll be all right."

Christmas Eve arrived, and they were about to leave for Judith's party when there was a knock at the back door. Blanche announced that Cacouette and several caddies were outside.

"They've been invited to M'amselle Friedmann's, but they don't want to go alone," she said.

Sarah and Merrick ran out and found them there in their Sunday clothes; Marie had a bow in her hair and Cacouette had smarmed down his with brilliantine.

"*Eh, bien*," he said. "Are you going to the Villa des Roses?"

"We thought you'd be there already," said Merrick.

"We're waiting for you."

"Well, we're just coming."

They locked up the cottage and went along the road together. Cacouette made polite conversation to Anne, but the other caddies hung back, and when they reached the lighted villa waited until Cacouette beckoned to them to follow him in. The party was being held in the big hall, the first time for many years it had been used. The piano was open, the pewter chandeliers blazed, lights had been lit beneath the sombre paintings and tapestries, and Christmas decorations festooned the walls. A long table was set with a sumptuous tea, crackers, and holly; excited children chased each other, while the British residents, with a few local French, stood about admiringly and told each other what a good idea of Judith's this had been. There was no sign of her, nor of Hans, but Frau Mayer had the party well marshalled, giving instructions to Emily, keeping the children from climbing over the piano, and making Merrick and Cacouette fetch chairs. Emilio arrived in a black suit and bow tie. Mr. Wake was talking to Mr. Ridgway, the parson; there would be a service tomorrow at the English Church, and Mr. Wake would read one of the lessons. Hillier the caddie-master was there with his French wife, and the caddies whispered when they saw him and shook hands with embarrassment; they remained together in a compact knot, gazing at the food, the furniture, the decorations. Judith emerged from the dining-room, closing the doors behind her, and whispered something to Frau Mayer. Frau Mayer clapped her hands.

"Attention, please!" she cried. "The tea is ready. All the children form up."

Everyone looked puzzled. Frau Mayer bustled about, dragging the children into file, the two smallest in front facing the dining-room door.

"By height," she kept on telling them—"everyone by height."

"What's this in aid of?" Merrick said, as she planted him alongside Sarah.

"It's the procession," Frau Mayer replied, frowning.

Even the grown-ups had to join the file, Anne with Mr. Wake, Emilio with Mrs. Hillier; when at last she had them stretching in a ragged crocodile across the hall, Frau Mayer nodded to Judith and the doors were opened.

Frau Mayer and Judith took the two leading children by the hand. The procession advanced, and as Sarah reached the threshold she caught her breath. The tree stood in an alcove at the end of the room; all the lights had been put out except the fragile candles on its branches. Slowly it revolved, a pyramid of glittering points, to the music of a carol; tinsel chains dangled in the dark branches, coloured balls reflected the candles, whose flames leant sideways in the motion of the tree, and a silver star gyrated on the summit. The children formed a gaping semicircle; the older people applauded, kneeling beside the children and pointing, and Merrick went forward to the stand to see what was causing the tree to revolve. The gramophone record playing the carol came to an end, but a musical box inside the stand continued to tinkle out the same tune. All in the room were silent, as if expecting a miracle. It ceased, the tree ceased to turn, and people crowded round Judith congratulating her, while the younger children gazed at her awestruck and incredulous.

She began to hand out the presents from a large pile. Frau Mayer had been given the list, and no one was omitted. The older people had simple but beautifully wrought ornaments and brooches off the tree; Anne guessed that Judith must have got them specially from Paris. The younger children were soon buried in tissue paper, unwrapping dolls, spotted horses, and boxes of games, rushing from one to another and showing off what they had been given. Judith came over to Cacouette, who was standing with Sarah, and said: "We had to leave yours outside. Would you like to come and get it?" She took them into a passage and pointed to a new bicycle. "We got one with the low handle-bars," she said. "If you'd like the other kind, we can easily change it."

Cacouette looked at the bicycle and then at Sarah. "I don't understand," he said.

138

"Is it for him?" Sarah asked in amazement.

"Of course it is. You said he wanted a bicycle."

"It's for you," she told him.

"For me?" He pointed at himself. "That's for me?" His manner seemed indignant, even unfriendly. He felt the bicycle all over, as if it were an ox, caressing the bright blue racing handle-bars and shining black spokes. "It's a fine model," he said at last. "But it's not for me."

"But it is," Judith laughed.

He felt it once more, straightened, and held out his hand to Judith. "Well, thank you," he said brusquely.

"You should thank Sarah," Judith replied. "She was the one who told me."

She went back into the dining-room, and Cacouette looked accusingly at Sarah. "You told her I wanted this?"

"I didn't, Cacouette. I just said once that it was a long way from Etaples to the golf-club. She must have thought of it herself."

He still seemed suspicious, and she could not understand him. She felt as excited as if she had been given the bicycle herself, and thought he should have been more demonstrative. Later she saw him chattering in a corner with Marie and the others, who all had parcels; after tea they slipped out and began to ride the bicycle up and down the road.

The party continued till after dark. Emilio did his famous imitation of the nightingales, and sang to Frau Mayer's accompaniment. Hillier's small daughter was sick, but everyone was cheerful and happy. M. Philippe, flushed with wine that Judith had kept for the men, whispered scandalous compliments to Blanche, and Merrick even had quite an amicable talk with Mr. Wake. Still Hans did not appear. Sarah did not like to ask what had become of him, and as she peered about in search of him she suddenly realized that Charlotte Wake too was absent. Frau Mayer had put on the gramophone and announced that "now there would be dancing." The tables were pulled aside, the younger children confined to the dining-room, and couples took the floor; Hillier paired off with Anne, and Anne noted with a smile that Merrick had invited Judith.

"Where is your sister?" Sarah asked Mr. Wake.

"She is at home, my dear. She goes out very seldom, and she is busy preparing for tomorrow."

Sarah felt outraged. How dared he come without Charlotte? She was certain he had ordered her to stay behind; probably she would be cooking, or pressing his green plus-fours. When no one was looking she slipped away and ran through the forest to the bungalow. The dark sky towered like one giant tree, hung with tinsel stars; white clouds floated between the pines. The clear cold air quickened her senses; her heart glowed with universal love, but in one small corner burnt a white-hot coal of indignation against Mr. Wake. Everybody should be at Judith's party that evening—everybody. A light was on in the bungalow, and through a window she saw Charlotte reading; the book looked like the Bible, the movement of her lips suggested that she was reading aloud. Sarah rang the bell.

"Do come to Miss Friedmann's," she said breathlessly. "We're all there, and there's singing, and everyone's been asking where you are."

Charlotte peered at her.

"Why, it's Sarah. Whatever's the child doing without a coat? You'll catch your death."

"Do come, Miss Wake. It's such fun, and it's Christmas Eve."

"Oh, I won't come out now, my dear. I've a headache, and I was just taking a nap."

"Won't you really come? Oh, you must come."

"No, thank you, dear," she said kindly. "My brother's there, isn't he?"

"Oh, yes, he's there, but it's you they all want. Please, Miss Wake."

"Well, that's very kind of them, I'm sure, but I really decided I wouldn't go out tonight. Thank you all the same, and I hope you're enjoying yourselves."

She closed the door, and Sarah saw the curtain drawn across the window. On the way back she met Cacouette and the caddies walking to Etaples.

"Wherever's your bicycle?" she exclaimed. "Aren't you going to ride it home?"

Cacouette looked embarrassed.

"I've left it," he said. "Your brother's looking after it."

"But aren't you going to show it to your family?"

"Well . . . not yet . . . no . . . you see . . . *eh bien*, I shall leave it with your brother for the moment," he stammered.

The others watched him, and she had an impatient feeling that they were keeping something from her. People disappointed her; Charlotte refusing to come, and now Cacouette, whom she had imagined displaying the gleaming bicycle to all the neighbours—how desperately they disappointed her!

The guests had gone, and only she, Anne, and Merrick were left among the debris. Hans had appeared at last; he stood by the piano, fingering the keys. Judith and Frau Mayer were relaxing.

"It has been a wonderful party," Anne said. "And what presents, Judith! You shouldn't have been so extravagant."

"Oh, it's Christmas," Judith replied. Her eyes shone, and her expression was happier than for a long time. "It's the first real Christmas I've had for years."

"In Bavaria they used to put little trees outside the houses," said Frau Mayer.

"What a good idea to make the tree go round," said Merrick. "Whoever thought of that?"

"Ah, that's a very old custom," Judith replied. "I found the musical stand in the boxroom. It was really that made me decide on a party."

Suddenly Frau Mayer touched her arm. "Look!" she said softly.

Hans had opened the violin-case. Without speaking or looking at them, he took out fiddle and bow and held them vaguely in one hand. He rested the fiddle beneath his chin, took it away, rested it again, and laid the bow along the strings. Frau Mayer sat forward, gripping the sides of her chair. He began to play. Anne recognized the first few notes of the Bach Chaconne.

"He would start with the most difficult," Frau Mayer muttered to Judith, but her eyes sparkled.

He played at first disjointedly, without flow, and even Anne, who had little musical training, could tell that he made mistakes. Frau Mayer's face never changed, but the fingers of her right hand tapped softly on the chair. Gradually he seemed to improve; it was as if the blood was visibly returning into his fingers, creeping steadily on, veining the bow, the strings, the violin itself. And as he played, Frau Mayer relaxed, sinking back contentedly and closing her eyes.

"What practice he will need!" she murmured to Judith at the end. "But it will be all right." Her tough expression softened. "Yes," she repeated, "it will be all right."

11

fter the new year Hans began perceptibly to get better. His play
ing had suffered greatly from lack of practice and the disturbance of his mind. He would stop in the middle of a piece and
fall into his old attitude of hopeless immobility, his head sunk into the violin, his bow drooping. His fingers had become stiff and clumsy; even
when he began to regain his technical skill his interpretations lacked life,
and the music seemed to be buried beneath a layer of ash.

"The great thing," said his mother, "is that he has begun to play. Now
he must practise, practise, practise. There is no point in going to a teacher.
He has learnt all the teachers have to tell him; now he must remember it.
And then we must just wait till the feeling in his heart unfreezes."

Quietly, efficiently, she took charge of his recovery, gradually increas-
ing his hours of practice from half an hour a day to three, to five, to more.
Sometimes he played alone, but usually with her, and Anne soon saw what
the relationship was that had made him refuse to leave Germany without
her. She was his discipline, as much as his kindred spirit. She saw to it
that he fed properly, she gave him fixed hours, she sent him to bed early;
and these were all part of a rule he needed. After he had gone to bed she
would discuss with Judith the progress he had made, and decide whether
he should go over the same work the next day or attempt something different. If he made a suggestion she always agreed to it, however ill he carried it out; though often she made him stop when he wanted to go on, thus
husbanding his strength. During their hours of practice they were relent-
less with one another, and Judith, passing behind the locked doors of the
hall, would hear them repeating the same passage over and over again on

violin and piano, until they were either stale or satisfied. Frau Mayer did not play particularly well, and as Hans got his spirits back he began to laugh at her mistakes, lower the bow and make her practise till she had corrected them; he was used to her, and it would be many months before either of them would let an unknown expert hear him. Anne was touched by the defiant patience with which Frau Mayer guided him back to life and the obedience with which he followed her. Once after supper they were sitting comparing the shape of their hands; jokingly they interlocked them, making a double fist, and it seemed to Anne that their spirits were so interlocked.

As he advanced, his mother found time for other energies. It was her nature to organize; with someone less purposeful than herself, she tended to dominate. She did not accept the situations which confronted her; she summed them up like a military commander, went straight for the point weakest in relation to herself, and installed herself on top of it. In Munich, ten years before, she had given lessons in history and languages to the daughters of well-to-do American and English families. Dozens of other German women were competing in this market at the time, all with more influential connexions; but whereas they, recognizing that what they wanted was money and what the girls wanted was a good time, had been ready to sacrifice education, Frau Mayer had told the parents flatly that their daughters were downright ignorant, and refused to do anything but teach. This was so unusual a prelude that she had become almost fashionable; her course acquired the reputation of a pedagogic tyranny, but a number of parents decided that their offspring would enter life handicapped without it. Her chief talent lay in teaching, and she loved it; by this approach she had also turned the meagreness of an elegant upbringing to her own and Hans's advantage.

Even when there was nothing for herself to be gained from it, she could not resist picking at chinks in the armour of wealthy and contented people; not from malice, partly from inquisitiveness, partly from an inverted resentment at the precariousness of her own life, mainly from a sense of mission. For Frau Mayer was an improver; and in her leisure hours she now set about improving Judith.

She mobilized upon a line of attack she had probed before: the breach between Judith's profession of liberal progressive ideas and her practice of them. She had discovered by careful inquiries what a large share in the valuable real estate of Oriol and Jacques-plage Judith had inherited from her father and still held; and she wanted to know what Judith did with the income. The two women had been friends for years; Judith did not object to a cross-examination which she might have thought impertinent in a stranger. Besides, she had a chronic sense of guilt about her wealth; though she had been giving it away for years, she still felt uneasy about it. A fresh benefaction entered her head, in reply to Frau Mayer's implied challenge; the children's adventure with the tee-boxes, the stories she had heard from them about Mr. Wake, and the new light in which people like Emilio and Cacouette put Oriol, also had something to do with it.

"We must have a new caddie-house," she announced. "What do you think of that, Anne?"

"I think it's long overdue."

"Elizabeth Mayer says the present one is unsanitary. I passed it myself the other day, and she's quite right. We ought to be ashamed of ourselves."

"I've suggested it several times," said Anne demurely. "Mr. Wake says it's not necessary."

"Of course it's necessary. Why should the members of the club have billiard tables and lounges and newspapers, and the caddies have a rabbit-hutch? They're human beings," said Judith indignantly, as if this was an entirely new discovery.

"He said that they're not inside it long enough to make it worth while building a new one. There's something in that. In the season they're out on the course most of the day."

"Oh."

Judith looked at Anne nonplussed, expecting Anne to keep her indignation stoked.

"All the same," Anne went on, "they should have something decent. When it rains, there's a whole crowd of them in that tiny space. There's no running water and only two lavatories."

"Of course it's disgraceful," said Judith, reassured. "I shall speak to André Lemaitre about it."

"You won't find him sympathetic. It's been mentioned to him."

"Why to him? Why not to me?"

Anne smiled. "I don't think anyone imagined you would be interested," she answered.

Judith looked embarrassed. "It's all my own fault," she said. "I never have been interested in Oriol until now."

She threw herself into the project with the fervour of righteousness. André Lemaitre was away; Mr. Wake, leaving the responsibility of opposing her to him, thought it politic to humour her. He agreed with everything she said. It *was* wrong to continue with the old building, it *was* insanitary, it *did* reflect upon the club, he was sure the membahs would think it excellent to have a new place, and of course the caddies would like it, but—he kept the "buts" for monologues to Charlotte and other conversations out of Judith's hearing—the old building was not so bad, the caddies did not expect anything better, would not appreciate it, would ruin it, would steal the furniture if it was to have furniture, and so on. When Lemaitre came back, he too said much the same; being a business man, he added that the club's profits were not as high as they had been, that 1929 would have been the time to think of new buildings, and that now, because of the crisis, it was imprudent. Judith had a stormy interview with him; in the end, as he had expected, she declared that she would put her own money into the project, and sent for builders to have it ready by Easter.

Her erratic imagination had to be curbed before it ruined this sensible and necessary scheme. Left to herself, she would probably have erected something between an exhibition of modern art and a home for juvenile delinquents; with Anne and Frau Mayer to watch her she agreed upon a respectable comfortable shelter, decently furnished and heated, with running water and adequate sanitation, in short, all that was wanted. She paid it visits at the beginning of the work, but left the supervision of her plans to Anne; Mr. Wake took the credit and was soon boasting that he had thought of it all himself long ago.

Frau Mayer was pleased, but not satisfied. She was slowly getting a hold over Judith which might have been sinister had she wished to use it for her own benefit; but the biggest hole she left in Judith's pocket was made disinterestedly. By indirections she worked up to it for some time. "You have been very good to *us*," she would remark, or "Hans and I have everything to thank you for," in a tone implying hosts of others for whom Judith had done nothing. One day she came out with it. Anne was at the Villa des Roses, and they had been talking about Hans's improvement.

"He will be ready to give a small concert in the summer," said his mother.

Judith was at once forward with schemes; she would arrange a party in Paris, and invite promoters, critics, musical acquaintances.

"I don't think we need trouble," said Frau Mayer. "He will, be recognized, he will make his name; you and I have both known that, since he was a boy. And as long as he needs me, I shall go with him. He is fortunate, Judith; he carries his livelihood in his fingers. So many people are not so lucky."

"Perhaps they don't have to work so hard," said Judith. "And perhaps, too, they are less sensitive."

"Oh, they are just as sensitive, I assure you."

"What sort of people?" Judith asked.

Frau Mayer stroked the white cat sitting in her lap, and looked at Judith beneath her eyebrows.

"We are not the only refugees," she replied. "There are thousands of them."

"I know, my dear, but . . ."

"If you choose," Frau Mayer interrupted, "you could help some of them."

"In what way?"

"For example—you have a large villa, of which one floor is uninhabited, even with Hans and me here; and you do not entertain. You also have two cottages empty. At least three families could be temporarily settled here, and I know of many more than three."

"In Germany?" Judith asked.

"No, in Paris, living in one room."

Judith was silent. Frau Mayer, stroking the white cat and watching her all the time, related the plight of these acquaintances. They were people she had known in Munich, poor people, she emphasized, and without influence or special gifts to recommend them; sooner or later they would make their way in a new country, but meanwhile they were living all on top of one another—"like the caddies," she added cleverly. The cottages in the grounds of the Villa des Roses had been built for a chauffeur and a gardener, but Judith had no car and the gardener lived at Oriol. The empty rooms in the villa itself could easily be converted into a self-contained flat; one would scarcely know that there were people living there. As Frau Mayer continued, both Anne and Judith recognized information they had given her in reply to questions she had asked casually in the past, and realized that she had asked them with an object. She had worked it all out; she even knew that there was a stove in the boxroom which could be brought out and repaired "if you choose, my dear Judith. I know it would be a bother, but it could be done."

"Very well," Judith said suddenly. "We'll do it. Why not?"

Frau Mayer turned her hands palms upward. "Why not?" she repeated.

"You'll have to work it out," said Judith. "Reckon up how much will have to be done, and what it will cost. It's your idea, and I give you responsibility for it."

"I accept it gladly."

Anne was alarmed at Judith's impulsiveness; it seemed that one had only to suggest a philanthropic venture for her to agree with it immediately.

Judith must have sensed this, for she said, after Frau Mayer had left the room, "You've been very quiet, Anne. I'm afraid you don't like Elizabeth. A lot of people have always disliked her and thought her bossy, but she has great strength of character. I wish that I had the same resolve."

"I haven't considered whether I like her or not," Anne replied. "She doesn't seem to me the kind of woman you like or dislike. You admire her or you don't. Personally I think she asks too much of you."

Judith looked thoughtful. "You must have people in your life who ask too much of you," she answered at length. "Otherwise you never do more than is convenient to you. This new plan will be extremely inconvenient." She laughed. "It will be hideously inconvenient. The place will be turned upside down. Yet I ought to do it. It stands to reason that I ought to do it. There are people without homes, and I can quite easily make room for them. Doesn't it stand to reason that I ought to do it?"

"Yes, it does," said Anne. "And I wish other people felt the same. If everybody saw their duty in that way, the world would be happier."

"Ah, but that's no excuse for me to avoid it."

"No, it isn't," Anne replied.

Afterwards she wondered if the characteristic in Judith which she took for impulsiveness was not simply clarity of mind. Judith had put it clearly; she had room, others had none, therefore she was bound to give up hers. And this led Anne to wonder further if generosity of spirit was no more than the drawing of obvious conclusions and the taking of action in accordance with them. She had never been in a position herself to be generous with money, but if people were in trouble she helped them. This had seemed obvious to her, and no particular virtue; it only appeared to be a virtue when contrasted with its absence in others. She did not know Judith well enough to detect that, in consenting so rapidly to Frau Mayer's proposal, she had really been arguing against herself. To have anyone else permanently billeted on her, and especially to have strangers, was one of the last things she wanted. She liked to withdraw into the seclusion of the top floor and to know that the emptiness of the floors below separated her from the rest of the world. Her sense of loneliness came from her physical ugliness and failure to attract, and would have remained with her in the midst of company. Had she married Sir Maurice Wildenstein, had she married anyone, she would still have insisted on opportunities for complete ramparted privacy, and her isolation in the Villa des Roses satisfied this craving to absurdity. Her unsilenced conscience told her that this was selfish; Frau Mayer knew that she knew it, and had picked upon it as her point of attack.

Judith was one of those honest thoughtful people of inherited wealth, whose honesty constrains them to spend a large part of their income on others, and whose intellect puts them in constant doubt whether they ought to have inherited an income at all. She foresaw that taxation would take more and more of it, and did not question this, considering it morally right and part of historical development. At present it was fairly intact, and she forestalled the rearrangements of society by distributing it herself in accordance with her own wishes. Hitherto she had chosen as her beneficiaries people whose tastes and talents coincided with hers; artists, writers, musicians, architects, who in her view had imaginative ideas and needed money to advance them. To give in these directions satisfied her own interests; it was generous, and agreeable.

Her generosity towards the persecuted Jews was different, like her generosity on other occasions towards the poor. She gave because she felt she must, but she was not deeply interested; only when friends of hers, artists like the Mayers, were in trouble, did she allow herself to become personally involved, and for the rest she merely signed a cheque or guaranteed a subscription. As one of a Jewish lineage that had become prosperous, she had for the resourceless, unknown Jews something of the embarrassed distaste which working-class families that have made money sometimes show towards those that have not, or those who have escaped from some awkward disability towards others who are still suffering from it. She was liberal by nature and in her mental attitude, and spoke of politics and international affairs in the language of socialism; but it was from the height and distance permitted her by her money. Those who disliked her did not fail to point out the discrepancy between the sympathies she proclaimed and the life she led; and though it was far less marked than is common among well-to-do "progressives," she was aware of it, and did not try to obscure it by talk, or to deny that it existed. She affected scorn for the rich folk who visited Oriol in the routine of selfish pleasure, and had not a good word for André Lemaitre, whose politics were of the extreme Right and whose factories were among the most iniquitously run in France; it shocked her now sincerely to have it brought home to her that she herself was a neglectful landlord, personally guilty of the evils which politically she condemned. The building of the new caddie-house, the limiting of the waiters' hours of work, and one or two other small interventions, gave her a chance to show that she at least tried to practise what she preached on her own estate. Nonetheless, though her indignation with these wrongs had been genuine, the attention she spared for their removal flagged.

The advent of refugees to her grounds, under her very roof, would force upon her a continued interest. Having decided upon it in a fit of morality, she now tried to see it cheerfully. It would be a kind of spite to the neighbouring villas; she relished the prospect, as each one would open to receive its annual freight of fashion, of the guests who would be descending upon the Villa des Roses. It would also give her something to do, and she lacked sustained occupation. A time had usually come with each of her cultural projects when she found she was no longer wanted. The theatre, the picture-gallery, the magazine she had helped to finance, were now carrying on admirably without her, and though their managers listened politely to her excellent suggestions, they contrived to give her the feeling that she had served her purpose. Besides, she had a doubt whether culture was enough, which became particularly strong whenever she met people who were only cultured; it might be enough for Hans, who had genius, but not for her.

Sometimes Judith reflected on the momentum of events which had brought her to this fresh stage of activity. All events could of course be traced back to the beginning of the world, and apart from this there was no such thing as a new beginning. Yet the day when Merrick and Sarah had alighted upon her seemed extremely like one. At that instant she had been on the edge of an abyss. Without knowing it, they had prevented her from falling over, and she had turned about and faced life instead. The same evening the letter from Frau Mayer had arrived, informing her that Hans's freedom could be bought, and the arrival in France of both of them had ensued. After that had come the goad and stimulus of Frau Mayer's company, and on top of it her own rewarding friendship with the children and the episodes of Emilio and the caddie-house. A few months ago the immediate future had seemed hideous; it was now the present, and it heartened her. The world's future was blacker than ever; her own, teeming with unknown happenings, seemed exciting, and she dated it from that summer's afternoon when she had seen Merrick's legs dangling through the skylight.

She now put forward a plan of her own which she had been thinking of for some time. Frau Mayer had refused to take more money as a gift, but had frequently said that she was willing to earn some. Judith suggested that she should give Sarah lessons.

"You know how to teach," she said, "and now that Hans is better you can easily spare a few hours a week."

It pleased her to have a proposal for Frau Mayer; so many had come from the other side.

"Willingly," Frau Mayer answered. "But what will the mother say?"

"She'll be delighted."

"She might think me a bad influence."

"Oh, what nonsense, Elizabeth! She's intelligent, and so is the girl. You can teach her history. She draws quite well. Teach her the history of art."

"Ask them, then," said Frau Mayer. "I'll start whenever they like."

She had already undertaken to organize the disposition of the refugees; it was a refreshing trait of this often forbidding woman that, however much work she had to do, she always seemed willing to do more.

12

Love, the awakening of the soul, desire, the awakening of the body, thought, the awakening of the mind: three windows waiting to be opened. In early childhood and in infancy some of the curtains round them are stirred, but not until later can they be flung wide. In many people one or all of them is never more than ajar throughout life. An excess of the first renders the character too ethereal; of the second, too gross; of the third, too frigid. Each of these three reveilles is usually sounded by some older person, either living, through direct influence, or dead, by way of books. The occasion is exhilarating, and is remembered for a long while, even if the encounter was brief.

Sarah remembered Frau Mayer as one of the first to have roused her mind. She had history lessons from her three times a week; they were supposed to last only an hour, but often, if Hans did not want his mother to accompany him, they went on a whole morning, and Sarah did not notice that the time had gone. Of course Frau Mayer had a system, a planned explanation of almost everything; but she warned Sarah in the first lesson that she taught in this way in order to fix an image in the pupil's mind, to simplify history and show it as a continuous story. She might be wrong; she wished Sarah to bear in mind that all the opinions she was now to hear might be wrong, so that when she grew older she might have the curiosity to find out for herself. Her chief aim, she declared, was that Sarah should not be bored, and she added that she would soon be able to tell.

She hung a map of Mercator's Projection on a wall, put her stubby finger on the Eastern Mediterranean, and announced that this was the cradle of civilization. "There we really began," she said, "and there, according to one legend, we shall end; Armageddon will be fought there." Sarah was not to trouble her head which particular emperor succeeded whom, or exactly when, or which precise areas had come under whose sway; it would be enough if she knew where Egypt and Greece lay, and kept a clear picture of the Eastern Mediterranean in general. Why had civilization started there? she asked. Because culture came from wealth, and wealth increased with commerce, and commerce flourished best where communications were easiest, and communications were easiest in the old days, before trains, where the people had navigable rivers and calm seas. In later lessons she explained how mariners, gradually gaining mastery over the great oceans, ventured farther, and how empires followed them away from the ancient treasuries; and she painted the great movements of gain and conquest, and the abandonment to desert of once-luxurious cities. "The sea," she repeated, "the sea meant wealth and power; that is why England has become so rich and so calm, by comparison with other nations, and why Germany is so explosive. Look ..." and she jabbed her finger in the map.

She described, with a generalizing sweep at which a meticulous scholar would have been horrified, the invasions and counter-invasions, the routes of armies, and the battles which she considered to have been historic. She represented them on the map by large red marks: Marathon and Thermopylae; Kossovo, Mohacs, Vienna; Blenheim, Malplaquet, Waterloo; Poltava, Smolensk, and the crossing of the Beresina; Ypres and Verdun. Why did the clashes have to happen there? she asked. Why do armies so often go the same way? Because they have to; the same way is the way that seems quickest and the hardest to defend, and the battles happen at the places which seem to the other side the easiest to defend. We shall see, she declared, if there is another war (to Judith she said "when," to Sarah "if"); the armies would advance and retire over the routes that they had taken for centuries, and they would be resisted at much the same points.

She pulled out Judith's albums of the great painters and set them alongside one another, and she asked Sarah what the difference was and invited her to guess which of them had come the earliest. She took photographs of styles of architecture and declared that there was a cycle which constantly repeated itself: first, a style of simple functional lines, economical as the human body, followed by the elaboration of ornament, and then by ornamentation for its own sake, after which there arose a new simplification. The height of ornamentation, she declared, was the beginning of decline, and precursors of the new austere style were usually contemporary with it; the phases of the cycle always overlapped, since there were always individuals thinking ahead of the fashion.

Although she repeated that no programme of general education had a right to the name unless it included the rudiments of chemistry and physics, she was glad to hear that Anne had read the children folk-legends and fairy-stories, for she said that the eternal conflicts of human nature and the ephemeral conflicts of nations and classes were distilled into them. She described, in simple words, the anthropological and social origins of the story of Cinderella, and she told Sarah that if anyone wanted to read the fate of Germany it was only necessary to glance at the myth of the Nibelungen; and together they glanced at it. Science, she said, should be approached as a legend, perhaps the most wonderful legend of all, since it was being enacted all round and every day; she detested the so-called classical spirit, which had put a kind of hoodoo on science, walled it off, and made the young who had no pronounced bent in that direction afraid of it. She never once mentioned the word Nazi, but she said that in Germany men had come to power who were terrified of science and played upon the people's fear of it; and she called anyone who shrank from science or was contemptuous of it a reactionary—the first time Sarah had heard the word.

She encouraged the fascinated girl to draw and study flowers, not only for their beauty, but for the understanding of change and growth they would give her. Sarah needed no encouragement to do this; and she learned from Frau Mayer that there was scarcely a flower in the field or garden that did not have some legend attached to it or, if it was of fairly modern growth, did not have some history. Frau Mayer pointed out flowers in the pictures of great masters and asked Sarah to identify them; and she claimed that all of them, and all the beasts and insects which crowded the paintings of Madonnas and Crucifixions and Adorations, had often been put there because they symbolized something and told some story. Frau Mayer's learning was a magic wand; under her spell flat canvases, maps, long-past events, printed words, came so to life that it was easy to imagine the brush held in the living hand, the armies marching and counter-marching, the pen dipped into the ink. Once she was discussing a picture of Albrecht Dürer; "And what is that little animal in the foreground?" she asked Sarah.

"It's a lizard, isn't it?"

"It's a kind of lizard. Its correct name is salamander."

"Oh yes," said Sarah, "I've heard of that."

"And do you know what it symbolizes?"

"No, Frau Mayer."

Frau Mayer glowered at her from under her heavy brows. "The salamander is the symbol of Death," she said; and at this moment a white cat leapt into her lap. Years afterwards Sarah would sometimes, for no reason at all, murmur to herself, "The salamander is the symbol of Death"; and though she later discovered that the salamander could live in fire and was rather the symbol of immortal life, she continued to believe Frau Mayer, and to see her thus, with Dürer's painting open on her knees and the white cat springing on to it.

She became so enthusiastic about these lessons that Anne began to come to them as well. Judith too was often there; now and then, after Sarah had gone home, she would disagree with something Frau Mayer had said, and Anne would sit listening to their argument. They would try to draw her in and appeal to her impartial judgment, but she preferred to listen, and felt ashamed of her ignorance. She had read a number of the English classics, and some of the French, and in her own childhood she had often sat beside her father while he sketched and talked to her about line and colour; but she had had so little time in recent years that she had forgotten nearly all her books except the favourites she read aloud to the children. It surprised her to find that Frau Mayer did not know Jane Austen; she lent her *Pride and Prejudice*, and Frau Mayer pronounced it a good delineation of a small corner of early nineteenth-century society. Anne asked her if the pomposities of Mr. Collins and Lady Catherine de Burgh had not made her laugh, and Frau Mayer replied that the satire was skilfully conveyed. Judith, who heard this, advised Anne afterwards not to expect a great sense of humour from Frau Mayer.

"It is not because she is German," she explained. "The Germans have quite a good sense of humour, when they are allowed to show it. It is because of what she has seen and been through that things which seem comic to you and me seem more serious to her. For example, we think a man like Mr. Wake a figure of fun, but I assure you that in Germany today a man of that kind might be a menace. In *Pride and Prejudice* Lady Catherine de Burgh is the type of haughty aristocrat, and now we laugh at her; Elizabeth probably thinks at once of the Prussian junker, who is far from being a laughing matter. A sense of humour is largely dependent upon one's distance from unpleasant events."

Sometimes Frau Mayer seemed deliberately to be provoking Anne. She would advance views on education which she thought Anne would not like, saying once that children who did not disagree with everything their parents told them were likely to grow up stunted. She tried to convince her that women had no freedom and were still members of a downtrodden sex, though she was herself a poor witness to this view. Anne took it all in, demurring and modifying, but never taking offence; between themselves the other two women attributed to her an attitude, which they called "typically English," of allowing some truth to almost every statement, but reckoning the degree according to the individual instance. Anne was interested in their theories, some of which she had heard before; when Merrick and Sarah had been very young she had read books about education, and Miss Wells, the free-thinker, had given her some good ideas. Anne expressed herself awkwardly, through lack of the habit; but to herself she thought, when Merrick put his arm in hers and paid her some gallant compliment, or when both of them sat by her in the evening and told her what they had done during the day, that she had all the rights she wanted and their upbringing was not misguided. And she could not help believing that Miss Wells and Judith would have talked to more purpose, though less eloquently, if they had had children of their own; as for Frau Mayer, she did not doubt that, whatever her theories, one of her first aims with Hans had been to keep his sympathy and impart her experience of life to him, and in this she had succeeded.

Anne welcomed Sarah's classes, knowing that it was time for something of the sort, and having been doubtful where to turn for it. Sarah spoke French fluently, and between Anne and the lessons the English residents arranged for the children in the town, she was at least as well educated as any girl of her age in England who went to school. Mr. Ridgway, the parson, had instructed her in the Bible, which she now read of her own choice; her gift for dramatizing everything that came her way, likely to be dangerous in some respects, had enabled her to enjoy it. She read it in the same manner that Frau Mayer taught history, as a story, and not from the disastrous sense of duty or compulsion that usually annihilates it for the young. Several of the characters were among her heroes, and if the pictures of them had been without such long beards they would certainly have been on her walls, together with Byron and Sir Walter Raleigh; she had had a particular liking for Peter and Thomas, with their obvious and understandable shortcomings. Mr. Ridgway had also prepared her for confirmation, and an itinerant Bishop had performed the deed; she had not known what it was all about, and Anne had been privately doubtful of its importance, but she had nonetheless gone through an intense religious phase, hiding crucifixes and holy pictures in the woods and resolving to be a nun. This had passed some time ago, and now history was the passion, and Anne was delighted that she had such a teacher. To draw was not a passion; it was in her blood to stay.

"I think Merrick ought to come to Frau Mayer," Sarah said, as the Easter holidays approached.

"Oh, you won't get him to do any more lessons," Anne replied. "He has enough of that at school."

"Don't you think he'd enjoy it?"

"He might. Tell him about them, and he can always go if he wants to. But I doubt it."

Sarah told him when he arrived, but Anne turned out to be right. He had no intention of going to classes during the holidays; after trying in vain to lure him on several evenings with vivid versions of the things Frau Mayer taught her, Sarah gave him up. He altered that year more markedly than at any time before. He bathed, played golf, beat them at Initials, and did the things he usually did, but Anne noticed that he was restless and

158

Sarah thought he was becoming conceited. He showed little interest in the story of Hans's recovery, and was disappointed when he heard Hans play. He went to the Villa des Roses on an unlucky evening, when Hans was practising rather than playing, and heard, instead of the melodies he had expected, a succession of disjointed repetitions. The music happened to be Bach, and Merrick thought it dull. He wondered at Hans's fingering, wishing he could do the same on the piano; but he said afterwards that he would wait till Hans gave a concert, and he did not like Frau Mayer. He had not cared for her bossy behaviour at the Christmas party, and suspected that she was getting too much control over Judith.

He did not himself know what was the matter with him, except that he felt ill at ease and wanted to get away. At times he would have liked to go off on a tramp-steamer, or on some journey of exploration; at other times he wished he had a friend of his own sex and age at Oriol, but when Anne suggested that he invite one, he could not think of anyone he wanted. Jerry was busy at the club, and Jerry was several years older. The horses were hired out every day; Mr. Masterton at the stables had none to spare for him. He rigged up a carpenter's bench in his shed in the garden, began to make a bookcase, and bought a book which told him how to make a boat; and he saved money to buy tools, putting it away in a drawer in his room. He spent much of his time wandering alone about the villas, full as usual for the season; he felt curious to know what the people were like who rented or owned them, and what sort of life they led.

Unlike Sarah, Merrick had few reveries to ease this inexplicable ache. He felt within himself no buried music or repressed yearnings. Sometimes he imagined himself skipper of a ship or winning the Grand National, and Anne and Sarah were included in these hopes. If he won the National, it was to be on a horse owned by Anne, who would lead him in, and all three of them would make a lot of money out of it; both of them were always aboard his imaginary boat. Merrick's ambitions were just possible, Sarah's never. She too dreamed of a boat, lovelier but less seaworthy than his, such as no known chandler would ever rig nor champagne launch; and though Anne and Merrick had their cabins, her captain was invariably some dark-haired lover.

His restlessness was noticeable but not obtrusive, except when he had an argument with Sarah. Life at the cottage continued like a small white cloud; the possibility of a storm existed, but none came yet, and on it went, now taking a joyous little leap, but mainly islanded, moving but scarcely seeming to move, in a blue sky. He returned at the end of July, and all was as it had been, except that the refugees had begun to arrive. He saw them on a walk the first day of the summer holidays, and decided that he would make their acquaintance; but something else happened which he found more interesting.

He was prowling home the same day when he came on a villa tucked away in the pines, which he had not noticed before. It was well off the main road and the trees had been cleared right back to make room for a garden, a large lawn, and a tennis-court. A circular hose was playing on the lawn. The name was written on a white board outside the drive: the Villa Harlequin. As he reconnoitred it, a girl came out on to the lawn. She had an independent air which attracted him, and he was just going down to talk to her when a woman, evidently a governess, called her in. She and the villa were the last thoughts in his mind that night, and the first when he awoke next morning; it would be something to do to get to know her, and he could visit the refugees afterwards.

13

Merrick decided he would stalk up to the white railings from the forest. If he still liked the girl's appearance, he might speak to her; if not, he would have a look at the refugees.

"Are you going to the beach?" he asked Sarah at breakfast.

"Are *you*?"

"I'm not sure."

"We could play tennis."

"I don't feel like tennis."

"Why not? It's going to be a lovely day."

"I just don't feel like it."

Sarah could be a great nuisance sometimes. She took it for granted that they would always do everything together for ever and ever, and when he determined to do something on his own she seemed to think she had the right to know what and why. He tried another tack.

"I think I'll go across and see Jerry. He might give me a lesson."

Sarah looked at him and said nothing, but felt rebuffed. Usually it was "come on," or "shall we go across to Jerry's?" or "we'll miss the tram, Sarah, if you don't hurry"; but now, and without looking her in the face, it was "I think I'll go."

Yet though she had not answered, and nothing prevented him from going, he could not bring himself to it for several minutes, and hovered about instead, picking up newspapers, staring out of the window, and strumming on the piano. They had frequently sulked, and had flaming arguments, and now and then a fight; all these had passed like summer storms. Quite often he had told lies to her and she, though less often, to him, and both of them to Anne; but this calculated deception in order to get away from them was something new. He felt shifty and unkind when he did leave, and resolved to do something to make up for it on his return.

"Where's Merrick?" Anne asked, coming in from the kitchen.

"I don't know. He just went out."

Sarah picked up a book of Michelangelo Judith had leant her, but Anne saw that she was not looking at it. The faintest of misgivings caught at her; and so, in the first five minutes, though the three of them had said so little, both Anne and Sarah had an inkling that some change approached.

Merrick went along the main road towards the Villa Harlequin. After all, he only wanted to know who lived there, and if Sarah had wanted to join him she had only to say so; or so he told himself, knowing that it was untrue. He even turned off the road into the forest, so that, if she had followed him, she would not guess where he was going. Why should they always be the same? He was a year older, and a time came to make new friends. He forgot her as he approached the red-roofed villa, and concentrated on not being seen.

It was a sunny morning; a fresh wind was blowing off the sea, stirring the flat tops of the pines, the sun had little strength in it, and the dew had not yet evaporated. Beaded cobwebs sparkled among the shrubs, and his shoes left their print on the glistening fairways. Nobody was about. There were no hoof-prints in the sandy rides; as he slipped between the trunks of the faintly creaking pines, it was as if no one had ever been there before him. A wraith of smoke loitered round the chimneys of the Villa Harlequin, and the green shutters had been thrown back from two windows on the top floor; but the lawn was empty, the hose was not playing, and the house looked as if it had been put under a spell. The long grass round the white railings was too wet to lie in; so he lay down on the pine-needles behind a tree and watched.

He soon heard a car started up on the far side of the house, which he could not see, and caught a glimpse of it driving out in the direction of the main road. Well, that was that; they must have gone into Oriol; he would have to come another time. Suddenly the shutters on the ground floor opened with a clatter, and then the french windows on to the terrace and the lawn, and the girl came running out. He eased himself forward behind the tree; he was a good fifty yards away, at the edge of the forest, and from years of conspiracies with Sarah he had plenty of practice in concealment.

The girl was talking to someone in the house. A man came to the french windows in shirt-sleeves and an apron, and reappeared with a deck-chair, which he placed for her on the lawn. They must be fairly rich, thought Merrick, for the servant wore a wasp-striped livery waistcoat, and from what he had seen, the car looked smart and new. He waited for the woman who had been there yesterday, but no one else came. The girl stretched out in the chair, facing the early sun that was rising behind the forest, and folded her arms behind her head. He did not dare to move, since she was looking straight towards him; the essence of his plan was that they should seem to meet by chance. He had been right about her being pretty. She had a smallish face, with very dark hair, which was not done up in any ridiculous bows or curls; he liked her all the more when she kicked off her shoes and he saw that she wore no stockings.

A black-and-white setter puppy dashed out of the house and jumped all over her. "Go away ... down ..." she called vainly, laughing. She began to play with it, sending it off on wild dashes by throwing a ball across the lawn, and catching it out by only pretending to throw. Merrick took a golf-ball from his pocket and flung it high in the air, so that it landed with a plop just beside them. The puppy seized it and began to chew it, while the girl stood stock still, gazing all round her. Merrick dusted his grey flannel suit and advanced. It was not as he had planned; he tried to be offhand, yet self-composed.

"Is it yours?" she asked.

"Yes, I hope you don't mind. I couldn't resist throwing it."

"You did give me a shock. What a thing to do! Here, Billy ... Billy.... Well, it's your fault if you don't get it back." She made a feeble effort to catch the puppy; but it ran round in circles, the ball between its teeth.

"If I could come in, I might get it," Merrick said.

"I bet you don't. Still, you can try."

It would be gallant to leap the railings, like Douglas Fairbanks in the Robin Hood film, but he might fall. He compromised and vaulted them, resting one hand on the top bar. After a tussle with the puppy, during which he was conscious of being observed, he wrenched the ball away.

"He has made a mess of it," said the girl. "Whatever made you do it?"

"Oh, I dunno."

They faced each other. She looked rather foreign. Her hair was black and drawn back from her forehead, and her eyes dark. She had an olive complexion. Her cheeks were round and soft, her lips curly, and she had a small round chin with a dimple.

"What's your name?" she asked.

"Merrick MacManus. What's yours?"

"Linda Selden. Merrick? That's a funny name."

"It's Irish. My father was Irish."

"How do you spell it?"

"M-E-R-R-I-C-K."

"It sounds more like a surname. I've never heard it before. We've got some friends who live in Ireland. Do you know them? They're called O'Hara. They've got a castle."

"I've never been to Ireland," Merrick answered. "We live here. I expect I'll go one day. I've never seen my father," he added grandly, anxious to bring out the exceptional. "He's alive, but he never comes to see us. He's in America somewhere."

"Why doesn't he ever come to see you?"

"Mother . . ." he corrected himself. "My mother and he are separated."

"So are mine. My mother's Lady Wildenstein now. She used to be Baroness de Leverson, and before that she was my mother. She's been married three times. My father's in America too."

She must have invented some of it, unless America was a place populated with separated fathers; the bringing-in of a castle and two titles sounded like showing-off. But she seemed to have said it all quite naturally, and if it was not true, then she was a better liar than Sarah; and the way she had kicked off her shoes, when she had not known he was watching, went in her favour.

"Can you throw that ball over the house?" she said.

"I should think so."

"Do it, then."

He thought this rather silly, but did it to please her. It went deep into the woods on the far side.

"I'll go and get it," he said.

"Oh, it doesn't matter. I can't even get it on to the roof. I broke a window yesterday. What are you doing here?"

"I just came for a walk."

"All alone?"

"I'm going to meet my sister."

"How old is your sister?"

"Fourteen and a half."

"Is she pretty?"

"She's going to be lovely. She's a bit awkward now."

"I've got a very good-looking cousin. He's half Russian. He's coming to stay with us in the summer. People don't often come this way," she went on suspiciously. "Mother chose here because it was off the main road. We've taken it until the autumn."

"The best places at Oriol are off the main road. People don't know what it's really like. Most people, I mean." There was something about this girl which made him assert himself as hitherto he had only done with grown-ups. "How old are you?" he asked.

"I was fifteen on February the seventeenth. How old are you?"

"Fifteen and a half."

This gave him an immense advantage. He had thought she must be older. "You should let me show it all to you," he began. It encouraged him to talk about Oriol.

"Come and sit down," she interrupted. Evidently she was very independent. They pulled two rubber mattresses on to the dewy lawn and sat there while he told her, and she listened, her bare legs tucked under her, now and then asking a question.

He told her about Jacques-plage, though not about the "castles," which seemed childish.

"It was named after my grandfather, you see," he said untruthfully. "He was the one who first found it, and then Mr. Friedmann came and put all the money into it."

"Who's Mr. Friedmann?"

"Oh, he's dead now, long ago. My mother knew him quite well. His daughter Judith lives over there in the Villa des Roses."

"My stepfather knows her."

"Everybody knows her by sight. She's rather odd to look at, and she doesn't mind about dressing well or things like that, but she's awfully kind when you get to know her. I'll introduce you to her if you like one day. She's got a chap staying with her who plays the violin wonderfully. I'm sure he'd let you come and listen. I'll ask if you like."

"I've been to a lot of concerts," she replied, not to be outdone.

"Sarah and me—that's my sister—often go to the opera here, but it's different when someone just plays for you and nobody else. When he gets worked up, he goes on for hours and hours . . . and," he added hastily, "if you get tired, you can go and he won't mind."

"It sounds lovely. Will you stay to lunch?" she asked.

"Well, I can't really." It was impressive, that she was in a position to issue such invitations. He began to think of excuses, but she seemed to have forgotten all about it.

"I've got a governess here," she said, "but she's rather dull, and she can't swim. I suppose you can swim?"

"Yes."

"Whereabouts is your hut?"

"We don't have a hut. We just go to one of the lonely parts and bathe there. It's much better."

"I'll come one day. When are you coming back?"

"Well, tomorrow, if you like."

"All right."

He looked back as he went towards the road, but she had begun to play with the dog again. He ran most of the way back, whistling and singing and jumping up at the pine branches. One of them, outside the Villa des Roses, was just out of reach. If I catch it, he said to himself, I shall marry Linda. He jumped and jumped, and at last he pulled it down. Sam Bryant came by.

"Hello, young fellow, what are you up to? Pulling the forest to pieces?"

"I'm just cheerful this morning. Aren't you?"

"I'm generally pretty cheerful. Whenever I'm at Oriol, anyhow. Why particularly now? Spring beginning, eh?"

166

"I expect that's it."

"You watch out. How's your mother?"

"She's all right, thanks, Major Bryant."

"Well, give her my love."

Merrick's vigorous manner reminded Sam Bryant of their father, and a host of recollections presented themselves: Johnny with Mrs. Hooper, Johnny riding in a race, Johnny with Anne, Johnny in a brothel in Paris, Johnny in the war, the *beau sabreur*. They had been friends in their early youth, but Sam had taken Anne's side, and there the friendship had ended. He blamed Johnny, but was in no position to moralize, never having married himself or remained long with any woman. Now he regretted his bachelordom; especially when he saw Merrick growing up and remembered that he himself was nearly forty-five.

Merrick meant to tell Sarah all about his new friend, but the cottage was in a state of crisis. Breakfast had not been cleared, nor the rooms done, and Sarah was standing about with a tragic look. She turned away and dabbed her eyes; he was afraid it had something to do with him, and felt angry. Anne entered and said:

"It's all right now. It's better to leave her."

"Is she in bed?" asked Sarah.

"She's resting. You two go off to the beach. I'll look after her."

"What's the matter?" asked Merrick.

"Blanche is not feeling very well."

"Is there anything I can do?"

"No thank you, darling. Just leave her, and be kind to her when she gets up. No teasing."

"I'll take something to the beach," said Sarah. "We can have lunch there." She was behaving in a manner that had come over her frequently of late, ignoring Merrick and talking to Anne as if something had happened which men could not understand. It was an impalpable exclusion; he could not put his consciousness of it into words, and resented it.

"Is another of her relations dead?" he asked.

"No, it's not that. She's just had a shock."

"What sort of a shock?"

But Sarah did not know herself. Blanche had suddenly burst into tears over the washing-up and gone rapidly into hysterics. Sarah too suspected that it must mean another death in her family, this time of someone closer than usual, perhaps her mother, or her brother in the Army; and she had been crying herself, in sympathy, and imagining catastrophes to Anne or Merrick. In fact Blanche had discovered an affair between Monsieur Philippe and a maid at the Pine Hotel.

On their way to the beach the children peered in at her window. She lay on her bed under a blue quilt, her face turned to the wall, her shoulders heaving so violently that she looked like a sack of potatoes with an electric current passing through them. They had never witnessed such a terrible abandonment to misery. Sarah's eyes filled again, and Merrick felt helpless. It made them forget the slight coldness between them, and on the beach he ventured to mention Linda, pretending that he had met her on a walk.

"She's rather nice," he said. "She asked me to lunch."

"Asked you to lunch?"

"Yes, she's more or less on her own. I don't think she does much. She'd never even heard of Jacques-plage. There's a governess or someone, but she doesn't pay any attention to her."

"What does she look like?"

"Oh, she's quite pretty. It's a lovely villa. Much more comfortable than the Villa des Roses."

"Did you see the villa?"

"Yes."

"You said you met her on a walk."

He went scarlet; he was not often caught out. "I did," he protested, "but we walked back to the villa. They've got a tennis-court and a car and a chauffeur. I should think she'd let us use them."

The word "us" mollified Sarah. "I told her all about you," he went on. "We might go round tomorrow, if we're not doing anything."

He mentioned her again at supper. Blanche had recovered sufficiently to leave her room, but not to appear at table. Sarah, furtively and without telling Merrick, had taken her a bunch of flowers and a note imploring her

not to be unhappy, and this had sent her into transports of renewed sobbing. Her tomato face looked quite thin, and her eyes were red with weeping. Merrick thought it a good moment to talk about something entirely
different.

"Do you know the people at the Villa Harlequin, Mother?"

"That's the one right in the forest, isn't it? Who's taken it this year?"

"It's some people called Wildenstein."

"Well, of course I know about them. You used to be in love with Lady
Wildenstein when you were about nine."

"I? I've never heard of her."

"She's had so many names I don't wonder you can't remember. She was
called Baroness de Leverson last year, and when you were in love with her
she was Mrs. Selden."

"Oh, that one."

He remembered now; for several weeks he had slept with her photograph under his pillow.

"Why do you ask?"

"I met a girl who lives there."

"She's probably the daughter of the first marriage."

"What are they like?"

"I don't know them at all well. Jerry used to give Lady Wildenstein lessons. Her picture's always in the papers. She's very smart. Why, you know
all about her. You used to think she was wonderful."

Preoccupied about Blanche, Anne did not read to the children that
evening, but spent a further hour attempting to console her. The girl's de-
voutness came to her assistance. Blanche had prayed for Monsieur Philippe and for herself, and her tears now were mainly tears of gratitude to
Anne for showing her affection. Anne felt sincerely sorry for her; though
she did not want to lose her as a cook, she would have given a great deal
for her to be happy, for Blanche was in danger of becoming one of those
women like Balzac's Eugenie Grandet, "created to be superb as both wife
and mother, yet with neither a husband nor children nor a family, and living in the midst of the world with no world of her own." Monsieur Philippe
had no obligations towards her. Her relationship to him was largely of her

169

own imagining, and he would certainly have been an unfaithful husband; yet Anne felt indignant with him, as she did with anyone who caused suffering.

In bed Merrick thought of Linda. She had asked him to lunch, as simply as that, on her own initiative. She had talked about grown-up people in a surprisingly grown-up way. She had asked him to show her Oriol and Jacques-plage; well, he would, and of course Sarah would come too. He saw Linda and Sarah as inseparable friends, linked by himself. Linda's small face and olive complexion shimmered before him, and he remembered the way she had sat with her legs curled beneath her on the lawn. She had assurance without priggishness and without trying to behave like a boy. There was nobody like Sarah; but she was younger than they were. He began to plan what he would show Linda and wondered if the things that interested him would interest her.

14

The encounter between Sarah and Linda took place next morning before Sarah's lesson, and was a success. Children judge on first impressions, and theirs were favourable. Merrick decided in advance that they were to be favourable, and his thoughts had already leapt on to what they would all do next; in particular how to combine showing Linda Oriol and Jacques-plage with the use of her mother's car.

They sat on the lawn of the Villa Harlequin, throwing twigs at the puppy. Sarah gave Linda clandestine looks from behind her hair, admiring her composure. The governess had gone out again.

"Can she take the car whenever she likes?" asked Merrick.

"If I don't want it."

Merrick and Sarah were silent, glimpsing vistas of opportunity.

"Do you play tennis?" asked Merrick.

"Sometimes. I'm supposed to be having lessons, but I'm not much good."

"We could bring our racquets next time."

"The court's terrible. It's all covered with weeds."

"Well, we'll pull up the weeds and roll it. You've got a roller." He had already taken a mental inventory.

"The gardener was going to do it," said Linda.

"You don't need a gardener. We can easily clear it ourselves."

They soon saw that she was helpless. Later, when they knew her better, it surprised them that anyone who had to do so little for herself should be so little spoilt. She was an only child. Everything had been arranged for her, brought to her. Her father lived in California, her mother all over the

171

place, taking villas at Oriol or the south of France, chalets in Switzerland, suites in London and Paris, floors of palaces in Italy. Linda had been attended by a succession of governesses, who used her mostly as an opportunity to have a good time. Their sojourn nearly always ended in a scandal; they stole, or took to drink, or wore her mother's clothes, or fell in love with one of the staff, and departed unwept to Germany, France, England, Scotland. And Linda remained, affected little by any of them, waiting for something new to be arranged.

"Miss Ogle was the nicest," she explained. "When we were in Italy, she used to go off and sun-bathe with nothing on, and there was a man who went past in a boat every day and looked at her with a telescope. We had a very nice butler then, and Mother found him in her room one night, so she sent him away."

"In your mother's room?" said Sarah, amazed.

"Good Heavens, no! What an idea! In Miss Ogle's room, of course. Mother thought Miss Ogle was bad for me, but she was awfully nice, and all the Italians used to smile at her and ask her to dance, and they talked to her very interestingly and said things in a whisper so that I couldn't understand. Wasn't it funny her being called Miss Ogle? This one's very fond of men too, but I don't like her. She's called Miss Patterson. She's in love with Redfern."

"Who's Redfern?" asked Merrick.

"He's our chauffeur. He's frightfully good-looking."

"Do you go to school?" asked Merrick.

"Oh, no. Mother's always talking about it, but I never go. In two years I shall be finished somewhere, and then I shall come out."

"What's finished?" asked Merrick. "You haven't started yet."

"And coming-out?" asked Sarah.

"Don't you know?" Linda looked shocked. "I thought everyone knew what coming-out was. It's when you wear long dresses, and have a dance, and then you can get married. You'll have to come out," she said to Sarah. "But as you're only fourteen, it won't be till at least a year after me."

"I don't want to. I hate dancing."

"You'll have to, all the same. And dancing is wonderful. I can do a waltz. Redfern dances a lot. He goes out every night with the car, though

172

he's not supposed to. He said he'd take me one night, but he hasn't yet. Can you dance?" she asked Merrick.

"Not much."

"You can, Merrick," said Sarah indignantly. "You're very good."

"Not really."

"I'll teach you," said Linda. "We've got a radiogram in the big room and we can roll the carpet up, and if Miss Patterson comes in and tries to stop us, I'll tell her what I saw Marshall do."

"What did he do?"

"He tried to kiss her in the garage, and she let him. He's always trying to kiss people."

At the idea of a dancing lesson she became excited, and when they had the carpet back and the gramophone was playing, she began to glide like thistledown over the polished cork floor, making Merrick restless to follow and Sarah feel like a lumber-jack. She knew all the latest steps and tunes. Merrick picked up the rhythms. She led; he followed, dancing away from her to watch her feet, and then together, improvising his own steps.

"You're going to be good," said Linda. "Only don't pump your arm like that, and be less jerky at the corners."

"Come on, Sarah," he said. "Your turn now."

"No, not now. I can't." She would have done it with him alone, or Linda alone, but not with an audience.

Linda put on a waltz.

"Come on, Merrick."

He could not reverse, and grew impatient with himself. She discarded him and danced alone, her eyes half-closed, humming and smiling to herself, like a feather wafted in the breeze, delighted to be watched.

"You do dance beautifully," said Merrick. Sarah shook her head enviously.

"What do you think of her?" asked Merrick on the way home.

"She's awfully nice. I didn't think I was going to like her before, but now I do."

"She likes you too."

"How do you know?"

"She told me so."

173

"When?"

"Don't you believe me? Why do you always have to know everything? She told me she wished she had hair like yours."

"I'd much rather be dark. She's awfully graceful. I wish I was as graceful as that. I know I shall never be able to dance."

"Don't be silly. We'll teach you. It's only practice."

The children began to show Linda round. They took her to the beach and out to the wreck. They showed her their sea-castle and their hide-out above the fifteenth hole, and they carved her name below theirs on the kiosk in the woods. They took her up the forest look-out, and up the terrifying spiral of the Oriol lighthouse, Merrick keeping on the outside to save her from looking down, and she even ventured out on to the platform at the top with the bearded keeper, who was supposed to be mad and muttered to himself, and felt the lighthouse swaying in the wind. She was green when she got to the bottom, but she did it. They introduced her to Madame Menard, and made Emilio imitate the nightingales for her. They sucked grenadines through straws in the club-house lounge and the bar of the Pine Hotel, sitting on high stools and chattering to Pierre in his white coat. They introduced her to Cacouette, who continued to leave his bicycle at the cottage and would not tell them why. They related the story of the lost golf-balls and the tee-boxes, with embroideries, and explained how good Jerry was and how dreadful Mr. Wake. Jerry was passing out of their orbit. Hans had dislodged him in Sarah's heart, and he had fallen in love himself with a girl in Oriol; but now and then he played golf with Merrick and the two girls walked round with them. They went for drives with Redfern, south towards the battle-fields, and along the coast, as far once as the forest of Crécy, and had picnics under the budding trees. Sometimes, instead of Miss Patterson, Anne accompanied them. She had the week-end free, and once she had made sure that it was quite in order to use Lady Wildenstein's car, and the children were not exploiting their new friend, she did not see why she should miss the chance; and all of them insisted she should come.

Anne loved France. Paris she scarcely knew, and did not want to know. She loved the ever-threatened, ever-reviving North, the immense stretches of ploughland and pasture-land with never a human being to be seen and the farms so scattered that she wondered how so much land could be so cultivated, and the cobbled streets and the churches with their thin steeples. She loved it indiscriminately, because she had been brought up there; whether it was the tall lines of poplars that flanked the national highways, or the advertisements for Byrrh and Cinzano and Dubonnet, or the *curé* bicycling past in his *soutane*, or the merry workmen in their berets and their blue overalls. A calendar in her office bore the motto: "Everyone has two countries: his own, and then France." If that had been written about any other country, it would have seemed presumptuous; sometimes she wondered if France were not her first country too.

It was a great treat for her to be taken on these excursions; she and the children had never gone so far on their bicycles. She liked to sit in the dicky, her hair blowing in the breeze, her cheeks red, one of the children with her, the others visible through the window. What a fool Johnny had been to forsake all this! If only he had stayed, his business would by now have thriven enough for them to buy their own car, and then, instead of the handsome Redfern, it would have been Johnny driving and Johnny unpacking the picnic basket, and they would all have been together. She said nothing to the children, not even when they happened one day to drive near the battle-field where he had been wounded; but there was always a certain look of Sarah's when she became obstinate, and of Merrick's when he laughed, to remind her, and, as they returned to Oriol, one or two places that were haunted with their early love.

Sometimes they went out across the estuary, where the tram made a sudden swing and dashed without warning to the opposite side of the road; and there would be the fishing-boats with their coloured sails furled, and the coppice of masts that her father had many times painted, and on the far side the cemetery where he was buried. Or they went the opposite way, towards the forest of St. Mathieu. The road rose slightly into a cleft between the high dunes, like a gateway with the gates torn off, the exit from Oriol, the entry into France. From the top of the dunes was an extensive view inland and towards the sea; on one side the ragged frieze of the dunes, with the sea beyond, a sparkle of blue and gold sloping up into the blue sky, on the other the hedgeless fields, the brown-tiled farm-houses, the willows, the poplars, the small streams, the one cow, the peasants, and

175

every summer's evening the caddies walking home. It was the end of Europe, the last battle-field before the sea, and made her think how fortunate the English were. It angered her to hear the things one or two of the visitors to Oriol said about the French. Mr. Wake, who had to do business with them, frequently complained that they never paid their taxes and nothing could be settled without bribery, and the Government was always resigning. No doubt it was true, and the peasants were close-fisted, and the middle class selfish and in many ways mean, but "we," she thought, were not perfect, not at all. And France was a woman's country; perhaps that was another reason she was prejudiced. She knew little about politics, and found it difficult to hate anyone, but she did not think she could ever, as a nation, endure the Germans.

When they came back from these drives, Linda usually had supper at the cottage, while Redfern made daring remarks to Blanche in pidgin French, not having been told about her experience of chauffeurs. The children discovered that Linda was almost completely ignorant. She knew no card games. They taught her Initials, but she could scarcely think of a single combination and had never heard of Sarah's quotations and characters from books. Sarah lent her the much-thumbed *Pride and Prejudice*, and *Jane Eyre* and *Wuthering Heights*, but she never got far with any of them. She had not even read the Bible. Her handwriting was appalling, devoid of punctuation, and full of elementary spelling mistakes, which Merrick pointed out to her with amazement; she seemed amazed at them herself, laughed cheerfully, and made them again. Miss Patterson paid scant attention to her, having a theory that children should not be forced to "do anything they did not want to do," which demanded the least possible effort from herself. Despite her travels and *savoir-faire*, the girl had been sadly neglected, and Anne felt sorry for her.

Something had been omitted. Lady Wildenstein, formerly Baroness de Leverson, did not seem to have been aware that most of a child's life is make-believe; if she was ever aware, she had been too busy to enter into it. She had never read to her, or told her legends, or sung her songs, or shared that luminous wood where fantasies flourish like wild orchids and the world is a voice or a stream or a green clearing. She had drawn no circle of enchantment round them, and Linda did not have to draw upon imagination, for she had the shallow realities of goodnight kisses from a mother nearly always in a ball-dress and diamonds, and of vigils over the banister to watch the dinner guests arrive, and of promises that one day all this would be hers. Anne knew, but Linda did not know, what she missed by possessing so much. She seemed already to have entered into "society," and to exist there like a waif, waiting to be a few years older. It is difficult to imagine a blonde waif; they present themselves to the mind as dark, and Linda was dark. She was more exquisite than lovely, with tiny bird-like hands and feet, and small sloping shoulders. She had a miniature, rather touching dignity. Having been taught deportment seriously, she held herself with poise; though she walked with a slightly undulant allure which she had copied from the films.

When the children first told Judith of this new friendship, her heart sank. She did not like Lady Wildenstein, for the obvious reason of her marriage, but also because she belonged to a part of the smart world which Judith detested. It reassured her to hear that Linda was alone at the Villa Harlequin, and she could understand that Merrick was attracted to her; but she hoped that the Villa des Roses, with its history and drawing lessons, with Hans and his music, yes and even with its shadows, would not lose its hold on Sarah, for it was Sarah she preferred.

She was oddly envious of Merrick. She supposed that he would grow up into one of those men to whom, by virtue of their good looks and easygoing manner, the world accords an easy journey. He possessed most of the charm that she herself lacked; consequently she tended to emphasize his intellectual weaknesses and to take the attitude that he was more superficial and less "interesting" than his sister. These criticisms were part of a revenge, in which she almost unconsciously engaged, upon all similar men whose indifference to her throughout life she had resented and at times suffered from. Although, with her complicated and tortured character, she secretly coveted the friendship of simple people, she compensated herself for her failure to obtain it by pretending that it was not worth having. When Anne had first told her that Merrick played the piano, she had reminded herself how the English hide their feelings and surmised that his cheerful extroversion hid the temperament of an artist. She did some conversational prospecting on him, but soon discovered that there was nothing there of the material she sought. He had no real gift for music. His playing was part of a natural facility he had for most things. He picked up a tune as he picked up a new game. He could scarcely read a note and had no intention of learning. So her interest in him had decreased.

She was too kind-hearted to let this appear, divining that if he had sensed dislike in her he would have been perplexed and hurt. Nor was there dislike. She detected a strain of intolerance and prejudice, planted possibly at school, in the way he sometimes spoke of foreigners and people who wore their hair long and dressed unconventionally, forgetting evidently that she, Hans, and Elizabeth Mayer, all belonged to these categories. She feared that he was insensitive. He had told her the story of poor Blanche; he seemed to think it funny, whereas she and Sarah thought it sad. She tried to correct this outlook. He listened solemnly, some of it sinking in, and then she warmed to him. His open face, his radiant health and attentive manners disarmed her, so that she could not wonder that Sarah worshipped him; and now evidently there was to be Linda too.

One day all of them went for a drive to the old walled town of Montreuil, about ten miles inland, but still called Montreuil-sur-mer. It had been Merrick's idea. He wanted Judith to get to know Linda, and Linda to get to know Judith and Hans, never doubting that they would immediately become the closest friends. He always assumed that people he liked would like one another, and was proud to show them off.

He sat in the front with Redfern and Linda, with Sarah in the dicky, and Anne and the others in Monsieur Philippe's taxi. They had to sit close, so that Redfern could reach the gears; even then his hand occasionally made a mistake and gripped Linda by the calf. Merrick hunched forward uncomfortably, his elbows pressed against his side.

"Why don't you put your arm round at the back?" said Linda. "You won't be so squashed."

"All right."

He rested it on the seat, just behind her neck, where it seemed to acquire a life of its own. It might almost have had eyes and a voice. It seemed to say. "I'm getting cramp. I should be more comfortable on her shoulder.

I'm sure it would be all right to let me lie on her shoulder, if you said I was getting cramp. Move me forward a little." He moved it forward.

"I'm getting cramp," he said.

Linda did not appear to notice anything. They admired the view, they talked about Judith and Hans, and all the time his hand, roused by the warmth of her shoulder, kept sending him interruptions. Several times he made up his mind, when there was a pause in the conversation, or when they stopped for petrol, or came to the next level crossing, to stroke her forearm; but each time his courage failed him. The wish survived all that afternoon. He lagged with her on the battlements of Montreuil, and at tea was inattentive to Frau Mayer's anecdotes from the history of France. He made sure that he was in the car with Linda on the way home.

This time he rested his arm on her shoulder immediately. The car bobbed over a cobbled square, down a steep hill, through a medieval gateway. One more street ahead, and then a turning into open country. Come what may, he would do it at this turning. His left leg trembled, and his stomach had the pain it had on the diving-board at school. Redfern changed down. Merrick lowered his hand over the short sleeve, until the fingers touched her arm. Again she did not appear to notice. He put a slight pressure on the arm and finally rested the hollow of his palm round it; and Linda, settling more comfortably into the crook of his elbow, put her other hand on his knee.

A ray of happiness shot through him. He pressed her arm fervently, and she responded with slightly more pressure on his knee. How lucky he was! Nothing he had wished for had come true so rapidly. The pain in his stomach vanished, his left leg ceased to tremble. The drive home was bliss. They talked again about the view, and Judith, and Frau Mayer, and the warmth of their two bodies seemed to be flowing into his thoughts and words. He glowed with affection for everyone; when they reached the links, and saw Mr. Wake fussing round the greens, Merrick waved his free hand and said to Linda: "He's a bit pompous, but he's not a bad old stick, really."

The cottage came in sight.

"Oh, I wish this drive could go on for ever," he exclaimed. "I wish we needn't stop till we felt like it."

He looked at her eagerly, like a cocker spaniel, demanding agreement.

"So do I," she answered, caressingly.

"Suits me," said Redfern. "I'll take you."

They stopped at the cottage gate and sat back, not wanting to get out, but the taxi drew up behind. When Merrick said good-bye to Linda, his eyes sparkled and his heart beat faster, as if she and he lived off a stronger battery than the others. The excitement continued indoors. He felt capable of anything. He laid the table before Anne and Sarah had taken off their coats, seized the potatoes from Blanche and peeled them in a minute or two, polished all their shoes, and cleared out a cupboard he had neglected for weeks. He went into his shed and put a plank in the vice, and suddenly he recalled what she was like. He thumped his fist on the bench. "I have someone," he said out loud. "I have someone."

He also had to tell someone. Anne was out of the question. Some parents boast that their children have always told them about their loves. These claims are not to be trusted. Few children can hide from their mothers for long that they are in love, but they do not "tell them all about it," knowing that the mother will wish to share it, and they do not want all of it shared. Only if there is a crisis does the truth come out in full; often then something is held back. But Merrick saw no harm in letting Sarah know a little. A secret was not worth having unless it was not a secret; one other person had to know. This secret made him feel bold and dashing, and that evening he told Sarah cheerfully, "I put my arm round Linda today."

There was a pause.

"Oh?" asked Sarah. "What did she do?"

"She didn't do anything. What do you expect her to do?"

"I wouldn't let anyone put their arm round me."

"I bet you would. Suppose it was Jerry? Or Hans?"

"They wouldn't be so familiar."

"They might be. Familiar? There's nothing wrong with it. It's just friendly. All the same, you'd better not tell Mother. She might imagine things."

"As if I would tell her!"

Sarah felt proud of him and pleased that he had let her into a secret. She bestowed a friendly thought on Linda, such as a queen, or even a queen-mother, might bestow on somebody honoured by the king. Linda had found favour in Merrick's eyes; she ought to think herself lucky. Sarah had a vision of them all, remaining exactly as they were now for the rest of their lives. Merrick would be in love with Linda, and marry her, but between herself and him there would always be something special which nobody else would ever have. There would be Judith too, and Hans, and Jerry, though he had been rather disloyal lately, and they would have the whole of Oriol and Jacques-plage to themselves, and nobody they disapproved of would be admitted.

It was a small and timorous vision, and in a few years she would have forgotten it; yet what often survives out of childhood, long after experience has tempered the joys, dispersed the fantasies, and rendered less final the despairs, and the home has been broken up and those who made it gone their ways, is this idea of a withdrawn world, carried about by the grown man or woman wherever they go, as the snail carries his house upon his back, but invisible and within. The people and the thoughts that populate it are admitted there not because they are useful or likely to assist success, but because they are loved. In these thoughts an infinite hope is deposited; in these people reposes an infinite trust. They are the individuals who desire your company, you believe, for its own sake and not for what they can make out of it; who will not willingly or wittingly deceive you, and will turn aside from the pursuit of their own interests to do some act on your behalf, as you will on theirs. If one day one of them tricks you, or abuses your confidence, the disillusionment is almost as acute and profound as the disillusionments of childhood, and no other is felt with more passionate intensity. Adults learn to make excuses and allowances which Merrick and Sarah did not make. Nonetheless, even to adults, the shock is often overwhelming, the wound at times impossible to heal; because it pierces a faith often unspoken, which by its nature is bound to be left without defences, and, if equipped with the elaborate ramparts of safeguards, provisos, and reservations which are customary in less intimate relationships, would cease to be itself.

Merrick and Sarah gave this trust without thought. The grown man desires to give it. Life becomes a mere battlefield without it. The grown man is reluctant entirely to abandon the ideas, the dreams which illumined childhood and which, if employed as a guide in after-life, would certainly lead to hardship and possibly to ruin. When first they came, they came spontaneously and were not arrived at by reasoning; dreams of success and triumph to be exercised unselfishly, thoughts of freedom and utter trustfulness, for which, as those who have imagined them grow up, the armies of the world lie in permanent ambush, demanding hostages or compelling separation.

Sometimes to all appearances they die. Sometimes they only wither, yet remain as a kind of irritation under the skin of the hardened heart, a diminutive soft spot. Sometimes they take complete possession, engendering the martyr, the recluse. But more often they are simply assisted to survive, reduced in scope and ambition, in a carefully kept reserve (as the children had their "castles"), where they shelter from the assaults flung against each new generation by the accumulated evil of history, guarded by those who recognized what would be lost if they were lost. They may continue to be present and active until death, together with the faces, or the memories of faces, which in this corner of the heart shared their exile from the remaining features of existence; and after death they survive in other people's recollection, like the wreath of flowers floating above a buried sailor, which remains fresh until the sea swarms over it.

These altruistic imaginings, this trustfulness, are as large a part of childhood as what is wilful and destructive. If the childhood is unhappy, they hide and yearn and feed upon themselves. If the childhood is happy, they are merged and interwoven with the outer world, the incompatibility of the two only becoming apparent afterwards; and very soon, for those who have to earn their living at an early age. Upon children such as these the world's attack is made not at the end of but during childhood, and abruptly; they are forced to learn what Thomas Traherne called its "dirty devices" immediately. Yet often the lack of distraction available to the rich helps to turn poor homes into a living place, pervaded with affection. The parents, knowing from their own experience what lies beyond, do all they can to give the children the assurance of somewhere kindly and apart, where laws of everlasting competition do not obtain; while children of more sheltered families may sometimes be brought up without warmth and give the impression of never having been children at all. Cacouette, the caddie, had never been a child. He had been at work since the age of eight. He had four brothers and five sisters. His father drank, his mother went out to work all day at the Etaples laundry. Their house consisted of three rooms. He did not ride home the bicycle which Judith gave him because he expected his parents to take it from him and sell it. Judith herself, in a wealthy family, had never been a child. Her mother had died early, her father had always been busy; her brain had developed too fast, and she had learned too many intellectual answers too soon. Linda had scarcely had a childhood, because her parents, who soon ceased to care for one another, had preferred to introduce her into their world as early as possible, and never entered hers. Merrick and Sarah were still children. They lacked the toughness of Cacouette, the avid studiousness of Judith, and the blithe sophistication of Linda at their age; but Sarah at least had more heart, and both of them were more impulsive.

15

Soon Merrick and Linda were seeing one another every day. He no longer stalked her at the Villa Harlequin; either he walked boldly in, or she came to the cottage on her own, where he waited for her, expecting her, yet excited when she came, and they would go off.

He grew impatient with Sarah, and plotted how to get rid of her, and she, in self-defence, grew haughty about her lessons. Whatever story it was Frau Mayer had been telling her, she would repeat it to Anne, pointedly leaving Merrick out. If he made a joke about it, she would lift her brown-gold eyebrows, or turn her back, and if she replied at all, give him to understand that these were things beyond his intelligence. And he, in turn ignoring her, would tell Anne that they could have Linda's car and suggest an expedition. "Sarah will be working, of course," he would say. Frau Mayer gave Sarah homework. She read or scribbled away, and if Merrick began to strum, then she would make a marked exit to her room.

"Sarah's turning into a bookworm," he said to Anne. "She'll probably end up wearing black stockings and spectacles."

"On the contrary, she's got a wonderful teacher. You ought to come and listen to her."

"That woman?"

"Don't you scoff at her. She's seen and read a great deal more than you."

"Oh, I dare say she has. She's older. I'm not saying she hasn't had a tough time. But has Sarah got to study the whole holidays?"

"Of course not, and she doesn't. Besides, you've got your own amusements."

He perched on the arm of her chair. "And you, Mother?" he asked, smiling at her. "You're a bit of a bookworm too, aren't you?"

"I like books. I thought you did."

"Oh, some. Mr. Masterton said the other day you used to be very good on a horse."

"I rode a lot once. All over Jacques-plage, before there was a single building."

"I should think you'd look good. He'd give you a horse any day, he said. Come out with me one morning. Why not?"

"Oh, I'm too old."

"You're only thirty-six. That's not old."

"And I've got no time now, what with you two."

"Oh, you have. Did you ride side-saddle?"

"No, astride."

"Yes, I can see you astride. I can't see you side-saddle. Not stately enough."

"I can be very stately when I choose," said Anne, laughing.

"I doubt it. I wish Sarah could ride," he went on. "It'd be good for her, and I think the Villa des Roses is a gloomy place to spend so much time at. The Villa Harlequin is much brighter. You can tell that the moment you go in."

The two houses were drawing the children apart. It seemed to Anne that they were the two influences, her own and her father's side, and Johnny's, pulling at them, trying to render them opposite and not complementary. There had been a debonair streak in Johnny she would have been glad for both of them to keep, but nothing more, nothing that could become dominant. Thinking of this separation, she kept the peace when they came home from their two haunts, praising Linda to Sarah and Judith and Frau Mayer to Merrick.

"Sarah's a nice kid," Merrick told Linda, "but she's a bit childish. She's crazy about history lessons now. It was the same when she was confirmed."

"What's confirmed?"

"Don't you know? I thought everyone had to be confirmed."

"I've never heard of it."

Perhaps Roman Catholics did not have to be confirmed, and Linda might be a Roman Catholic; there was something mysterious about the Roman Church which suited his idea of Linda.

"Are you an R.C. ?" he asked.

"Whatever's an R.C. ?"

"If you're not a Protestant, you're an R.C. ," he explained.

"I don't think I'm either. I think I'm Church of England," Linda said.

"That *is* Protestant. Then you'll have to be confirmed."

"Mother's never said anything about it. Perhaps it'll be when I come out. What happens?"

"Oh, it's nothing much. As a matter of fact, it's rather a lot of fuss about nothing. Sarah's made a business of it because she likes to attract attention. She wants to show off now about her lessons. Perhaps you won't have to be confirmed."

"If everyone is, then I ought to be," said Linda. "All kinds of things seem to happen to other people that never happen to me. I think Mother forgets," she added wistfully.

Merrick reassured her, although once again her ignorance surprised him; like Anne, he considered that she had been neglected and, interpreting this to suit himself, decided to provide her with male protection.

Sam Bryant chaffed him about her.

"I see you have a girl friend."

"Oh, Linda? Do you like her?"

"I don't know the young lady, and you don't leave the rest of us much chance. And I won't risk being your rival. But I admire your taste."

"She's awfully nice," Merrick replied, making it clear that looks weren't everything.

"I'm sure she is. She's also extremely pretty."

"Yes, she is, isn't she?"

He went red, but it made him feel grown up; and after all, it was true.

Anne smiled upon his courtship. It pleased her that a girl as pretty as Linda, who had met so many people, should be drawn to her son. She told herself that it was because he had a straight-forward character as well as good looks; but in her anxiety to prevent him becoming conceited she hid her gratification and paid more attention to Sarah. Perhaps Linda and

Merrick would tire of one another before Lady Wildenstein arrived; she did not like what she knew of Lady Wildenstein and shrank from the prospect of having to call on her, thank her for letting Redfern take them out in the car, and discuss Merrick with her. From pride she hoped that Merrick would discard Linda, but it might be better for him the other way round; it was time he had some setbacks.

She felt little jealousy or possessiveness. This was part of his development, another step, like going to school, across the frontiers of the cottage; she had brought up both the children with this inevitable voyage in mind, never vainly conspiring to keep them anchored at her side. It was expressive of her that though she had read them innumerable folk-stories and fairy stories, and though the dog-eared Green, Red, Yellow, and Blue Fairy Books remained on their shelves, from which she sometimes took them down herself, she had never read them *Peter Pan*. When she thought that the time for legends was temporarily past, she had gone straight to the Kipling of *Kim, The Jungle Books*, and the ballads, to the Brontës, Stevenson, Jane Austen. Stevenson was more for Merrick, the Brontës for Sarah, Kipling for both of them. Jane Austen had been a biased choice of her own. She relished every delicate note of irony, and responded warmly to the contempt for hypocrisy and pretentiousness beneath it; Miss Austen would have lingered long over Mr. Wake and the Duchess of Mendoza. She skipped a good deal; but each time it came to Mr. Collins, Sir Walter Elliott, and Lady Catherine de Burgh, not a word was lost, and her own reflections added acid to the acid already there.

She could never detach herself wholly from either child, even for a short time. All the same, they were interesting, they were a drama. Situation by situation, they unfolded, casting old skins, emerging in new; challenges were presented, fresh characters entered. All this Johnny had missed. And what she herself had missed by having no one, after they had gone to bed, with whom to laugh about them, to discuss them, to imagine what they might become! There was no man; only Blanche. Often Anne would sit for hours in the downstairs room recalling the children's words, looks, and gestures, until loneliness began to oppress her and she would go up to bed and read.

She took Merrick's devotion to Linda lightly, chaffing him like Sam

Bryant. Each morning she asked him what they were going to do. Sarah would be off to the Villa des Roses or to Mr. Ridgway.

"And I suppose we shan't see *you* all day," she would say, turning to Merrick. "You'll be at the Villa Harlequin."

"Yes, Mother, I shall be at the Villa Harlequin," he would reply in the same vein.

Then she would tell him to invite Linda to supper, or to join them on a picnic, arousing a glow of affection in him for her understanding and dissolving his faint, very faint sense of guilt.

"She's a wonderful woman," he told Linda. "She's just like us, really. You wouldn't think she was old at all, and that fool Wake would be absolutely stuck without her." It embarrassed him that she worked for her living; he hastened to explain it and make it sound romantic. "You see, after my father went away we didn't have any money, and so she decided she'd make some. She could have got married again any time, lots of people wanted to marry her, but she wanted to be on her own. As a matter of fact, I believe Mr. Friedmann wanted to marry her."

"Who's Mr. Friedmann?"

"I told you the other day. He's the one who started the whole place. I showed you the picture of him."

"Oh, yes."

"If she had married him, we'd all have been frightfully rich. I'm not so keen on being rich, though. I'd like you even if you weren't rich."

"Would you, Merrick?"

"Of course I would. Lots of rich people are just snobs. I like you because you're you. Same with Mother. She wouldn't care if you were rich or not. Her father was a painter," he added inconsequently.

"It's nice to be rich, all the same," said Linda. "Not that we're as rich as all that. We've only got two cars. Mr. Mazarian's got four."

"I'm glad you're not like him. A lot of people think he murdered his wife to marry the one he's with now."

He told her the legend of Mr. Mazarian's first wife, planted in his and Sarah's imagination at a more gullible age and never uprooted; she listened eagerly, storing it up to pass on to her mother.

She was the first girl he had thought of as an equal. (He did not "think of" Sarah at all; she was Sarah, she was there.) Having grown up with a sister a year younger than himself, he had become used to being the one who led and was looked up to. He admired achievement more than anything. He respected Jerry for his easy swing and Hans for his amazing fingers. If he had come across a girl who was a champion swimmer, or could beat him at tennis, or dare him over the jumps, he would at once have been interested in her; but the best had been no more than pretty. From an early age they had followed him in submissive groups, marshalled by Sarah acting as his self-appointed lieutenant; he had felt their dog-like gaze watching him behind his back, and gone miles to avoid them.

So Linda's attraction was surprising, because she had never "done" or was likely to "do" anything. He tried to interest her in his carpentry, and showed off the things he had made and was making, steadying her hand while she endeavoured to plane. She listened to his instructions attentively, as she did to anything new, but was no good at it and soon gave up. Her thoughts wandered. She liked going to the cinema; the evening performances were too late, and he disliked wasting the summer afternoons indoors, but usually she got round him without his knowing it had happened. She preferred love, he adventure and real events; their tastes joined at films which appeared to combine the two, and they saw *Mayerling* three times. At each visit Linda offered to pay for her seat, but this he could not allow. It gave him a thrill to walk up to Madame Jeanne at the Kursaal and say, "Two, please, in the balcony." He bought the most expensive seats, held open the swing doors so that Linda could go in first, and helped her off with her coat. It occurred to him that he might put his arm round her in the darkness, but it was difficult to invent a pretext and seemed unsuitable, and the film took his mind off it; however, her hand usually rested on the velvet arm between them, where his joined it. The projector at the Kursaal was always going wrong; the figures shot abruptly off the screen, or jammed half-way, accompanied by alarming crackling noises, whereupon Merrick and the other boys in the audience called out indignant comments. He did it to impress Linda; it flattered him to be able to explain what had happened and as they went out into the soft evening sunlight to have Madame Jeanne smile at him over her knitting and say, "*Au'voir, M'sieur, M'amselle.* Your enjoyed yourselves?"

"Yes, Madame Jeanne, we enjoyed ourselves very much."

"Then I give you the programme for the next week." And she would hold up the queue to do so. These little attentions raised him in Linda's esteem.

He had one anxiety. The money in his drawer dwindled. Seats at the Kursaal and tram fares mounted up. He bought Linda sweets from Madame Menard, and sometimes they took Paul's fiacre. Merrick had Mr. Micawber's attitude to money; something would turn up. He wished his birthday were not so far off; but in September would come the gymkhana, and if he won the under-sixteen competition he would be able to pawn the cup.

At night in his room he had the day to remember and the morrow to look forward to, and all his many reasons for liking her to review. He liked her because she did not easily get excited, except by things which he thought deserved it. She was never in the way. If she quickly forgot almost everything he taught her, if she continued to make her ludicrous spelling mistakes, and never learned to swim more than a few breast strokes, he did not mind, because she had never asked to be taught; he only felt puzzled and tender. "I'm awfully stupid," she once said, laughing, and was content to leave it at that; the struggles of Sarah and other girls to be practical and do the things boys did usually ended as a nuisance. Sometimes he almost forgot Linda was there, and this seemed to him a great merit, which no one else had had; even Sarah expected to be noticed.

Linda was fresh and bewitching, but not "childish"; she did not follow him about or gaze at him or grow speechless. She arrived at their meetings just late enough for him to become anxious, but not late enough to annoy him or make him think that "all women were the same." When she dissolved the deep turquoises of her eyes upon him, he fancied that they had something important behind them and had returned from contemplating things a long way away; which was roughly true, for they had usually been contemplating nothing. They were the first eyes whose colour he had noticed, except the lighter blue of his own.

He had never met anyone his age who had seen so much. She told him about her journeys over Europe, about her mother's parties, and the grand people who came to them, and the misdemeanours of her governesses, with a quiet knowledge of the world which impressed him and made him jealous and emulous. Suspecting that she had invented some of these stories, he met them with exaggerations of his own; but she backed them up with the evidence of photographs and signatures in books, and, besides, there was the sumptuous villa, the large staff, and the car. Linda had been brought up among men and women whose doings were in the papers; she had never known the awe which most children feel even at their names. She mentioned them casually, and Merrick, trying not to be impressed, would ask equally casually, "Is she a friend of yours? Do you know him?" There they all were in the photograph albums, not as Miss Ferguson photographed people, but intimately, informally, with Linda amongst them in different stages of growth. It laid his suspicions to rest; there could not even be a doubt that she had met the Duke of Windsor.

One day, on the beach at Jacques-plage, she announced that her mother would be arriving the same evening with several guests. His heart sank.

"You might have told me before," he reproached her stiffly.

"But I didn't know, Merrick. Miss Patterson only got a telegram this morning."

He became moody, wanting them to remain as they were, imagining behind her her mother, her mother's friends, all those "people," and behind himself no one except Anne. He dramatized his unimportance.

"I'm sorry," he said. "I suppose we shan't see so much of each other."

"Why ever not, Merrick? Of course we'll see just as much."

"No, you'll not be interested in me. You'll forget."

Flattered by the sullenness in his voice, she gave him her melting look.

"I shan't," she replied softly. "I never shall. I'll introduce you to my mother, and all of them, and you'll be able to come to the villa even more." As an afterthought: "And Sarah too."

"Oh, Sarah's too young."

He had spoken as he had, so that she could answer as she had; but his spirits were really low. An inferiority complex was developing. He doubted his own self-confidence; if Sarah were to come too, they would certainly be thought a nuisance. Linda divined his fears.

"Our friends aren't at all grand," she said. "They do the most extraordinary things, and you can be exactly as you like. When it's hot we have meals on the terrace, and no one wears anything except a bathing-suit."

"I don't want you to be different," he said in a strangled voice. He stared into the sand, and began to go red. "I like you more than I like Sarah, more than I like my mother too," he added almost desperately. "More than anyone I've ever met."

"Do you really, Merrick?"

"Yes."

It was said. He had put it into words. Relieved, he looked up to see its effect. Her tiny ears, the sloping shoulders, the dimpled chin, and graceful poise of her small dark head, made her an enchanting contrast to the bare white background of the dunes; she was like a little Arab princess.

"I like you too, Merrick," she said, turning her eyes on him. She had not committed herself far, but whenever she responded to him, even this much, he seemed to levitate. There was a long silence, during which he wrote a large M in the sand and interwove an L with it.

"There," he declared. "That's a cipher. That means we'll never be parted."

"I wish I could take it away."

"Do you? I'll buy you one one day. In diamonds."

"I'll buy you one."

But he did not want anything from her. She was a woman, and women should not give presents; it must all come from his side.

They bathed before going home, and wrote their full names in the sand at high-water mark, challenging the sea to efface them; and the sea effaced Merrick, but not Linda. They dressed behind two separate dunes; as he sat waiting for her he could not help feeling disconsolate, for it was the last time they would be on their own.

She emerged, with cheeks glowing and hair still hanging wet and limp.

"I can't get it drier. You do it, Merrick."

Kneeling behind her he rubbed it vigorously while she laughed and protested, and the waves of the ebb-tide, yapping like little glass dogs, receded from her name. The summer haze, like a swarm of mother-of-pearl midges, shimmered at either end of the deserted beach. Towards Berck-

192

plage a black speck, so indistinct that it might be either coming or going, was all that moved. It enlarged and became a fishing-woman, padding with bare feet and skirt hitched up by the water's edge; her wicker basket sat high on her back, and she carried a huge shrimping-net. She scarcely gave them a glance, but padded rapidly on till she was a speck again at Oriol.

They rose to go, their hands clasped.

"You can kiss me if you like," said Linda unexpectedly. She held up her face, with her eyes closed, and he kissed her on the cheek. She was afraid of being late for her mother, and they ran most of the way back.

In the cottage he thought hard about the kiss. The act had not been interesting, her cheek had been cold, and he was not agog to repeat it, but the offer had taken him aback; it was so unusual for Linda to show initiative about anything except a film. He felt abashed. Obviously he should have proposed it himself. She must think him terribly backward and cowardly. Perhaps she had been waiting for days for him to kiss her. People were always kissing each other in the films. He remembered that at these moments her hand would stir beneath his, and suddenly he was in a cold sweat. He had disappointed her, there was no doubt of it, and this evening her mother arrived, perhaps was already there; her mother with all those friends, young men sure to be among them. He was on the point of dashing round to the villa. No, it was too late; what on earth could he do to make up for it?

"Aren't you hungry?" Anne asked.

"No, Mother."

He had forgotten he was having tea.

"I've got to go into Oriol," he said abruptly, pushed his plate aside, and ran upstairs. Hurriedly, clumsily, he went through the notes in his drawer. Roughly fifteen hundred francs, over a thousand in hundred-franc notes, the rest in grubby tens and fives, some of them stuck together with adhesive tape, all he had saved, all he had in the world, all the finance for the shed. He swept it into his pocket, even the one or two franc coins and the centimes with holes in the middle, and dashed down the narrow stairs, colliding with Sarah and knocking all the books out of her hands.

"You are the limit, Merrick. One of them's the Bible too. Can't you look where you're going!" She was down on her knees, retrieving pressed flowers, treasured pictures of her heroes, postcards of the infant Jesus, drawings of Jerry and Hans and photographs of mannequins, and snatching at secret scraps of drawings.

"I'm sorry, I'm sorry. Here you are. Here's the Bible. It's not damaged, and if anyone goes to Hell it'll be me. Here's *David Copperfield*. Here's *The Prisoner of Zenda*. Here's . . . what's this?"

"You're not to look, Merrick. It's private." She went scarlet and seized it; it was a drawing of Hans.

"All right, all right. I don't want to see."

"And next time please look out," she said virtuously.

He ran through the forest along the tram-line and arrived breathless in the rue St. Jean. Which shops would be the best? None of them had their prices in the windows, that was so annoying of them; you had to go in, and once you were inside it seemed rude not to buy anything. He walked several times past the glittering row before he saw the one he was looking for. An elegant woman with a hat made of coloured feathers was inside. He waited for her to come out, restless, furious. At last she went. He slipped in, clutching the notes. A slender attendant in a grey dress came towards him, her hands clasped together as if she were praying. "*Monsieur désire?*"

He put on a firm voice, as if he made purchases there every day.

"I saw something in your window . . . I want to give a birthday present to someone."

He pointed it out. She drew in a tray of monograms and charms, such as women wear on their bracelets. It was important not to ask the price at once. He must pretend he didn't care about the price. What would it be? Two thousand five hundred, perhaps, at the most. He would ask them to keep one for him and borrow the other thousand. But it might only be two thousand, or even fifteen hundred. It was wonderful to finger them; to be behind the window, feeling the things. The charms were made of gold, with little jewels stuck into them. If only there were a cipher!

"Could you make a special one?" he asked, avoiding her eyes.

"Oh, yes, monsieur. What would monsieur like?"

"Well . . . how long would it take?"

194

"If monsieur would give the design, we could have it from Paris in a few weeks . . ."

"Oh, as long as that . . ."

"There's a lot of work in it, monsieur."

"Yes, they're lovely. . . ."

But it would be too long. He must give it at once. Linda must know that he had gone straight off to buy it, as he had promised. He had said in diamonds, but diamonds were sure to be too much, and it would be enough if she knew that it came from a good shop.

"What is it monsieur is looking for?" asked the grey spirit. Another had emanated from a door that he had taken for a mirror, and he thought they smiled.

"It's two initials," he said rather aggressively. "M and L together."

"Ah, together." What scent she had on; like hyacinths! "Here they are separate, monsieur. They could hang together . . . so," and she laid them against her own bracelet.

"Well . . . that might do . . ."

He fingered them avidly, burning to possess them and present them.

It could be delayed no longer. He crossed his ankles and without looking up asked: "How much would they be?"

"If monsieur takes both, it will be twelve thousand. If one alone, six thousand five hundred."

Twelve thousand francs! Twelve thousand for those two little things! He nearly dropped them.

A crimson flush spread from behind his ears. He felt the blood rising and saw it in several mirrors. He could almost hear the two spirits smiling.

"Thank you." His voice sounded a long way away. "I really wanted them together."

"We will send to Paris, if monsieur desires. It will be no more expensive."

"I wanted them now, really . . . thanks very much."

She lifted her shoulders ever so slightly and ever so slightly raised her eyebrows. He opened the door the wrong way and caught his coat in it. They must think him a perfect fool. Twelve thousand francs! And those fat sallow-faced men bought things like that like tram-tickets. He felt deeply mortified, hating to be smiled at and found unequal to an occasion. Now he had nothing for Linda at all. Flowers or sweets weren't enough, didn't last; besides, Madame Menard had gone. When he got home, he ran up to his room and wrote to her.

Darling Linda,

I felt awful because you had to go so early this afternoon. It was wonderful on the beach today, especially one thing, and I expect you know what that was. I thought of you all the time afterwards and I went to Oriol to buy you our initials as I said I would, but they didn't have anything I liked. I expect you are awfully pleased now that your mother is back. I am longing to meet her.

I meant what I said. I like you more than anyone I've ever met, more than my mother or Sarah. Anyhow Sarah's going through a silly phase.

For ever yours,
Merrick.

He slipped out after dark and dropped it in the letter-box of the Villa Harlequin. The light in her room was not on. He crept round to see if they were on the terrace, but the shutters were closed over the french windows. Chinks of light shone through from the long living-room. He heard laughter and then a voice singing softly, it seemed to a guitar; and he wished that he belonged there.

16

Next morning Merrick was working in the shed when the green Buick shot past, driven by a young man in a speckled shirt. There was another man in the front seat with him, and a pretty girl wedged between who waved. Merrick stared at them in surprise and waved back. They all waved and disappeared towards Oriol, laughing. Behind, more sedately, came Redfern at the wheel of a large white Packard.

"Whew! that's a car," Merrick said to himself.

Redfern, now correct and demure in livery, lifted a finger to his cockaded cap. Two smartly dressed woman sat in the back, talking to a man in a white suit; Merrick recognized Lady Wildenstein. They seemed to fit into the part of Oriol he knew least: the Oriol of fashion, Miss Ferguson, and the illustrated papers. Linda had evidently been left behind.

"Lady Wildenstein must have her house full," said Anne at dinner; the mid-day meal was always called dinner at the cottage.

"Why, Mother? Did you see them?"

"Did I see them? You could see them a mile off."

Lady Wildenstein's party had arrived in clothes clearly not intended for golf, causing looks of distaste among Sam Bryant, the young men from the City, and the regular players. Sam had been in Anne's office as they approached along the pergola walk.

"Good God!" he said, "who are these birds of Paradise?"

"They're the party from the Villa Harlequin."

"Oh, that crowd."

Their appearance aroused the same kind of resentment that the presence of a Christian might arouse in a mosque. Sam, like most of the old inhabitants, objected to the invasion of Oriol by people who in his opinion came only to be seen and photographed. If they had to come at all (and as they brought money with them he supposed they were necessary), he wished they would stick to the shops, the smart hotels and restaurants, and the Casino. They were much too exotic for the Pine Hotel and the golf-club.

"They drove past here this morning," said Merrick. "They've got a super car."

"What are you going to do about Linda now?" Anne asked.

"Well, she did ask me to go round this afternoon," he said awkwardly.

Anne hoped she was right in thinking that they were not the kind of people who appealed to him. An echo sounded from her days with Johnny. She knew little about them, except what she had heard and read; her prejudice came from their manners. Their clothes, though colourful, were extravagant, and one or two of the men had drawling voices and affectations which repelled her. At the golf-club they had obviously been aware of the hackles rising against them, and obviously enjoyed it; she supposed that they throve on shocking people.

Merrick put on a tie and walked round in the afternoon. It was unusual for him to feel nervous about meeting new people, but the knowledge that there would be a lot of them there and that Linda would want him to be at his best made this a special occasion. What topics should he talk about? He guessed that they would all be rather artistic, and art was one of his weakest points. He could tell them about his grandfather; perhaps they would like to see one of the paintings. He could play the piano. That was a good idea, as long as they did not give him a score or ask him for something he did not know. He wondered if Lady Wildenstein would like to hear that he had once slept with her photograph under his pillow. He must remember to stand up when one of the women spoke to him; this would not be difficult, for it came naturally to him. He felt his pocket; yes, the matches were there, to light their cigarettes. Perhaps he should have bought some cigarettes. He magnified his own importance, assuming that they would all have heard about him and have their eyes on him.

The Buick and the Packard were parked outside the front door, and Redfern was polishing the white bonnet.

"Well, what do you think of this job?" he said to Merrick.

"Pretty good. Twenty-eight h.p., isn't it?"

"Yes, it's their latest."

"I'd like to learn on that."

Redfern grinned. "You'll have to ask her ladyship." He looked at Merrick and winked. The past two weeks, the drives, the whispers he had heard in the front seat between Merrick and Linda, and the caresses reflected in the driving-mirror, had made Redfern a kind of accomplice. Merrick moved closer to him.

"What's she like?" he asked softly.

"Lady Wildenstein? She's not bad." He went on polishing for a minute and gave a quick glance behind him. "Keep on the right side of her," he murmured, "you'll be all right."

The villa had certainly come to life. The gardener was lugging trunks into the garage, a footman was clearing a laden table, a clatter came from the kitchen, and maids ran up and down stairs. The shutters had been thrown back, the windows opened. The gay colours in the living-room sprang out to the sun, the dull red carpet looked burnished. The girl and one of the men he had seen in the car were whispering together on a sofa, their heads together and their feet curled up. A man in leather shorts and Tyrolean braces was playing the piano and another strumming on a guitar. They paid no attention to Merrick.

He went on to the terrace. Lady Wildenstein was playing backgammon with a fat woman wearing a floppy straw hat. She smiled vaguely at Merrick. Some people were on the tennis-court, but not a sign of Linda. Lady Wildenstein shook the dice-box and said to him:

"Are you looking for someone?"

"Well, Linda asked me to come round."

"She'll be down in a minute." Her eyes darted back to the board. "Have you moved?" she said.

He stood there not knowing what to do and feeling intensely aggrieved. Evidently Linda had not even mentioned him. The men were all in open-necked shirts with short sleeves; his neat grey flannel suit, his tie, must make him look stiff and out of place. He took a dislike to them all; Lady Wildenstein might at least have welcomed him.

He stood by the board, pretending to be interested. The fat woman gave him the same vague smile.

"Sit down," said Lady Wildenstein. "Do you play?"

"No, I'm afraid I don't." He had a spasm of affronted pride. When the two women set the board for a fresh game without another word to him, he decided he would go home. He would be extremely polite, but he would go, and if Linda wanted him she could come to fetch him; that would show her.

Suddenly she ran out; she had put on over her dress an embroidered apron of the kind the Austrian peasants wear.

"So there you are, Merrick. I thought you were never coming."

He greeted her drily and she gave him a quick anxious glance, which flattered him.

"This is Merrick," she said proudly.

"I guessed that, darling," replied Lady Wildenstein without looking up.

Linda slipped her arm in his. "Do you like my present?" she asked.

He glanced at it with studied lack of interest and nearly said what he thought. It did not suit her. It might have suited a fair girl, but it did not suit her. Lady Wildenstein's eyes hovered over them, guessing at their relationship.

"It's very pretty," he answered.

"Only that? I put it on specially for you."

Her voice had a pathetic note of disappointment, relaxing his inner tension against her. Her hand pressed his arm.

"Come and watch them play tennis," she murmured, drawing him away.

Lady Wildenstein, entertained by this by-play, leant towards her partner. "I think the young man is sulking," she said in French.

Linda and Merrick sat on the lawn, but he was not going to start the conversation. He could not blame her for being upstairs when he arrived, but it had hurt his self-conceit to be ignored, especially when he had been set on making a good impression. The resentments piled on one another; he was wearing the wrong clothes, he was younger than the rest, he had looked foolish.

"You're angry, Merrick," she said. "Why are you angry?"

"I'm not angry. I didn't seem to be expected, that's all. I thought I might as well go home."

"Go home! Why ever should you go home? We've all been looking forward to seeing you. I told Mother all about you."

He took this to be a lie. Everything seemed to have changed, as he had thought it would and hoped it would not. There were strangers in the living-room, strangers on the terrace, strangers on the tennis-court. They had taken over the places which had been his and hers alone. Worst of all, they had taken her. In that silly apron, making those winning faces at him, she was no longer the girl whose name only yesterday he had mingled with his, to whom he had written the only letter he had ever written to any girl, whom he had thought about half the night. Her background had reclaimed her.

"What's the matter, Merrick?" she asked.

"Nothing's the matter," he said calmly, meeting her eyes and feeling dignified.

"Something is, all the same. It was sweet of you to write that letter. I loved getting it. I thought of you too after you had gone. I nearly wrote to you, but you know what I am."

He considered it an unfair ruse to play on this, for her spelling had become one of their most affectionate jokes, one of the passwords between them.

"Did you really go to Oriol to buy something?"

"Of course I did. I said I would."

"It was sweet of you. You oughtn't to have done it, all the same. Oh, Merrick, please don't be angry. Mother's awfully absent-minded sometimes, and I did tell her all about you. She said we could have the car whenever Redfern's free."

Her blue eyes swam. She was genuinely fond of him; as fond as she could be of anyone. It was true that she had told her mother about him, eagerly, lovingly, with some pride. He was her beau; she had found him by herself, he had come to her of his own accord, out of the forest, and they were in love, and she wanted all the rest to see it.

He pulled at the grass, beginning to ask himself if he were not the one who had behaved badly. He was quick-tempered, but not particularly vain. He wanted to be sure that during the past weeks she had not been attentive to him merely because there had been no one else. There had been a pact between them. Perhaps on her side it had only been a game; if that was so, he was ready to pretend it had been nothing more to him. But if she had already asked her mother about Redfern and the car, perhaps she wanted to go on as before.

He relented inwardly and began to loosen his tie.

"Who are all the friends?" he asked.

"Well, the lovely one on the sofa is Sandra Carlisle. And the man with her is Guy Ilfracombe. Don't you think he's awfully good-looking?"

"Everyone you know seems to be good-looking or lovely," said Merrick, mocking her. "Even Redfern. Don't you know anyone ugly?"

"There's Delia. She's the fat one playing backgammon with mother."

"She looks like a marshmallow," said Merrick.

Linda laughed. "Yes, she does rather. She's frightfully funny on the stage, though. Have you ever seen her?"

"No." He had never been inside a London theatre.

"We'll go to her next first night, Merrick. First nights are thrilling. I've only been to one, but there was such a crowd outside I was nearly squashed. And they all thought Mother was a film star. What do you think of her, Merrick?"

"Well, I've hardly seen her yet."

"Don't you think she's beautiful, though?" Linda asked in an eager little voice.

"Why, yes, I . . ."

Impatiently he broke off. This eternal indiscriminate praise for everyone and everybody connected with her had begun to vex him. She expected him to surrender his own judgment to a mutual admiration society, and his quills went out. He resolved, to assert his independence, that he would select at least one of her friends to dislike, and immediately picked on the man in leather shorts. It cost him no effort, for it was Mr. Aldrich—that was his name—whose voice had jarred on Sam Bryant and his mother, and no stranger ever took to him on first acquaintance. He strolled across the lawn, turning his head with swan-like languor; he was tall, but too thin and lacking in muscle for his fancy dress. The white stockings were wasted on calves and knees not meant for display, the short grey jacket with green facings belonged to the gamekeeper or the mountaineer, but not to him; and his body seemed to be slipping through the hitched-up shorts. He was affable to exaggeration.

"Darling Linda," he said, patting her hand. "In her little *dirndl*."

What a voice it was! One breath of it brought Merrick's embryo preju-dices to arms: the prejudice against the aesthete, the prejudice against the *poseur*, the prejudice against the effeminate, the prejudice against the un-accustomed. The battle-cry of a thousand steady virtues, and of as many persecutors, awoke in him at the sound of Edwin Aldrich's voice. It was almost unbearably drawn-out; the voice of somebody fatigued with ec-stasy, the voice of an ageing faun.

"How idyllic you look!" he uttered. "Like a little shepherdess. I must do a drawing of you."

Merrick felt acutely embarrassed by him, and wondered that Linda did not shrink away; but she sat there composed as ever, actually smiling at the compliments. Lady Wildenstein called Mr. Aldrich from the terrace, and he sauntered away. Merrick wanted to laugh; but perhaps Linda would be offended. Already he had begun to suppress his first impulses in order to please her; already curiosity about these unusual friends had begun to alter him. The plans he had made earlier to impress them were discarded. He was on unfamiliar ground; it would be wisest to say noth-ing and observe, difficult though this was for him.

The younger man he had noticed at the piano appeared in a pair of bathing-trunks and walked over to the horizontal rails between the lawn and the forest. Resting a hand on the top rail, he stood on one leg, ex-tending the other in a supple arc. He was deeply sunburnt and, though small, powerfully built, with the muscles of a young god.

"Is he a dancer?" Merrick asked.

"Don't you recognize him?" said Linda. "It's Paul Walker. He's quite famous."

Merrick remembered the young man's photograph in the papers. He ad-mired his athletic physique; he was doing exercises Merrick could not even have attempted.

Afterwards Paul came and sat beside them.

"I'm stiff," he complained. He lay on his back and did piston exercises with his legs.

"You don't look it," said Merrick.

"I'm as stiff as an old gentleman in a club. I've got hopelessly out of practice."

"I'd love to be a dancer!" Linda exclaimed.

"Well, why not? You're about the right height. So is he. Come on, I'll give you a lesson. Come on, Linda."

"Merrick too?"

"Of course. Both of you."

She jumped up laughing, and, kicking off her shoes, stood with him on the grass. He placed himself behind her with his hands on her slender waist. Obediently she following his instructions, pointing her feet in the first position, and rising on her toes; turning in an unsteady circle she ended facing him, one hand lightly at rest on his bare shoulder.

"Bravo!" cried Paul. "Now again."

She was naturally graceful, apart from the lessons in deportment, and seemed to know in advance what she should do. "Bravo, bravo!" Paul repeated with genuine delight. Lady Wildenstein clapped her hands, and Redfern in his shirt-sleeves looked out admiringly from a first-floor window. Merrick was struck by Paul's strength. For a sustained period he could take her whole weight on his extended forearm without a tremor. Resting her hands there as if on a parallel bar, she bent forward with her head up, her eyes shining with excitement and success. Slowly she raised one sun-burnt leg.

"Higher, higher!"

"I can't," she gasped.

"Higher, just a little higher. Don't bend it."

Her thin white dress slipped back above the knee and her body, slim and flexible, quivered with stress. Without being told, she bent back her foot and toes to complete the curve.

"Oof!" she gasped, coming back to earth.

"Now on my shoulder!" he cried.

"Oh, Paul, I can't do any more."

204

"But you must. You have to work if you want to be a dancer. I'll hold you. All you have to do is balance, and put your hands above your head ... like this."

He made an arch with his arms, wrists and fingers bent, and cocked his head a little on one side.

"Come on!"

He held her again at the waist and with a quick light movement lifted her to his shoulder. Flexing one bare foot on his chest, she extended the other leg, pointing the toes as if she had done it all her life. Her hand clutched his head. Waveringly one arm lifted, the other joined it, and there she poised for a dazzling instant, needing nothing but the gauze skirt and diamond coronet to be Swan Queen or Sleeping Princess. Everyone applauded.

"Bravo, bravo!" cried Edwin Aldrich. "Pavlova!"

Linda slid to the ground; Paul made her a ceremonious bow and led her forward to her mother. The slight undulation of her behind suddenly struck Merrick as incongruous and comical, and he wondered if he dared to tell her so. He overcame a twinge of jealousy for Paul and joined in the superlatives. She was wonderful, marvellous, she had just the face for a ballerina, just the figure, she was born to it. Lady Wildenstein squeezed her hand affectionately.

"Isn't she exquisite?" she said to Merrick. "Darling Linda. You never told me you could dance. You never tell me anything. Aren't children secretive?"

"I didn't know I could myself, Mother. It was Paul."

"You looked just like a star," said Merrick.

"Did I? I thought I was going to fall over backwards."

She looked up at him with a deprecating flutter of her eyelashes; her eyes sparkled, her cheeks glowed with the warmth of the exercise.

"Do you think she could really be a dancer?" Lady Wildenstein asked Paul, going back to the backgammon board. "Isn't she too old?"

"Not if she works. She's a little too thin at present, but she will be the right height and she has grace."

Edwin Aldrich wanted to send her to a ballet school at once. He imagined a triumphant future for her, picturing her first appearance at the

Opera House; they would all be there with bouquets. Linda and Merrick wandered off.

"You were awfully good," he told her. "Honestly, haven't you ever practised it before?"

"Never, honestly. It seemed quite easy. Oh, Merrick." She tucked her arm into his. "At last there's something I can *do*."

"You can do lots of things."

"Oh, I can't. Everyone can do things except me. I can't ride, and I can't swim, and I can't spell, and I can't play tennis. And now I can dance." She did a few steps on the lawn, attempted a pirouette, and fell into his lap. He caught her by the shoulders, holding her there.

"Merrick!" She struggled to get up. "You mustn't do that when Mother's here."

"When can I do it, then?" he asked, releasing her.

She sat at a distance from him, smoothing her dress, and replied in a voice full of propriety, "You mustn't do it at all."

"Why not?"

"Because you mustn't."

She had become prim and on her dignity; he saw that he was expected to look abashed, but something inside him chuckled. She looked so comical when she was being proper, and he did not believe she meant it; after all, she had been the one who had first suggested kissing.

Later in the afternoon Miss Ferguson arrived to take photographs. The public she served disapproved strongly of Lady Wildenstein and her coterie, but insisted on reading about them, and she knew they were good for a whole column. They had no false modesty, but they refused to appear in a conventional pose; it must be something original, something witty.

"A Victorian photograph!" cried Mr. Aldrich, clapping his hands. "In profile, all looking different ways. Paul, you must recline in front. And Helen," he marshalled Lady Wildenstein on to a chair, "you in the middle of course. Three-quarter face, darling."

He organized them, giving one a tennis racquet, another a golf club, suggesting that they should dress up and regretting they had no false whiskers. Miss Ferguson took the spirit of it. She enjoyed parties like this; they were so much more entertaining than her usual subjects.

"What about us?" said Linda.

"Little Linda! We've forgotten all about her."

The group was rearranged so that Merrick and Linda should recline on either side of Paul. Lady Wildenstein, assuming a gracious pose, sat behind them encircled by her guests.

"I feel like Queen Victoria and the Empire," she said, when the photographs had been taken.

"You should have been dressed up as Britannia," Mr. Aldrich exclaimed, "and we could all have worn turbans."

"I have a wonderful idea," said Lady Wildenstein. "We'll have a patriotic ball. Everybody must come as an Empire-builder."

Mr. Aldrich clapped his hands. "Darling, it would be heaven. We'll cover the house with flags and have a brass band. And a cotillon. We simply must have a cotillon."

They became animated, discussing the dresses they would wear. Mr. Aldrich was to be Cecil Rhodes "with a frock-coat and one of those little bowler hats." Miss Ferguson, foreseeing a page-full of photographs, led them on and made certain of being invited.

"And Linda must be the spirit of something," said Lady Wildenstein. "Linda and Merrick together as the spirit of the future, leading us all forward."

Everybody was delighted. Merrick heard Miss Ferguson say to Lady Wildenstein, "Who is the boy?" Evidently Lady Wildenstein had forgotten, for Miss Ferguson turned to him:

"How do you spell your name?"

He spelt it.

"I've seen you before, of course. Isn't your mother the one at the golf-club?"

"Yes," he said brusquely. He thought that everyone was looking at him, and went red. Miss Ferguson turned away without writing down his name.

"*Vous le connaissez?*" asked Lady Wildenstein.

Miss Ferguson lowered her voice. "*Je crois qu'il comprend,*" she said, and they walked off. Merrick knew they were talking about him. He thought Miss Ferguson was a detestable creature, even though she had once bought a photograph of his; really she only cared for people who had titles. The tone in which she had mentioned his mother's job had stung him. His mother could easily have married again, everyone knew that; it was better to do a job like hers, on which the whole club depended, than to sneak about prying into other people's affairs and cadging invitations. All the same, he longed to know what the two women were saying and what impression he had made on Lady Wildenstein.

The afternoon went fast and the shadows of the pines lengthened on the lawn. Trays of drinks were brought, people he recognized or had read about arrived in cars from Oriol and other villas. There was no one he knew well, and he felt much favoured when Lady Wildenstein took his arm and said, "Come and sit beside me. I want to hear all about you and Linda. She never stops talking about you."

"She's been awfully nice to me," said Merrick. "I hope you don't mind me coming here so often."

"Come whenever you like, my dear. Edwin's got a car, and I've got the big car, so you can have the Buick whenever Redfern's free. How old are you?"

"Nearly sixteen."

"Where are you at school?"

He named it. "You won't have heard of it," he said. "It's quite small. My mother thought I ought to go to school in England."

"And your mother works at the golf-club?"

"Yes."

"Of course, I've often seen her. And your father is dead?"

"No. He's in America."

"Is he working in America?"

"I don't know. I've never seen him."

"I understand, my dear," said Lady Wildenstein.

The footman came up to know how many there would be for dinner. "Edwin!" she called. "Have you asked anyone tonight?" No. They would only be eight. "Sir Maurice may have asked someone," she added, as if it did not matter, and Merrick wondered where Sir Maurice was. Lady Wildenstein leant back and made several remarks to different people, forgetting Merrick. After some minutes these conversations ran out and she became interested in him again.

"Now tell me how you met Linda," she said. He began to describe their first meeting, but she soon interrupted: "She's like a little Infanta, isn't she? Everybody says that I ought to have her painted." Her restless eyes wandered to her daughter. "You know," she said, with a searching look at Merrick, "if anything happened to her, I should kill myself."

"I'll look after her," Merrick said gallantly.

"I'm sure you will. What have you been doing together?"

"Well, we go to the beach, and once or twice we've played tennis, and we go for walks, and once or twice we went riding."

"I don't think Linda ought to ride."

"They always give her one of the quiet horses. And we don't stay out for long."

"All the same she's so fragile, Merrick, and she's all I have. You will take care of her, won't you?"

"Of course I will, Lady Wildenstein." He wanted to say something affectionate about Linda, but the words stuck in his mouth; besides, she had again forgotten the conversation and was calling out to Edwin to know where Lord Ilfracombe and Sandra Carlisle had gone. "Those two," she sighed. "They're crazy about one another."

"I think I ought to go, Lady Wildenstein."

"Very well, my dear. Come whenever you please. I like you." She smiled sweetly and began to talk to someone else.

Linda walked with him to the main road. "You did make a hit with Mother," she said. "I've never known her have such a long conversation with anyone."

"I like her," he replied. "She's natural." He waited for a car to pass. "Come here," he said.

"Why?" Linda looked proper again, and suspicious.

"I'll kiss *you* good-bye this time," he said, laughing at her.

"As long as it's only a kiss," she said.

He drew her into the bushes. Her cheek was warmer this time, and he kept his lips there longer. They parted with a lingering hand-clasp.

"And you're not angry?" she said, turning back.

"Why ever should I be?"

No, he was not angry, not at all, but he felt glad she had remembered that he had been. His heart danced. The afternoon which had begun so ill had ended in a parting even better than yesterday's. He had enjoyed it all, except for Miss Ferguson; and she did not matter, she was only a hanger-on.

When he got back to the cottage, Anne and Sarah had begun supper. Sarah said in a disapproving voice: "You're late."

"I know." He turned to Anne. "I'm awfully sorry, Mother. My watch was slow." He fetched his plate from the kitchen.

"Let's see your watch," said Sarah. He ignored her.

"Have you been at Linda's all this time?" Anne asked.

"Yes, it was rather fun."

"Who was there?" Sarah asked, and began at once to talk about Frau Mayer, pretending not to be inquisitive.

He went on with his meal, thinking what a silly little girl she was. Later he said to Anne:

"Do you know someone called Paul Walker, Mother?"

"I know of him. He's a dancer. Was he there?"

"Yes, he gave Linda a lesson. It's amazing the things he can do. Like a contortionist." Sarah pretended not to listen, but her knife and fork paused in mid-air; he continued, getting his own back: "He was going to give me a lesson, but Miss Ferguson came. He's rather decent. Not a bit conceited."

"Did Miss Ferguson take photographs?"

"Yes, I don't like her much. She's a snob. I like Lady Wildenstein. There were lots of people there. There was a Lord someone-or-other. Rather good-looking," he added casually.

Sarah's eyes were popping and she gave up her pretence of eating. She knew all these names from the illustrated papers. She had a photograph of Paul in her album; that was where Merrick had seen him. Incapable of acting, she surrendered to inquisitiveness. "Are they all staying with Linda's mother?" she asked.

"Yes, it's a house-party."

Anne gave him a quick look. The word jarred her, making him sound sophisticated. She went into the kitchen for the pudding, and when she came back Merrick was well launched into an account of the afternoon.

He became quite spirited in praise of Linda's friends, satisfying his unwillingness to yield wholly to their charm by poking fun at Mr. Aldrich. It was natural to him, whenever he made a new acquaintance or a fresh discovery, to want the others to share it. Usually his enthusiasm was infectious, but this evening Sarah's censoriousness annoyed him, leading him to show off in front of her and adopt a rather patronizing air, which repelled Anne as well.

"It all sounds very wonderful," she said without sympathy. He detected or imagined a note of irony, and guessed that she disapproved of the villa and its guests. She began to clear the table, and Sarah picked up a book. There was a hostile silence. His happy mood subsided. He was just going in to the kitchen to help Anne and explain again how much he had enjoyed himself and what good company they were, when Sarah put down her book and forestalled him. She passed him without a word, tacitly reproaching him for not having gone in first, almost with her nose in the air, and he experienced a strong dislike for her. He went to bed early, taking with him some of the old illustrated papers she collected. They contained photographs of Lady Wildenstein, and one of Lord Ilfracombe at the wheel of his Mercedes, and one, full-page, of Paul Walker dressed for a ballet in tight white hose and a velvet doublet. He wondered what they were all doing now. Probably sitting on the terrace in the moonlight; Lady Wildenstein would be playing backgammon with Delia, and Lord Ilfracombe and that dark girl would be whispering on the sofa, and someone would be playing the piano. They would all be in evening dress. And Linda? Now that these people had come, he could scarcely bear to be without her. She danced so well. He was certain that they had rolled back the carpet and were dancing. Perhaps Paul was giving her a ballet lesson. The vision of her returned, perched so lightly on Paul's shoulder, her foot pointed, her arms arched above her head, and the links that he and she had formed on the beach and during their drives with Redfern seemed vulnerable, tenuous, easy to break. He remembered how she had fallen into his lap and how he had held her by the shoulders; it had excited him in a strange way, and the excitement remained, so that for several minutes he read his sailing-book without grasping a word.

Anne sat downstairs mending Merrick's socks and Sarah was curled up on the window-seat. They picked up their books, but neither of them read; Merrick's departure had left an electric charge. Lifting her head, Sarah looked furtively at her mother.

"Do you like Lady Wildenstein?" she asked at last.

"I hardly know her, darling," Anne replied at once, as if she had had her answer ready. "I'm sure she's very hospitable."

"I think Merrick's in love with Linda."

"In love?" Anne smiled. "I don't think he's old enough yet to be in love." There was a pause.

"When are you old enough to be in love?" asked Sarah.

"It depends. Perhaps in a few years. Some people never fall in love. It depends who you meet and when you meet them."

"How do you know when you're in love?"

"You'll know, darling, when it happens to you. You won't need to ask me."

"I'll tell you, all the same."

"Will you, darling?"

After another pause: "In *Wuthering Heights*, Mother, was Heathcliff in love with Catherine Earnshaw?"

"Oh yes," Anne said emphatically. "He didn't know how to express himself, but sometimes those are the people who love most."

"I thought so."

Sarah moved back the curtain, and watched the darkness gathering over the level deserted golf-course and the rugged dunes; she imagined them to be the Yorkshire moors. Her life was still all dreams, thought Anne, and Merrick's was reality. A disquiet came upon her, as if the world had drawn up to their door to claim him.

And in the Villa Harlequin Lady Wildenstein was saying good-night to Linda. She wore a long dress, ready for the Casino, and Redfern was waiting at the door with the white Packard. Linda, in bed, gazed at her in envy.

"It's a new dress, Mother."

"Yes, do you like it?"

"It's lovely."

"I like your young man," said Lady Wildenstein.

"He's good-looking, isn't he?" said Linda anxiously.

212

"He's got a cheerful face. Where did you find him?"

Linda pretended to be indignant. "He found me, Mother. He's very good at games and things like that. He won a prize at the gymkhana."

"Did he?"

Lady Wildenstein's voice was inattentive. She put her still cold face to the mirror, frowning a little and touching her eyelashes. Linda wanted to go on talking about Merrick. She wanted to hear everything her mother had thought about him.

"I like that kind of face," she said. "And he's got curly hair. And very good teeth."

"Has he, darling?" her mother replied vaguely. "Yes, he's very healthy-looking; but you'll see hundreds more faces. Hundreds and hundreds more. These ear-rings are too short," she said irritably.

"I like them, Mother. You do look beautiful. Will you be back late?"

"Heaven knows. I expect so. Now don't excite yourself, darling."

It saddened Linda that her mother had so many things to do. She wanted to say how strange it was that Merrick's father too did not live with his mother, but she did not dare. She lay back in her large bed, watching the way the lights moved over the dress. The dangling ear-rings glittered as her mother bent above her.

"Good-night, little Linda," she said. "Don't dream too much." She kissed her good-night, but when she had gone downstairs Linda ran across the passage and watched them leave. They were standing under the electric lantern over the porch. Edwin wore a black cloak with a red silk lining; her mother had drawn on a pair of long white gloves and was fastening the clasps of her bracelets over them. Redfern held the door, and as they drove away Linda had a glimpse of the glove resting on the window-strap; it was crinkled at the wrist and the diamonds glittered on it.

How she longed to be like that! Instead of getting into bed, she sat down at the face mirror and made herself up with cosmetics stolen from her mother's dressing-table. Her appearance delighted and amazed her; the lipstick made her look twice as pretty. She turned in front of the cheval glass, looking over her shoulder and posing in her nightgown in the positions Paul had taught her. Perhaps she would really be a great dancer. She saw herself as Edwin had imagined her: the bouquets, the first night, the

213

people cheering. It was a new picture, but most of all she loved to imagine herself as a bride, sailing between crowded pews on the arm of her seldom-seen father. She took the mosquito net from the cupboard and draped it veil-like over her small head. The Wedding March, the only classical tune she remembered, rang in her ears. She lifted her face to an imaginary husband. "I will," she murmured. How wonderful it would be to marry! And what a pity Merrick was not famous!

17

Merrick would have been an unusual boy if the Villa Harlequin, even without Linda, had failed to beguile him. Life there was free and easy, and formal good manners were not expected of him. The guests had their meals at such irregular hours that food and drink were on the table from late in the morning until very late at night. Visitors continually came and went; occasionally they were invited, more often they invited themselves, or just arrived. Lady Wildenstein was glad to see them, the more the merrier, but hospitality did not burden her; she took it for granted that they knew how to entertain themselves, and left them to it. Though fashionable and unoriginal in her own clothes, she liked the guests to wear what they pleased, and their choice was usually eccentric. Sometimes, but rarely, when luminaries of orthodox society were expected, she would insist that Edwin Aldrich wear something other than cowboy trousers, or whatever his fancy dress was for the day, and that the others change out of bathing-suits and put on dresses and jackets; and then they would make it a stunt, a diversion, to be "respectable." Her house was open first to the brilliant and entertaining; then to the beautiful and good-looking; then to those who made up for dulness or ugliness by being famous or notorious. The mortal sin in her calendar was to be a bore.

She decided that she liked Merrick's appearance. His name attracted her. She thought Irish blood romantic, and encouraged him to make the most of it. Women love an Irishman, she told him in one of those intimate conversations which broke off so abruptly, and several times she smiled at him knowingly and said, for reasons obscure to him, "Ah, that's the Irish in you"; these allusions flattered and heightened his personality for him. She observed that he had ease of manner. He laughed infectiously, and though he had little to say, said it gaily and without earnestness; so she took him on, and for lack of heart opened her doors to him.

Besides, he was a male, and it never mattered how many of them there were; they were expendable. It was particularly convenient to have about the house a boy of Linda's age, evidently addicted to her and ready to look after her. Having satisfied herself that he was not sexually precocious or likely to fill Linda with unwholesome thoughts, Lady Wildenstein left them to their calf-love. She treated Linda as a feather in her own cap and pictured her as an enchantress of the future, with hearts dangling from her wrist in scores. Merrick readily accepted the position of favourite *en titre*. It gave him a kind of status in the house. He remembered that he had promised "to look after" Linda, and attended her with proprietary gallantry without turning into a slave. Under the impulse of the moment he moved from one advance to another without the least plan or conception where it might lead; and since Linda was willing to be "looked after," their amours progressed blithely from embrace to embrace until their achievement had reached the limit of his imagination. It was not at that time a long journey. He suspected very indistinctly, from Linda's primness at certain movements which he had not intended as advances, that she had an inkling of territories beyond, but her prohibitions did not put him in a fever. He still looked at statues and pictures of naked women without relating them to real life. At school he had been told the facts of life, but since they coincided with nothing he happened to be searching for, and meant little more to him than logarithms at the time he was still learning the multiplication table, he had soon forgotten about it. His curiosity about the human body, his own or anyone else's, was not yet at all lively. To kiss Linda, to hold her hand, to put his arm round her, to caress her arm, seemed a necessary and natural rounding-off of their friendship. Without it he would have been wretched. With it he thought himself completely happy. The strange sensation he had had when she fell into his lap was submerged in all kinds of different new experiences next day. There was too much going on for him to brood; only his assertion on the beach that he preferred her to his mother struck him profoundly and stayed long in his mind. He had meant it, but it seemed an extraordinary thing to have said; unable to think Linda could believe it, he repeated it several times.

Now that he had seen her world, he discerned how intimately she belonged to it. Its manners, inflections, the way it reacted to those alien to it, its occupations, the pleasures it looked forward to, had delicately printed themselves upon her as the dappled forest on the antelope. She knew of nothing different and wanted nothing different. Why should she? He could not be surprised that she had not taken to carpentry and swimming and the things he preferred, or to the books Sarah preferred, when her own life moved amid such luxury.

There was always something happening, there were constantly more people. It was not always an artist or a beauty or a Bohemian. It might be a man who knew about politics, for though Lady Wildenstein preferred scandal to all other talk, it brought her prestige to have authorities on the state of the world at her table; besides, the state of the world was exciting and everyone wanted to hear. If Edwin happened to be telling a witty story, or Paul was describing a new ballet, she would tap on the table and say with mock admonition: "Now stop, all of you, and listen! This is very important. So-and-so has just come back from Germany . . ." and So-and-So would take the floor. Her eyes flickered over her guests, making sure they were impressed. "Isn't it terrifying?" she would exclaim in a voice weary with outrage. "Can you imagine it?" The adjectives all changed from "marvellous," "heavenly," and "fascinating" to "terrifying," "frightful," and "unbelievable"; but soon the gaiety would return and Edwin resume his story. He had a gallery of acquaintances whom he caricatured with disarming ridicule. Lady Wildenstein would implore him to describe one of them; and after protestations that they had all heard it, and counter-protestations that they longed to hear it again, he would begin with an accentuated exaggerated indulgent "*Well* . . . ," and they all leant forward in their gay blouses and shirts, among liqueur glasses and flasks of Chianti. Often luncheon went on well into the afternoon, and Merrick would forget that he had planned to take Linda to the beach.

Edwin Aldrich's voice continued to upset him, but there was no denying that he was extremely entertaining.

"What do they all do?" Merrick once asked Linda.

247

"Do? Well, Guy lives in the country, and Anthony's in business in something, and, of course, Paul dances, and Edwin . . . well, he's just Edwin."

Edwin belonged to that small recurrent group who put style and manner before all else and are taken by some writers as typical of an entire age, as if no one else had lived in it. He had the air of an eighteenth-century French aristocrat, and could easily be imagined with powdered hair and quizzing-glass; but although he would have been at home at the court of Versailles or in England during the Regency, and had even revived expressions like La and Lud, he had had enough originality to adapt the elegance of former to modern times, mixing it with cosmopolitanism, informality, and a sharp sense of business. His father was a clergyman, and lived with his mother, whom he adored, remotely in Warwickshire; though not born into the world one of whose arbiters he had become, Edwin had learnt its foibles and was steadily exploiting them. He saw that it was unable, through its lack of force and huge panoply of comfort and tradition, to express itself in new ways, and constantly craved a mode, a fashion. These fashions he had set himself to create and by persistence and talent had succeeded, as Disraeli and Oscar Wilde in their particular ways conquered the society with which they had no ties by birth. He had not their genius, and it was perhaps typical of the time in general that one of its most vivid notes had to be struck by a man whose profession was the minor arts of interior decoration, theatrical scenery, and the entertainment of house-parties. He had launched into portraiture, and without much talent for it put well-known people into such arresting and blandishing backgrounds that it became almost a social necessity to be "done" by him; he had himself said jokingly that he would be commissioned to stage the Coronation. But unlike Brummel and Wilde, he had not got where he was by arrogance; wit, an amiable imagination, a touch of malice, and a succession of attitudes self-confidently assumed, had helped him on his way and he had integrated himself on disintegration.

He came past the cottage with Paul when Sarah and Anne were out and Merrick working in the shed. He stopped and exchanged a friendly word, and Merrick asked them in. Edwin wore his usual leather shorts, white stockings, a green Tyrolese hat, and sun-glasses; he carried a heavy stick with a polished handle.

"I didn't know you were a craftsman," he uttered.

"I'm not," said Merrick.

"Oh, but you are." He looked airily round. "Why don't you make furniture?" he asked. "People buy such frightful furniture."

"Well, I might try."

"Oh, do. There's quite a future in it, and really you see the most shaming things. Are you making this?" he asked, picking up the beginnings of a bookcase.

"Yes, it's not much, but . . ."

"But it's so good. You should give it a bit of a scroll. Something like this."

He sketched a quick design on the tracing paper, which Merrick thought well-drawn but too ornate. Edwin asked to be shown indoors.

"Oh, there's nothing really to see," said Merrick. "You can come in if you like."

"I can't resist other people's houses," he said, and they went in. He was extremely affable to Blanche and took in the upright piano, the open fireplace with the fender, and the faded chintzes, placing them in a category. "I like that," he observed waving the sun-glasses at the painting above the mantel.

"My grandfather painted it. It's the fishing-boats at Etaples."

"It's rather lovable. Something faintly Turner about it." He peered up the narrow staircase, but the cottage did not interest him enough to see more; he pronounced it "endearing" and "lived-in."

"How many of you are there?" he asked.

"Just my mother and sister and me. Oh, and Blanche, of course."

"It's so English, isn't it? And the garden." He surveyed it from the front door, like a nobleman surveying a vista. "I love the garden."

He went off with renewed encouragements to make furniture.

Merrick watched them curiously. Edwin was describing sweeps with his sun-glasses, analysing the Pine Hotel and pointing to the dunes, as if devising a landscape of his own. Merrick preferred Paul; but when he went back to the shed and looked at the sketch, he decided that there was something in it, and, modifying it to his more austere taste, began to work on it.

219

He informed Anne rather proudly of the visit. She did not share his pride.

"Oh, I know he's got that awful voice," said Merrick, "but he's frightfully amusing."

"Frightfully amusing?" She smiled at him. "You're beginning to talk like them."

Usually he took her raillery in the same spirit as she did his, but this time he became offended.

"Well, he *is* amusing," he said. "You ought to hear him."

"I can do without him," she replied.

Her relationship with Merrick became less easy, less spontaneous. He spent almost every weekday at the Villa Harlequin, and she grew tired of hearing about it. He pretended not to be impressed by a title, but if there had been a Lord there, it acquired a roll off his tongue. He called Lord Ilfracombe Guy, and repeated the Christian name unnecessarily often. He talked showily about the women's jewels and the big cars. He even brought back scraps of gossip and discussed well-known people in front of her in a familiar way that began to reek of condescension. He let her see that he got on with them, and thought she should be proud of him for having made his way into this privileged world; when she did not respond, he became resentful. At supper one evening he declared: "I think I ought to have a dinner-jacket, Mother."

"Well, you can't," she said firmly. "They're very expensive, and you'd have grown out of it in a year. Besides, what on earth do you need one for?"

"If I start going out at nights, I shall have to have one."

"Where are you going to go out at night?"

"Oh, I don't know." He fidgeted with the table-cloth and could not look her in the face. "People might ask me."

"You've got your blue suit. Nobody would expect you to have an evening suit at your age. Your grandfather never had one the whole of his life."

"I'm not my grandfather."

"Well, when you're older, we'll see."

He got up abruptly. "All right," he said. "If you want me to look a fool in front of everyone, I will," and walked out.

"Oh, don't be such a baby," she replied to the shut door.

Formerly these fits of his passed rapidly; this time he sulked for two days, and she made no effort to conciliate him.

"Sometimes he's exactly as his father used to be," she told Blanche. "He gets that same sullen look and thinks his stupid pride has been insulted. Women aren't half as vain as men."

Blanche shook her head. "He'll be a handful, that one."

"He's always been a handful. If only Sarah bothered half as much what people think of her! She won't even comb her hair."

"Ah, she is like Madame. She is kind and thoughtful. She thinks of others. But him . . ." Blanche sighed, but she still had a soft spot for Merrick.

He began to think his mother unreasonable. She did not prevent him from doing anything he wanted to do, she gave him no advice, and spoke not a word against his new acquaintances, but her attitude bespoke disapproval. It became almost disagreeable to come home, and after the Villa Harlequin the cottage seemed dull. There was nothing to do there. Nobody came to visit them except Hillier or Jerry or someone like that who had nothing to talk about. Judith had gone to Paris; besides, he knew that Judith did not like Lady Wildenstein, and put it down to jealousy. Hans was always practising, and he was not going to spend his time with Frau Mayer. He had lost interest in carpentry, and began to adapt himself to the Villa Harlequin. As long as Linda had been alone, his had been the stronger pull; now the magnet was reversed, and in the struggle of influences the life, the incipient character, the occupations he had been creating for himself succumbed. He did not set out consciously to succeed. Had chance endowed someone like Cacouette with good looks and by some impossible heave cast him upon the Villa Harlequin, he would no doubt have behaved craftily and with cunning, studying the foibles and weaknesses to turn to his advantage. Merrick was absorbed unconsciously and changed almost without knowing it. An air as if of a masque wafted perpetually round the villa, bringing to his ears the soft music of a modern Lotus-song. Everyone had some minor accomplishment, and this fête of life was of their own making. Several of them played the piano far better than he did. Delia sang songs from old musical comedies. Edwin Aldrich mimicked celebrities. Paul danced on the lawn with the forest for a back-cloth. Lord Ilfracombe took Sandra, Linda, and Merrick out on to the Paris road and drove his Mercedes at a hundred miles an hour. They did not pay dancers and musicians; they were the dancers and musicians themselves, and all they said was in jest, if at times too subtle for him. They appealed to Merrick's admiration for achievement of any kind as well as to his love of gaiety, and Lady Wildenstein, all of whose guests had to have a personality, continued to flatter him, telling him how Irish he was, how fond Linda was of him, making him somebody. It was only when he went home to the cottage that he felt a conflict and wished that he, or Anne, were somebody who mattered.

Sir Maurice and he took a liking to one another. Sir Maurice was sixty; far from decrepitude, but approaching premature decline. He was a great connoisseur of china and had an expert knowledge of medieval manuscripts; when he talked about them, his mind was agile and interesting, but his wife's friends seldom evoked his scholarship. It was his *roué* past they wanted to hear about. Edwin had characterized him in his verbal portrait-gallery as a courtly old beau, who in youth had quizzed ballerinas from stage-boxes, spent huge sums on jewels and bouquets, and until well past middle age was still to be imagined entertaining beautiful women at little tables in front of a log fire, waited on by a discreet manservant in white gloves. He was an eminent financier; Lady Wildenstein had married him for his money and his position. He had married her in the hope of ending life with a home instead of in one; he dreaded the fate that had befallen some men older than himself, whom he caught sight of now and again in London and Paris, ancient shadowy lechers haunting the apartments of expensive prostitutes. He kept a mistress somewhere, but Lady Wildenstein was not inquisitive. She made him seem older by never permitting him to speak of things to which he had given his intellect. She preferred him as an antique, egging him on to talk about the old days; and then, with slow elegant sentences and apologetic digressions forgiven for their faded charm, he would bring before them the Viennese court before 1914, and describe his visit "on a little mission" to St. Petersburg, and the week-end when he had accompanied King Edward VII round Paris. His stories were too long, his hearers never sure when the end had come, but he contrived to show up a quick nervousness and lack of finish about their own manners, and to accumulate behind himself the ghosts of generous

222

beauties who sinned not in the corners of flats, but in majesty in four-posters.

Sir Maurice had one peculiarity of speech; this was to use, with an interrogatory rise at the end of sentences, a word that sounded to Merrick like "nit."

"What does it mean?" he asked Linda.

"I don't know. He always says it."

They took to saying it themselves, "Good-night, nit," "Shall we go to the beach, nit," and had bets on the number of times he would bring it in in a quarter of an hour. Sometimes he would seem to have finished a sentence and suddenly flick it out . . . "nit," like a hiccup. They could hardly keep a straight face, and supposed it was a form of nerves. But nobody paid much attention to Sir Maurice apart from encouraging him to reminisce. He slept late or sat in the sun with a catalogue or collector's book. In the afternoons he usually went to the Casino and came back, winner or loser, with a present for Linda and his wife. He preferred Lady Wildenstein's political friends, and could be relied upon to occupy any diplomat for an hour. During these conversations he spoke French, with a German accent, or at least used the French terms. "What are they saying in the *coulisses*?" he would murmur, drawing the visitor aside. "Do you expect a *démenti*? I fancy I detect a slight *détente*." He never spoke of the French or German Governments, but always of the Quai d'Orsay and the Wilhelmstrasse, and it delighted him that many of the problems about which the world was preparing to go to war were almost exactly the same as those he had studied in his youth. If no diplomat happened to be present, and if the others were too busy for him or had gone on some expedition, he seemed quite happy with Merrick and Linda. "We were all more peaceable in my youth," he would sigh. "A boy like you doesn't know what peace means. In my youth nobody troubled about wars. Mind you, those of us who thought about it could see the signs. I was a Liberal. That's old-fashioned now, but at that time some of the clubs wouldn't have a Liberal at any price. What are the young thinking now? The students—what is the feeling?"

Merrick didn't know what he was talking about and politely said so.

"Are they for Chamberlain, or against?" asked Sir Maurice.

Merrick replied that if there was a war he would go into the Navy.

"It's all very sad," Sir Maurice sighed.

When Merrick thought it all right to change the subject, he asked, "Can anyone get into the Casino?"

"Ah, so that's what you're interested in, eh? Don't you do it, my boy."

"But what happens inside?"

"One does a lot of foolish things, believe me. One swears not to do them again, and one does them all the next evening. They say one leaves one's heart at the Casino. Do you know why?"

"No, Sir Maurice."

"You've read the Bible, nit?"

"Yes, Sir Maurice."

"And what does the Bible say? Where your treasure is, there will your heart be also."

He smiled, his eyes twinkling behind his pince-nez, and Merrick forced a laugh. Sir Maurice, who had made this joke before the First World War, at Karlsbad, watched closely to see that he had understood. Later Merrick, who despaired of getting a straight answer out of him, slowly corkscrewed a circuitous explanation of how to play baccarat. It sounded a ridiculous game, and he supposed Sir Maurice had given him an inadequate explanation of it. He longed to get inside the Casino and see the gaming-tables.

"It has a charm, it has a fatal charm," Sir Maurice told him vaguely, but he seemed unable to describe the rules. Merrick learnt backgammon, however, and lost half the money in his drawer to Lord Ilfracombe. Ilfracombe suggested that he should play another day for revenge. Merrick made an excuse, but he did not like to back out, imagining that Lord Ilfracombe thought him cowardly or, what then seemed almost worse, too poor.

He came home punctiliously for meals, but had little to say, his thoughts full of Linda and the Villa Harlequin. He no longer asked Anne each evening what had happened in the office or made jokes about Mr. Wake. He slept later and came to her room less often in the morning. She still read to them at night, but sensed that he was not listening. Sometimes Anne saw him by accident with his new friends, patrolling the rue St. Jean or dashing past in the green Buick. While he had been alone with Linda, she had not felt anxious, but these others were too old for him; too old, and much too smart. He seemed to be losing his good manners; his former politeness had changed to off-handedness, and he no longer paid her his joking compliments. She kept all this to herself, afraid of the outcome and pondering what it would be best to do.

One Sunday she saw him at the races. Blanche went out on Sundays, first to Mass and afterwards to visit one of her countless cousins. It had been their habit for years to have dinner at a small restaurant in Oriol where the shopkeepers went once a week with their families, tucking the napkins into their waist-coats and gazing reverently at the food. The Grand Prix d'Oriol was to be run that afternoon, and she assumed that Merrick would come with her. Before the meal he said awkwardly: "Do you mind if I go off early? I promised to take Linda to the races."

"Surely she can go there on her own? You can meet her there."

Anne felt angry with him; Sunday was also her free time, which she had always spent with the children.

"I said I'd take her," he answered stubbornly.

"Well, if you promised her, I suppose you must. But with all their cars ... besides, Mr. Masterton is coming. He'll be disappointed."

He did not answer, was silent during the meal, and hurried off before Mr. Masterton arrived. Sarah said nothing; she looked covertly at Anne, worried about Merrick's behaviour to her. Anne knew that Sarah was on her side, but it distressed and vexed her that there should be sides.

The race-course lay along the Oriol side of the estuary, and from the stands one could at moments watch three gears of speed simultaneously: the jockeys bent over the thudding horses, the fishing-vessels with their coloured sails moving out to sea, and beyond, passing the military cemetery with its giant stone angels and five thousand crosses, the Paris-Boulogne express.

Anne sat high up in the public stand among the townsfolk and went through the card with Mr. Masterton. He was an old flirt of hers: about fifty, a hard-bitten coper with a multiplicity of wrinkles.

"Why don't you ride again?" he asked, as he always did.

"Oh, I'm too old," she smiled.

"Too old! You? Nonsense. I'll give you a horse."

"Well, one day, perhaps. And with a leading-rein."

They went to the paddock before the second race and leant over the rail next to Hillier and his French wife. Anne saw Sam Bryant with a pair of glasses over his shoulder, escorting a new girl; and Jean de Moutiers was in the ring, wearing leather breeches and an English tweed coat with two slits in the back.

"Well, what do you fancy?" said Mr. Masterton.

"I like the look of Parsifal."

"She's the best of the bunch, and that's not saying much, but she won't win," said Mr. Masterton mysteriously. He bent over her card and whispered confidentially, "I should take this one." He put a mark against Phantom.

Parsifal led the whole way round, but in the last furlong fell back for no obvious reason, and amid groans and expostulations from the crowd allowed Phantom to romp home at fifteen to one.

"It looked put up to me," said Anne.

"It was," said Mr. Masterton.

A large crowd collected round the paddock before the big race, for which M. Mazarian's mare Venturous was favourite. Anne passed Sam Bryant.

"Hello," he said. "How are you making out?"

"Well, I won on the last race."

"You did? How the devil did you know?" He interrupted himself to stare at the entrance. "Here they all come," he exclaimed in an amused tone.

Lady Wildenstein's party were just arriving; it was impossible for them to arrive anywhere without attracting attention, and the crowd round the paddock turned to watch them.

"Merrick's got into an odd bunch," Sam remarked.

"He's got a passion for Linda," Anne said, wishing to dissociate him from the others. She avoided being seen by him, but when they were back in their places and Mr. Masterton had his eyes on the parade before the race she watched him. Lady Wildenstein had a box in the members' stand. She did not know a hoof from a fetlock, but whatever the spectacle was she always had the best position. She wore a light tweed suit made specially *pour le racing*. Edwin Aldrich had excited almost as much attention as the horses; he wore a pepper-and-salt check with drainpipe trousers and a light coat buttoned almost to the neck, a carnation in his buttonhole, and a grey bowler hat with a curling brim. A picture of studied elegance, he looked as he had intended to look, as if he were playing at being a racing man.

All along the front of the members' stand were the private boxes, bowered with hydrangeas, and as Anne surveyed their occupants—Lady Wildenstein, the Duchess of Mendoza, Madame Agyropoulos, Monsieur and Madame Mazarian, Mary Stiles in a nest of courtiers, Miss Ferguson bustling from one to the other—she thought to herself how fortunate they were and how little she envied them. Involuntarily she looked across the estuary at the great cemetery where her father was buried and, not far from him, Arthur Friedmann's son; and she wondered if her old friend would have been pleased today to see the result of his enterprise. It had triumphed, of course, it had paid itself back many times over, but she did not think he would have been among any of those gay parties; or if he had been, he would be sitting aloof from them all, and not listening to them. Judith was not there, though she owned a box. It occurred to Anne that Judith had a remoteness, a frustration, in common with her father, and had found no outlet for her energy; there was something lonely about both of them. And suddenly she saw him as he had been that first day, the blue smoke curling from his cigar, and heard his guttural voice proclaiming to her mother: "Here there shall be a view." How amazing it was that one man could have created all this from nothing; yet what was it worth now that it was done? He had foreseen it from the beginning, as he had foreseen so many things, including the failure of her marriage; yet she was convinced that he had gone away in order not to see it as it was now, at its gayest and most brilliant. She believed that she had understood him, although they had never talked intimately together. Had he remained, had he lived, he would often have visited her at the cottage, his gift to her. She wished that Merrick had known him; Arthur Friedmann would have given him good advice, and Merrick needed advice.

The horses had cantered past and gone down to the starting-gate. People had begun to stand up and focus their glasses. She noticed Madame Menard, dressed very prosperously, with her shy daughter, and Emilio in a straw hat, gesticulating; it always surprised her on occasions like this to see these old acquaintances out of their working clothes. Only Mr. Masterton stuck obstinately to his gaiters and squashed felt hat. And there was Sam Bryant down on the rails, his arm linked with his new girl; it was time, more than time, he married. There was a sudden buzz and a pressing forward all round her.

"They're off!" said Mr. Masterton, handing her his glasses.

M. Mazarian's horse was lying fifth the first time round, and she knew that it would win. She followed the race as it went out to the big loop alongside the estuary. A group of fishermen were watching from the embankment. The horses flashed past, thinning out. She admired the way M. Mazarian's jockey held Venturous in; at the turn down by the aerodrome he was lying sixth, but as they came into the straight he gave the horse its head. Fifth, fourth, third . . . and the two jockeys in front of him had their whips out.

"Well, that's that," said Mr. Masterton, and they sat down as Venturous tore past, the winner by several lengths. The crowd cheered. Edwin Aldrich waved his bowler hat, and Lady Wildenstein's guests made such an exhibition that Anne heard people commenting on them.

Merrick, his cheeks flushed, flung his arms round Linda and kissed her.

"Damn fools!" grunted Mr. Masterton. He did not appear to have recognized Merrick, and Anne hurried him off to collect their winnings, so that he should not. She thought she must be getting old and hypercritical, and that Merrick would imagine she wanted to crab his pleasures. He never bottled up his enthusiasms, and when he was with her she loved to see him merry and excited; but he should not get into the habit of behaving so conspicuously in public. What should she do, what should she say to him?

She felt more troubled that evening, waiting for him to come back. She had met him before the last race at the *pari-mutuel*, with a fistful of money he was putting on for Lady Wildenstein, and he had tried to avoid her. It had horrified her. There had been no mistake. He had not wanted to speak to her, and he had driven off in the big white car without a word to her. The light had faded, it was time for supper. Sarah was reading an illustrated paper in the window-seat; every time she heard a noise outside she looked up, but Merrick did not come in. Anne went into the kitchen and got out the plates. Suddenly Sarah rushed in and pushed the paper in front of her.

"Look, Mother, look! It's Merrick."

It was the photograph of Lady Wildenstein's house-party. There was Lady Wildenstein in the centre, with Edwin at her back in his Tyrolean costume, and others whose names she knew from the gossip columns posed in profile with tennis-racquets, and Paul reclining on the ground in front; and on either side of Paul were Linda and Merrick. The years rolled away. Her heart sank; and she put her hand to her eyes.

"It's quite a good one of him," she said, lighting the gas and trying to appear unconcerned.

"They haven't put his name, Mother. Look, he's just called 'a friend.'"

It was true. The others all had their full names and titles, but Miss Ferguson had not thought Merrick worth a name; he was "Linda Selden and a friend."

"He'll be awfully annoyed," said Sarah.

"Why should he be, darling? You don't want your name in the papers, do you?"

"No, but Merrick might. And it's awfully insulting just to be a friend."

Anne laughed. "I don't expect he'll mind," she said, knowing that he would. "Anyhow, don't you show it to him. If he sees it, let him see it for himself."

She had to discourage Sarah from girding at Merrick. Sarah had such passionate devotions, springing immediately and emotionally to the side of anyone she thought unjustly done by. She knew that Merrick was behaving badly and, watching her mother minutely, guessed that he had upset her. She bristled at the grand tone in which he spoke of the Villa Harlequin, and this supercilious caption in the newspaper would have given her a revenge upon his vanity. Anne made her promise to leave him to find it for himself, and to say nothing wounding when he had. She pretended to treat it as a joke, but the photograph had come to her like an icy wind. It was almost like going into a room long after someone had died and finding the corpse still there. She had never forgotten the photograph of Johnny with Mrs. Hooper; it was even the same paper that had published it.

Late in the evening Monsieur Philippe's taxi stopped at the gate. Sarah jumped up.

"Here he is," she said.

But it was Judith and Frau Mayer; they wanted Anne to come to the new film at the Casino theatre and have supper at the Villa des Roses afterwards. Philippe handed her a note.

"I was at the Villa Harlequin," he said. "Your son asked me to give you this."

Dearest Mother,

Lady Wildenstein asked me to stay to supper, so I said I would. I hope you don't mind and haven't been waiting for me, but I couldn't ask you because we'd all been to a party after the races and we've only just come back. I hope you won some money. I did quite well. Hope you don't mind me staying here.

Love from
Merrick.

"All right," Anne said to Judith. "I'd like to join you."

Sarah's supper was ready, and Blanche would be back before dark. She felt angered at Merrick's casualness, and though the film was a good one, her impatience and disquiet continued during it. Night had fallen when it finished, and as she and the others came out on to the lighted portico of the Casino she suddenly saw Merrick and Linda arguing with the commissionaire. They were cajoling him to let them inside, and he was smiling and shaking his head. Merrick tried to take his arm and tripped, and Linda laughed at him. His face was flushed. He tried to cover his embarrassment at seeing Anne with an exaggerated heartiness.

"Oh, hello, Mother!" he exclaimed. "Hello, Judith. Have you been to the film? This is Linda. Linda—my mother—Miss Friedmann. My mother —Miss Friedmann—Linda—oh, and Madame Mayer. We've been trying to get in. Linda wanted to see inside, but this chap says we're too young."

His voice was unsteady, causing Frau Mayer and Judith to look at Anne. He was not at all drunk, but it was obvious that he had had something to

230

drink. Cars were drawing up, and in front of all these people she did not want a scene.

"I think you'd better go home," she said coldly; and as M. Philippe arrived at that moment, she walked straight past Merrick and got into the taxi. She stared ahead of her as they drove away, but from the corner of her eye had a glimpse of Merrick swaying slightly and looking foolishly indignant. Neither of the other two women spoke; the accented silence compelled her to say something herself.

"That was a surprise," she said lightly.

Frau Mayer, who had been longing for a cue, said: "The young gentleman appears to be having a night out. Does he often do that?"

"He does very much as he pleases," Anne replied, "but I didn't expect to see him at the Casino."

"And who is the girl?"

Judith replied: "It's Lady Wildenstein's daughter." She explained Linda's background, with some remarks in German which Anne took to be unflattering to Lady Wildenstein.

"So," said Frau Mayer to Anne, "your son is in the smart world, then?"

Anne wondered if she said these things out of native tactlessness or deliberately to provoke. Frau Mayer was considerate enough not to mention that Merrick had been drinking, but Anne knew that both women had noticed it and would discuss it as soon as they were alone; they would certainly say to one another, with a touch of satisfied jealousy, that the upbringing she had given her children was not perhaps turning out as well as she had hoped. At supper they talked of the film, and she tried to appear unconcerned. Frau Mayer had not forgotten, since at one moment, for no other reason, she remarked that it would be a good thing if Casinos were to be forbidden by law; and when Anne left to walk home, said: "I hope your errant child will have returned."

"I hope so too," said Anne.

The moment she turned the key of the cottage, Sarah was at the door.

"Merrick hasn't come home," she said dramatically.

Anne knew now that she was really anxious.

"Hasn't he, darling?" she answered. "I think there's some kind of a party at Lady Wildenstein's. I expect he's enjoying himself."

"It's past eleven," said Sarah, disappointed with Anne's nonchalance. "He's never been out as late as this."

"And what are you doing, my darling? Why aren't you in bed?"

"Oh, I was only reading."

"You go to bed. You'll tire your eyes."

"Aren't you coming?"

"Soon. I've just got some letters to write."

After she had kissed Sarah good-night, Anne took a book and waited. She tried to read, but could not. Midnight struck from the clock on the mantelpiece. Again time rolled back and her memories stepped out of the mirror into life. She sat exactly as she had sat years ago waiting for Johnny. Had it not been for that, she would have been less worried. Someone had probably given Merrick a drink or two as a joke, and it would naturally have gone to his head; there was no reason why he and Linda should not have gone to Oriol, though he could have told her first. But where was he now, and why did he not come back? She walked to and fro, arms crossed. Several times she drew the curtains aside and looked out; cars went past to the hotel, but none stopped.

She had done it all before, in the same room, at the same hours of the night. When two o'clock struck, she could stand the anxiety no longer. She walked to the hotel and asked the night porter to get her the Villa Harlequin on the telephone. Lady Wildenstein answered almost at once, in a bland surprised voice, and Anne guessed that she had just come in from the Casino.

"It's Mrs. MacManus speaking," Anne said. "Merrick's mother. I'm so sorry to worry you at this time of night, but I've lost my son." She tried to make her voice light-hearted. "He hasn't come home, and I wondered if perhaps you know where he is."

"I do indeed," came the bland voice. "I've just seen him this very moment. He's asleep on my terrace."

Anne felt relief first, astonishment afterwards.

"On your terrace? What has he been up to?"

"He looks quite comfortable. He's got a sleeping-bag." Lady Wildenstein did not add that Linda had another one next to him. "Do you want me to send him back?" she asked.

232

"Well, if he's asleep . . ."

"Oh, he's asleep all right. Breathing very heavily. If you don't want him now, I'll send him round in the morning."

"It's very kind of you," Anne said coldly. "I'm sorry to have given you this trouble, but I was anxious."

"Oh, it's rather amusing. I wish you could see him. And we all like him here so much. Good-night."

"Good-night."

Anne did not think it amusing. Angry and disturbed about Merrick, indignant with Lady Wildenstein, she slept badly. Still, there was nothing the matter with him, there had been no accident.

18

The sun woke Merrick at half-past six. Linda was curled in her sleeping-bag like a papoose; her dark head looked charming and one arm rested beneath her chin; but the sight did nothing to cure Merrick's headache. His temples were throbbing, his head seemed to weigh a ton, and his tongue felt like a stocking. He looked at his watch. Anne might not know that he had been out all night, and at the cottage were aspirin and a comfortable bed. He wrote a note for Linda, folded it, and put it beside her with a stone on top.

Darling Linda,

I think I'd better go home in case my mother gets anxious. It was wonderful sleeping out, and you did look beautiful this morning. I wish I could have stayed, but I ought to go and I'll come round later. One day we really will get into the Casino, but even though we didn't it was a marvellous evening and I shall never forget it.

Love from
Merrick.

He made the ending staid in case someone else opened the note before she awoke; nor did he feel in the mood for tender eloquence.

It was a perfect morning for an early walk, but he did not enjoy it. He had never had such a dreadful headache, and as he sluggishly remembered yesterday evening he began to feel angry with Anne. She had made him look ridiculous in front of Linda and Judith and that conceited Frau Mayer; Monsieur Philippe too had seen him, and might tell Blanche, and if Blanche heard she would tell Sarah, and Sarah would put on her goody-

goody manner. They would all say he had been drunk. This he did not mind; it made him feel dashing. He had been a little drunk. At supper Edwin Aldrich had kept on filling his glass with wine, and he had swallowed it like orangeade. Linda had had a little too; afterwards, when the others had gone to the Casino, they had been left alone with a feeling that they must do something. It was Linda who had suggested that they should go to Oriol and see what it was like at night, and Redfern, who was to meet a girl at one of the cafés, had taken them. They had visited the floodlit fun-fair, and sat in the garden of the Normandy bar and had a crême-de-menthe, and they had danced at the little Casino on the front where all the townsfolk went. When neither of them had any money left, they had walked the glittering gauntlet of the rue St. Jean. Jewels flashed behind grills in the windows of the Paris houses, and many of the shops were still open. On all sides they had been lapped by music, down from behind shutters, out from the bars, up from night-clubs in cellars. The streets had been as crowded as in day-time; dozens of young French couples were out in gay clothes, laughing and flirting, and Linda and he had walked among them arm-in-arm. Through the huge plate-glass windows of the Casino restaurant they had seen people at shaded tables in evening dress and waiters hurrying round a crowded dance-floor, and when Linda had pressed his elbow excitedly and wished that they could get in, he had boasted that he could take her. He was still sure he could have managed it; the commissionaire, an old friend, had just been about to yield, when Anne appeared and spoilt it all.

Not quite all. Redfern had picked them up and brought them away, and because Redfern's girl obviously had to sit with Redfern in front, Merrick and Linda had sat in the back. They had been ecstatically affectionate. For the first time he had kissed her on the lips. He had put one arm right round her waist and drawn her to him, and they had stayed like that the whole way back to the Villa Harlequin. At the time he had scarcely known what he was doing; Linda, the night, the wine, a surge of exhilaration inside him, had swept him away. Now, remembering it all, he felt shocked by the strength of his emotions and admired it; and Linda had yielded to everything. It had been impossible to go back to the cottage. The whole villa was theirs. They had stood on the lawn and looked at the moon, and he had kissed her again by the white roses that climbed up the netting of the tennis-court. And somehow, he did not know whose suggestion it had been, they had pulled out the sleeping bags and got into them, and they had talked until they went to sleep.

It had been perfect, idyllic; and now he had a headache. He knew from the curtains drawn in the kitchen and the smoke rising that Blanche was up. The back door was open, and he found her sweeping out the living-room.

"Good morning, Blanche," he said softly.

She started round with a little scream and put her hand to her heart.

"I didn't mean to frighten you," he said, but this time she chose to be genuinely angry. He tried to calm her down and asked her not to tell the others that he had only just come in. She tossed her head and turned her back on him.

"You speak to your mother," she told him.

"Of course I'll speak to her. But you needn't tell her you've seen me, need you?"

"You speak to her about it," Blanche repeated, and that was all he could get out of her. Unluckily they were not on good terms. Merrick had caught her reading a novelette entitled *I Shall Love No More* and had made a joke about it to Sarah, which she had overheard. She had decided that he was quite heartless "like all men"; she was sick of the lot of them, and at present intended to live the rest of her life with Anne, or else go into a convent.

Merrick crept upstairs, took an aspirin and did not wake up till noon. When he came down he was surprised to find Anne in the sitting-room. She was talking to Blanche, who at once went out; Merrick assumed that she had sneaked.

"Well, you're a nice one," said Anne. She was even-tempered now, curious and at the same time reluctant to learn if he would lie about last night.

"I've got a headache," he answered.

"Is that why you didn't come home last night?" she asked, letting him see that she knew.

"Yes, it is, really."

She waited for him to tell her that he had been at the Villa Harlequin, but he said nothing, looking stubbornly at the table.

"Didn't it occur to you that I might be worried?"

"Oh, I was all right, Mother. You know I'm always all right," he replied, lifting his eyes and at once lowering them.

"That's a very dangerous thing to say. It's tempting Providence."

"Well, I shan't be like I was last night again."

"I should hope not."

"It wasn't my fault. Edwin Aldrich kept on giving me more to drink." He changed the subject. "Aren't you going to the office this morning?"

"I waited to see you, and then I shall have to see Lady Wildenstein." There was a pause.

"Oh?" said Merrick. He realized that if Anne did not know where he had been all night she would soon find out, and now he began to wonder how much she knew. If it was only that he had slept the night at Lady Wildenstein's she might not mind; if she discovered that he had slept out with Linda, she might try to stop him meeting her. He did not like the idea of her going to see Lady Wildenstein, though he did not think Lady Wildenstein would tell her; he ranged her on his side against Anne. "I slept at the Villa Harlequin," he admitted, in what he hoped was a straightforward manner. "I got a sleeping-bag and slept out on the terrace."

"Well, of course I know that," said Anne. "Do you think I just went to bed? I sat up for you till two, and then I telephoned."

"You telephoned the Villa Harlequin?" he repeated, amazed.

"Of course I did," Anne said, trying to show him how ridiculous he was. "What do you expect me to do? I don't see you all afternoon, I come across you by accident at the Casino, rather tipsy, and then you don't come home. Anything might have happened to you. I don't mind your going to the Villa Harlequin so much, and I don't mind your being with Linda, but I don't want to have to spend my time chasing you. I should like to know where you are, that's all, and I think you should come home at a reasonable hour." She was going to add that he was not yet sixteen, but checked herself.

If Merrick had had more common sense at that moment, or perhaps felt less surly—his headache had not gone—he could have reassured Anne on this score and the interview could have come to an end. Instead he concluded that she knew he had slept out with Linda; this appeared to put him in the wrong, and he began to defend himself.

"I'm in love with Linda," he said.

"You may think you are," Anne replied, "but by next year I expect you'll have forgotten her."

"No, I shan't. She's more likely to have forgotten me. She's got hundreds of friends. She's been all over the place."

"Oh, all over the place," Anne said. "Here, then the south of France, then somewhere else. All the same people, all the same things to do. I don't call that all over the place. And it's not difficult with the money they've got. It's dull, really, darling. A lot of people like that are bored, and you'd soon get tired of them."

"They don't seem bored to me," said Merrick. "And they're the most interesting people I've ever met. You don't know them, you just hear what other people say against them. And if they're dull," he added, glowering at her, "what are we? We never even leave here."

Anne did not answer. She turned away, and he knew he had said something transfixing and calamitous. He had not meant to say it, but the feeling of being in the wrong had led him to accuse her, and the inferiority complex about lack of money, about Anne working at the club, about being of no importance, which the Villa Harlequin had developed in him, rose violently to the surface.

"If you are bored here," said Anne quietly and without looking at him, "then we must do something about it. I thought you enjoyed the holidays, and it seems to me you have a pretty good time. You're left a great deal to yourself. But if you're bored, then we must find something that will interest you. Only I don't think the Villa Harlequin is the best solution."

She spoke without sarcasm, which she never employed on either of the children, and she felt none. She had taken him more seriously than he wished to be taken, because she could understand and had often thought that one day soon both the children, and Merrick especially, would find the cottage and her company a limitation to them. It was as well that Merrick should think this, since it meant that he had initiative and ambition and was not going to be tied to her apron-strings. This had not pained her, but the thought that had bruised her heart was that he should prefer Lady

Wildenstein and the Villa Harlequin; and again she seemed to be with Johnny, after he had come back from his encounters with his rich new friends and had informed her, in that tone implying it was something beyond her, how entertaining they all were and what a fine time they had.

And again she felt bewildered. One voice urged her to tell him at once what she thought of the Villa Harlequin, of Lady Wildenstein, and the fatal ease with which such society could corrupt him, to tell him the whole story of his father; another voice warned her that he would think her meddlesome, never believe such things of people he found so engaging, and merely be the more attracted to them and resentful of her. If she told him about Johnny, he might well inquire why she had stayed at Oriol, if she thought it such a snare; and she would reply that it had been her home, that only one part of it was a snare, and the other part, the beach, the forest, Jacques-plage—but he knew that part himself, and till this point had been content with it. Johnny too had been content with it up to a point.

Sarah was at the gate, and saved her a decision then.

"I haven't told Sarah anything about this," she said quickly, "and I'd rather you didn't."

"Oh, I shan't tell her. Are you really going to see Lady Wildenstein?"

"I don't want to, but as you seem to be making rather free with her house, I must at least meet her."

"I'll take you," said Merrick, who preferred that the interview should take place with him there, and liked the idea of introducing them all to Anne.

"No, I think I'll go alone," she replied.

"I'm sure you'll like her," said Merrick, as Sarah came in.

But Anne did not think she would like Lady Wildenstein; nor did she when she went to call. She went prepared and hoping to believe that she was quite wrong. It was certainly a beautiful villa. The guests were polite and offered her drinks. She saw no reason why they should not wear unusual clothes if they wanted to; during the summer at Oriol most people wore as little as possible. She did not like Edwin Aldrich's voice, and she found it beyond her to feel anything but distrust for Lady Wildenstein. Lady Wildenstein was affable to a degree, but gave the impression that she had taken no trouble to understand Anne's feelings, and cared for nothing in Merrick's character except that he should be entertaining. Their conversation took place in the big living-room. Her eyes wandered. Frequently she interrupted to talk to other people, and once, after she had come back from a telephone call, she appeared to have forgotten why Anne had come. Anne thought her face singularly frigid; it struck her as the face of a woman who often smiled but never laughed. She had seldom seen beauty so completely without character; Lady Wildenstein did not even look discontented.

"Merrick's such a sweet boy," she said. She talked with a monotonous and languid emphasis on adjectives and adverbs. "And of course he adores Linda. Linda is an angel," she added as if thinking of something else, and in the same flat tone went on, "I dread to think of anything happening to her."

"I like Linda very much," said Anne. "But Merrick sometimes forgets that he is only fifteen and tries to behave as if he was much older."

"Linda's just the same," said Lady Wildenstein. "She wants to come out next year, and you know she plucked her eyebrows when she was twelve. It was quite unnecessary, too. She had lovely eyebrows. She is lovely, don't you think?" She smiled fondly towards the garden, where Paul Walker was giving Linda a dancing lesson. "So graceful," she sighed.

It occurred to Anne that had Linda been in love with Merrick, or even deeply attached to him, she would have taken more interest in what was being said in the living-room; certainly Sarah would have hidden herself somewhere and watched every expression of the two parents.

"Linda has no father," said Lady Wildenstein. "I think that draws her to Merrick. You are so wise in not letting Merrick see his father at all."

"His father has never asked to see him."

"Really? Linda's father insists on it, and legally of course he has to. It upsets the child."

She continued to praise Linda in a sentimental way, until Anne brought her back to the subject.

"I'm glad Merrick and Linda are friends," she said. "But I would be grateful if you could see he comes home early. He loves an excuse to stay up late, and if you would send him off . . ."

"Of course I will, my dear. Linda is just the same. She'd be up till dawn if she had the chance, and she's far too young. I don't know when Merrick is coming next, but we'll only be here another week. I'll see that he's home in good time."

"I didn't know you were going."

"I must get back to London. There are so many things I have to do."

"Is Linda going with you?"

"Oh yes. I couldn't leave Linda behind," replied Lady Wildenstein, although she had left Linda happily enough throughout the previous month.

This piece of news was for Anne the most satisfactory result of their talk. Merrick's holidays would last another three weeks, and she had expected that he would be regularly at the Villa Harlequin all that time; if he was only to have a week, perhaps she need not trouble herself, and the whole affair would pass and be forgotten by next year. As she was going Linda came running in.

"Here's my little imp," said Lady Wildenstein. "We've been talking about you for the last half-hour. This is Merrick's mother."

"Oh, I know her," said Linda, smiling and holding out her hand. "How's Merrick?"

"Well, he's got rather a headache this morning," Anne replied.

"I should think so. It wasn't his fault. Edwin kept on filling his glass."

Anne liked the promptness with which she took Merrick's part, and went away thinking that with anyone else as her mother she would grow up into a sweet-natured as well as an attractive girl. She felt sorry for her, as she had the first time she met her, remembering the touching way she had laughed at her own ignorance and the cheerful evenings she had spent with them at the cottage. She wished it could have been Linda coming to them, instead of Merrick being drawn to the Villa Harlequin. She feared that Linda was bound to become spoilt. Certainly she would stay ignorant; and though Anne did not consider a good education an elixir, she thought that a few weeks with Frau Mayer would have done Linda a lot of good. She wished too that Sarah could have been able to travel as Linda did.

She told Merrick of Lady Wildenstein's promise about early hours, but not that they were only staying another week, and it surprised her that he did not know. He was immensely inquisitive about her visit. Had she met them all? What did she think of Lady Wildenstein? Had Lord Ilfracombe been there, and didn't she think Sandra Carlisle beautiful?

"There seemed to be a lot of people," she replied, "and Lady Wildenstein said some very flattering things about you. I don't think you deserved half of them."

He asked Linda that afternoon what had happened.

"I don't know," she replied. "It looked as if they got on quite well. Is your mother angry?"

"She was this morning," said Merrick, exaggerating to make his courtship more risky. "I told her we slept out, but I didn't say we were together."

"Mother saw us," said Linda. "She said we looked like cherubs."

"I wish we could do it every night," said Merrick.

"So do I," said Linda, and pressed his arm.

"Wasn't *your* mother angry? It was my fault. I'll tell her. I'd better apologize."

He fancied that this would be gallant and appeal to both of them.

"I think she'd be awfully pleased if you did," said Linda. "She was a little annoyed, but not very. She made me tell her everything we'd done."

"You didn't tell her about being in the back of the car?" Merrick asked.

"Of course not."

He wanted to remind her of this part of the evening, but felt embarrassed; he hoped eagerly for a chance to repeat it, but thought it would be difficult. Perhaps it had only been due to the wine; and he wondered how much he would need to produce the effects of the evening without those of the morning.

He waited until Lady Wildenstein was alone and then apologized to her.

"You're very wicked," she said. "Come and sit beside me, and tell me all about it."

Nothing passed the time for her more pleasantly than news of other people's romances, and now that Linda was growing up she had become inquisitive about hers. She had her own quorum of courtiers, but she preferred admiration for herself and love when it happened to others. Her hospitality did not spring from warmth of heart, but from an inability to be long alone; left to herself, she soon grew bad-tempered. Linda was a

242

part of her own setting, and she took it for granted that the girl would make conquests.

It had suited her to have Merrick as Linda's companion; but since he was not of their world, and Linda would soon cease to see him, she had taken no more interest in him than to note that he knew how to make himself agreeable. She enjoyed the fascination her household exercised upon the respectably brought-up young and the anxiety this caused their parents. It gave her a kind of revenge upon the conventional society which disapproved of her and blinded itself to cravings to which she gave scope; she told herself that, frown as they might, they did not understand how to give their children a good time, and she did, and Anne's visit merely supplied further evidence.

Merrick sat beside her on the sofa, flattered by her attention and disarmed by her broad-mindedness.

"I had a long talk with your mother," said Lady Wildenstein.

"Yes, she said she was coming to see you."

"She's very worried about you. I told her that I was perfectly happy about you, and I'm always glad to see you here. I know you're in love with Linda, but last night you were very disgraceful," she added without any particular expression.

"Yes, I'm awfully sorry. It was such a lovely night."

"Ah, it's always a lovely night. But one must acquire a sense of responsibility, Merrick." She looked at him solemnly, and he looked solemnly back, believing that she was showing a different, serious side of herself. She paused, and said abruptly, "You never see you father?"

"No. I believe he saw me when I was very young, but I don't remember anything about him."

"He never writes to you?"

"No, never."

"Mm." She gave him a thoughtful glance which made him feel interesting, and then asked, "You get on well with your mother, don't you?"

"Oh yes, Lady Wildenstein."

"And she's looked after you all this time?"

"Yes." He was going to put in something about the offers of marriage Anne had received, and to say that it had been her choice and not compulsion to work at the golf-club, but Lady Wildenstein went on: "Of course there may be something of your father coming out in you. What did he do?"

"He owned horses," said Merrick, "and he used to ride them himself."

"I expect he was very dashing?"

"Well, I believe he was. Major Bryant used to be a friend of his. He was rather wild."

"That's what it is, my dear," said Lady Wildenstein. "You must beware of that side of you."

He had ceased for some time to think much about his father, but Lady Wildenstein, under disguise of warning him against the past, had made it sound romantic again, and he saw himself as a young man with a secret.

"Linda is very fond of you," said Lady Wildenstein next. "You should be flattered, Merrick. She is very fastidious."

"Linda's wonderful," he said. "She's awfully natural."

Lady Wildenstein looked unusually pleased, and for a moment her face was almost illumined.

"She is, isn't she? I've brought her up just to be herself. It's so uncommon, and she's sure to have everyone all round her. But she'll always have a special place for you," she added hastily.

He wanted to tell her about the days on the beach and at the cottage, but again she forestalled him.

"You haven't been going up to Linda's room, have you?" she asked, with a searching but not accusing look. He must have shown that he was puzzled, for she added, "After dark, I mean?"

"No," said Merrick, with genuinely innocent surprise. It occurred to him that Lady Wildenstein was disappointed. Their conversation was interrupted at this point, and he returned home early. He could never remember what Lady Wildenstein looked like. He had a clear impression of her face when she was there, but when she had gone it had gone too. What she had said stayed in his mind. The question about going up to Linda's room, and her attitude to his reply, made him think that perhaps he should have gone up there; even that both Lady Wildenstein and Linda had expected it of him. Her reference to his father had set other fancies stirring, and in his bedroom he took out a photograph of Johnny he had hidden a long time ago and compared it with his own face in the looking-glass. There was certainly a resemblance, especially when he put his face in the same position. He was not so good-looking; but, then, he was much younger, and photographs always showed people with such clear splendid features. After all, it took two to make a son, and there must be something of his father in him. He began to think about it again and, though now was no time to mention it, he decided that Anne had done wrong not to tell him more. An idea came to him which he had laughed at when Sarah had put it forward; perhaps they were illegitimate.

Anne was his mother, and could do no wrong. She could only, perhaps inevitably, because she was older, fail to understand, and be anxious about him when there was no cause. Lady Wildenstein had asked in the friendliest way whether he got on well with her, and of course he did; all the same, there was something to criticize, he was growing to a stage a little beyond Anne, and there were emotions in him she could not be expected completely to grasp. He must be tolerant and polite, and do nothing that might hurt her if it could be avoided; and in this new mood, and as a sign of contrition, he resolved to spend more of his time with her and Sarah. That evening, although his thoughts were of the Villa Harlequin, he played Initials with them and asked Anne to read. He apologized to Blanche for startling her, and promised Sarah that next morning he would accompany her to the Villa des Roses. Anne recognized that he was making an effort to atone and to placate her, but it was not what she had hoped, and her pleasure was mixed with regret that it should so obviously be an effort; formerly he had simply enjoyed being with them, but now love appeared to be stiffening into duty.

In the morning he started off with Sarah, a letter for Linda in his pocket. They were walking along the main road. Suddenly they heard a clattering of hooves, and a dark boy on horseback, about Merrick's age, dashed round a corner brandishing a whip and shouting.

"What the devil's this fool doing?" Merrick exclaimed. "Cantering on tarmac! He'll kill the horse if he doesn't kill himself." He stood out in the middle of the road and shouted, "Hi, you! Stop! Don't be a fool!"

More hooves clattered, and Linda and the party from the Villa Harlequin trotted up on Mr. Masterton's hirelings, a gay and precarious cavalcade. Linda jogged uncomfortably on the sleepy chestnut that was usually given to Sarah. The dark boy reined in and trotted back. Linda stopped because the others stopped; she could not have done it alone.

"Who is that fellow?" Merrick asked her.

"He's my cousin Boris. He's got Russian blood."

"Well, he might learn to ride decently. He's a public menace."

"He's ridden for years," said Linda indignantly. "He was showing us how to be a Cossack."

"Well, tell him he's a damned fool. He'll break the horse's leg on this road." Merrick's face was flushed, and Sarah could see he was really angry. "Suppose a car came round the corner?" He glared at Boris. His feet were out of the stirrups and he had let the reins lie; he seemed to fit the saddle, and it did look as if he had ridden before.

"He's not an idiot at all," said Linda, and tugged on the reins, trying to move the chestnut.

"Here, you've got them all muddled up," said Merrick. He straightened them and slid them between her fingers. The chestnut lowered his head and munched grass, pulling her forward.

"Oh, he is a nuisance," she exclaimed, tugging at him.

Suddenly Boris dashed up a sandy ride into the forest, followed by the cavalcade. "Tally-ho," cried Edwin Aldrich, who was wearing a high-necked yellow pullover. Linda, powerless to do anything the chestnut did not want to do, was borne sedately after them, bending her head to avoid boughs, leaning sideways to avoid trees. Merrick looked anxiously after her, frowning.

"She might have told me she was going out," he said. "Look at them. And they don't know the way or anything."

He turned to Sarah. "And what's the matter with you?"

She was standing out in the road, her lips parted, her hand keeping the hair off her forehead, gaping after them.

"Who was the dark one, Merrick?" she said, half whispering. "The one in front?"

"Some cousin of Linda's. I suppose he's just arrived. What a damned fool!" He looked at her suspiciously. "Don't tell me you're going to fall in love with *him* now," he said indignantly.

19

The children went on to the Villa des Roses. After her lesson Sarah asked Merrick if he wasn't going to call on Linda. He was surprised, having thought that because she knew he had upset Anne she was against him. He had had the virtuous intention of bringing her straight home. During her lesson he had repelled temptation to slip away to the Villa Harlequin and wait for the riders to come back, and gone instead to talk to the refugees. In the first cottage a baby was screaming, and the mother too busy to talk to him; in the second they had smiled politely and wished to be friendly, but none of them spoke French or English. So he had sat in the garden, listening to Hans practising and revising his letter to Linda. He wanted to remonstrate, without being rude; she had gone off with a lot of people who knew nothing about horses and a fellow who galloped on the main road. He would give the letter to Redfern. There was nothing to prevent his giving it to her himself, and nothing to stop him going to the Villa Harlequin, but he liked to think that there was; it made him a martyr for her, and the letter more colourful. When Sarah suggested going, he answered that they might as well, for a minute, but "we oughtn't to stay long."

The riders had just returned and had not yet changed. Sarah saw Boris again, and fell in love with him. She fell in love entirely, in rapturous secrecy, with a hopelessness that was entirely without wretchedness, since she had no far objective for which to hope. She did not even imagine an objective, except to see him. The knight had ridden at last to the drawbridge. For Jerry she had had hero-worship, for Hans compassion, but this was unlike and transcended all, absorbing, engulfing her. He was her true love, who had come to her on horseback.

He made every other tenant of her thought an outlaw and reigned there. She dreamed no more, day or night. He was with her when she went to sleep and when she awoke; he galloped through her dreams, dispersing them. She felt sorry for others and more than usually affectionate towards them, because they had nothing like this. Frau Mayer seemed ponderous, Judith forlorn, Anne was merely the mother who cared for her but had no other life. For Blanche she had a small particular glow, since Blanche had loved Monsieur Philippe.

She walked on air. The forest had a voice. The sea, the dunes, disclosed a beauty beyond and beneath the beauty that had always been there, and an animation, the existence of which she had guessed vaguely at moments, was now there in reality. Day was not morning, noon, evening, meals, lessons, but a reach of time along which she must somewhere cross his path. This had to be done, some fresh detail added to her store of him; when night came, she took them out and peopled it till she slept. It became her rule, the crown of each day, to go with Merrick after her lesson to the Villa Harlequin. It suited him well. He supposed that its charm had been too much for her and that she was repenting of her priggishness, and he took a forgiving attitude, careful not to say "I told you so." He drew her into his conspiracy; she entered willingly and without cunning. They agreed, without ever mentioning it, not to tell Anne about these visits, but Sarah had no sense of guilt; something was happening that was for her alone.

She saw that the guests at the Villa Harlequin did as they pleased, and if she did not want to join in no one would make her. She scarcely noticed them. The more there were, the thicker the shield of conversation and movement behind which she could look at Boris. Most mornings he played tennis. He wore white flannel trousers and a blue vest, and played with enthusiasm, rushing to the net immediately after he had served, crouching with an excited expression to receive the service. She longed for him to play well, knew that he would, and he did. She never spoke to him of her own accord, and he was hardly aware that she was there; but once, after a game, when they were all sitting on the sunlit lawn, he offered her a glass of lemonade. Her heart beat furiously as she waited for the moment when he would hand it to her. She smoothed back her hair while he fetched drinks for the others, and when he came to her made a violent effort and looked him in the face. Something must have arrested his attention, for he prolonged his own look, and afterwards, when everyone was talking, he said suddenly: "Have you lived here long?"

She was nervous, not knowing what she would do if he began a conversation, and longing to return to her silent absorption. She replied:

"Yes, quite a long time."

Someone else spoke to him, and he turned away, and she felt idiotic for not having said it was her home.

On the way back to the cottage Merrick would talk about them all and say how original they were.

"I don't like Boris as much as the rest," he said.

"Why not?"

"He's too conceited. He shows off."

She had to say something. So she said, "He's very Russian-looking."

"Is he? I've never seen any Russians before."

"Oh, you know what I mean, Merrick."

"I don't. I though they all wore high boots and looked like bears and had whiskers."

"Oh, that's just what books show them like."

He glanced at her. It was unusual for her to scoff at books; that was more his role.

"The way he was riding that horse was terrible," he said, switching. "Lucky for him Mr. Masterton didn't see."

"Perhaps that's the way Russians ride."

He decided that it was true, she had found a new hero. They ceased to talk much about Boris. Merrick was slightly jealous of him, though Linda had explained that he was just a cousin she had known "all her life"; and Sarah was not going to give herself away.

She saw no particular fault and no particular virtue in him. She did not think about his character, and he no more had qualities for her than a spirit or a faun; but she could trace each line, each feature. Black hair and eyes, curling black eyelashes, broad high cheek-bones, and heart-shaped face. At home she invented excuses, so that she could go upstairs and do drawings of him. Sometimes she found herself doing them on scraps of paper in the living-room, and hid them hurriedly when Anne or Merrick came in. She buried one drawing in the woods and went back two days later to unearth it. She carved his name and hers on a tree; the kiosk in the woods, where so many lovers had engraved themselves, was too ordinary for her. She wrote him a message, put it in a ginger-beer bottle, and hiding it under her coat ran to Jacques-plage and committed it to the waves; she returned next day, and ranged the water's edge to see if it had been washed up. It had not; she imagined it bobbing away, tossed and becalmed, until at last someone in England or America discovered it. She had a secret so tremendous that it could be confided only to the woods and ocean. People would talk about it and destroy it; but the elements would hold it, as it was now, for ever.

She saw him one morning at Oriol. She was with Merrick, he with the others, going the opposite way on the opposite side of the street. She made an excuse to leave Merrick, and darted round a block in order to pass Boris. Out of breath, she turned a corner and came on him looking into the window of a jeweller's. She went slower and pretended to be looking at the shops herself. He did not see her, but she heard him say: "It's time for lunch. I should like to drive back in a nice old cab."

She raced off to the stand where Paul kept his fiacre.

"There's someone for you," she said, panting. "The people from the Villa Harlequin. They're up there by the Normandy."

"*Merci, M'amselle.*"

Paul grunted to Jamais, and they jogged off. Boris and the others got in, and passed her; but he did not see her. She did not mind whether he saw her or not. She wanted to see him and do things for him, and that was enough.

Anne suspected nothing, attributing her abstracted manner to her lessons. Frau Mayer and Judith were absorbed in the world crisis. Czechoslovakia was about to be invaded. They took all the papers, read every word of the political news and comment, and analysed them all morning, breaking into bitter attacks upon the Western Powers. Judith made telephone calls to Paris, while Frau Mayer bent forward listening, gripping the arms of her chair, and Hans, oblivious, played on in the sombre hall. The refugees came in constantly, asking what was going to happen, and Frau Mayer translated the papers for them. Often Sarah saw them, squatting on the steps of the two lodges with grave faces; but the gloomy atmosphere of the Villa des Roses did not pierce the golden ring she walked in, and the same compunction which had prevented Anne telling the children the true condition of mankind came over Judith and Frau Mayer. A short time ago they had censured Anne for failing to teach the children politics; but now that the armies were mobilizing, they were themselves silent in front of Sarah, as people are in front of children when a family skeleton or black sheep is mentioned. Why should they tell her all about it? As long as it lasted, let her stay a child. They would be talking in Judith's sitting-room, the table strewn with newspapers; suddenly she would enter, sidling round the door, her note-books under her arm, and Judith would turn down the wireless and Frau Mayer say gruffly: "Well, here's my young pupil. Have you done me a good essay?"

But she noticed that something in the child was altered. The essays were less painstaking, and one day she forgot to write one at all. She asked fewer questions, and no longer turned the pages of the picture albums without waiting for Frau Mayer. Frau Mayer elaborated a comparison between Bismarck and Disraeli, but when she asked Sarah which of them she preferred, the girl was gazing out of the window at the copper-red pine-trunks. She did not interrupt, and Sarah continued to stare, until the note-book slipped off her knees and made her jump.

"Come, come," Frau Mayer said. "You're not paying attention."

Sarah went red.

"I'm sorry . . ." she stammered.

Frau Mayer, remembering the evening at the Casino, guessed that there must be trouble at the cottage, and tried to worm it out.

"You're thinking of something else, Sarah."

"Oh no . . . well, I was just absent-minded . . . I heard you, though." She paused, struggling to recollect. "Bismarck was a dictator," she said vaguely.

"I said more than that. Perhaps you'd rather be outside on a lovely day like this. Perhaps you'd rather be with your brother."

"Oh no, Frau Mayer."

"We'll leave our lesson today, my child. There's enough of Bismarck, anyhow, more than enough. And what does your brother do all day?"

"Oh, he does carpentry, and he bathes."

"And he goes to the Villa Harlequin?"

"Oh yes."

"He is in love with Linda, I think?"

"He's very fond of her."

"That place is a bad influence," said Frau Mayer.

"Oh, they're awfully kind, really. They don't bother you at all."

Frau Mayer grunted. She had not expected this from Sarah, whom she had thought safe within her own and Judith's orbit, and a few days ago Sarah might have agreed with her. Now all Boris's surroundings were within his halo. She felt tender and understanding towards Merrick, because he too was in love, but she could never have spoken about Boris as he spoke about Linda. She kept him inside her, an intense hidden flame, burning in the forest of her innocence; no paths had been cut into the world, and no one could reach it or set eyes on it. It lasted its week, then flamed up furiously for an instant, and went out, consuming her first incarnation with it.

Linda, informed almost accidentally by her mother that they were leaving, had to tell Merrick. She felt that she was unhappy, but enjoyed the prospect of a tragic farewell and was already excited about the future. Lady Wildenstein had taken a house in London and was to give a party for Sandra Carlisle; Linda had been promised she could have a new dress and stay up for it.

"Oh, Merrick," she said. "It's so wretched. I'd much rather stay here with you."

His morose face fanned her into a gust of love. Several films came to mind. There would be the final kiss, the lump in the throat; they would exchange presents and write letters across the Channel.

"You'll come to see us in London, Merrick darling. You'll come to our new house."

"Will I?"

"Of course you will. Perhaps you'll be able to come to Sandra's party. Oh, that would be wonderful. It's going to be on November the seventh."

"There'll probably be a war by then."

"Do you think so?"

She looked alarmed; if there was a war, Sandra's party might have to be cancelled.

"Everyone's talking about it."

"I know. Isn't it awful?"

Merrick saw himself in uniform, coming to say good-bye to her.

"My stepfather says it'll all blow over," Linda declared. "I heard him say so. He'd been talking to someone very important, and he says they're going to agree about whatever it is."

"I could come to your party from school," said Merrick. "Yes, I could do that."

He would run away. He would get leave to go to the dentist and then he would take the afternoon train, and climb in at night. One boy had done that, and been expelled. Well, he would be expelled; then Linda would see what she meant to him.

"Oh, Merrick, could you really?"

"I should probably be sacked," he said with glum relish, making it clear.

"It would be lovely if you could come. You oughtn't to be sacked, though."

"I don't care if I am."

He felt really downcast and could not speak of it to Anne or Sarah, who did not know yet. Anne guessed, and said gently:

"What's the matter, Merrick? You're very silent."

"Oh, nothing."

She began to talk to Blanche about the week's food. The unfeeling conversation made him want to explode, but he let them go on, so that when he made his announcement they could feel how trivial they had been.

"Lady Wildenstein's leaving," he said abruptly.

Blanche gazed at him with her mouth open, amazed at the violent in-

253

terruption. Sarah too was looking at him, thinking at once of Boris, her eyes wide.

"Is she?" said Anne. "I heard they might be leaving."

"They're going on Monday."

"And Linda too?"

"Yes."

"That is a pity. I'm sure you'll be sorry."

He did not answer, expecting sympathy, but rejecting it when he got it.

"Are they all going?" Sarah asked, her head up.

"Yes, all of them."

Sarah would miss Boris, or think she would, but she could have no right to feelings like his. She just imagined she was in love with people, and she scarcely knew Boris. But he and Linda had been together for weeks, they had kissed every day, he had held her in his arms, a cord was woven between them.

"Well, this is Wednesday," said Anne. "Would you like to do something for her before she goes? We could ask her here and take her to a film."

"Oh, I don't know."

He resented the word "we," seeing the end of their idyll travestied into a polite dutiful return of hospitality, with mothers and people asked.

"What would you like to do?" said Anne.

"Oh, I don't know," he repeated disagreeably. "There's nothing much we can do, is there?"

Again came this hint that the cottage had nothing to offer, but this time Anne merely felt exasperated with him. He was altogether too like Johnny in these moods, wilful, petulant, determined to be accorded superior characteristics.

"I think Linda would enjoy coming here," she said. "She used to love it."

She longed for Linda and her mother, and all of them, to go away, and be quit of them.

"I think we'll just go out one evening," Merrick said. "Just Linda and me."

"It's as you like."

Sarah was silent. He's going away, she thought. I shall never see him again, I shall never speak to him again. She must know where he was going, she must find out his address, but she did not know how to do it. There was no one she dared to ask. Redfern—perhaps Redfern would tell her, and she would make him promise not to tell Merrick she had asked. Or Blanche—she could ask Blanche, and Blanche could ask Monsieur Philippe perhaps, and M. Philippe could ask Redfern. Or she could go to see them off—Merrick would be sure to see them off—and look on the luggage labels. But he was going, and that nothing could stop; another week, and he would be gone. She wrote the days in a book, and multiplied them into hours, minutes, seconds. Helplessness and despair crept over her.

Merrick and Linda agreed that they would go to the beach on her last night and make their farewells there. It would be like the time last month, he told her, when they had been alone together, and she said yes, that would be wonderful, better than anything else; besides, she had seen all the films. But the next day she said:

"I'm awfully sorry, but do you mind if Boris comes?"

He could not believe it.

"Of course I mind," he said fiercely. "It ruins everything."

"He asked, Merrick. I couldn't help it."

"But why tell him?"

"I don't know. I just said something . . ." she filled in the words with an appealing look.

"Oh, damn! After all, we may never see each other again."

"I didn't want him to come, but I couldn't refuse. He's so pushing."

"Of course you could have refused. I haven't told Sarah, and if she'd asked I should have said no."

"I'll tell you what, Merrick. You ask Sarah, and then Boris can look after her."

Linda had learnt about pairing people off from her mother.

"And who else shall we ask?" Merrick said bitterly. "What about your mother, and mine, and Mr. Wake, perhaps?"

"Oh, Merrick, don't be angry. We'll tell them we want to be alone. We'll leave them."

He hated the whole plan now. He had thought her free of the convention which compelled the inviting of people who were not wanted. She had

255

always escaped from Miss Patterson or Lady Wildenstein when she had chosen, and he nearly renounced the evening entirely. But she apologized so sweetly, and explained so remorsefully, and promised so faithfully that she would spend the whole time with him, that he relented and asked Anne if Blanche could prepare some food. Anne consented unwillingly that Sarah should go, and made him promise not to stay out later than half-past ten.

He went into Sarah's room to tell her. It was impossible to keep up a pretence of casualness, and surely Sarah, who had shared all or nearly all his secrets in the past, would understand now. She hid something when he opened the door. He sat on her bed, uncertain how to begin; for the first time it was he whose emotions were in knots.

"What are you doing?" he asked.

"Oh, just drawing."

"I expect you're learning a lot from Frau Mayer," he said, being friendly, and did not miss her suspicious look. "I wish you could do one of Linda."

"I'll try, but I'm hopeless at girls. It's awful she's going, isn't it?"

"Yes, awful. It really is. It's terrible being in love, Sarah, really in love. It gets worse and worse. I've said all kinds of things to Linda. You wouldn't believe what I've said."

"What have you said?" she asked shyly. Almost more than anything on earth, she wanted to know what they said.

"Oh, all kinds of things. I couldn't tell you. I never know what I'm going to say. It just comes out."

"And does she say them back to you?"

"Oh yes. Not so much," he said candidly, "but then she's a girl." He fingered her sheets of drawing-paper; she had never known him so solemn. "Listen, S," he went on. (A long time ago, when they were reading spy stories, they had called each other by their initials, or by a number.) "You'd like to come bathing tomorrow night, wouldn't you?"

"At night?"

"I've asked Mother. She says it's all right for you, if we're back by half-past ten. Blanche is going to give us something to take. Linda's coming. She's going next morning. And Boris."

"Boris!" She started violently, giving herself away. Their eyes met.

"Did you ask him?" she said accusingly.

"No. Linda did."

Knowing she liked him, he did not tell her that Boris had asked himself and was a nuisance.

"Linda and I may go off," he went on. "You needn't worry, though."

"Go off?"

He grinned. "Oh, not run away. Though I wouldn't mind, and I don't think she would. Just go for a walk. You'll be all right, won't you?"

"Of course I'll be all right," she answered indignantly, imagining herself accused. "What are you going to do when you go off?"

"Oh, S, we aren't going to do anything," he said kindly. "Just go for a walk."

"Well, why shouldn't you?"

"No reason at all. I'm only telling you in advance."

"How long will you be?" she asked, picturing it.

"I can't tell now. It depends, when the time comes."

She wanted to say that Boris might be annoyed to be left with her, but could not even say his name. Her stomach went icy. She would be alone with him. Alone together, on the beach, after dark. Oh, how wonderful—and terrifying! What would she do, what would she say? She summoned her heroines. How would Jane Eyre behave? How would Elizabeth Bennet behave? Catherine Earnshaw? Queen Flavia?

And suddenly they all withdrew. Their examples became quite meaningless to her. She was isolated, she would be isolated, herself, Sarah MacManus, a real person, and she did not know what she would do. She was in a fever that she would make herself ridiculous. She would be tongue-tied, or give him another idiotic answer. If only she could ask Anne, as she did before going to a party! But it was impossible, and here for the first time was a position of utter nakedness, he and she and no one else, and no counsel to depend on but her own. "O God, don't let him think me silly," she repeated; and as the hour approached she trembled increasingly.

They were waiting on the road outside the cottage. Merrick carried the picnic-basket. Her heart was like the heart of the murdered man in that story, that thumped and thumped and thumped through the floor-boards, but when Linda and Boris arrived it was just like any other meeting, and they walked cheerfully over the dunes, croaking back at the million frogs. Merrick made howling noises to frighten Linda, and Boris and Linda pushed him down a dune. Sarah ran after him, rolling him in the sand. The nearness of the sea, the rising of the moon, excited them and drew them all together, and it was as though she had known Boris all her life.

The sands had poured into their neglected "castle," and Merrick tore planks from it to make a fire. The sun dipped over the horizon, leaving a crimson wake, the oncoming night paused, and between, in a yellow and green no-man's land, the evening star arose. Sarah gazed at the long beach and the sea, grey now except far out beneath the sunset, and seeming to mount in a vast swell to meet the night.

"There's a picture like this," she murmured. "It's by Turner. Only the sea's rougher in it."

"Do you like pictures?" Boris asked.

"Oh yes. Do you?"

Worlds seemed to hang upon his answer.

"I like everything. Everything and anything."

"And everyone?" she asked, and could have bitten it back.

"My God, no." His eyes made a moment's leap, like two black salmon. "A few people. A very few people very much."

He jumped to the fire and began to throw all the logs on top of it, annoying Merrick; but as Linda was in her most affectionate mood, he did not say anything. She was being deliberately aloof with Boris, showing him that this was Merrick's evening, making no eyes, practising no coquetries, but standing quietly by the leaping fire with her hand in Merrick's. The other two were so naturally excluded that Merrick could even be exceptionally attentive to them, after he had done everything for Linda. He dug her a sand-chair by the edge of the fire, and she installed herself there like her mother in Miss Ferguson's photograph, but fresh, lively, her eyes dancing, spring and not the pose of spring. Boris sat cross-legged, poking the planks and humming to himself, and Sarah could watch him to her heart's content. His eyes glittered among the flame-shadows on his face. He appeared to be far away, and suddenly would leap up out of his reverie with an idea for them. He was the older, but he was quite content to let Merrick arrange everything.

Linda too had brought food. They ate until they were gorged. Night drew down, and the lighthouse flashed out at them. They counted the flashes in unison. Six, and then eleven. They each said "Now," when they thought the flash was coming. Sarah watched the beams chase one another across the sea and began to feel mesmerized, entranced.

She was sitting with Boris at the foot of a dune. Suddenly she heard him chuckle and say:

"Yes, there they go."

She looked quickly at him and beyond his profile saw two figures melting into the dark, Linda in a white dress, Merrick with his arm in hers. The moment had come. She began to tremble again. All the evening's joy had gone, though all she most wished for had come. Alone. No one for miles to either side, wilderness behind, and in front no one for hundreds of miles, except on ships. The pools glimmered, and the silver feathers in the moon's highway turned to silver fish and danced. High-water mark was an infinite black rope, woven of seaweed, twigs and shells. A bottle had been thrown up among them. Suppose it should be hers, and he should see it and open it! She wanted to say something to distract him, but the words stuck.

"The lovers," he murmured, gazing after the two. He lay back, arms behind his head. "What a beautiful night! Have you ever been in love, Sarah?"

She trembled fiercely. "No, I don't think so," she answered. The words came out with a jerk. "Have you?"

"Oh yes."

For a long time he was silent. She edged back, so that she could see him better. The moon was on him, making him look savage.

"I wonder what that blue star's called," he said.

"Perhaps it's Aldebaran."

"What's Aldebaran?"

"It's one of the brightest. The blue ones are the brightest."

"How do you know?"

259

"Frau Mayer told me."

"Who's Frau Mayer?"

"She gives me lessons. I think she knows everything. She's like an owl, she knows so much."

Boris chuckled. "Like an owl," he repeated.

"I should like to know everything," Sarah said.

"There's only one thing I want to do, and that's fly. My brother flies. He's going to take me up one day, but I should like to fly most by night."

He spoke firmly, without yearning, and she knew that he would do as he said.

"What do you think of when you look up now?" he asked.

She was imagining him up there with his brother, like Icarus, but she answered: "I imagine I have a boat, and I go from one star to another, and then I look down and I see here."

"I shall be a pilot," he said.

Slowly she felt peaceful. It was easy to talk to him now. Her terrors floated away from her like veils of mist, and into the empty spaces they left flowed the rustling waves, Boris's voice, and a pervading tranquillity. She could stay like this for ever, listening to him and talking, she could tell him unabashed everything she had wished or thought. He leaned on his elbow and smiled at her, and she was able to meet his eyes.

"How old are you?" he asked.

"Nearly fifteen. You're seventeen, aren't you?"

"Eighteen next month. So you're only a year younger than Linda?"

"Yes, I suppose so."

She put her head on her knees, hugging her bare legs, and said, "I wish I was like Linda. She's so unselfconscious, and she never minds how many people are there. She always seems to know what to say, and what she ought to do, and I ... oh, sorry. . . ."

Her ankle had touched his hand, and she drew it away.

"And you?"

He sat up, nearer to her. Her confidence rose with his friendliness and gentle voice; in her heart she paid him the highest compliment she or Merrick knew, that he was "natural."

"Oh, I get so terrified," she answered. "I think everyone's looking at me, and I say something absolutely silly, and I think they're laughing at me. The other day at the villa ..."

"Go on."

"Oh, it wasn't anything, but it's what I mean. It was when you asked me if we lived here, and I said we had quite a long time, and it was so stupid, because we've always lived here. I don't know why I said it, and I felt such an idiot."

She laughed softly, quiet and relaxed. Never before, not even to Anne, had she spoken to anyone like this. Her words came easily, and an immense tide of relief flowed from her. Abruptly, as if another tide had met it and clashed, she felt a shock. A paralysing thrill began in the calf of her leg and moved up along her spine. His bare hand had touched her ankle and was stroking it. She sat still, frozen, petrified.

"It's natural to be scared when you're young," he said gently. "You won't be later."

She could not stir. He raised himself, and his other arm was at her back, feeling round her waist, his body close to hers, against hers. An appalling terror seized her. He pressed to her so that the palm of his hand was holding her between the ribs and hip. His eyes had become narrower and more elongated, his red smiling mouth seemed enormous.

"Don't, don't!" she gasped.

She jumped up, but he caught her hand.

"Come on, Sarah," he said, smiling. "Sit down."

She stared at him horrified, and as he tried to bring her towards him she wrenched away her hand and ran, stumbling up the dune. He ran after her, laughing. A clutch of his hand on her heel made her desperate, as if a wolf were after her, and she ran wildly from the sea, falling in the loose white sand, stumbling up the dunes on hands and knees.

"Sarah, Sarah!" he was calling. "Come back! Sarah!"

She found the path and ran on until his voice was lost, fell, and lay where she had fallen behind the shoulder of a dune. Her whole body shuddered and between sobs and panting gasps she repeated, "Terrible, oh it was terrible. . . ." She rolled her head on her arms. "No, no, no," she cried, sobbing. After a while she lifted herself and peered above the dune. She could hear Merrick calling her now, then Linda, and Boris again.

"Sarah.... Sarah.... Sarah...." Their voices floated to her over the croaking of the frogs, and far off, in flashes of the lighthouse beams, she saw their three figures silhouetted on the last dune before the sea.

What was she to do? She could not go back. She could never see him again, never be near him again. At each recollection of his scarlet mouth and glittering eyes she shuddered. But she had no shoes. She had left her shoes behind, and she could not go home barefoot. She waited, straining for a glimpse to tell her if they were chasing her, but the voices died away and the silhouettes disappeared. She crept forward. She would fetch her shoes and go home. She came near the beach and saw Boris out by the sea in his bathing-trunks, scattering the phosphorescent waves. She knew where she had left her shoes, slithered to the top of the last dune, and felt her heart leap as though it would jump into the sea. Merrick and Linda were lying in the fold of sand beneath her, in each other's arms, kissing each other. She checked like a shot stag, her eyes distended, then she dropped and rolled out of sight.

20

Everything was at an end. One word hammered in Sarah's head: betrayed, betrayed, betrayed. She skulked near the cottage for Merrick's return, and saw the three of them go past, Merrick carrying her shoes, his arm round Linda's waist, Boris—she could not look at Boris. They went on to the Villa Harlequin, and Merrick returned, running. She slipped out, startling him.

"So there you are!" He was enormously relieved, dreading the stories she might have told Anne. "What on earth happened to you?"

"Give me my shoes," she muttered.

"All right, all right. But what happened? Did Boris do anything? Do tell me, Sarah."

She put on her shoes, refusing to answer, and he became anxious.

"Look here, Sarah; you're shivering all over. We're late, and Mother's sure to ask what happened, and I'm the one who'll have to explain. You ought to tell me at least something. Or else pull yourself together."

She turned on him and answered fiercely, "Oh, you'll be all right. You needn't worry. I shan't say anything about you."

"Well, what is there to say about me? I know about myself. I want to know what happened to you."

But she would not answer. Anne had a glimpse of a pale drawn face as she hurried to her room.

"What's the matter with Sarah?" she asked.

"Oh, I don't know. She's in a state about something."

"But what?"

"I don't know, Mother. I don't really," he answered desperately.

Already the memory of the evening was being killed. Linda among the dunes, Linda's farewell at the Villa Harlequin . . . these were moments to be secured in all their details. The idyll had passed, she was no longer with him; but an image like her, and moments only a little less blurred than the real moments, came to sit for portraits of the reality, be locked away and hoarded. And now people stepped between, who had nothing to do with it; mothers, sisters, people.

Anne ran up to Sarah's room. The door was locked.

"You can't come in," came a muffled voice.

"Are you all right, Sarah?"

"Yes, Mother, I'm perfectly all right. Please leave me alone."

In the morning she had a temperature. Merrick came back from seeing Linda off to find the doctor at the cottage, Anne looking worried, and Blanche tragic in general and hostile to him in particular. He felt lifeless now, heavy-hearted, but of course no one was thinking of him. Anne began a cross-examination at once.

"Something must have happened yesterday evening," she said. "The doctor thinks Sarah has had a shock."

"Well, what kind of a shock could she have had, Mother?"

He felt an active anger against them and a craving to get away. He thought of the cars, moving now along the road to Boulogne. He had hoped to go to Boulogne with Linda, and come back with M. Philippe, but there had been no room; a big disappointment, because he wanted at least to see her out of France. Once she was on the sea, or in England, something irrevocable had happened; as long as she was still in France, it seemed possible still to recall her.

"Where did the child go yesterday evening?" the doctor asked.

And who was this creature to be talking about yesterday evening? To Merrick it seemed that the only people who could have had a yesterday evening were himself and Linda, and no one else had a right to talk about it.

"They were on the beach," said Anne.

"Ah. Perhaps a chill?"

"But it was a very warm night. Otherwise I would not have let her go. Do you think she could have got a chill, Merrick?"

"I don't know," he answered, disgusted with Sarah. "She might have. She came back without her shoes."

"Without her shoes!"

More questions. Impatiently he explained that she had been alone with Boris "for a few minutes," and when he and Linda had come back, she had vanished.

"Boris?" said Anne. "Who is Boris?"

"Linda's cousin."

"You never told me he was going."

"I didn't know. We didn't want him."

"How old is he?"

"Seventeen."

Anne saw the doctor looking at her.

"I would have expected you to know how to look after your sister better," she said.

Merrick blazed up. "I would have expected her not to behave like a silly little fool. If you want to know what happened, why not ask her? How the devil should I know?"

He walked out, went to the Villa Harlequin, and sat among the ruins of Lady Wildenstein's house-party. He told himself that here was his true home, and heard Lady Wildenstein murmuring, "You get on well with your mother? And you never see your father?" She was right, his father's nature must be coming out in him. Well, he preferred it; it made him feel defiant, himself. People—and now he meant Anne—had tried to render him into something other than he was, and it would not work. In the living-room he found a sheet of notepaper marked Villa Harlequin, lay on his stomach on the lawn, and wrote to Linda. ". . . Everything is frightful now you've gone" . . . and so on. In two days she would get it. Already they would be at Boulogne. He saw the cars drawing alongside the boat, the porters swarming, Mr. Harris the purser showing Lady Wildenstein to a cabin, passengers staring at Edwin Aldrich, who had been wearing a check travelling-cape, and sailors admiring Linda. All round would be bustle and struggle, women selling fruit, newsvendors, and she would be serene, aloof, observing. "I imagined you at every moment," he wrote. "I imagined you the whole way back to your house in London." He longed now for the holidays to end, so that he and she could again be in the same country.

If things had been easier at the cottage, his feelings might have been less violent, but in his anger with Anne and Sarah, Linda's world gleamed like a white house in thunder. He persuaded himself that he was being blamed for things that were not his fault, denied freedom, and expected to develop sedately, inch by inch, in a kind of cottage world, where everyone was good and kind and never did anything wrong, anything explosive.

Sarah became delirious for a short time, and Anne found out part of the story. She was enraged with Merrick, as he had never known her before. Her lips tightened, her mild eyes blazed. She accused him of failing to look after Sarah. She had seen the evil genius of Johnny in him; now she saw it at work through him upon Sarah, and this was something beyond her tolerance. He might go in that direction if he chose (and at times it seemed natural that he should), but Sarah never; that she would not have. They had the worst row of their lives, and Merrick was astounded at Anne's vehemence.

Sarah remained in bed, recovering. Judith and Frau Mayer visited her; they were informed she had a chill. Charlotte Wake came, and left a tract; Anne threw it away, not wanting a recurrence of Sarah's religious crisis on top of everything else. She now knew the whole story, except about Merrick and Linda. That Sarah would never tell to anyone; their code survived even delirium. She had nightmares, but horror soon changed to an obsession that she had been disgraced, and she told Anne that she was going to have a baby. Disabused of this, she grew calmer. Nothing, of course, could ever be the same again. She did not know what would become of her, but supposed she would go on somehow, like Blanche. Boris, as a human being, was soon forgotten; he vacated her thinking mind for a kind of box-room, out of which he emerged for nightmares and warnings, looking like a wolf with lips.

She became forgiving. Having loved and lost individually, she forgave universally. When Merrick came to see her she was embarrassed, but the shock of what she had witnessed on the dune had diminished and left a haunting wonder mingled with respect. She had her secret too. He did not know that she had seen, therefore he did not know that she had told no one, and she cherished her unrecognized loyalty by herself. He too was embarrassed; also vaguely respectful, because this unknown something, this experience there had been so much fuss about, invested her with mystery. He asked how she was, and they talked about nothing in particular; deep down their curiosity about each other had increased, though it took time to show itself.

From Linda there arrived a letter full of affection and spelling mistakes. Merrick put it in his pocket and took it with a throbbing heart to the dunes. It was in reply to his, not a native impulse. She told him she missed him, and would never forget the list of events he had reminded her of in his letter, but she did not mention any of her own. She had had a smooth crossing, and the new house was very nice. London was lovely, and everyone pleased there was not going to be a war. He must come to the party on November 7. Linda hoped Sarah was well, and his mother too, and sent all her love. It would be wonderful when they met again; he must not be too gloomy, and he must remember that There's Always Tomorrow, and write to her again. He wrote at once, but did not get an answer before going back to school.

He wandered about Oriol and Jacques-plage and paid sentimental visits to the Villa Harlequin. The gymkhana had been cancelled because of the crisis, though he did not see what the crisis had to do with horses. The season was ending, crowds came now only at the week-ends, and during the week Mr. Masterton could let him have a mount. He got up early to see if there was a letter; when, each morning, there was not, it was a relief to gallop on the beach, and he stayed out as long as he could. He went to the empty race-course and practised over the jumps in the far corner; it was not allowed, but he knew a way in, and no one saw him. He groomed the horse himself afterwards, and often stayed to help Mr. Masterton; he enjoyed it anyhow, and wanted to remain away from the cottage. Sometimes, after a silent supper, when Anne had gone to Sarah's room, he would walk into Oriol and re-live his evenings with Linda among the gay young French couples. Madame Jeanne at the Kursaal asked where she had gone.

"To England."

"And now you'll find another?"

"Oh no, Madame Jeanne."

"Ah, you're one of the faithful ones."

All the same, he noticed other girls, compared them with Linda, and smiled at them in the street. Anne, preoccupied with Sarah, did not seem to care how late he stayed out. She was no longer anxious about Sarah, but had to stay with her.

One evening, well after dark, he was returning past the rear entrance of the Casino when he noticed a narrow iron ladder running up to the roof. He could seldom resist forbidden entries, deserted buildings, or attics; he had the instinct of a burglar without the compulsion or desire to steal. He lay on a mound opposite the kitchens, and watched the chefs in their tall white hats and the busy waiters balancing trays. Next door was the stage door of the theatre, and the ladder between. He ran across, scrambled up it, and went like a squirrel over a shoulder of the roof, which was flat, with concrete walls jutting up, that boxed in offices and gave him cover from the searching lighthouse. He tried a door. It was open, and led into the attics.

He crept along, bent double, towards a narrow beam of light, full of dancing dust, which seemed to burst like a fountain out of the floor. He knelt down, and looked through a tiny hole straight on to the stage, high above the gallery, high above the drop-clothes, high above everything, like a young god gaping out of the sky. It was the last act of *Carmen*, and the procession into the bull-ring was just ending with a noisy chorus. His circle of vision was diminutive, but Carmen herself crossed it for an instant, black lace cascading from her mantilla, her train a white waterfall of lace beneath it. There were dark shudderings from the orchestra, and the harsh voice of the man who was going to murder her; but as Merrick could see nothing, and hear little, he crept along to another attic, in the middle of which rose a dome of illumined glass. He guessed that he was above the main hall. To his excitement, he found the dome was made of dozens of quite small panes, which he could lift and remove. He lay full-length on the filthy rafters, eased his fingers under the glass, moved it away and looked down.

It was as if he had stumbled upon the skylight of some King Solomon's cavern, or was gazing at a secret bazaar where nothing was sold and no one moved that did not glitter. Sconces looped with necklaces of glass held fans of shaded lights towards the walls, and from the centre, like a canopy over an Oriental emperor's throne, hung an immense chandelier, terraced and tiered with crystal and blazing with a thousand candles, that shivered and turned almost imperceptibly, displaying the rainbows in their hearts. The smoke of cigars and cigarettes lifted heavily upwards, dispersing in bluish wisps about the roof, and making the people below seem mysterious and shielded. They were curiously quiet, grouped about what he knew were the gaming-tables, like priests around a sacrifice, and the quick cries of the croupiers had a ring of authority and command. Some twenty tables had been filled, each one bare and startling as an operating-table, and lit by arc-lamps whose spreading beams prolonged the pyramid sides of their immense shades and drew in the arms of the seated players. The green squared cloths, the flickering wheel, the bright counters, the shadowy figures of bystanders swaying forward to watch the spun ball settle, glimmered like the submarine glimmers of a lagoon; a white or a gold stone shines, or a sunbeam falls, or a tendril of seaweed trails, and here, as there, every movement was leisurely, except the fish-like darting of the croupier's gilt rake.

"*Messieurs, mesdames, faîtes vos jeux,*" called the dispassionate voices, and then, mechanically, almost bored, "*Les jeux sont faits. Rien ne va plus!*" There was a pause like an indrawn breath, and then, in a hubbub of whispers and sighs, broken by a gasp or exclamation, "*Le numéro onze.*" Sometimes the croupiers seemed to give the number a lingering roll off the tongue ... "*le numéro o ... o ... onze, le numéro hui ... ui ... uit,*" sometimes a brusque finality, as if turning a key ..."*le numéro un ... le numéro vingt-deux*"; in an instant the rakes were darting in and out, pulling in a heap of coloured plaques, pushing out another, and the monotonous call, like a muezzin, would be heard again—"*Messieurs, mesdames, faîtes vos jeux! Les jeux sont faits! Rien ne va plus!*"

The roulette tables were long rectangles, or T-shaped; the wheel, supervised by two croupiers, spun in a shallow crater in the middle. There were other tables, much smaller, the shape and colour of the leaves of water-lilies, without wheels, but with two or three cards floating on the green surface. A crowd several deep hemmed in the smallest, at which about a dozen people were seated. By each pair of hands was a heap of plaques, red, blue, and green, most of them square and the size of an envelope. It seemed that nothing at all was happening at this table. The hands, ranged in a circle like the numerals of a clock, seldom moved except to push one of these plaques forward, or to tap it on the cloth. The players were not even holding cards. The cards lay on the table, and they lifted a tiny corner.

Merrick remembered that Sir Maurice had told him about something called "the big table," which was in fact the smallest in size, and where all the richest people or the greatest gamblers played. Sir Maurice had said that they played for hundreds of pounds. This must be it. They would be playing baccarat. Merrick guessed, and he was right, that there might be thousands of pounds there. The lack of movement on the still green pool made the game uncanny, as if the people playing it were deaf and dumb, communicating by signs he could not see. Astonishing things must be happening, for the people watching frequently turned to one another with a gasp, or shook their heads, and the crowd never grew smaller.

Through the smoke he began to detect the features of the players. They were all in evening dress, the men in soft white shirts with black bow ties, the women in jewels and long dresses. There was one young man who seemed rather nervous, for he was constantly turning round and making comments, or trying to get the other players into conversation; Merrick noticed that they merely smiled, or made a gesture in reply, as if he had jarred their silence. He recognized Monsieur Mazarian, immobile as a debauched Buddha, his face sallow and expressionless, heavy rings under his eyes. His wife, the former mannequin, was not playing, but had a chair behind him, and now and then leant forward to whisper in his ear. She was very beautiful, and many years younger than her husband. From the laboratories of Monsieur Germain, who was playing at the same table, she had her perfumes. Hundreds of eyes which never saw their final work had bent for weeks above her dress, and round her neck and in her ears hung rubies, for which thousands had laboured in the Burmese mines and a few timely telephone conversations with the money markets paid. Merrick suspected her, because of the quite baseless tale he and Sarah had invented long ago that her husband had murdered his first wife to marry her.

Many people thought her common, and the Duchess of Mendoza, forced by the deprivations of civil war to a less extravagant table, did not speak to her.

There was a movement, a craning forward in the crowd, and the croupier pushed a pile of square red counters to the impassive merchant, bowing and smiling and retaining one or two, which he dropped into a slot beside him. Merrick thought Sir Maurice had told him that these red counters were the most valuable, and worth about fifty pounds each. M. Mazarian paid no attention, but with a slight movement of a pudgy wrist diverted half of them to his wife, who put them into her bag. A host of eyes followed them there; it seemed almost that she had put the eyes in too.

Suddenly, somewhere along the attic, Merrick heard a noise. He wriggled back and sat alert, peering into the darkness.

"Someone's playing the violin," he said to himself. He was tense and motionless. The faint sound, reaching him in stray catches, alarmed him, not because he was afraid of being caught, but because it was so thin, so mournful, so disembodied; as if a ghost were playing. His eyes were smarting from the smoke of the gaming-rooms, and he eased the glass pane back into its frame and slid away, dust all over him. The lighthouse beams fled like white shadows across a skylight, illumining some shabby French and English flags and packing-cases filled with straw. He had seen enough for one evening, and wished that he could only have found that ladder before Linda went, and brought her up here. What a sight it would have been for her! How she would have loved it! He thought he would go home now, but the eerie music drew him, and he followed it in the dark into another attic, with another illumined dome.

The sound was quite strong here, and as he lifted the pane a deep note surged up at him with unimpeded clarity and force, like the sea at Jacques-plage when the last dune was reached. He looked down and caught his breath.

"It's Hans," he said aloud.

The room below was the great ballroom, where the citizens of Oriol brought their young for *thés dansants* and gala evenings. All the lights were out except one shaded bracket in a corner, and Hans, in a black suit, was playing in its glow. High mirrored walls and curtains shutting out the forest dwarfed him, making him look lost, solitary, and yet resolute, as he had seemed that first night he had played at the Villa des Roses. Hundreds of empty chairs stared at the bare floor, but in one, half-hidden and like a shade herself, sat Judith. Her head was hunched, her cloak pulled shapelessly about her. Hans's head seemed to be embedded in the violin. He and it were one, mingled, passing and returning into one another's lives; he swayed very slightly as he played, and a giant shadow on the wall swayed in time.

Gamblers on their way into the rooms or from them entered quietly and sat down to listen, but neither he nor Judith noticed them. When he ended, a woman in a white fur cloak applauded, but stopped abruptly. Judith looked up, then sank her head into her shoulders again. Hans stood swaying, his bow lowered, his white face lifted, and it seemed almost as if he were drunk. Once more he played; and perhaps someone had told the gamblers, for so many people were thronging in to listen that a man by the door rose and fastened it back for them. Among them Merrick recognized Monsieur Ferrand, the manager of the Casino. He had an agitated air, and Merrick knew why he had come; business was being spoilt. When Hans next paused, he bustled up to Judith, who listened to him without moving. He spread out his hands, and made polite faces. Ignoring him, Judith walked over to Hans, and together they went out. Monsieur Ferrand, with infinite apologies, acting ecstasy, acting regret, steadily shepherded his customers back to the gaming-tables and chained the ballroom doors.

Merrick clambered down the iron ladder and walked home through the star-lit forest. What an evening of discoveries it had been! He was indignant with fat old Monsieur Ferrand, and thought Judith should have resisted him. He would have resisted. He would have appealed to all the people. "Don't you want to hear him?" he would have cried to them, and they would have refused to go. He wished Sarah could have been there. Linda would have been excited by the gaming-rooms and the crowd, and it would have been romantic to listen to Hans with her, up there on the roof, but Sarah would have enjoyed it most; it would have meant something special to her.

Had he known, he would have had even more cause to remember that evening, for his father had been in the crowd round the big table. Johnny was on his way from America to Paris, and for old times' sake had decided to stay the night at Oriol. He had intended to pay a call at the cottage, but shirked it at the last moment and lost a few thousand francs at roulette instead. Anne heard of it some days later, but did not tell the children. Had Merrick met him, in the mood he was in at that time, it could have been dangerous to Anne and to Merrick. And yet Sam Bryant had spoken to him, and told Anne that he had lost his looks and grown coarse; if Merrick had seen him, it might only have scattered the last embers of his romance.

Part
Three

21

Sarah told no one, apart from Anne, about her "experience," but later she began to feel rather proud of it. A change had come over her, and she knew that it had come. It was like a game she and Merrick used to play at parties, when they had to go out of the room and come back as someone different. She had come back as someone different, or rather as two people. One was like her old self, awkward, with secrets, reveries, and ardent loyalties. The other was very small and not always there; more a voice than a person, a voice that looked on, an eye that spoke. It watched her and said, you are Sarah MacManus, you are doing this or that. And though she was now two people, or one and a fraction, she had moments when she felt exposed and alone. She guessed that the world might be her enemy. Till now it had unfolded itself in objects; now she had an inkling of its nature, and sometimes felt scared and vigilant. It was as though she had been sailing up a river in exploration of a continent, abandoned to her discoveries and to her dreams about them, when suddenly an arrow had quivered in the sail, and a face looked out at her from the banks, and she knew that the country on all sides was full of faces. They might be friendly, and they might be hostile, but they were there.

The membrane of unconsciousness was broken, and something had stepped through the enchanted circle with which she had been surrounded. She thought that she now understood what Merrick meant when he talked about "people" and wanted to get away from them. They pressed upon her new exposed self. Often it excited her, because they were now more real, and even someone like Mr. Wake appeared more interesting.

She did not like her old drawings; they were much too romantic, and she tore a lot of them up. At times she was alarmed and felt a need for caution, whereas before she had merely been shy. She turned more to Anne and depended more on her; yet she looked at her in a more detached way.

She no longer idealized their relationship. They were not just Anne and Sarah, mother and daughter. There was more to it than that. She realized that she had been born. In the previous year Anne had explained the facts of life to her, which Merrick had been told at school. She had listened gravely, and at the end, when Anne asked if anything was not clear, she had answered, "I don't understand about Macduff."

"Macduff?" said Anne, bewildered.

"Yes, in *Macbeth*. It says he wasn't born of woman."

"Does it? It's years since I read *Macbeth*."

Anne got out the Shakespeare. "It's right at the end, Mother, almost on the last page." Anne found it and read it out.

> I bear a charmed life, which must not yield
> To one of woman born.

"And the next bit," said Sarah.

Anne read on.

> *Macduff*   Despair thy charm;
> And let the angel whom thou still hast serv'd
> Tell thee, Macduff was from his mother's womb
> Untimely ripp'd.

"What does it mean?" asked Sarah.

Anne thought hard, not having expected anything like this; it was important to give a correct answer.

"I think it means this," she replied, and explained a Caesarean operation.

"But he was born of woman all the same, wasn't he?" said Sarah.

"Yes, he was, but poets are allowed to pretend things that aren't exactly true. He wasn't born as most people are. That's what it means."

"But everybody has to be born of woman?" Sarah insisted.

"Oh yes, darling. Everyone."

After that Sarah considered that Shakespeare had cheated her.

The thought constantly returned to her at this time that, in order for her to be born, Anne and her father must at some period have made love to one another, and with amazement, almost with incredulity, she imagined Anne in bed with the man whose photograph she had seen. She wanted desperately to know what Merrick had been doing with Linda. It had seemed to her, on that awful night on the dune, that they had had nothing on. It was not true, but she could not be certain, and longed to know more.

Merrick spent Christmas and part of January with a school-friend in the West of England. Anne had encouraged him, not because she did not want him back, but because it would be good for him to go somewhere else. The summer holidays had ended so unpleasantly, but it had been inevitable that they should have a row, and she was glad now that Sarah's experience had brought it out, and they had got it over. She thought of asking Sam Bryant, when next he came, if it would not be possible later to get Merrick a job that would take him on journeys to those distant countries that Sam knew about—Africa, India, the East. She had some money saved for a purpose such as this, and it might lead to work that suited him.

She missed him. It was the first time he had been away from Oriol in the holidays, and it saddened her not to have him there at Christmas. He wrote to her, describing a day out with the local farmers' hunt. The master had blooded him and he had been given the brush; he asked her for some money so that he could have it mounted. She sent it to him, and he sent back a photograph of himself at the end of the day's run. It was one of the best ever taken of him; Sarah and Blanche both asked for copies.

The cottage was warm and snug, and usually Anne enjoyed the winters at Oriol. With the closing of the Casino, the hotels, and the Paris shops, the little town seemed to revert to the state in which she had first known it. Dry leaves blew about the empty squares and netless tennis-courts, and piled up at the steps of the Casino; soon there was nothing but bare branches, empty flower-beds, and shuttered fronts. A few shopkeepers hurried along the rue St. Jean, head down against the wind. The sea was white and raging, the sand heaped itself against the embankments and blew across the deserted promenade, as if fighting to recover in those few months all that had been taken from it, and after a storm the greens and fairways looked as if they had been sown with sand. Only the pines kept their green, creaking and swaying wildly, like an anchored fleet struggling to break its moorings. Oriol became bleak and Jacques-plage desolate, yet it was then that Anne felt it to be her home, and where she belonged; and she and Sarah went for long walks, returning with a voracious appetite to Blanche and the open fire.

Yet this year she felt depressed. Everybody was talking about war, forcing upon her fresh anxieties about Merrick. He would soon be sixteen; his father had not been much older at the outbreak of the first war. It seemed to her that she had made her preparations against every possible trouble except this. She had worked, so that the two of them could go to school; had brought them up according to the principles she believed in, so that they should not turn out like their father; and apart from that had left them free to develop in their own way. Two or three years longer and their circle would be broken. He was restless and adventurous. She could not afford to send him to a university. He would have to look about for a job; anyhow, he would want to do something. And as these thoughts came to her, another part of herself listened in amazement. University . . . job . . . departure . . . all this could surely have nothing to do with Merrick; for was it not only yesterday he and Sarah had turned the tee-boxes round, and not long before that he had won the prize for the under-fourteens and fallen through the dining-room roof at the Pine Hotel? And war—call-up? These words she could dismiss more easily, for if war came, then a machine took charge and there would be little any mother could do to help her son, any wife to help her husband, except think of him, write to him, and survive.

She read his letters over and over again as she lay in bed, as if they were the letters of a lover, imagining him and no one else at the events and meetings he described. She had had the photograph framed, and often looked at it. It showed him bending over the pony's neck, covered in mud and elated with his success; she could just imagine him. She wrote him her own long letters, letters that would have surprised many of her friends, full of narrative, characters, and good-natured gossip, a winter's tale. She told him about the people whom she knew he was interested in, friend or foe: how Emilio was going to London at last, to open a little restaurant of his own, how Hans might be offered a contract in America, and how religious Charlotte Wake was becoming (she frequently went to Oriol and played the harmonium in the empty church, and she left tracts with everyone). Anne liked to think of him reading the letter as she was writing it, at night, in a small room at the top of a Devon farmhouse, with the window open and the moon shining on the frosty hills. Probably, when he had read it, he would pick up a book on sailing or horsemanship; but now and then, before he went to sleep, he would remember that she was there, and even perhaps imagine her.

He returned for the last fortnight of the holidays. She and Sarah met him at Boulogne. As usual, he wore no hat or coat, despite the cold, and was leaning over the rail talking to one of the sailors. When he saw them he waved eagerly and, suit-case in hand, ran down the gangway reserved for the porters, ahead of the passengers; Mr. Harris, the purser, had arranged it as usual, though in winter with so few aboard it was not necessary. Careful not to be too demonstrative at such moments, Anne seldom said what was first in her thoughts.

"No coat!" she exclaimed instead, as she kissed him. "We don't want you in bed with flu for the rest of the holidays."

"Oh, it's not really cold, Mother. It was pretty rough, all the same. Almost everyone was sick except me."

He kissed Sarah, said she was even taller, and shook hands with M. Philippe. He was full of stories about Dartmoor and the hunting, but the moment they came in sight of the estuary and crossed the bridge to Oriol he forgot everything else. How was Blanche? Was Emilio really going to London? What was Judith doing? Was Mr. Wake still making a nuisance of himself? He jumped out at the cottage gate, hugging and tickling the protesting Blanche. Frou-frou ran to and fro in a semi-circle, jerking on her chain; and he had not been back half an hour before he and Sarah had to race off to the dunes, to watch the great white winter sea thundering in along the beach.

Anne was curious to know if he still thought of Linda. He did, but tried to keep it from her. He wrote her letters in his bedroom, which he did not give to the postman; instead he took them himself to the letter-box at the entrance to the Pine Hotel, where Anne had first met his father. He told

Linda about the hunt, hoping that she would be impressed, and at the end of each letter he wrote "Have you changed? I haven't." For several weeks she had not replied with letters, but she sent him postcards with views of Italy on one side and bald statements on the other like "This is a lovely place." "We are having a wonderful time here." "The hunt must have been great fun." She wrote to him as "Darling Merrick," and his heart beat fast when he read it; she "wished that he was there," but she never answered the question whether she had changed, and though disappointed he put it down to an inability to express herself.

He walked several times to the Villa Harlequin, approaching it through the creaking forest as he had the first time, and imagined that she would be there again playing with the spaniel puppy. There was sand on the lawn and terrace, the shutters were all closed like closed eyelids, and the house had withdrawn into itself. He remembered it as it had been a few months ago, but the laughter, activity and guests were only a background for his memory of her. He wished that she could be there alone again, as they had been before her mother arrived; those first days already seemed far-off, the days that followed had interposed themselves, and the recollections of her that came first were on Paul's shoulder, or curled up on the sofa, talk and music all round, among her friends. If only it were Easter, not winter! Perhaps at Easter she would come alone.

Anne knew that he still thought of her. She said nothing. She would have preferred him to have forgotten Linda, but his faithfulness touched her. The fortnight was far too short, and when he had gone her depression returned. The spirit had not left the house, the two women and the girl had more than enough life between them to keep it cheerful; but a spur, a spark had been removed. Certain people seem to have been born with a gift for making any place and any situation more alive. When they come into a room, everybody there awakens; when they go, those remaining become awkward, thinking of something else, as if they had been made aware of their own want of buoyancy. Some of them, still under the spell of the person who has gone, will perhaps try to imitate him or her; but it does not come off. Often nothing else distinguishes those who bring with them this heightening effect, and certainly "brilliance" is not needed to create it; it is merely that they have some native quality, delighted with the smallest detail, and curious about everyone, which is like the mountain air. Merrick was one of these people.

So Anne was left again to Judith, Mr. Wake, and the little colony of permanent residents. Judith made frequent journeys to Paris, returning gloomier each time about the international situation, each time with a longer list of refugees. There were now three families quartered on the Villa des Roses. Frau Mayer controlled them with efficiency, and continued to give Sarah lessons. Hans had played at several successful concerts in Paris and according to his mother there was little doubt he would be invited to America.

In the middle of February, to Anne's astonishment, Blanche asked if Anne thought she should get married; and to M. Philippe, of all people. He had offered her a lift to Oriol, insisted that she should sit in front with him, and suddenly proposed to her. Blanche related every detail.

"Well, my little one," he had said familiarly, ogling her. "When are we two going to make up our minds?"

Blanche's heart had started to thump. "What about?" she had asked, staring at the windscreen.

"*Eh bien*, about getting married."

"What a scandal! You!" Blanche had exclaimed; she felt she would have a heart attack.

"What's wrong with me?" he laughed. "My business is all right, and I'm not so bad, am I?" He stopped the car and bent towards her, leaning on the steering-wheel and stroking his thick moustache.

"You and your girls!" said Blanche indignantly, keeping herself tightly to herself.

"Oh, that's all over."

"That's what men always say. How do I know? Besides, you don't even go to church."

"I can go," he said. "I'm religious. Look!" He opened his shirt and brought out a medallion of St. Christopher.

Blanche glanced at it haughtily, noticed that he had hair on his chest, and turned away. "What about it?" said M. Philippe.

"I shall consider it," said Blanche.

"*Eh bien*, consider it."

283

He drove on, several times reminding her what a fine man he was, what a good business he had, and how he had not been to church lately because he had not had time.

"I shall consider it," Blanche repeated.

She had considered it at once, and made up her mind at once that she would accept him. She guessed, with the hotels and villas so empty, that Anne must at least be thinking of leaving. She would willingly have gone to England or Timbuctu with her, but this was probably her last chance of a husband, and she still wanted M. Philippe. She only asked Anne's advice because she wished to talk about it.

"What do you think?" she inquired. She was fatter than she had ever been. The oil she put so liberally into her cooking seemed to exude from her red face and hands; Merrick had once said that she would make an excellent steak.

Anne was sad, because they had been together so many years and Blanche had been her confidante. She had helped to nurse the children, she had seen them grow up, she had taught them French. But obviously it was best for Blanche to marry while she still had the opportunity; M. Philippe was a bit of a rascal, but Anne's experience of Frenchwomen told her that Blanche would be well able to manage him. Her own disappointment had not made her cynical about others' hopes; she had been much younger when she had married, and perhaps looked for too much, and Blanche was going into it with her eyes open.

"I think you should take him," she replied. "I shall miss you dreadfully, Blanche, but it will be pleasant for you to have a home of your own."

"I shall never forget you," Blanche declared. "I shall come to you whenever you want me. I shall do your washing . . ." she seized Anne's hands, kissed them fervently, and burst into tears, but soon recovered. "I'll teach him if he tries to trick me!" she exclaimed. "Let him try, and I'll show him what kind of woman I am." She wagged a red finger menacingly; and perhaps, if M. Philippe had seen her then, he might have changed his mind.

Sarah could not believe it. She pushed her hair back and looked straight at both of them, her lips parted, her eyes wide.

"Blanche! Going to get married! But you said you would never marry!"

"She's changed her mind," said Anne.

"But, Blanche, you were going to be a nun!"

Blanche shook her head regretfully. "It is not the life for me," she answered. "I am not good enough. I shall have children. Six children. Three girls and three boys. Perhaps more."

She had begun already to live in the future. At present M. Philippe occupied a room above the Pine Hotel garage. He would have to give that up, of course, though he would continue to drive his taxi. They would buy a little house at Oriol, somewhere near the beach, if it was not too expensive. She cut advertisements out of the papers and discussed them with Anne. She would take in washing, but Anne's she would do free. Sarah shared her excitement, although it shocked her that Blanche could change her mind so quickly.

Blanche informed M. Philippe that she accepted him, allowed him to kiss her, rejected other suggestions of his, and brought out of her bag an announcement of the engagement, which she and Anne had composed. It was to be published in the *Echo d'Oriol*. M. Philippe asked why there was such a hurry, but she insisted, and it was published the same week. Even then she remained formal and correct with him, allowing him nothing but an occasional kiss, repelling his practised hands, and waiting until he had been signed, sealed, and delivered before her own surrender. She drew most but not all of her money out of the account Anne kept for her, and Anne and Judith both gave her cheques. It was to be a white wedding, at Oriol, in the church of St. Pierre, in front of *monsieur le curé*. All the surviving relations were to be invited; she had made a list of nearly forty.

"Ah, if only Maman were alive to see me!" she sighed. It distressed her deeply that she had no dowry to speak of, but she consoled herself with the thought of all the aunts, cousins, and second-cousins, who had scoffed so subtly at her chances, watching her as she sailed along the aisle. "Why, *cousine Angèle!*" she exclaimed to Anne. "Her father is a baker, and doing well enough, and she is not much younger than I am, and still she has nobody."

Anne offered her more time off so that she could have everything ready; she would not take it, and went about the house-work with her habitual zeal. But every night the light in her bedroom burned on into the small hours, as the plump red fingers stitched away at the trousseau and the white dress, and Anne suspected that she was already making baby-linen.

"Ah, it is beautiful to be getting married," she said once to Anne. "Why do you not marry again?"

"I? Why should I want to get married?"

"Ah, it is so beautiful. Of course, it could not be in a church, that would be a pity. But *monsieur le maire* would marry you, and you could be in white all the same."

Anne smiled. "No, thank you, Blanche," she said. "Not even to be in white."

Long ago she had put the idea out of her head. In the early years after her separation she had thought of it for the children's sakes; it would have helped her with their education, she had not by then grown used to the office at the golf-club, and it might have done Merrick good to have a step-father. She had refused two offers, and now the thought no longer even suggested itself. She would at once have forgotten Blanche's remark, but for a surprising interview the same day with Mr. Wake. It was early afternoon, and she was just about to turn off the fire and shut up the office, when he came in from the course. Neither of them spent long at the club in the winter, for there were few players and little work; some days she did not go at all.

Mr. Wake wore a woollen scarf and a thick overcoat, and had a red nose.

"Infernal weather we're having!" he growled.

"It's all right if you keep moving," she said.

"Nowhere to move to. Everything's shut. What on earth do you do with yourself?"

"Oh, I read, and I go for walks."

"Humph. I can't settle down to a book. Of course you've got those children of yours to look after." He fussed about, picking things up and putting them down again. "I hear that housekeeper of yours is getting married," he said.

"Yes, she is."

"Humph." He blew his nose. "M. Philippe, eh? Well, that's not a bad match for her. I wonder what made him pick on her."

"She'll make a good wife."

"Oh, I don't doubt it. Capable creature. But Philippe's a rogue. Always out with the girls, eh? I suppose it's the threat of war, and all the rest of it. People getting restless."

"It may be that," Anne answered; she had wondered about M. Philippe's motives herself.

"You ever thought of marrying again?" Mr. Wake asked abruptly.

It surprised her greatly that twice in the same day she had been asked a question that had not been put to her for years. She was about to reply when she saw Mr. Wake's face. He had put in his monocle, and was favouring her with the kind of look she could only think of as "meaning"; it gave him the air of a villain in an old-fashioned melodrama.

"I gave up all idea of it long ago," she said.

"Humph. It's a pity. You're a capable woman. And your children'll be growing up one of these days, eh?"

He followed up this innuendo with a still more meaning look. She repeated her reply, and got rid of him as soon as possible. His remark about the children had annoyed her, but on the way home she burst out laughing. There was no doubt of it; he had been taking soundings.

"So it is to be me," Anne thought. "A capable woman. That's what he wants. The old fox!"

She laughed so much that she almost had to tell Blanche. She decided against it out of kindness to Mr. Wake, which she knew was misplaced, and because she might have guessed wrong. She did not think so, and she had not. For several weeks she became the object of meaning looks and weighted allusions. Then his manner changed to courteous consideration, even gallantry, which made work at the office pleasanter and slightly comical; but had no other influence on her.

22

owards the end of March Judith came round to see Anne. Her face was drawn, her hair untidier than ever, and her agate eyes had lost their colour; she fumbled nervously and continually with the folds of her cloak. She hunched forward by the fire, taking off an old felt hat, and Anne's dismay must have shown in her expression, for Judith said at once in a dead voice:

"How frightful everything is!" and added jealously, "Doesn't it have any effect on you?"

"Sometimes," said Anne. "I shall be glad when the winter is over."

"I shan't even be glad of that. At least wars don't break out in the winter."

"Oh, the war," said Anne thoughtfully.

"I'd forgotten. You don't read the newspapers."

"I read them, but it seems to me there's nothing much we can do about them."

"I suppose not, I suppose not." Judith's eyes strayed round the room. "You're so tranquil and English, Anne," she said. "Sometimes I admire and sometimes I detest it. You're all the same. Wherever you go, you take your private Channel with you. Even you, and you've lived in France all your life."

Anne was tolerant of Judith's ill-humour; for years people had assumed that she had no anxieties of her own.

"Anyhow, I didn't come to talk about politics," Judith went on. "I want you to put some of my business affairs in order. Can you spare the time to do some secretarial work for me?"

"Of course. How long would you want me for?"

"It shouldn't take more than a couple of weeks. You can type and do shorthand, of course?"

"Yes. Would you want me each day?"

"Oh, you can suit yourself about that."

"It's only that some mornings Mr. Wake wants me. I'm free most afternoons and evenings."

"You must have the patience of a saint to go on working for that man. I can hardly stay in the same room with him."

Anne smiled and shrugged her shoulders.

"I'll pay you the usual rate for such work, whatever it is," said Judith. "Would you rather have it in francs or in sterling?"

"You needn't pay me," Anne replied. "My salary goes on the whole year round. I'd be glad to help you."

"Oh, nonsense! You must be paid."

"I'd rather not."

"Well, I shall pay you, whether you want it or not. I warn you, there'll be quite a lot to do, and I've always had my own way of looking after things. I'm pretty sure it won't have been your way." She lifted her jaw, pressing forward the upper lip. "Elizabeth Mayer would choose this moment to leave me," she said.

"Oh, so it's definite?"

"Yes, it's definite. Hans is to give a coast-to-coast tour in America in the spring, and he's got engagements for the whole summer in Paris. They sail in a fortnight." Her eyes brightened. "It's exciting for him," she said affectionately. "It's his big chance to make his name."

"You've done a great deal for them," said Anne. "I'm afraid you'll miss them."

"Yes, I shall miss them. Elizabeth is an old martinet, but she's been company for me, and she's kept things in order. And Hans I've always been fond of. I knew when he was a little boy that he was a born musician, and I never cease to tell Elizabeth that he'd be better now on his own. He ought to go to America without her, but she won't leave him. She's to be his wet-nurse and publicity agent and campaign manager and Heaven knows what, all rolled into one."

"I think it's a pity, too," said Anne. "But I suppose she's got no one else."

"She ought to find someone else," Judith declared vigorously. "I've known several infant prodigies—not that Hans is any longer an infant— and the one essential with all of them at a certain point is to get them away from their mothers. It'd be much better for him if he had a completely impersonal manager who didn't know Schubert from Paganini." She sat up and darted a look at Anne. "What would *you* do if that Merrick of yours were a genius?" she asked; she did seem to be in an aggressive mood that morning.

Anne laughed. "What would Merrick do?" she replied.

Judith sat back, huddling her cloak. "Yes, that's probably the answer. I expect Hans and she will have more rows, and then he'll fall in love. Still, they both deserve a success. They've stuck to one another." She got up; Anne noticed how bowed her shoulders were. "Well, when will you come?"

"As soon as you like."

"They leave this week-end. Shall we say your free mornings to start with, beginning on Monday?"

"Isn't that too soon for you? You don't look well, Judith."

"It's my own fault. I allow things to upset me too easily. And I abominate the winter. I wish my father had chosen his Oriol in the south." She pulled on the felt hat without troubling to look in a mirror. "I'll expect you at ten o'clock on Monday. There's a typewriter at the villa. I'm most grateful to you."

Judith was again on the verge of a breakdown. For months the organizations with which she was in touch had been sending her reports concerning the treatment of Jews in nazified Austria; on each of her visits to Paris she had met new groups of refugees and heard more horrors. She could not take these events calmly. Those who refused to believe them, seeking for an excuse to turn a blind eye and a cold shoulder, roused her to violent fits of rage. She would condone nothing, she would listen to no explanations. Although she continued her subscriptions to cultural societies, she had abandoned her personal interest in them and now concerned herself solely with relief. Despairing of rousing humanity, or even a Ministry, to her own pitch of indignation, she confronted her wealthy fellow Jews with their responsibility, joining committees with those who were already active, and chiding on those who were reluctant, to subscribe, to adopt, to agitate. She became the bane of many and the admiration of many; her arguments were unanswerable, and her eyes burned with the exaltation not only of a woman with a righteous cause, but also of one who has at last found a part in which she believes she can achieve results worthy of herself. Something noble arose in her. She expected no gratitude, and often got little; she acted with selfless conviction, forgetting even the persecutors in her devotion to the victims, rescuing those whom she could rescue, helping, restoring, and rehabilitating. There was an element of revenge in all she did upon the confusion of her past life, which now seemed to her, unjustly, to have been futile and wasted. One of her old friends in Paris said that she now reminded him of the prophetess Deborah in the Old Testament, or of Judith with the head of Holofernes.

While she was thus employed, her personal troubles flew away from her. She did not care what was said to her face or behind her back; she took even less thought for her appearance. But her work, and the terrible stories that prompted it, exhausted her. She had no gift for organization; her role was to rouse, to enlist, and to provide money. She was not even capable of sustained effort over a long period, but rather of feverish bouts of energy such as had resulted the year before last in the freeing of Hans and his mother, and in recent months of others. When these were over, she collapsed and sank again into moody foreboding isolation; Frau Mayer, who had been the organizer of her work, had then taken charge of Judith herself. The occupation of Prague had coincided with one of these sombre fits. Already the reports were beginning to reach her from Czechoslovakia, and on top of all this had come the news that Frau Mayer and Hans were leaving.

When Anne went to work for her, Judith tried to disguise the state she was in. She did not mind admitting her state of mind to Frau Mayer, who was also Jewish, had experienced misery, and known her so long; but pride forbade her to betray herself to Anne. Anne guessed a great deal. Old Emily was continually sighing and muttering that Judith should go away for a rest, while Judith's almost haggard appearance and irritable impatience told their own story. Consequently Anne treated her in her own mind as an invalid, using the opposite technique to Frau Mayer's; where Frau Mayer had been despotic, Anne was persuasive and soothing; subtle, where Frau Mayer had been blunt; where Frau Mayer had responded to Judith's outbursts with a quick, harsh retort, Anne yielded, said little, and in the end achieved the same result, so that within a few days Judith recovered some of her spirits and was in better health.

Anne was a quick worker, but as she only had a few weeks to spare she went to the villa most afternoons and often stayed to supper. After she had answered the day's letters, she turned to Judith's past business, and it seemed to her that Judith was a woman entirely without method. Her life appeared to have been a conglomeration of impulses, some of them merely capricious, which she had pursued eagerly for varying intervals in the past and then abandoned to those who benefited from them. Her desk and cupboards were often their only witness, for she had evidently forgotten about many of them and left the paying of subscriptions to her Paris lawyer, who had a sum for this purpose and sent her the receipts. These Anne found mixed up with private letters, bank balances, reports of annual general meetings, and appeals for money; several had not even been opened. Judith had thrown nothing away, hoarding the relics of her enthusiasms with an impartiality that would have been the delight of a biographer, and a disorder that would have been his despair. Some of them, like the Picasso, a few letters from Proust, and a number of limited editions, were valuable and she knew where they were; but scattered in several rooms and a dozen drawers Anne unearthed stacks of letters and expensive short-lived magazines which might have had some value and were all evidence of a period. As a traveller carries on his luggage the labels of hotels he has stayed in, Judith had accumulated at the Villa des Roses the labels of intellectual phases she had voyaged through: labels of dadaism, cubism, surrealism, communism—there were heaps of pamphlets, some correspondence, and an acknowledgement of a donation—Buddhism, Yogi-ism, and so on. She had read most of the modern Europeans in their original language, and there on her shelves, worn and faded as if with their recent arrival at immortality, and not yet refurbished as classics, were the novels of the first world war, *Sergeant Grischa, All Quiet on the Western Front*, Barbusse, together with Huxley and Pirandello,

Gide and Thomas Mann, Shaw and Joyce, Wassermann and D. H. Lawrence, and the banned monuments of the time, like *Lady Chatterley*, *Ulysses*, and *The Well of Loneliness*, in their unexpurgated editions. She had read them all, and taken them in; she understood the faults of each, she knew what each stood for. Downstairs, bought rather than collected by her father, were the old masters in their gilt bindings: Goethe, Tolstoy (in French), Shakespeare, Racine, Cervantes, Dante, and the rest. She had read them too, or most of them.

It astonished Anne that a woman of such culture should be so messy. Anne imagined that her financial affairs must be chaotic, unless the lawyer had complete control of them; she thought with concern of all the rascals and charlatans who must have imposed upon her during the last twenty-five years, of all the intellectual bubbles she had helped to blow up, the lost causes she had helped to lose. But when she met the lawyer he gave her a different picture. He was a small fragile Jew with deep-set eyes and delicate hands which, as he spoke, seemed to flutter of their own accord. He had acted for Arthur Friedmann at the birth of Oriol.

"I know, I know," he sighed. "She has always been like that. She would never take a secretary, no more than she would buy a car, until Frau Mayer more or less forced herself on her. It surprises me that she has even entrusted you with so much. And yet, in their way, her private affairs have been better ordered than those of many more conventional people."

"I'm glad to hear it," said Anne, smiling. "But I find it hard to believe."

"I've known her since she was a child. You knew her father, I think?"

"Yes, I knew him well."

"A man of great ability, but he paid too little attention to her. He cared only for the son. She grew up without family care—why, imagine going off to America, Canada rather—you remember?—and leaving her behind! She had plenty of money, but she had too little affection. That was always my opinion, and I told her father so."

"I'm surprised," said Anne. "He was such a kind man."

"Kind, yes. His gift to you, for example; that passed through me. But with Judith he had a blind spot. After the son died, I don't think he wanted to have anything to do with his family. And she was left to herself. Ah," the pale hands fluttered, "the things she did when she was young, the friends she made, the societies she joined! I used to see her . . ." His voice trailed away in horror from the memory.

"Surely a lot of people must have exploited her?"

"A few at that time, a few. But she soon learnt about them. You say she has no method, Mrs. MacManus. Perhaps not, as you and I understand it, but she has an instinct. That came from her father, if nothing else in her character did. Her investments . . . you know she does them all herself?"

"I've found letters about them all over the place."

"Oh, of course. All tangled up with her private correspondence and poems from promising young men, no doubt. Yet they have all been successful, or nearly all. I used to implore her to put them in the hands of a broker, or at least to take advice; and now . . . well, I almost ask her for advice myself. Even her most eccentric purchases. . . ." They were in Judith's sitting-room, and his hands gestured at the walls. "These paintings, for example, these to me meaningless triangles and squares—they go up in value every year. Some of the young men she has started off are now celebrities." He mentioned one of them.

"She's a strange mixture," said Anne.

"Is she? Is she?" murmured the little lawyer. "You know, as I grow older I become less interested in my clients' business and more fascinated by my clients. I always tell my writer friends that if they want to know about people they should consult the lawyer, the accountant, and the doctor. We are the ones who know. A priest may be there at the end, but we have been there all the time and we *must* be there at the end. And I have to be there after the end; often for months and months, settling debts, arguing about taxes, with the present delay in Ministries. And I amuse myself in trying to discover a thread in people's lives. What is the thread in Judith's life?"

Anne thought for a little. "I should say she was a woman of the mind," she suggested, and added: "All the same, she is tremendously generous, and generosity comes from the heart." She thought that this had been a foolish answer, contributing nothing.

"An intellectual, of course. And, as you say, generous. But what is the thread?"

He gazed at her, questioning, as if she were a projection of himself, and answered himself. "She should have married, Mrs. MacManus, she should have married. The thread has been that she has never found a husband. Men have been frightened of her brain, her quickness. And of course her looks, her height, her appearance—all that has been against her. It has been her tragedy."

"Did she have no offers when she was young?" Anne asked.

"Offers, yes, of a kind. And she had her young men," said the lawyer, dismissing it. He seemed to have other confidences about her, but was not intending to pass them on. "She did not allow herself to be hoodwinked, not after she had learnt; and she learnt quickly. She has never allowed herself to be hood-winked since. I can promise you that she knows where everything is in this house, and the contents of everything; even of the envelopes you say are unopened. She has not opened them because she knows they are not worth opening. Let me see one of them."

Anne gave him one at random.

"1931," he said. "An invitation to a ball."

"Isn't that worth opening?" Anne said, laughing.

"Presumably not, in her opinion. Besides, she never goes to such affairs."

"But why does she keep them?" Anne asked.

He shrugged his shoulders. "I've no idea. Some people do."

"It makes it difficult for a secretary," said Anne.

"Ah, well. Till now she has never bothered with a secretary. It has all been here," he tapped his forehead. "All perfectly orderly. And her memory is phenomenal."

Despite this information, Anne insisted on introducing her own version of method into Judith's affairs. She made an inventory of the whole house; Emily accompanied her suspiciously, like a witch. She catalogued the books, the pictures, and the gramophone records. She put the letters together and tied them up in bundles. She filed the correspondence; one file for Judith's investments, another for her artistic ventures, another for her philanthropic ones, another for the property in Oriol, another for the Pine Hotel, the golf-club, the Villa des Roses. She enjoyed herself, for she liked order, and the subjects were full of interest and memories. She discovered a yellowing old photograph of Arthur Friedmann as a young man; rather dandified, with a high stiff collar and even then a rose in his buttonhole, even then a remote look. She would have taken him for a poet rather than a business man.

"Do you want this?" she asked Judith.

Judith glanced briefly at it. "No," she said. "You can keep it."

But when they came to a photograph of her brother James, she held it to the light and gazed at it for some time.

"You never knew him, did you?" she said abruptly.

"No." Arthur Friedmann had once showed Anne this same photograph. She had forgotten it. The brother, though ugly and with glasses, had a lively intelligent face. He looked far more Jewish than Judith. Judith had a hooked nose; but with her height, and her sandy hair, Anne had never thought her particularly Jewish in appearance.

"Oh, how clever he was!" said Judith. "I was so envious of him. My father named Jacques-plage after him. There's no Judith-plage," she added, with a hint of sourness. "No one has immortalized me." She sat down holding the photograph in front of her. "How long ago it all is!" After a silence she laughed, and added with gaiety: "Shall we name something after me? One of the golf-courses? Or a restaurant? The restaurant Judith. That would sound good."

Sometimes she helped Anne with the work, but she was more hindrance than help. For a few minutes, sitting on the floor among a heap of papers, she would get on with it, but soon she came across a letter or a magazine and began to read it; it would remind her of something else and start her on a search, and so whole mornings passed. She still wanted to pay Anne and suggested the same weekly sum that she got at the golf-club; but Anne refused, telling her it was a labour of love. "Besides," she said, "you've been very good to Merrick and Sarah. It's I who owe you something."

One day, in the attic, she came across a large cardboard box. Inside, carefully wrapped in tissue paper, was a collection of small ornaments: artificial flowers and jewellery, made out of beads, wire, scraps of glass, and metal, with here and there a semi-precious stone. They were like the presents and decorations she had admired last year on the Christmas tree, and she wondered where Judith had bought them. It occurred to Anne that she would have liked to buy one of the brooches for herself.

"What would you like done with these?" she asked.

Judith's eyes suddenly lighted up. She took several from the box and turned them over in her long fingers, tenderly, affectionately.

"Do you like them?" she said.

"I think they're lovely. Where do they come from?"

"I made them myself," Judith replied. She sat with her amber beads dangling, gazing at the ornaments with her dark eyes and fingering the workmanship, like a child fingering a new toy. "I could have earned my own living all right, if I'd had to. Sometimes I wish it had been necessary."

"But they're works of art," Anne exclaimed.

"Yes, I really believe they are." Judith put them back in the box. "Leave them in the attic, Anne. Perhaps there'll be another Christmas." She lingered over the last one, ruggeder than the others in design but beautifully wrought: a figure of one of the Etaples fishing-girls. "Yes, it can be restful to work sometimes with your hands," she said, "but I suppose only sometimes. It calms the mind. Perhaps that's why your young Merrick is even-tempered." She laughed. "Compared with me, anyhow. Or perhaps he gets it from you. Were you always so calm, Anne?" She turned to her with a look in which there was no trace of mockery.

"I don't think I was ever temperamental. When I was a girl, I was less placid."

"There was your marriage. Wasn't that unsettling when he left you?"

"Oh yes, for a time. Then I started again."

"I should like to start again," Judith said: and then, with the cynicism which was one of her defences against self-revelation, "but I suppose it would all be the same again."

Judith came to supper sometimes at the cottage, and played Initials and Analogies with Anne and Sarah. Sarah and she had in common their sensitivity to injustice and their passion to end it; Sarah's ubiquitous, childish and astonished, Judith's concentrated and implacable.

"I'm glad you had her brought up in France," she told Anne, with whom she would often stay talking till late at night.

"It was necessity rather than choice, though I'm glad of it now."

"You made a virtue of it. Those English girls' schools! And the German ones were worse. France is the only place to bring up children."

Anne reminded Judith that Merrick was at school in England, and seemed to be happy there.

"Well, perhaps England is the place for boys," Judith conceded, and at once contradicted herself. "That's the trouble. It's too much the place for boys, men, the male," she said, scoffing at the word "male." "Everything is done to encourage a population of solid males. Sport for males, education for males, careers for males, a whole huge Empire, all for males. The only reservation I would make in England's favour is that the mania was never carried as far as in Germany. Of course Merrick is happy. He's good-looking, he plays games well, he rides horses, he's fairly sensible without being too obviously clever, and I should say he'll carry out whatever male job is laid at his feet efficiently. But if he were an artist, if he had anything at all irregular about him, his life would be a torment."

"He's not a complete clod," Anne said pleasantly.

"No, he's not a clod. Far from it. He has charm and good manners, and I do find him intelligent, but he'll never have a struggle. England was created for and by boys like Merrick. If he hadn't lived in France, and had your excellent upbringing, he would already have begun to look down on the French. In a year or two he would be calling them Frogs and saying they were dirty and unreliable. And in middle age he would talk publicly about their immorality, whatever that means, and sneak off to Paris privately for lascivious week-ends. As he has lived here, we shall be spared all that."

One night Anne took Judith into Sarah's room. They had been talking late, Sarah was asleep, Blanche in bed, and the moon shone invisibly above the cottage, bathing the garden in a radiance of pearl-grey light and olive shadows. The room was like the inside of a luminous grey shell, and along one wall stirred the reflection of a curtain ruffled by the breeze. Sarah lay on her side, her arms and shoulders beneath the blankets; her hair made an aureole round her head, and Anne remembered Judith's saying that one day she would be beautiful. She longed to caress the calm forehead, but feared to wake her. There were books on the bed-table, the window-ledge, and the floor by the bed, and on the walls the pictures and photographs of Sarah's heroes; her drawing-paper and box of crayons were on her chair. Anne turned to Judith, and saw that her eyes were full of tears. She showed her Merrick's room, with its pictures of ships, the fox's brush, and his adventure books. Judith gave it a quick glance.

"Yes, it is as I would have expected," she said. "By the way, what about Linda? Is he still in love with her?"

"I don't think he was ever exactly in love."

"Of course he was, my dear. I hear that frightful mother of hers is going to open up the villa again at Easter."

"I hadn't heard that." Nor was Anne pleased to hear it; she had hoped that she would see no more of Lady Wildenstein.

"He'll go back there, I suppose," said Judith. "Lady Wildenstein knows how to give people a good time. What will you do about it?"

"I don't know," Anne replied. "I suppose I shall wait and see."

"The old British motto. Well, it's no good my trying to give you advice. You manage things far better than I ever have. You're a clever woman, Anne."

"I?"

"Well, perhaps not clever. But you have common-sense, and in the long run that is probably more valuable."

23

Spring arrived, spring of 1939. Once again the shutters were being taken down from the pavilions and Trianons in the forest, once again the Renaults, the Rolls Royces, and the Packards began to glide along the rue St. Jean, once again Madame Menard, wrapping her shawl about her shoulders, took up her pitch outside the Casino, the Italian waiters returned, Mr. Masterton let out some hacks, Jerry reopened his shop, and the caddies resumed their trek from Etaples. But this year anyone could have seen that things were different. Not all the villas opened, and the value of property was sinking; the estate agents had on their books several "desirable residences" which in previous years had been unprocurable. Some of the big shop-keepers were trying to sell their branches at Oriol; finding no buyers, they closed them down and left iron grills across the once-glittering façades. The luxurious hotels opened only one wing or a couple of floors; the remainder were not to see the sun again until, three years later, it came in through shattered roofs and the swastika waved over them.

A week before Easter, Anne started again to go regularly to the office. Entries for the Easter meeting at the golf-club were still large, and she had finished her work with Judith. They were sorry it was over. It had meant company for them both. Anne, concerned about Judith's health, persuaded her to take a secretary three mornings in the week and went round with Sarah in the evenings to visit her. She was glad to be quit of one part of the work. She had had to read the reports about the treatment of the Jews; indeed, Judith had taken a kind of fierce pleasure in forcing them upon her. Although she had chosen to live her life within such a small compass, she did not flee from what she knew to be evil or pretend that it was not there. Her recollections of the maimed and wounded men she had cared for in girlhood, at the end of the first war, had never left her; she had been present when her father, convinced to the last moment that he would survive, had died in her mother's arms. She found it well-nigh impossible to believe that human beings could commit, in the twentieth century after Christ, the acts that the Nazis were committing, but the evidence was there. Its effect upon her disappointed Judith, since she did not show it to the full; but she thought deeply, unhappily about these things, and even then felt that she herself, if only by remaining apart, bore some responsibility for them. She went sometimes to the English church, and prayed for the victims to be saved and the hearts of the persecutors to be turned, and she prayed in her room and in the depths of her own heart.

One evening she took the tram to Etaples and walked out to the military cemetary on the far side of the estuary. She laid flowers on the graves of her father and of James Friedmann; on James's there was already a fresh cluster, with a few words of remembrance in Judith's handwriting. The lighthouse sprang out across the water, swinging intermittent beams over the five thousand white tombstones and making them seem like a camp of sleeping Arabs. On her knees, gazing into the starlit sky, she implored the spirit that was her God to avert war; Merrick was constantly in her thoughts, but she tried to think of mankind. She remembered the good people and good acts during her life and set their tiny weight against the Goliath of evil-doing. Her own troubles, such as they had been and were, appeared infinitesimally small to her, the pomposities and grotesque attentions of Mr. Wake pathetic; but the dislike she had always felt for the self-indulgence of many of the visitors to Oriol grew stronger.

When Merrick returned for the Easter holidays, one of his first questions was about Linda. Anne and he were sitting together in the back of M. Philippe's taxi. Deliberately he had said nothing about Linda until they were passing the side-road to the Villa Harlequin; here it seemed natural to mention her. He tried to speak casually.

"Are the Wildensteins back?" he asked.

"I don't think so, but Judith told me they were coming. Have you heard from Linda?"

"I had a postcard about a month ago. She said they'd be here for a few days."

"I expect Linda will come round as soon as they arrive."

"I should jolly well hope so," said Merrick, and changed the subject.

He had arrived uncertain whether he still cared for Linda, but the sight next morning of the Villa Harlequin, with the trees turning soft green, the primulas out, and rosebuds beginning to form on the wire round the tennis-court, left him in no doubt that he did. The windows were open, carpets were being beaten, and blankets had been set out to air on the terrace. He recognized one of the maids.

"When are they coming back?" he asked.

"In a few days, I think."

"Do you know who's coming? I mean, only Lady Wildenstein, or a lot of people?"

"Oh, the house will be full. There is to be a dance."

"Oh!" He felt disappointed that Linda had not told him of this; but perhaps, when she last wrote to him, it had not been decided. He walked away, not having brought himself to ask if she would be coming. But of course she would be, if there was to be a dance; probably it was being given for her.

His old anxiety returned about not having a dinner-jacket. At a dance everyone was certain to be in evening dress. Merrick did not like to mention it to Anne again; besides, a dinner-jacket had to be made, and there would not be time. He went to see Jerry.

"Hello," said Jerry. "Back again?"

"Yes. How's it going?"

"Not bad. More people than I expected. Want a game?"

"Any time you're free. By the way, how tall are you?"

"Five foot ten. Why?"

"You haven't got a dinner-jacket you've grown out of, have you? Something that'd fit me."

"Good Lord, no. I haven't got one at all. What on earth do *you* want one for?"

"Oh, I might have to go to a dance."

"Nobody wears them in Oriol, except at the Casino. I hate the things myself."

"So do I," said Merrick, "but this is a dance at a villa. I suppose I ought to have one."

"Lord, no. No one'd expect you to. Go in a suit."

"I'll have to."

"You'll be all right," said Jerry, laughing at him. "Where's it to be?"

"Lady Wildenstein's."

"Oh God, is she coming back? I should think you could go in a bathing-suit there, and it wouldn't be noticed."

The Wildensteins arrived, and Anne began to hear about the dance, which was evidently to be a big affair. Judith had already received her invitation. She was indignant that people should spend so much money now on such things, and had sent a curt refusal to Sir Maurice. As soon as he arrived, he telephoned her to express his regret.

"Won't you stay just for that night?" he begged her in his suavest tones. "Paul Walker is going to dance, and Helen will be so disappointed if you don't come. Stay for that night."

The voice at the other end startled him. "I am staying," Judith retorted. "I shall be here at my own house."

"You're not ill, I hope, my dear?"

"No, I'm not ill. I disapprove of your party, or dance, or whatever it is. That is why I am not coming."

"But, Judith . . ."

She interrupted him vehemently. He was in his wife's bedroom. Lady Wildenstein lay in bed giving instructions to a relay of servants, and Judith's voice, strident as it poured through the receiver, made her look up in amazement.

"What on earth's the matter with her?" she exclaimed. "Tell her not to shout."

He held the receiver away from him, put his hand over it, and shrugged his shoulders.

"I think she has a bee in her bonnet," he apologized.

"Why isn't she coming?"

"Oh, she is mad . . . My dear Judith," he resumed courteously into the telephone, "I can hear you quite well without your shouting. Really, I think you are exciting yourself about nothing . . ." he went on, polite and conciliatory, for some time, before realizing that she had rung off. "She really is mad," he said irritably, putting down the receiver.

"Well, go on, tell me. What is it? Why isn't she coming?"

He threw out his hands.

"If you please, she thinks we should not give a dance. We should spend every penny we have on relief funds, it seems, on refugees, Heaven knows what."

"You mean to say *that's* why she's not coming!"

"It seems so."

Sir Maurice felt unhappy. Judith had been almost insulting, and his wife was seldom in a good temper before her face had been made up.

"Well, that settles that," she declared, and taking her list of guests from the bed-table she scratched out Judith's name. "She never comes into my house again, that's certain. What cheek to . . ." Her maid came into the room, and she went on in a level tone of surprised indifference, "What an astonishing idea! If no one's going to be allowed to enjoy themselves whenever there's an international crisis, isn't the world going to be a gay place! Have those electricians come, Jeanne?"

"Yes, milady. They're waiting downstairs."

She turned to her husband. "Maurice, I think I shall have the platform for Paul to dance on put over the terrace. Part of it's under cover, and if it did rain, people could watch from indoors—it'd be too awful if we had to cancel it. Don't you agree?"

"Yes, that will be excellent," he answered vaguely, "excellent."

He was still thinking of Judith. He sat on the lawn, turning the leaves of a superb new book, in which all the museum collections of china in Europe were illustrated; he had contributed a chapter himself, but still he could not get her out of his mind, and without telling his wife he went indoors and wrote Judith a cheque for her funds.

Merrick could not understand why the invitation did not come. He could not believe that Linda had forgotten him; only a month ago he had had a postcard from her. He knew that she had been at the Villa Harlequin two days, without a word to him. He was too proud to go there himself. If he had not heard about the dance, he would have gone, but now it would look as if he were cadging an invitation. He took the postman aside, and asked him if he was sure he had not forgotten something, but in front of Anne and Sarah he pretended that he didn't care, and had heard anyhow it was to be a party only for older people. He felt humiliated. They both understood him, and were indignant with Linda and Lady Wildenstein, and this suspense and sense of insult united them.

On the morning of the day before the party the envelope arrived, addressed to Anne. His heart gave a bound, but he pretended not to have seen it. The invitation was written out for all three of them.

"Well, I shan't go," said Anne.

"Oh, Mother, you must. You never go out, and it'll be wonderful."

"I enjoy myself all right," she said.

"But you must, Mother." The delay, the humiliation, were forgotten at once. "I'll dance with you. Sam'll be there, and dozens of people you know. I expect Mr. Wake will be there. I'll make *him* dance with you."

"That settles it," said Anne. "I certainly shan't come. And if you think I should have to fall back on Mr. Wake . . ."

"Oh, I didn't mean it like that, you know."

"No, I shan't come. Seriously. They're your friends."

"I shan't either," Sarah said.

"Oh, *you* will."

He tried to persuade Anne, but she had made up her mind. He would enjoy it much more without her; if she went, he would know that she was there, and imagine that she was keeping an eye on him. Besides, it would be a very smart party, and she had no dress for it. He gave up the attempt. At heart he knew that he would prefer to be without her, and that she too knew this. But he insisted that Sarah should come. He wanted to show her off, and as there would be a crowd he could not expect to be alone with Linda for long; so Sarah could not be an embarrassment. It was time that she was seen a little. She would be younger than all the rest, but so much younger that it would not matter; and she looked unusual, and he wanted her to gain confidence in herself.

"I'll look after her," he told Anne. "I really will this time. I'll know all the people. She must come."

"Well, I don't know, Merrick. Will that cousin be there?"

"Oh." He had forgotten about Boris. "I'll find out."

It was no longer difficult to go to the villa. He ran round, hoping vainly for a sight of Linda, and found the place in confusion. A van blocked the drive, and gilt chairs were being taken out. Redfern told him that everyone was at Oriol.

"Are there going to be a lot of people tomorrow night?"

"Are there! You coming?"

"Oh yes. Who'll be there?"

"All the old crowd from last year. And half Oriol."

"Is Boris staying at the villa?"

"Boris? He's in America or somewhere. Why, are you jealous?"

"Certainly not," said Merrick. He wanted to ask about Linda, but it would give away that he had not seen her.

"You see," he told Anne. "It'll be perfectly all right. Do let Sarah come."

"Well, you ask her. If you can persuade her, and promise you'll look after her, she can. Though I don't know what she can wear."

Sarah took a lot of persuading. She was longing to go, but dreaded it; and the fearful problem of clothes seemed to settle it.

"But no one will expect you to have something from Paris," he said, persistent. "What about that blue dress?"

"Oh, Merrick ..." She laughed at his inability to understand such things. "It's frightful."

"If you brush your hair back and hold your head up, you'll look stunning. If you don't go, I won't."

"I bet you will."

"I won't. Don't you want to go?" She was silent. "Of course you do. I'll stay with you."

"You'll be with Linda. Besides, that'd be obvious."

"All right, I won't. Whatever you like. But please come, Sarah. You've got to get used to people one day, and there aren't often parties like this."

Furtively she asked Anne's advice.

"I could make you rather a nice dress," Anne said thoughtfully. "As a matter of fact I've been meaning to. There's that frock you were confirmed in. I could do something with that."

"Oh, Mother, that white one! I couldn't go in that."

"Of course you could. You'd look very good in it." Anne saw a challenge, and took it up.

"But white! . . ."

"White is perfect," Anne replied, thinking that there would be very few others at the party with the right to white. She brought the dress out, and held it up to Sarah. "We'll make it a bit longer, and cut these long sleeves and puff them out," she said. "And you can have that coral sash of mine."

She agreed with Merrick about Sarah's squeamishness, and grew ruthless. All day and half the night she and Blanche worked at the dress, lengthening, puffing, taking in and taking out. They tried it on next morning. Sarah shook her head, almost in tears.

"It's hopeless, Mother. I can't go. Don't you see . . . I can't." They made more alterations and tried it on again with the coral sash.

"It's too short," Sarah moaned.

"Don't be absurd," said Anne. "It's just right."

She and Blanche dressed Sarah in the evening, kneeling round her with last-minute pins and needle and cotton. At last it was ready, and they stood back.

"*Belle, belle*," Blanche cried, clasping her hands.

"Yes, it's a success," said Anne. "Only hold your head up."

Sarah looked at herself in Anne's long glass. It was not as bad as she had expected, but still she was uncertain.

"Must I wear this sash, Mother?"

"Oh yes. It matches your necklace and your shoes perfectly. Doesn't it, Blanche?"

Sarah turned sideways, beginning to feel excited.

"Well?" said Anne, when Merrick saw her. They waited; what he said would decide Sarah. He said nothing for a moment, unexpectedly touched by her.

"It's better even than I imagined. You look a knock-out, Sarah. If you don't dance every dance, I'll give you my camera."

Anne lent Sarah her evening bag, made sure that everything she did want, and nothing she did not want, was in it, helped her into her coat so that the dress did not crease, gave her hair a last comb, and sent them off. Blanche stood beside her in the doorway.

"Like a lily," she murmured. "Like a lily of the valley."

"How do you feel?" Merrick asked on the road.

"Awful."

"Don't you worry. You'll see. Oh, and by the way, be careful of the drinks. Sometimes they put something in them."

They reached the Villa Harlequin. A space had been cleared outside as a car-park, and several big cars were standing in the drive. Redfern said good-evening to Merrick; he was looking forward to the party, having arranged with his cronies to divert a little lobster and champagne for a gathering above the garage. A footman took Sarah's coat, explained that her ladyship was still at dinner, and ushered them into the living-room. A log-fire blazed on the immense hearth, chairs and sofas had been pushed back to leave a dance-floor, and the band were unpacking their instruments at the far end. No other guests had arrived; the children heard talk and laughter in the dining-room.

"How awful!" murmured Sarah. "We're the first."

Merrick too felt diffident, but pretended not to be. "Well, we can have a look round," he said boldly, and began to warm his hands at the fire. "Looks pretty good, doesn't it?" He surveyed the room with his proprietary air. Huge sheaves of irises, lilac, and magnolia stood on tables against the wall; under the ceiling and between the crystal brackets hung festoons of almond and cherry blossom, and the chandelier in the centre was wreathed with lilac.

"Look, the garden's flood-lit!" Sarah exclaimed.

Merrick walked on to the lawn. "Oh, come and have a look at this!"

He pointed up at the house. The windows on the first floor had been ornamented to represent boxes at the opera. Tasselled draperies flanked and canopied the framework, through which the lighted rooms glowed like the inside of a flame. Sarah caught her breath. It was something undreamed-of, evoked by a magician. The house, the garden, were all an illusion, and would surely vanish in an instant. Concealed arc-lamps dappled the garden thickets, tree-trunks and young leaves; one had been subtly placed in the encircling forest, illumining the sombre tapestry of the pines. The air was like summer, and even the stars, winking in a velvet sky, seemed to have been set there as a decoration. Since rain was out of the question, the platform for Paul Walker's dance had been placed at the end of the lawn; an organ-grinder, with a charcoal fire beside him for hot chestnuts, had been engaged from somewhere, and Madame Cheiro, the fortune-teller from Oriol, had pitched a tent beneath the trees.

"Edwin Aldrich did all this," said Merrick knowingly. "What a party! Aren't you glad you came?"

"It's beautiful, Merrick. I wish we weren't the first, though."

"Oh, there'll be dozens of people soon. There's nothing to worry about."

"I'm not worrying, but I wish there'd be more people I know."

"Oh, there'll be lots of them."

All the same, she was unconvinced, the fantastic splendour of the villa making her feel uneasy as well as captivating her; she was again conscious of her dress, and the coral sash seemed more than ever a mistake. They returned to the big room; the pianist had begun to strum, and the rest of the band were tuning up.

The door from the dining-room opened, and Lady Wildenstein with her women guests, shimmering and glittering, appeared to float towards them on a beam of light; the men were just visible, standing in the background. As this armada of colour and jewels approached them, both the children had a disheartening sense of their own drabness and isolation. Merrick could not even look for Linda; for a moment all individuals were lost in a single impression of glowing brilliance. Lady Wildenstein greeted them with friendly apologies and introduced them. Sarah knew no one, though she recognised and had heard the names of several of them. With so many eyes upon her, her attempts at self-confidence collapsed irretrievably. Luckily she was not expected to shake hands with them. They gave her friendly smiles, but her head sank lower and she could not look them in the face. At last the introductions were over. She found a chair for herself, and watched them covertly in her old way; now she felt terrified again, dreading that they would try to bring her into the conversation.

Merrick scarcely recognized Linda. She wore a white dress, with a white gardedia in her dark hair, and though fresh and appealing as he remembered her, and prettier than he had ever imagined she could be, he had at once the feeling that she must be older than he was. Her turquoise eyes rested for a surprised instant on his blue suit, but she greeted him affectionately.

"You look stunning," he told her.

"Do I, Merrick? I'm so glad you think so."

He did not know what to say to her. He had had so many things to say, but in this setting all of them appeared unsuitable.

"The decorations are wonderful," he said.

"Aren't they! Edwin spent hours over them. You must have your fortune told."

"So must you, Linda. I'll come with you."

He thought that this might lead to something, but another girl was speaking to her and she had not heard him. They were all several years older than she was, but she talked to them with entire ease, sitting up eagerly on the sofa. Her eyes shone with excitement.

"You look like a white crocus," he said gallantly.

"Oh, Merrick, how sweet of you! But don't you like my gardenia?"

"I like it very much. All the same, you look like a white crocus."

Linda and Lady Wildenstein took the women upstairs; when they returned, her friends began to gossip. They paid no attention to him, rousing the desire to assert himself that he had felt last year, the first day he met her mother. They were discussing the tunes the band should be asked to play and mentioned several he had not heard of. He had to say something and suggested *Tristesse*, though he did not particularly like it. Linda made a comical face.

"Oh, Merrick, really!" she exclaimed. "It's years old."

He felt put out and offended; the more so because Sarah had heard, and he wanted her to think that he was on easy terms with them all.

310

The men came in: Sir Maurice, Paul Walker, Edwin Aldrich, Lord Il-fracombe, and others he did not know. Quickly he asked Linda to dance.

"Of course, Merrick."

"What number, then?"

"Well, I don't know. I'm getting in an awful muddle already."

As she did not suggest a number, he asked for number five.

"All right, Merrick. Number five. Don't forget."

She was surrounded by other partners, and he went over to Sarah.

"Come on," he said. "I'll introduce you to them."

"No, I don't want you to, please."

"But you must meet them, Sarah. You can't sit here the whole evening. And they're awfully nice."

"Is that Paul Walker?"

"Yes, I'll introduce you to him."

"He's rather small. I thought he was much taller."

"You wait till you see him dance. Come on."

Reluctantly she let him lead her across to the young men. They said how do you do pleasantly, but did not ask her to dance; Merrick began talking, guests were arriving, and she slipped back to her chair unobserved.

She shrank into herself, especially when she saw Mr. Wake. Like all the other men, he wore a black tie and dinner-jacket; most of them had soft shirts, but his was starched, with a stick-up collar, and his monocle dangled on a white waistcoat. He was being affable to several people at once, but when he saw her he said, "Hello, Sarah. Enjoying yourself?" and hurried past without an answer. Miss Ferguson was there, taking mental notes, her sharp eyes roaming for celebrities; she had left her flashlight and camera in her car, but intended to use them later. It was big game tonight: two important film stars, several politicians, some rewarding eccentrics, and a mine of titles. The band struck up, and dancing started.

Lady Wildenstein presented Merrick to a large plain girl, and he saw that he was expected to dance with her. She had no partner for the following number, so they danced that too. At the beginning of the third he escaped into the garden. The one after next; that would be with Linda. He felt nervous and uneasy. He had expected her to make a reference to the previous year, which would have given him his own cue; but she had been like a stranger, and he could not think how he would work it in himself. The house was filling, and couples emerged on to the lawn, exclaiming at the barrel-organ with its dolled-up monkey, the hot chestnuts, the lighting, and the gaily draped windows, where other couples sat leaning out, listening to the enchantments of the night. Despite Linda's remoteness, or because of it, he felt fonder of her than ever, longing to shine in her eyes and detesting his blue suit. He blamed Anne bitterly for allowing him to come here in it; she must have known that it would be wrong.

He waited till he saw the band getting ready for the fifth dance before going in; he did not want Linda to see him waiting, alone and obvious. She appeared after a few minutes and he went up to her.

"You see," he said, "I haven't forgotten."

"Oh, Merrick, is this ours? Of course it is." She apologized to a scraggy youth. "I'm terribly sorry. I did promise this to Merrick."

The youth looked sour, and Merrick's heart leapt; at least she had remembered him and preferred him to someone. Mercifully the dance was not a waltz, but the floor was already so crowded that he had little chance to show his skill.

"I suppose you're terribly busy," he said.

"Isn't it awful? And I don't know half the people here." Her eyes wandered, reminding him of her mother.

"Can we dance again later, when you don't have to bother so much? What about number twelve?"

"I expect so. Number twelve," she replied vaguely, peering round his shoulder.

"I've got lots of things to tell you."

"Have you, Merrick?" She smiled and gave him a fleeting look.

"We'll have to go to the beach again. I wonder if your name's still there."

"I don't know if I'll have much time. We're only staying three or four days."

Three or four days! He could not speak, but she seemed aware of no shock, and while she smiled and chatted to people round his shoulder he danced on mechanically; her dark hair shone, and he could smell the gardenia-scent.

"Do you mind if we dance towards the door?" she said. "I think Mother wants me."

Lady Wildenstein came up.

"Darling, you must help me," she said, without looking at Merrick. "People keep on arriving. I'm worn out."

Linda detached herself. "I'm so sorry, Merrick, but I'll have to go."

"Of course you must. We'll wait till number twelve."

Perhaps she did not hear. Certainly she had not glanced at him, and already the crowd engulfed her. He struggled to the buffet and gave himself a glass of champagne; then he took refuge in the garden again, and sat on the white rail dividing it from the forest.

The moment had come and gone for which he had waited months. Indeed, he had waited for it. He had dramatized his sentiments a little, there had been long periods at school during which he had scarcely thought of her, but on his horizon there had always been the landmark of this moment. And when he reached it, it had evaporated. He had said nothing, he had reminded her of nothing. He had no inkling of her feelings towards him. People had separated them; not just her mother, but everyone—people. It depressed him that she had been so distraite, scarcely giving him a look or hearing what little he had said; but he could not blame her for it, for after all she was the hostess. Alone, she would be quite different. He must get her away from the people, that was it. Only three or four days. . . . Of course she would be coming back. He had forgotten to ask her that, and wanted to dash over at once, whoever was with her, and ask. Even in three or four days she would surely have time to come for a walk, so that he could tell her everything. Music filtered out to him. The villa gleamed and glittered, ensheathing her, dividing him from the person he knew her really to be. At the twelfth dance he would bring her into the garden, and talk to her alone. He planned the way he would do it, the things he would say, and went indoors cheerful enough to dance a third time with the large plain girl.

Sarah remained meanwhile in her chair behind the sofa, furtively

343

watching the dancers and noting the handsome men. Nobody spoke to her, nobody invited her to dance. She dreaded that somebody would ask her, for she still danced badly and had no small talk; whenever any young man approached, she lowered her head and searched for an imaginary something in her bag. As more guests arrived, she imagined that she was becoming prominent and that people's eyes were on her. Sir Maurice and M. Mazarian stood in front of her for some time, talking in low voices about Germany, the markets, and "the situation"; as they moved away, Sir Maurice tripped over her. She blushed and longed for an obscure corner. If only she could be invisible!

She found another place, but scarcely had she settled there when the number ended and the dancers left the floor. Several couples approached, looking pointedly at the empty place beside her, and she again told herself that she was in everybody's way. There was a single chair on the far side of the room, almost concealed by one of the french windows, but the floor was now bare and she had not the courage to attract attention by walking across it. She waited until the next number had begun, and the centre of the room was again thronged. As she sidled along the walls, Sam Bryant saw her.

"Hello, Sarah. Not dancing?"

"No."

He was all right. She felt at her ease with him, and thought how well he looked in black coat and white silk shirt. The lines down his lean weatherbeaten cheeks were like scars; she would have liked to draw him.

"What about a dance with me?" he asked.

"Oh, I can't. I can't dance, really."

"Nonsense," he said cheerfully. "Come on, come and have a try."

The touch of his hand on her bare arm embarrassed and disturbed her, but she allowed him to steer her on to the floor. It terrified her to have to start; her stiff body seemed to belong to someone else, her steps were jerky, and she could not hold her head up. Sam attempted nothing difficult, guessing her stage-fright. Her acute shyness and secretiveness probably concealed an emotional character; it was a compliment that she had consented to take the floor with him. She came above his shoulder, and though unyielding was light and slender. It was a long time since he had held a girl so young, and Sarah's innocence, the slight flush on her neck, the gleams of golden light in her hair, even her clumsiness, touched him. One day she would be nearly as tall as the Edwardian beauties, but mercifully less regal and more primitive; something between Lily Langtry and a wood-nymph.

To take her mind off dancing, he made conversation.

"This must be almost your first party," he said.

"Yes, it's the first big one. It's lovely, isn't it?"

"They've certainly thought of everything. I'm not sure what I'm doing here."

"Weren't you asked?" came a surprised voice.

"Oh, I was asked all right." They were edged against Lady Wildenstein and after easing Sarah away he added: "This isn't my set at all."

After a pause Sarah added: "What do you mean, set?"

"Well, they're all very artistic. I thought they looked down on me. I'm a Philistine."

"Lady Wildenstein's awfully kind," replied Sarah. "Oh, I'm awfully sorry."

Her feet had got in his way and she had nearly fallen.

"You can't help it, my dear. It's the crowd." He kept her in a corner, where there was less danger.

"I saw that brother of yours," Sam said. "Isn't Anne here?"

"No, she let us come on our own."

"She ought to have come too. She used to love dancing."

"Did you dance with her much?"

"Oh, yes, in the old days. We used to do the polka together."

Sarah stored this up to repeat to Anne; she would have liked Anne to have come, so that she could watch her dancing with Sam Bryant. And where was Judith? Anne had promised she would be there, and she would have been someone to talk to.

When the number finished, Sam shepherded her back to her place and remained talking with her till the next began.

"What about a drink?" he asked. "Orangeade, or something?"

"No, thanks, really."

"Champagne, then?" he suggested jokingly.

She smiled and shook her head.

"You haven't chosen a very comfortable seat."

"Oh, I like it here, honestly. I like watching. Thank you for asking me."

Filled with admiration, she saw him dancing a Viennese waltz, his partner like a reed in his arms; they turned and turned in small neat circles, reversing with equal ease, his left arm held high outstretched, yet never in anybody's way. What he must have thought of her! If it had not been for him, she would certainly have fallen.

Merrick had disappeared, as she had expected. She felt glad, for she did not want him to see that she had no partners. She knew that the young men to whom he had introduced her would not invite her; she was too young, and they did not know her, and obviously they would not want to dance with a girl in a silly dress. Merrick was so optimistic; he always thought people would do the things he wanted them to do. She felt thirsty and hungry, and wished she had allowed Sam Bryant to bring her an orangeade. In another room a dazzling buffet of cold patés and lobster salads had been laid, and couples were sitting at smaller tables lit by branched silver candlesticks; but she did not dare go in alone. She longed to be less self-conscious, to hold her head up, to talk brilliantly, to allure, to be asked to dance every dance. She wanted desperately to make Merrick proud of her and to hear him telling Anne what a success she had been, but she could not do it. She knew that people could not all be smiling at her; yet they seemed continually to taunt her, and whenever a stranger seemed about to speak to her she began to tremble.

Edwin Aldrich stood forth in the middle of the floor and, tapping with a long pointed wand, announced magniloquently, "My lords, ladies and gentlemen, the ballet is about to begin. You are requested to take your seats upon the terrace." There was a hum of excitement, chairs and cushions were carried out, and the band transferred themselves to the far end of the lawn beneath the platform, substituting flutes for saxophones. The arc-lamps in the garden were turned out, and a soft blue light illumined the platform, on which Paul Walker appeared wearing a skin-tight costume sewn with leaves, his hair curled taut in the Grecian manner, two little horns upon his temple, and danced *L'Après-midi d'un Faune*. Sarah stood in the shadows entranced; now at least she could forget herself. The

316

languorous passion of the flutes, blue pool, background of pines, the lights from the house chequering lawn and tree-trunks, and the moon above in cloudless onyx, perfected the illusion. Clapping and chatter afterwards destroyed it. He danced several times, and ended with a run across the lawn, a pirouette, and an obeisance on one knee to Lady Wildenstein.

Sarah could have watched him all night, but the band returned and struck up a dance-tune. How thin and trivial it sounded! She remained in her corner, gazing at him in his cluster of admirers; black pencil elongated the slanting corners of his eyes, reminding her of Boris, and his muscles rippled beneath the lights. She was disappointed that his hair was fair and, close to, he looked so much smaller. She slipped closer to hear what he was saying, and followed the group round him along the terrace. Smiling and excusing himself, he went away to change, with gestures of his hands like flowers unfolding; when she walked back to her place, she found to her horror that the chair had been removed.

There was nowhere else to sit. An agony of shyness seized her. Everybody else was either dancing or talking. She was the only one alone; conspicuously, glaringly alone. Her hands and arms seemed suddenly to have become a hideous encumbrance. For something to do she again fumbled in her bag, dropped it, and out flew her mirror. A young man picked it up, but she could scarcely speak to thank him. Now she knew that everyone was looking at her and could feel the crimson rising. She must go home at once. There was no point in staying. She must find her coat and go home.

She hurried into the hall, and opened a door which she thought led into the cloakroom, but it was the kitchen. A group of waiters gaped at her. Redfern put a champagne bottle down guiltily.

"Oh, I'm sorry," she muttered.

Emilio came after her.

"Are you looking for something?" he asked kindly.

"Oh yes, Emilio. I'm going home. Do you know where they put the coats?"

"They're upstairs. I'll show you."

"No, no. I can find it."

But she could not. All the bedrooms seemed to have been turned into sitting-rooms and were full of couples who stopped talking to stare at her.

She saw a girl coming out of a room at the end of a passage, and there at last on a bed was a heap of coats and furs. Several women were making up their faces at mirrors, waited on by a maid in starched cap and apron. Sarah thought miserably of her shabby coat. She could not bear to ask for it in front of these other women and hung back, longing for them to go. The maid asked if she could help her.

"It's my coat. Could I have my coat, please?"

"What is the number, *M'amselle*?"

"Number?"

"Was *M'amselle* not given a ticket?"

She had forgotten it. Of course, Merrick had put it in his pocket. She went through her bag, pretending to search.

"I've lost it," she said.

"If *M'amselle* could tell me what the coat looks like."

She wished the maid would not talk so loud. A woman at the dressing-table was leaning forward, staring at her through the mirror.

"It's just a brown coat," she murmured, almost in tears.

The maid began to turn over the furs: minks, sables and brocades, but no sign of a brown cloth coat. More women came in, talking and laughing. The maid's efforts to help drew more attention to Sarah.

"It doesn't matter. Please, it doesn't matter. My brother's got my ticket. I'll come back. Please. . . ."

She almost ran out. A woman behind her laughed, and all the miseries of her imagination welled up pitilessly. She would not go back. She would tell Merrick she was leaving and go without it. It didn't matter if it was lost; anything rather than go back to that awful room.

She found him at last alone in the garden, talking to the chestnut-seller. He had now danced four times with the large plain girl. Recognizing from Sarah's face that something was the matter, he felt guilty for neglecting her.

"I'm going home," she said rapidly. "Will you bring my coat, Merrick? You've got the ticket."

"All right," he replied at once. "Just wait till I've had my dance with Linda. It's the next one. Then I'll come with you."

"No, you stay. Please. I'll be quite all right."

"I'd like to come. As a matter of fact I'm not enjoying myself much."

An emotion, an understanding never put into words, passed between them.

"Please stay," she repeated. "I'm sleepy, anyhow." She saw him watching her.

"Have you danced much?" he asked.

"Major Bryant danced with me."

"What about the others? The ones I introduced you to."

"Oh, they didn't ask me." Anger blazed in his eyes. "It didn't matter, Merrick. And Paul Walker was marvellous."

"Not one of them asked you?" he exclaimed.

"No. It doesn't matter, really, Merrick. I enjoyed watching much more."

"What a bunch!" he said bitterly. "What beautiful manners!" Tenderness for Sarah surged in him. "Wait just ten minutes," he said. "I'll have my dance with Linda, and then we'll go. Here . . ." he gave her a hot chestnut. "Have some of these and stay here."

The next dance was just beginning. He passed several couples whispering in the shadows of the terrace. Indoors a buzz of gaiety mingled with the music. Late guests were still arriving, and beyond a doubt the dance was a triumphant success. Lady Wildenstein glided like a column of ice among her guests, receiving congratulations. Sir Maurice talked confidentially on a sofa with a diplomat, his expression grave. Linda entered. She saw Merrick at once and looked away, but he knew that she had seen him. Turning her back, she began to dance with Guy Ilfracombe. Merrick walked up to them.

"I think this is my dance," he said politely.

"Oh, Merrick, is it? How awful. It's all my fault." She turned an innocent look on him. "I promised Guy," she said. "We two will have another dance later." She gave Merrick her most bewitching smile. "Don't be angry," she pleaded. Ilfracombe guided her away, and as they went Merrick heard him saying, "How extraordinary to come to a party like this in a blue suit!"

His stomach seemed to contract violently. His fists clenched. The faces and voices round him became blurred, and for an instant he stared at the revolving couples like a cataleptic. Wave after electric wave rolled up;

pride, a resolve not to provide the spectacle of an outburst, made channels and dispersed them. He walked back to the garden, and when he saw Sarah, Linda went suddenly from his mind.

"Come on," he said, "we're going."

"What about my coat?"

"Blanche can fetch it in the morning. Come on. I'll get you something to eat at home."

He had to go at once, and take Sarah with him. He knew that, and knew that he would not return. Linda did not matter; perhaps there had been some excuse, but it did not matter. He remembered only Guy Ilfracombe's voice, and the young men who had refused to dance with Sarah. They walked together to the garden gate.

"Oughtn't we to say thank you to Lady Wildenstein?" Sarah asked.

"No."

She looked sidelong at him; his lips were compressed, his face set. He seemed not to notice what he was doing, and instead of turning left at the main road went straight across to a sandy ride between the pines.

"Where are we going, Merrick?"

"I don't know."

She followed as she had often followed him, forgetting her coat, and regardless of the sand in her thin shoes. Stars glittered between the pines, and dew was rising. Tall wet grass clung to her dress, but he and she were together, united, and that was all she cared for. He took her arm; she felt his feverish trembling, and when suddenly he burst out his voice was pent-up, passionate, as she had never known it.

"I hate them all," he said.

24

Merrick neither saw nor tried to see Linda before she left Oriol. The pattern showed him that she was indeed "changed," and had tired of him, and he was not going to pursue her. Sarah's passion had been intense, of a different kind. It had been brief and swift, and her recovery was brief and swift. Merrick had become enamoured far less intensely, and more slowly; the recovery too was slower. He went through minor emotions about Linda, such as being hurt and being bitter; but it was more her world that he blamed, and against this he felt with force. This other anger mingled with the personal disillusion; the latter healed, the former remained. He did not forget Lady Wildenstein's ill-manners, and when he recalled Lord Ilfracombe's sneering remark and, above all, the ignoring of Sarah, he went into a cold rage.

Sarah described the ballet to Anne, and Merrick said that he had danced with Linda but the party had been "far too crowded." Anne could not fail to notice their lack of enthusiasm, and when she saw that he did not go to the Villa Harlequin, she knew that it was all over. And she had other things to think of, for in the week-end after Easter Charlotte Wake went off her head.

Her brother was out on the course at the time. Anne saw Charlotte from the office window; she was approaching along the last fairway, and carried a banner made out of a sheet, with words cut roughly out of red flannel. There were a good many people sitting in the sun, though no longer the usual crowd. Leaning the banner on the railings of the first tee, Charlotte began to address them in an unnatural high-pitched voice.

"Oh, my friends, beware the wrath of God! For he that is just shall be rewarded, and he that is unjust shall be cast out. Thus saith the Lord. Even so. Amen. O, my friends," she lunged, throwing out her hands, "let us cease from the pleasures of this wicked world and consider the words of the Lord . . ."

They stared at her dumbfounded. Hillier was trying to reason with her, but it had no effect except to make her raise her voice. She spoke in the high monotone of an orator without training, who has learnt his speech by heart. "O my friends! turn from the vengeance which is to come, and hear the Word as it came to the apostle Paul . . ."

Ripples of laughter spread among the members; some looked upset and sorry for her. The caddies had come out, and were giggling and pointing.

"It's terrible," said Anne suddenly. She walked out and took Charlotte by the arm.

"Come with me, my dear. We'll walk home together." Hillier took the other arm. People gathered round, Miss Ferguson among them. "Who is she?" she was asking, feeling for her note-book. Anne did not answer, and Charlotte consented to be led away, still at her harangue, her eyes behind her steel-rimmed glasses staring and exalted. They put her on her bed, where she lay stiff as a corpse, her lips moving. Anne knelt by her, smoothing her hair.

There was a bustle in the hall, and Mr. Wake rushed in, his monocle bouncing on the yellow waistcoat.

"What is it?" he exclaimed. "What's the matter with her?" His eyes grew wider, his lips parted as he heard. "In front of the club-house? In front of all the membahs? Did they see her?"

"Couldn't help seeing her," said Hillier.

"She must be ill," he said, gaping irritably at his sister.

"Of course she's ill," said Anne.

"But I had no warning of this. No warning at all. What did she say in this . . . in this speech?"

"Sounded like the Bible to me. Wasn't it, Mrs. MacManus?"

"The Bible!" exclaimed Mr. Wake, turning from one to the other.

They did not reply, and their manner checked him. He saw that his attitude had given a bad impression, and took his sister's hand perfunctorily.

"There, there, Charlotte," he said.

She raised herself on her elbows and launched upon another declamation. Anne tried to press her back on to the bed, but her shoulders were squared, her body amazingly stiff and unyielding.

"Behold, I shall send my chosen into your midst," she cried. "For he that doeth my Word shall have everlasting life, and he that doeth it not shall be cast into the everlasting furnace. This is my judgment upon the nations, that is gone into all lands . . ."

She was taken to the Roman Catholic hospital at Oriol that evening, her hand locked with Anne's the whole way in a tense grip. The nuns received and absorbed her without a trace of surprise; it was almost as if they had expected her.

Sarah was horrified and upset, for Charlotte had been the first of a string of single women who had taken an affection to her—Miss Wells the scientist, Judith, and, till now, Blanche, were others. Merrick was sorry for her, but pleased about Mr. Wake's discomfiture. He had his report of what had happened from Jerry and Cacouette.

"And she really did shout at them?" he asked Anne.

"Oh, she did. Poor Charlotte! You oughtn't to laugh at her."

"I'm not laughing. It must have stirred them all up. Who was there?"

"Oh, the usual ones," said Anne. "Miss Ferguson . . ."

"Was she there? I hope Charlotte screamed at her. Jerry says she threatened them all with hell-fire."

"So she did."

"Miss Ferguson wouldn't mind being in Hell. All the people she writes about would be there."

"That might be the Hell," said Anne.

He laughed, and they seemed to be back on their old footing. She paid several visits to Charlotte in hospital, taking excuses from Mr. Wake that he was "too busy." Sarah came with her, and Merrick once. They stood uncomfortably at the end of her bed, while she stared at the ceiling, made vague remarks, and patted Anne's hand; when they went, she blessed them repeatedly. On the way back Merrick talked a little about Linda and told Anne that she had become too grand for him. He came to her bedroom in the mornings and slowly began again to confide in her.

They were together one evening in the living-room. Sarah had gone to bed with *The Conquest of Mexico*. Anne was stitching rings to a curtain. Merrick, in shirt-sleeves, had squares and protractors on the table and thought he was designing a boat. Suddenly, without looking up, he said:

"I suppose I've been a nuisance to you."

"When in particular?" Anne asked.

"Last year, mainly. About the Villa Harlequin and all that."

"Oh, that. It wasn't so much you I was worried about. It was so terribly like what had happened before."

He looked puzzled. "Before what?"

"Long before you remember."

"About my father, you mean?"

She put down her work.

"I've never told you," she said. "I was going to one day, but I wanted to wait till the right moment."

"Why not tell me now?"

"Do you want to hear now?"

"Yes."

He pushed the instruments away and sat forward, fingers in his close-cropped hair. Anne did not speak at once. The time had come, but these memories had been lying so long to be gathered that they could well wait a few more minutes.

"He was an attractive man," she began. "Handsome—people called him irresistible. I thought so too. I'd never met anyone like that. Oriol was quite different then from what it is now, and Mother and Father and I had lived quietly up there in the forest—quieter even than here. Then during the war I was in the hospital, and my father died."

"You were fond of him, weren't you?"

"Yes, very. I wish you and Sarah had known him. Sarah's like him in some ways."

"I reckon she gets her drawing from him."

"Yes, that's from him."

"My father was a very good rider, wasn't he? That must be my side. Not that I'm very good."

"You have his looks. And his charm. Charm," she repeated with a grimace. "I've come to dislike the word. It was just after you were born . . ."

She looked down at the fireplace, and began to tell him the whole story. It had been the one pivot and crisis of her life, and the happenings of those weeks seventeen years ago stepped straight out of their engravings in her mind, until Merrick could imagine his father in the room. He listened, leaning on the table, without stirring. Anne often paused, not from emotion, but to recollect clearly what had come next; she told him the tale as if she had been reading a book, relating happening after happening in their proper order. When she described how Johnny had begun visiting the smart villas, and not come home, and turned into a snob, Merrick shifted and felt himself going red.

"And then you divorced him?" he asked at the end.

"Yes."

"And he never wrote to you?"

"Once or twice. It was mainly about money. He soon stopped."

"And you've never seen him since? Not once?"

"Never. Sam Bryant saw him here last year, but I didn't know he'd been till afterwards."

"He was here, at Oriol?" Merrick exclaimed.

"For a night or two, it seems. He was staying at the Sunset Hotel."

"And he never came to see you, or told you, or anything?"

"Oh no."

This was the condemnation, although neither of them pronounced it. What had led to the divorce had all happened so long ago that high-sounding sentiments, whether of outrage or forgiveness, could not fit it; only its reflection upon the children mattered. But his entire indifference, his failure to visit them in the years between, were to Anne a continuing wrong; for Merrick it was decisive that he had come to Oriol and ignored Anne. It meant disillusion, and would to Sarah too. They had always expected this unknown figure to appear to them one day, and had imagined many forms for him. Once they had hoped dramatically for a reconciliation. Merrick had pictured him returning from America, penitent in a dignified way, and rich, with a string of racehorses; Sarah had envisaged someone who would watch them from distances, a mysterious rather mournful and hypnotic stranger. But that was that, Merrick said to himself; now they need not trouble about him.

Anne brought herself to say something she did not want to say.

"You have a right to see him, if you choose. Later, if you want to write to him, the lawyers will give you the address, if he still has an address. I should like to know, that's all."

"No," he answered. "I don't want to write. I'm not interested in him."

As he said this, Merrick had an uprise of emotion, the cause of which he did not exactly know; but there was an obscure feeling of something finally renounced, of a parting. He got up, and went to the curtained window.

"I understand," he said. "I don't wonder you were worried. You saw all the same things happening again."

"I was afraid of what might begin. It's such a terrible thing to watch someone being ruined—ruined at the root, I mean."

"How?"

So far it had been clear to him. "Snob" was an appalling word, but he saw that this was what his father had become, and what he was on the way to becoming. He saw too the glittering face of Oriol, which was the dangerous face, and understood that it had taken his father away from Anne, and last year had taken him. He did not understand what she meant by "the root."

"It's difficult to explain," she said. "Each of us has an integrity. Each of us has something which is our own . . ."

"A personality," Merrick suggested helpfully.

"No, that's something else." She said what she meant. "Each of us has an immortal soul. Things come to break it up and pollute it, and we either succumb or we do not. I don't want you to succumb. When you have lost that, you have lost everything. A lot of all that I have seen come to Oriol is polluting; and yet it was started by a man I admired."

"Judith's father?"

"Yes. He gave us this cottage."

"Did he really? I never knew that. What was he like?"

"I always think he should have been an artist of some kind. He had such imagination, such an instinct."

"He must have made a lot of money."

"He couldn't help it. And yet so much of his energy seemed to have been wasted. I don't think he was ever a very happy man."

"Judith looks unhappy."

"Yes." She looked at him and smiled. "You notice people, don't you?" Later she went on, as if defending herself before him and her own conscience. "I stayed here at Oriol after the divorce because I thought it a wonderful place for children. And it was my home. Perhaps, with all its temptations, I should have left, but I didn't see why I should."

"Why should you, Mother?" He drew the curtain. "It's a fine night. Let's get some air." On the doorstep outside he took a deep breath. "Expelling the cobwebs," he explained. "All of them." There was a mild breeze blowing from the sea; the course was dark, the stars intermittent behind clouds. Merrick flicked a pebble at Frou-frou. "Why should you leave Oriol?" he repeated, taking Anne's arm. "You were here first, and you are the real Oriol. And the real Jacques-plage."

"And that is a real compliment." She answered lightly, but the depth of her heart was reached. "Oriol," she murmured, and later, "I wonder what you will do, Merrick."

"I wonder."

"I read in the paper that there's some scheme to take boys of your age exploring. They go in the summer, and it's not expensive. I don't know if it's too late to apply for this summer. It said they were going to Northern Canada."

Merrick had seen it too, and longed to go. All the same, he said, "I'd rather stay at Oriol this summer—unless you *want* to get rid of me," and he began to tell her about the boat he meant to build.

Often she looked back to that evening, for it had redeemed so much. The conflict with Johnny had never ceased, despite his absence. Many times she had wanted such a conversation with Merrick, and he had given her the lead himself. The evening had really been a moment of triumph for her and what she had lived to guard; yet she thought of it with peace and reassurance rather than triumph.

327

It redeemed anxieties he had caused her in the past, and lightened some of those she felt about the future. It had become clear that she and the children might have to leave Oriol and go to England, and so many dangers appeared to lie in dead ground in relation to Merrick's judgment. Until he had grown up more himself, he needed someone by him with a higher trajectory of vision who could detect them. She was ready to yield or share her place with anyone she could trust, but at the moment there was no one else with the same influence. She had feared she might be losing it, but this conversation showed that it was still strong, and that she could and must continue to contribute something of value to his life. Consequently the thought of a possible migration to England, though dismal in many ways, troubled her less on his account. For Sarah it might be an advantage; Merrick had at least been to school there, but to Sarah it was almost a foreign country.

All round them now appeared emblems of depression and disquiet. They did not need newspapers to tell them that the storm was drawing near. Villas owned by or usually let to English people were closing for the first time, and the big hotels no longer thought of opening even a wing; the Pine Hotel shut up its big dining-room, and in June and July never had more than thirty visitors. Emilio had chosen his time well to start in London; there was no future for him at Oriol, and even had it been possible for him, he did not want to live in Italy. Madame Menard too had achieved one of her ambitions. The Confiserie des Fleurs was hers; she sold her pitch outside the Casino, discarded her shawl, and reappeared in her true colours, a prosperous shopkeeper in black satin, behind hillocks of chocolate pralinés and nougat.

"Ah, it has been hard work," she told Sarah. "And now, just as my labours are to be rewarded, they are going to start killing one another. *Mon Dieu*, what a world!"

"And what about your daughter, Madame Menard? How is she getting on with her singing?"

Madame Menard tossed her head. "Jacqueline is a little fool," she replied. "I have told her she must study and work hard, as her mother has worked. And what does she do? *Imaginezvous*! She falls in love."

"But surely she can still sing?"

"Oh, it is love, love, love, night and day. I'm tired of her. And in another year she would have been ready. She would have sung Mimi. She would have gone to Paris." Madame Menard sighed. "Well, the young are like that. I was the same."

She never mentioned Monsieur Menard, nor did either of the children ever see him. In her new position she no longer thought it suitable to sing in the chorus, and the last performances of *Bohême* and *Carmen* had to do without the flash of her gold teeth and her majestic coquetry; that summer, though a few gaming-tables at the Casino remained open, the opera closed down.

Old friends came frequently to the cottage to discuss what they should do. Jerry was leaving for a new job in England and thought he would join the Territorials. It surprised Sarah that this affected her so little. Two years ago she had worshipped the ground he walked on and surreptitious sketches of him crowded her folders. He looked pleasant, his freckles still gave him charm, and his happy-go-lucky nature reminded her of Merrick; but he no longer caused her heart-beats. Her past had begun, and he became one of the first inhabitants of it.

Sometimes, returning from shopping in Oriol, she and Anne would take Paul's fiacre. The old man was despondent; if war came, he said, it would ruin what the cars had left of his business. Jamais looked more ramshackle than ever and seldom broke even into spasmodic canters when a car frightened him; he jogged along in forgetful senility, jerking his head and whisking his undocked tail against the flies. When they reached the cottage, Blanche would come out with the apple for him, and the nip of something strong for old Paul, but Paul remained mournful.

"And you'll be going too?" he said to Anne.

"Oh, not yet, Paul. Perhaps never."

"Everyone is going. *Il n'y a plus d'Oriol.*" He rested his hand on Jamais's neck. "He and I might as well go together," he said. It took some time to recover from the gloom he left.

Things were bad too for the caddies. There were no longer enough golfers for them all, and though most of them would get employment during the harvest, no other jobs were available near home. Hillier mentioned this casually to Anne, who passed it on to Judith, and Judith arranged that all who had worked at the golf-club for a certain number of years, and were no longer wanted there, should receive their average wage until they found another job. M. Lemaitre objected violently, saying they would cheat, if they really wanted work they would get it, and with its already reduced receipts the club could not afford it. She had another row with him and again overruled him; financially he was quite right, and she again paid out of her other sources of income.

"She's a good woman," Cacouette told Sarah. "She thinks of other people."

He was indignant with some of the caddies, who were saying that it was all a trick.

"Of course she's rich," he said, "and she doesn't notice money, but she's put her hand in her pocket. That's more than most of them will do, unless it's for themselves."

"Who do you mean, Cacouette?" Sarah asked. She had found him crossing the golf-course, taking the short cut home. He wore a bright yellow pair of shoes which had not fitted one of the members, an old sporting coat of Sam Bryant's that was much too big for him, and his own patched trousers. He told her what the caddies thought of M. Lemaitre, clearing his throat and spitting loudly. He still sniffed and wiped his face on the back of his hand, and his slang was as difficult as ever; from the scraps she could understand, and the expressive wrinklings of his monkey face, she gathered the story of Judith's row. She had not heard it herself, but Cacouette had picked it up somewhere.

"And Wake? What does he think about it?" asked Cacouette.

"I don't know. Anyhow, he's not important enough."

"He's a pig." He looked slily at her, and added, "He's making eyes at your mother, eh?"

Sarah was amazed.

"You haven't noticed it?" asked Cacouette knowingly. "He's making eyes at her all right. She's not going to marry him, eh?"

"Good Heavens, no! Mr. Wake!"

"I should hope not. He's a proper pig."

At Etaples bridge he shook hands with her abruptly and ran on to join the others. Leaning over the parapet, she watched them disappear into the back streets. The tide was out, the fishing boats moored, sails furled, by the wooden struts of the quay. One of the women padded past with bare feet, her wicker basket high on her back. Etaples was a dirty little town. The narrow houses opened on to narrow cobbled streets except by the quay, where the main road from Paris to Boulogne joined the Oriol road. The walls were peeling, and shreds of old advertisements for cinemas, political meetings, a circus, hung loose from them. Men in jerseys lounged by the quay, while children played in the gutters, shouted at shrilly by women gossiping at street-doors; one or two old people sat outside on kitchen chairs.

A big car, the grid laden with suitcases, crossed the bridge; a chauffeur drove, and Sarah caught a glimpse of Madame Agyropoulos in the back. Men stared without expression, turning to watch it round the corner towards Boulogne. A woman jerked her head up and said something to her neighbour. Perhaps it was due to Sarah's conversation with Cacouette, certainly a seed was germinating in her own nature; whatever the immediate cause, that moment came upon her with the piercing impact of a revelation. The gleaming car, the piled-up luggage, the fur rug, the smartly-dressed woman; and on the other hand the decaying houses, children in gutters, poverty. She remained stock still, as if something had happened which she could not believe. The two opposites were so close together, why, the wheels had even splashed mud over the children, and yet so utterly apart that the car might have been a visitant from another planet. In the unmodified clarity with which simple facts appear to children, it was suddenly astounding, and incredibly disgraceful, that such things should exist side by side and no one appear to consider it strange. The thought receded slowly as she went home, but each detail of that moment imprinted itself ineradicably on her memory; in later years, when she knew what a revelation meant, she called it so.

The first group of refugees left the Villa des Roses and "moved on"; others took their place. Judith sent for her lawyer again and told him that she wished to make a new will. He remained several days, bringing his own version of her affairs and going through the files Anne had prepared. On this occasion Judith did not ask for Anne, because she intended dispositions in her and the children's favour, and did not want her to know about them till the will had been drafted. She met Anne one day by chance, and shocked her greatly by saying that if Germany invaded France, France would probably give in. Anne accepted that Judith knew much more about politics than she did, but this was too much for her. She had vivid memories of the French soldiers in the 1914 war and could remember Verdun. It seemed scandalous, almost a crime, for Judith to go about talking in this way, and she said so.

"My dear Anne," Judith replied sadly, "I'm afraid I shall be right. The country is split from top to bottom."

"It always seems like that, I know. The Government's always falling, and so on. But if they're attacked they'll resist."

"Some will, but not enough. They have no leaders. Everyone is wondering how he can save his own skin. I can hardly go to Paris now, it depresses me so much. What are you going to do?"

"If there's a war, I shall take the children to England. Anyhow, I shall stay here until I have to go."

Judith looked gravely at her. "Please don't call me an alarmist," she said. "But you should think seriously about it. You should make some kind of preparation."

Although Anne knew that Judith liked to provoke people, especially "the complacent English," her manner this time had no spite. It made her think; and when she spoke about it to Hillier, the caddie-master, who had lived at Oriol from the beginning, he appeared to agree with Judith. Other indications disturbed her. Mr. Wake borrowed Blanche for a "little party" to which he invited Anne, and Jean de Moutiers and M. Lemaitre, with their wives; the two Frenchmen had a political argument and almost came to blows.

It was a disagreeable evening in every way. Anne liked Jean, though she wished he would stop trying to be an Englishman; his manner had become offhand to the point of rudeness. She did not know why she, the secretary, should have been invited to meet M. Lemaitre, the director, whom she thoroughly disliked, until she realized that she would be the only unmarried woman there and was evidently expected to play the hostess. Mr. Wake had even invited her a quarter of an hour before the others, and used it to indicate his wishes. "If you would not mind doing the honours. . . . If, after dinner, you would be kind enough to show the two ladies to my poor sister's room . . ." He behaved towards her in such a way that the guests certainly assumed that he and she were about to get married, or worse; he referred their praise of the meal to her, instead of to Blanche, and paid her elephantine courtesies. Even his manner towards the guests was studied to impress her. She was obviously intended to take their presence as an honour, and frequently, after mentioning some important person by Christian name, or delivering himself of a pompous comment on world affairs, he would glance at her to observe the effect. He was all the more attentive now; since Charlotte's illness he had no one to look after his clothes.

They were discussing the inevitable subject. M. Lemaitre said people had to choose between Hitler and revolution, and he preferred Hitler. Jean did not see it so simply, declaring that if the Germans attacked they must be fought. He grew excited, becoming French and himself. Their voices rose, their wives sighed, and Mr. Wake poured oil on both waters. Anne knew that he was signalling to her to rise, but she ignored him deliberately, made a remark which stopped both of them, and began to talk to Jean about the old days. She got up when she felt like it and went home early with Blanche, whom Mr. Wake had angered by giving her only fifty francs, never even complimenting her on her cooking. After this Anne hoped that he would consider her an unsuitable mate; but next morning he only reproached her, almost roguishly, for leaving him in the lurch, observed how intelligently his guests had talked, and trusted she would come again.

Blanche was married at the beginning of the summer holidays; she had waited on purpose, so that Merrick could be there. "*Il était toujours mon flirt,*" she said archly, but, investing herself in advance with her new dignity, no longer allowed him to hug and tickle her. Anne had lent her the cottage for the reception; the relations had behaved with despicable meanness, but M. Philippe had stumped up, and Anne, without Blanche knowing, was paying for the rest. For several days before, Blanche had alternate fits of despair and exaltation; now she was imagining the children she would have, now she felt certain that M. Philippe would desert her on the altar-steps. Her dress did not fit, there would not be enough taxis, the organist had rheumatism, the choir wanted another five hundred francs.

The day came, however, and Blanche was wed. Anne, Judith, and the children sat among the relations. The service seemed long and complicated, they did not know when they should sit, stand, or kneel, but at last the bells rang from the belfry, the organ pealed, the choir anthemed, the relations got up with an excited clatter, and there she came, red as a huge beetroot in a white parcel, beaming triumphantly, with her quarry on her arm. When the reception was over, and she had to say good-bye to Anne, she burst into floods of tears, pressing Anne's hands and declaring she would never again meet anyone like her. The children stood by embarrassed, with handfuls of confetti, while M. Philippe's cronies dug him in the rubs and whispered bridal jokes. The car drove away festooned with white ribbons, the relations ate and drank what remained of the wedding breakfast, and Anne and the children were left alone.

It was a strange feeling to be without Blanche. For as long as they remembered she had brought in the big china soup-tureen, her shining greasy face sweating in a wreath of steam. Sarah wanted to cry; the music, Blanche with her white veil and bouquet of white carnations, the nuptial pomp, had excited her imagination, but Merrick could only talk about the greed of Blanche's relations. Anne felt her absence most. To go into the kitchen and not find her there, to see her empty bedroom neat and characterless as a hotel bedroom waiting to be let, depressed her like the first shiver of autumn on a summer's evening. Four people, and twelve years. . . . Now they were three; Blanche was the first to have left the cottage since Johnny. How many years, how many months even, remained? It seemed to her like the beginning of the end.

~

Yet that last summer was the happiest of all. Nearly as deserted as in winter, Oriol and Jacques-plage seemed to belong to them alone, and the sun shone all day long. Sarah and Merrick became again as devoted as they had been in earlier years, and Merrick returned to his natural occupations, carpentry and riding. Mr. Masterton had horses now whenever he wanted them, and in the evening he worked again in the shed, finishing the long-neglected book-case. Impelled by a vague homesickness, a farewell sense, they revisited their old "castles"; sand had entirely covered the hut in the dunes, but their names, with Linda's beneath, still stood out clearly on the wooden kiosk. They climbed the light-house again. Merrick took Sarah on the Casino roof and lifted the glass pane above the gaming-rooms; but it was dull, there was scarcely anyone there. Three new words "Do you remember?" had crept into their conversation; slowly, in minute patches, the past was beginning to grow round them. Linda and the Villa Harlequin were too recent memories, but Sarah could already make shy jokes about Boris. It was all behind them. They believed that they would soon be leaving Oriol, and Merrick felt excited. The place had a stronger hold on Sarah, but his eagerness infected her and made her ask questions about England. They had their voices recorded at the Oriol gramophone shop, and Merrick and Emilio did an extremely convincing rendering of two Italian songs; Anne was nearly taken in when she heard it.

Unobtrusively she made her own preparations. If they did have to go, they had better be ready for it in time; when Sam Bryant came over for a lonely week-end at the beginning of August, she had a long talk with him about her prospects. She had saved throughout her life, but so much had gone or was reserved for Merrick's education that she had only enough left to live for a few months without a job; perhaps not even months. Sam did not doubt that she would get a job at once in England if she had to, and much better than her present one.

"I see you at the head of a vast organization," he said. "The indispensable one, who runs the whole show."

"I think I should like that," said Anne.

"Of course you would. And you'd do it damned well. You're wasting your time here."

"Oh, I'm a vegetable. I've got used to being here, and I've taken roots."

"Uproot yourself. I do, every five years. It used to be every year, but now it's not so easy."

"And yet here you are year after year, back again at Oriol." She laughed at him. "You're as much a creature of habit as I am."

"Ah, Oriol's different. And why? Don't you often wonder why? Look at

335

it. It's not much." She looked; sun, pines, dunes, a flash of the sea. "I've seen dozens of views that make this seem like an old billiard-table. Africa. You should go to Africa, Anne."

"Should I? You find me a job that'll take me there, then."

"Such names, too, the places have. Black Ghost Mountain, Valley of the Blue Moon. And still I come back to Oriol. Why?"

"It's our youth, I suppose," said Anne.

"I suppose it's that." They turned their heads, and their memories smiled at one another. Both had ridden the years well. Anne still had her fresh English complexion, and only a few grey streaks in her auburn hair. He was spare, as he had always been, but more lines and the tightening of flesh over his cheeks had given him character; she preferred his appearance now.

"And now another war," he said. "I wonder who'll have me. Last time I had to pretend I was older. This time I'll have to pretend I'm younger. It'd be strange, wouldn't it, if they had a hospital here again, and a gunnery camp and all the rest of it. I shouldn't be surprised."

"I can't think of it," said Anne. "Only twenty years, and all the same talk again . . ."

She broke off, thinking of Merrick. Sam too remembered that she had a son and wished he had not spoken. For all his restlessness, in which there was something of the soldier of fortune, he had hated the 1914 war; he might perhaps have been at home as a bandit or a partisan, somewhere among mountains, but he did not need to kill for his adventures, nor did he yearn for male comradeship. When he had it, he enjoyed it, but he could exist without.

Suddenly Anne laughed. "I must tell you a secret," she said, changing the subject. "You're not to make fun of it, and you're not to tell anyone."

"Of course not."

"Well, I am being courted."

"That doesn't surprise me. I've admired you for years."

"Dear Sam. And I you. But I am being seriously courted with a view to marriage. And by whom?" She paused for her effect. "By Mr. Glanville Wake."

"I don't believe it."

"What? Am I not good enough for him?"

"It's grotesque. Why, it's an insult."

"It's the greatest compliment any man can pay a woman," said Anne with mock gravity.

"How do you know? What are the symptoms?"

"I shouldn't need to tell *you*. It's been going on for weeks. Compliments, and *oeillades*, and invitations to dinner, and this morning a bunch of roses."

"Roses! From Wake?"

"Certainly. Red roses. He thought they would brighten my office, and they do. None of the members have ever brought me red roses," she added pointedly.

"If you become Mrs. Wake, it's an end to my faith in human nature. I may add that both your children will leave you."

"Oh, there's not the faintest likelihood of it. I'm a little sorry for him, and I must say I'm touched by the roses; but he only wants me as a house-keeper. I don't know what to do. I can't tell him not to waste his time and money, because he hasn't said anything direct. It's all innuendo."

"A very subtle technique. I shouldn't have thought it of him."

"Oh, but it isn't at all subtle. It gets more obvious every day. What on earth shall I do?"

"Marry me," Sam answered.

"What an idea!" For an instant or two her heart had beat faster, and she had almost thought him serious.

"Why not?"

"You, Sam?" She smiled. "I believe you'd be worse than Mr. Wake. At least he'd be at home the whole time. You'd always be away. You'd be a dreadful husband."

They talked on jokingly, each wondering at the back of it how serious the other was, like people who have known each other too well and too long. He was going back to London the next day, and promised that he would look round for a job that might suit her.

"You must be firm with Wake," he said in parting. "I know it's difficult for you, with that good nature of yours, but you'll have to snub him. Do something rude."

"I'll try," she answered.

She thought about Sam afterwards, remembering and disturbed by the moment of agitation. He had made his suggestion so abruptly that her instinctive response had betrayed her own feelings to herself. It was ridiculous, of course; they were old friends, and would never be anything more. How strange, almost comical it was, all these men thinking of marriage: M. Philippe, Mr. Wake, and even Sam. She took it as a joke and thought no more about it, but this glancing indication that men, real men, still found her attractive, made her lighter of step, lighter of heart, and that night she looked at herself in the glass for at least a minute.

Her preparations to leave cast her back upon the past. At every turn she was reminded of things that had happened years ago. She found old photographs of her parents, of the children, and one or two of Johnny. She could not bring herself to tear them up; there was one of him with Merrick, a few months after Merrick had been born. She brought out the deeds of the cottage, signed in Arthur Friedmann's handwriting; what would become of it, if she left? What would become of her furniture? She could not take everything with her. One evening, when she was looking through old papers, she heard the front door bell and Merrick rushed excitedly into her room.

"Guess who's here," he exclaimed.

"I've no idea, darling. Who?"

"Guess."

"Greta Garbo."

"No. Mr. Wake."

"What on earth does he want?"

"I don't know, Mother. He said he'd just looked in."

"Have we got anything to drink?"

"There's some sherry left over from Blanche's wedding. Shall I give him some?"

"Yes, you look after him. Tell him I'll be down in a minute." She felt certain he had come to propose marriage, and was glad that she could now bring his absurd philanderings to an end. He rose to greet her, wearing his turf-green suit and canary waistcoat, the monocle dangling on its black ribbon.

338

"Ah, the lady of the house," he declared. "I thought it was high time I paid you a little visit."

"It's a long time since you were last here," she replied. She felt guilty for not having invited him back to supper. "Won't you stay and have something to eat?"

"Well, that's very good of you. If it isn't too much trouble . . ."

"I'm afraid my cooking isn't up to Blanche's standard."

"I am sure it is excellent. So you look after yourselves now?"

"A girl comes in every morning, but I usually cook the evening meal myself."

"I'm sure you do it excellently, my dear."

He sat down, and Anne took the chair opposite him. The children leant on the table and watched him silently, fascinated by the presence of the arch-enemy.

"Yes, things are difficult now," he went on. "We are all being left to ourselves. The hotels closing, and the membahs all leaving us."

At this word Merrick glanced quickly at Sarah, who went scarlet and turned away. Mr. Wake did not notice; if he had, he would not have understood. He talked on about the empty golf-links, the crisis, the departure of Madame Agyropoulos, the financial losses of the Casino. "And the little theatre, where one used to hear those charming performances of the opera. I miss that greatly."

"Are you fond of music?" Merrick asked.

"I have always been a devotee, my boy. Besides, one used to meet everyone there. Monsieur Mazarian frequently let me have his box. And my poor sister, as you remember, was quite a musician." He sighed heavily, and Anne remembered how little he had cared for his poor sister.

"How is Charlotte?" she asked.

"I hear from her now and then. She is well looked after, and in quite good company, but I fear she will never be the same again."

He sighed again and paused to let the tragedy sink in. Merrick got up suddenly.

"I've got some work to finish," he announced. "Will you excuse me?"

"Of course, my boy."

"Come on, then, Sarah."

"What do you want me for?"

"You said you'd help me."

Anne saw him wink at her and felt horrified; it looked as if they were being deliberately tactful.

"Don't be long," she said. "I shall want some help with supper."

"Oh, we won't be long, Mother."

Outside he seized Sarah by the arm and said excitedly: "I've got a wonderful idea. Why not try that gramophone record on old Wake?"

"Which one?"

"The one I did with Emilio, of course. The sham one. He says he's fond of music. Let's see if he recognizes our voices."

The slow smile illumined her.

"Supposing he doesn't?"

"If he doesn't, he doesn't. It's only a joke."

"He'd be furious, Merrick. And what about Mother? She's heard it."

"She wouldn't say anything. We could ask her not to."

"But it's so rude."

"It's a joke, Sarah," he said, more impatient because the idea was his. "If he can't take a joke, that's his look-out. We'll do it like this, you see. . . ."

When they came back, their demure faces betrayed a conspiracy.

"What are you two up to?" Anne asked.

"Oh, it's nothing, Mother." They had decided not to tell her. "You wouldn't mind a harmless joke, would you?" Merrick asked, accentuating "harmless."

"It depends."

"But you wouldn't like to spoil it, would you?" he said coaxingly.

"It depends."

At supper Mr. Wake talked patronisingly about the cottage and the beauties of home life. "It is a little lonely at my place," he said, as if the bungalow were an old country home, "but I endeavour to entertain as best I can. We had an agreeable little party the other night, did we not, Anne?"

She gave a non-committal answer.

"These Frenchmen get so agitated, but one becomes used to that. I like de Moutiers, but I fancy Lemaitre had some compelling arguments. Of

340

course, he is a man of great experience. Oriol is quite a plaything to him. His business at Lille is an immense affair."

"Is it?" said Anne.

"Oh, immense. He has invited me to visit it." Mr. Wake went on to lament the closing of so many villas. "Such charming places. I don't expect you've been into many of them. You have your own nest. But really you should have been at some of the dinner-parties. I recollect once, at Madame Agyropoulos's, we sat down twenty to table. Yes," he said, "Oriol has had style. I think we must have had half the celebrities in Europe at the golf-club, eh, Anne?"

"I dare say so."

His manner angered her, but he was unaware of it. She knew the children were drinking in every word, and that Merrick would imitate him afterwards. Sarah seemed on the point of exploding with laughter, and had to leave the table; but Merrick, gravely in control of himself, was a model of good manners, with a "Really, Mr. Wake?" and "Is that true?" and "Will you have another glass of sherry, Mr. Wake?"

After supper he suggested innocently, "Would you like to hear some gramophone records?"

"By all means," Mr. Wake agreed, settling in the armchair. "What have you got?"

"We've got some of *La Bohême*."

Mr. Wake took a cigar from his breast-pocket and flourished it.

"Ah, *Bohême*," he murmured. "What melody!"

Merrick put on Musetta's waltz. Sarah sat in the window. Emilio had taught them the words, and she could say them now by heart. She saw the cafés, the gay throng of men in furry top-hats and women in crinolines, the lovers, the flash of Madame Menard's teeth. She knew each lilt of the music, and she knew when Musetta, pretending to twist her ankle, would interrupt it with her humbug scream.

"*Quando m'en vo* . . .

> When I walk through the street,
> Then all the people stare at me,
> All the young men are aware of me. . . .

341

"I remember going once with the Mendozas," Mr. Wake interrupted in the middle, and told a story which spoiled the music and had no point except that he had gone to the opera with the Mendozas. Merrick caught Sarah's eye and picked up another record.

"We've got this one of an Italian folk-song," he said. "It's not very well known. Would you like to hear it?"

"By all means. Who is singing?"

"Oh, two Italians. Cavalcanti and Merrichio."

"Ah," said Mr. Wake profoundly.

Sarah edged into a corner, so that he should not see her shoulders shaking. Anne knew now what the joke was, and that she should stop Merrick, but Mr. Wake's supercilious tone had exasperated her. Merrick put on the record and also sat out of sight; when the song began, he had to hide his head in his hands and watch through his fingers. Sarah looked from under her hair. Anne sat upright, looking at no one. Emilio sang the first verse; his voice was plausible, though having heard the record before she now recognised the exaggerated timbre. Merrick's, to her, was unmistakable. He sang in tune, but he seemed to be so obviously guying the lyrical richness; surely anyone could tell it was not a real singer. The record ended, and Merrick took it off.

"Ah," said Mr. Wake. "There's nothing like a true Italian voice. Nothing to beat it. Charming."

Merrick stood with his back to them, and Anne could see him quivering. The whole room seemed to tremble with suppressed laughter.

"Would you like to hear another?" Merrick asked, when he could get his voice under control.

"I think that's enough," said Anne, having difficulty with her own.

"Oh, just one more. What do you think, Mr. Wake?"

"One more, then," he replied. "Quite a little concert."

Merrick put on the other side, which Anne had not heard; Mr. Wake began to wave his cigar in time. It was another folksong, pleasant and easy to sing, but the two voices had the same plausibility, the same overtone of caricature, the same plushness. Half-way through they suddenly broke off and Merrick's real voice announced in flat English: "This programme is coming to you by courtesy of Emilio Cavalcanti, of the Pine Hotel, Jacques-plage, and of Merrick MacManus."

The silence seemed to heave, as when the lit fuse reaches the dynamite. Mr. Wake's cigar stopped in mid-air, and suddenly Merrick began to laugh. He laughed bent double, as if he was going to be sick; his face was white and scarlet, his shoulders leapt up and down. He tried to speak, but he could do nothing but laugh and laugh until he had a stitch and had to go out. Sarah lowered her head to her lap, tears pouring from her eyes. Mr. Wake rose.

"Not a very good joke," he remarked grandly. "A joke in extremely poor taste."

"I was nearly taken in myself," said Anne hurriedly. "They played it to me, and I . . ."

"It occurred to me at once that those were not true voices," said Mr. Wake coldly, "but the common decencies of politeness prevented me from saying so. However, it seems to have afforded your son some amusement."

He went towards the door.

"Oh, don't go," said Anne.

"Thank you. If you have any other jokes, perhaps you would let me know in good time, so that I can enjoy them. Goodnight."

The door closed. Sarah exploded.

"Now he's mortally offended," said Anne. She began to laugh.

"Wasn't it wonderful?" Sarah gasped. "Wasn't his face funny? Did you see him listening? I thought I was going to burst."

"Well, we're all equally to blame," said Anne. "I ought never to have allowed it. Why ever did Merrick let him know?"

"Oh, Mother . . . we couldn't have missed it . . . you couldn't have stopped it."

"It's all very well for you," she said. "You don't have to see him every day. I shall have a nice time at the office." But she continued to laugh, and that night in bed, after she had put the light out, she heard the children through the wall of Merrick's room. Sarah was laughing, egging him to re-live the incident for her. His mock Italian voice floated in through the window, and then more laughter as he imitated Mr. Wake.

343

"Those Italian voices. Nothing to beat 'em, my boy."

It was the last time Mr. Wake came to the cottage, and nearly the last time the children saw him. Whatever his intentions towards Anne had been, he did not pursue them. His manner next morning was aloof and insulted, and he called Anne Mrs. MacManus. When, insincerely, she apologized for Merrick, he replied frigidly: "I have often thought that your children have been allowed too much latitude. I hope they will not give you cause to regret it." He became again brusque and domineering, the master to the employee. She saw that it was useless to remonstrate with him, and felt relieved that his attentions were evidently at an end. Besides, she, and the world, had more important things to think of; the fire in the East was blazing up and the hour-glass had only a few grains left.

A fortnight before war began, she received a long envelope with a typewritten document and a short note from Judith inside. "You needn't bother to read all this," she had written. "What concerns you is on page five. When you've had a look at it, let me know, and if there's anything that isn't clear we can have a talk."

She spread the document out.

> I, Judith Louise Friedmann, spinster, of Villa des Roses, Jacquesplage, near Oriol, France, solemnly declare that this is my last Will and Testament, and I hereby revoke and declare void all other Wills made by me . . .

She turned the sheets. They were divided into three columns: in the first a name and address, in the second a profession or degree of relationship, in the third an item of property or sum of money. She came to the fifth page and read at the bottom:

> I give devise and bequeath the residue of my real and personal estate whatsoever and wheresoever . . .

She saw her own name and the children's and the words blurred. She sat back, looking at the wall, smoothing the wide sheets, and after a minute read again:

> . . . the residue of my real and personal estate . . . in the following proportions, namely (1) as to one half to Mrs. Janet Anne MacManus, at

present of The Cottage, Jacques-plage, near Oriol, France, to be held on trust by her until her children, Merrick John MacManus, and Sarah Moira MacManus, reach the age of twenty-one, and then to be divided into three equal parts among herself and her two children ... (2) as to one half to be divided equally among the following Jewish societies and relief organizations....

Anne's first feeling was that this was impossible; then of bewildered gratitude; then it occurred to her that this document was meaningless, since Judith was alive, scarcely middle-aged, and would live many years. Anxiety seized her that Judith might have some illness of which no one had been told. She scarcely thought of the money, since she had for years been accustomed to knowing that she had little and had made all her plans accordingly; nor did she want money at the expense of Judith's death.

She went back to the beginning and read the whole Will. Its thoroughness astonished her until she remembered Judith's German blood and supposed that had something to do with it. The legacies to be distributed free of duty comprised nearly a hundred items, each one identified by its appearance and its position either at the Villa des Roses or in her Paris apartment. Had Judith been dead, the consideration with which she had marshalled and distributed her possessions would have been more lovable; but Anne found something macabre about the sight of this living woman, descending as it were into the grave, and reaching back a skeleton hand to dispose of objects among which, if Anne chose to walk a few hundred yards, she could see her sitting, eating and talking every day. Nevertheless it was an imposing document, as much a shred of history as a personal testament; between the lines could be read the tale of that pauseless dispersion of Jews westward which had begun so many centuries ago, scattering in search of freedom and in pursuit of wealth and quiet, breaking out at such moments as now into terror-stricken flight, rolling on to ever further corners of the world and casting up on each shore a Rothschild or a Proust, a Disraeli or a Karl Marx, and countless families, who, restored perhaps with a new name, still kept in their blood the flow and culture of the world rather than of any nation. Judith's kin had been fortunate enough to quit their birthplaces when the epidemic of persecution had been at a comparatively mild phase. A few generations ago they would have been cobblers, tailors, pawnbrokers, owners of one-room shops, people doubtless like certain families to whom she herself had given refuge, who in their turn would "move on," some to make their name or fortune in whatever way the age and the country which finally harboured them afforded. She had made small provisions for a number of groups she had encouraged in the past, but the beneficiaries among whom her and her father's personal belongings were one day to be divided were no longer poor or struggling. They had already inherited a position, or had made their way; they were great bourgeois dynasties with seats on boards and in banks, with influence in society, and books and collections in their homes. There was no longer the consumptive son who studied the violin in a back-room, or scribbled revolutionary pamphlets with fevered fingers; musicians played for them, and the world's classics were arranged in order on their shelves.

Item 10. To Jean Kahn, cousin by marriage, now of Avenue de Wagram, Paris, formerly of Prague, my late father's set of diamond and gold studs and links.

Item 32. To Eugenie Oppenheim, first cousin once removed, now of New York, formerly of Vienna, my Dresden china tea-set in the wall-cupboard on the first floor landing.

Item 41. To Hans Mayer, violinist, lately resident with me and formerly of Munich, the Picasso drawing in my upstairs sitting-room.

Item 57. To Emily Thill, domestic servant, of the Villa des Roses, Jacques-plage, the sum of £2000 and all the contents of her two rooms at the Villa des Roses and in my Paris apartment.

Everything was there, separately allotted, down to silver-gilt work-scissors, a pair of mother-of-pearl opera-glasses, and "a small tortoiseshell box, inscribed A.F., on the French writing table in the corner of the study." The exactitude of these bequests seemed to petrify the house, as if nothing there would ever be moved again, but an ominous paragraph had been added at the end:

If some accident befalls my villa or apartment and their belongings, I rely upon my lawyer to identify such as may be kept safe or recovered and to dispose of them according to my wishes herein expressed.

The sense of homelessness came through. Where was Judith's home, after all? She had absorbed much of the civilization of France; yet she was not French and had not been wholly absorbed by France. Her name was German, but had she returned now to Germany she would have been murdered. Czechoslovakia, the country of her father's birth, meant next to nothing to her. If Anne had to leave France, England would be waiting for her; and somehow, without great difficulty, she would be reabsorbed. Judith would find influential friends and relations in many other countries; but she belonged nowhere, and of her own family she was the last.

She greeted Anne cheerfully the next morning. She had begun to work again on her beads and metal ornaments, a sign that she was distressed in her mind; bright objects, hooks, needles, and scraps of cloth lay all over the table.

"Well," she said, "have you read the great document?"

Anne knew that the joking manner was a disguise and replied seriously: "Yes, I've read it, and I don't know what to say."

"I hope it's all clear. That dreadful legal language . . . !"

"Yes, it's quite clear. You shouldn't have done it, Judith."

"That's a nice thing to say. Am I not even allowed to make my own will?"

"You shouldn't have done this for me. . . ."

"You and your children," Judith interrupted.

"For any of us. I'm so touched by the thought. I can't tell you how touched, but you should not have done it. I don't like to think of you making wills."

"We all have to, some day." She paused, and said without expression and without looking up from her work, "There is about to be a war, and I don't think I shall survive it."

"Don't say that, Judith, please."

"I have an intuition, my dear, and my intuitions have nearly always been right."

"You shouldn't talk like that."

"Shouldn't I? Well, then, let's hope I'm wrong." She put down her work and smiled at Anne. "You and your children have been a bright spot in the last year or two," she said. "I was in the gloomiest state of mind when they first came here, and they cheered me up."

"They broke in," said Anne. "That's hardly a reason to leave them money."

"Yes, they broke in. They came in through the skylight in that next room. Sarah nearly hit me on the head with a tile. It was a moment in my life, an important moment, I needn't tell you why, and I have enjoyed being with them. Let me have the pleasure of acknowledging it."

Anne walked over and kissed her. Judith turned her head slightly, and her fingers moved. Her heart rose with a longing to express itself; but the habit of reticence drove it back. Secretly she had waited for this moment with eagerness, imagining to herself Anne reading the will, taking it in, and then arriving at the villa; and as she looked at her now, she saw the eyes shining with affection that she had pictured. Money seemed to have corrupted so many of her friendships, and was again an intermediary; but this time she believed, and she was right, that the affection would have been there without the money, and came before it.

"Don't have such depressing thoughts," said Anne.

"How can one help it? Have you seen the news?"

"Yes, but all the same . . . there are still good people, Judith, and you are one of them." She paused. "What are you going to do?"

"I? I really don't know. I am rather English in that way. I shall wait and see. There is one thing I want to ask you, Anne. Are you likely to be in need of money now?"

"It's kind of you to ask, but really I am not."

"But if you have to leave—all the business of transporting things, and starting again. It will cost a lot."

"I have enough, thank you."

"And to continue the children's education?"

"Yes, I have enough. You should not trouble about me. I can easily get another job."

"I hope you won't send Sarah to one of those terrible girls schools."

"Oh, no. So much will depend on the way things are in England."

Anne was just going to say that she would have liked to send Sarah to a drawing school or to the university; but Judith would at once offer to pay for it, and she did not want that. So far she had managed by herself; she wished to go on in that way as long as possible.

When she had left, Judith sat for a long time without taking up her work. Since the arrival of Hans and his mother, activity had protected her to some extent from introspection; she had been doing something of obvious value, she had helped many people and could see the results. She had now relapsed into that gloomy brooding which had its origin in herself but was always ready to respond, like a sullen echo, to the unhappiness of the world. She had tried not to read the newspapers, had tried to shun the grim narratives of the refugees, to avoid meetings at which the only subject was sure to be the coming war; but the habits of a lifetime were too much for her. The force of her own feelings embroiled her in arguments. Her mind, a machine that seemed now to work ceaselessly off a current of its own, clamoured for more fuel and drove her automatically to the news, the wireless, the latest reports. It could not stop; dissecting, foretelling, it laid before her the outline of all that was likely to happen and amidst the fate of nations hinted at her own fate. She had not a moment's doubt that war would break out; for many years, since at the latest the occupation of the Rhineland, she had expected that. No illusions about the state of France blurred the clarity of her analysis; but she no longer wished to convey it to people like Anne, envying them their confused optimism. She foresaw shocks and disasters concealed at that time from many other people; yet they, when those disasters came, would survive, and Judith was convinced that she would not. Consequently she had made her new will, wishing to leave behind her the means to achieve some good and hoping to be remembered. Her relations might think of her for a few days. The institutions to which she had devised half the remainder of her estate would not remember her, for institutions do not have memories. But Anne and the children would remember, and keep a place in their hearts for her.

It was a strange thought, and might surprise her family, that so much money would descend to three people who had no speck of Jewish blood in them. It was strange to her that, preoccupied throughout her life with ideas, she should be making this tribute, at root emotional, to a woman and two children who had concerned themselves scarcely at all with the things that had interested her. But she believed, when the time came, that it would be well used. For a moment she had considered leaving everything to Sarah, the nearest to herself in many ways; but she had decided that no good reason existed to make a distinction that might trouble them. Nor was it necessary to write in stipulations or express wishes; they understood her, they would know what her purpose had been.

Anne told the children nothing about the will. The kindness in it was immediate, and she thought of it often. The material value was vague, and she believed distant, and not to be thought of except by way of Judith's death. It had no influence on her plans. During the next few days she saw Judith frequently; there was an awkward constraint between them, and little time remained to overcome it. On the day war was declared Judith walked to the cottage, turning to them for company. She found it as calm as usual. Merrick and Sarah were reading the papers and listening to the wireless with serious faces. Hillier and Emilio came in. There was no telephone; had there been, all that remained of the British colony would have been ringing up.

"So it's happened," Judith said.

"Do you think there'll be bombing?" Merrick asked.

"I don't know. There might be anything."

"There'd be no point in bombing Oriol."

"No, there'd be no point in that. We can all sleep with our boots on tonight," said Judith, attempting to joke.

Sarah gave her a worried look.

"What are you going to do?" she asked.

"Oh, I shall stay here a little. I've a houseful of people to look after, remember. Perhaps I shall go to Paris later."

"Will you be all right?"

"Oh, I expect so. They'll have to build a special shelter to get me inside."

She put the question to which she knew and dreaded the answer. "And what will the MacManus household do?"

"We're going back to England," said Merrick. "Anyhow, the holidays end in three weeks. I wonder if there'll be convoys across the Channel."

He was interested in the future, and Judith thought that natural. But Sarah gave her the same worried look, and said nothing; and she knew Sarah guessed all that she was feeling.

She was with them a great deal before their departure, since Anne had

350

a lot to do and was glad that Judith should have them with her. There were bills to pay, lawyers to see. Anne had to pack up all the belongings of her life that could be sent away and to arrange for disposal of the rest. There were letters to write and farewells to be made. She had no time for half the things she meant to do. She wanted to talk more with Judith. She wanted a whole day clear so that she could take a long walk round Oriol and Jacques-plage; but opportunities failed to occur. Time flew, and the car was waiting at the gate to drive them to Boulogne; she scarcely had time even to turn before getting in and say good-bye to the empty cottage, the deserted golf-course, the pine-trees, the encircling dunes, warm and smiling in the autumn sun. The children had taken their leave of almost everyone and everything, but she had had no time; and perhaps it had been best to be so busy.

Most of the luggage had gone ahead. M. Philippe had brought the larger of his two taxis. Blanche, already beginning to dominate him, had insisted that he should not charge them for it. "If you dare ask for a single franc," she had declared, wagging her finger, "then I shall leave you." She sat in front with him; Anne, Judith and the two children were in the back. They were not talkative. Merrick had caught the saddened look on Anne's face as they drove away. He stared through the window, reminding Sarah of the landmarks; the long pavilion of the Pine Hotel, all shuttered; the villas with their bright gardens; the turning to the Villa Harlequin; the bridge at Etaples and the fishing boats; the military cemetery and the last view of pine-clad Oriol across the estuary; the sea with scarcely a ripple on it; the advertisements for the big hotels; the ten red-brick houses opposite the cement works; the first glimpse of Boulogne Cathedral, a dome above the shoulder of a hill; slopes, turnings, level-crossings, all known blindfold; then the port and the beginning of cobbled streets. They were held up at the last level-crossing. Merrick pulled the window down excitedly.

"Look! look, Mother! It's Cacouette."

Writhing over the low racing handle-bars, Cacouette raced abreast. "What are *you* doing here?" Merrick exclaimed.

"Well, what do you think? I've come to see you off."

The boat was waiting for them, already camouflaged, the anti-aircraft mounted. Porters in their faded blue blouses recognized Merrick and gathered round; Mr. Harris the purser smiled at him, and a sailor called out in English from deck.

"You might be a film star," said Judith.

"Oh, he knows them all," Blanche said.

Cacouette dashed up, red and mopping his face. They stood talking awkwardly on the quay till it was time to go aboard.

"Well, good luck," said Cacouette in English, shaking Merrick's hand. "We'll win the war, yes?"

"Of course," said Merrick.

Blanche wept, though less distractedly than in the past, and M. Philippe shook hands. Sarah could not trust herself to speak. Anne and Judith stood apart, their hearts heavy.

"I shall miss you all," said Judith.

"We shall miss you desperately. You must tell us the moment you come to England."

"Oh, I will." A siren hooted. "Good-bye, my dear, and bless you."

"Good-bye, Judith."

The two women kissed, and Anne followed the children up the gangplank. Leaning over the rail as the ship slid out, the three of them watched and waved at the group on shore: Cacouette calling out and brandishing his cap, Blanche dabbing her eyes, Judith tall, motionless, gazing at them. Anne felt Merrick's arm beneath hers.

"It's sad for you," he said.

"Yes, it's sad. We've been there a long time." But she was not thinking of the cottage; she was thinking of the Villa des Roses, and of Judith driving back alone. The ship slipped between the arms of the harbour; they felt a breeze and the swell of the open sea. The waving figures were hidden. The steep streets, the sunlit coast, began to fade.

The three of them remained on deck, watching it all disappear, and Anne knew that something was over for ever. They were not being uprooted, only transplanted with their roots intact, but into a less protected world and life. The thoughts and principles the children had absorbed from her at Oriol would now be exposed to greater dangers and more chilling winds, but she believed that what was best in them would abide. The memory of the cottage would remain with them. For sixteen years and more she had poured all her own life into theirs, and silently, like an unseen angel, fought for them the battles they had been unable to fight themselves, strengthening them till they would be strong enough alone. She thought of Merrick's eagerness and enthusiasms, his candour and wish to be honest, and of all his gifts, and now would come their conflict with the world and with temptations. They were the new generation, who would have ideas bigger than hers had been. Her circle had been no wider than the cottage; theirs, and Sarah's especially, would extend to all that lay beyond. Sarah would want justice and love for everyone. She read history, she would be of the age, with its new disclosures and its new demands; and somewhere, one day, the horseman she dreamed of would come riding to her, and they would create their own enchanted ring within the tortured compass of the world. All this had been written in her during childhood, in the years that were now ending; the invisible ink that time would bring out.

And above them all hung the shadow under which their generation had been born and grown up, the shadow of war. In two or three years Merrick would be drawn into it, be called up, and sent away from her to unknown perils. Anne tried not to think of it, though now it thrust itself at her on all sides, the armed ship was evidence of it, the darkening sea a symbol. She remembered the only day in the last weeks when she had been free for a few hours to say a kind of good-bye to Oriol and Jacques-plage. The three of them had gone together to the empty stretch of beach, the golden-brown sand, sparkling with crystals, the pools reflecting the sky, the sea blue and smiling in the sun; and the shadow of a cloud had passed across the deeper blue beyond, making it almost black. Is that what awaits us? she had wondered; and at once another thought had answered, and the past years risen radiant to her side. How happy, how wonderfully happy, they had been together. It had been so, those years had happened; come what may, no one and nothing on earth could alter them.